S0-BIH-725

PRAISE FOR A MAJOR
NEW NOVEL

"A banished god, Siddhartha, Binder of Demons, and then (as a deliberate move against his former colleagues and in imitation of Earthly history) a reviver of Buddhism with himself as the Bodhisattva, sets out to fight the heavenly Establishment ... None of the above gives more than a slight idea of the brilliance of LORD OF LIGHT, of the manner in which the mimicked Hindu culture is both splendidly described and splendidly explained in the purest science-fiction terms. ... The two worlds never conflict; they are always as one, and that is a triumph."

Magazine of Fantasy and Science Fiction

Lord of Light

Roger Zelazny

 AVON
PUBLISHERS OF BARD, CAMELOT AND DISCUS BOOKS

*All of the characters in this book
are fictitious, and any resemblance
to actual persons, living or dead, is
purely coincidental.*

AVON BOOKS
A division of
The Hearst Corporation
959 Eighth Avenue
New York, New York 10019

Copyright © 1967 by Roger Zelazny.
Copyright © 1976 by Mercury Press, Inc.
Published by arrangement with
Doubleday & Company, Inc.
Library of Congress Catalog Card Number: 67-19099
ISBN: 0-380-44834-3

First Avon Printing, January, 1969
Thirteenth Printing

AVON TRADEMARK REG. U.S. PAT. OFF. AND
FOREIGN COUNTRIES, REGISTERED TRADEMARK—
MARCA REGISTRADA, HECHO EN CHICAGO, U.S.A.

Printed in the U.S.A.

To Dannie Plachta,
of friendship, wisdom, soma.

Lord of Light

i

It is said that fifty-three years after his liberation he returned from the Golden Cloud, to take up once again the gauntlet of Heaven, to oppose the Order of Life and the gods who ordained it so. His followers had prayed for his return, though their prayers were sin. Prayer should not trouble one who has gone on to Nirvana, no matter what the circumstances of his going. The wearers of the saffron robe prayed, however, that He of the Sword, Manjusri, should come again among them. The Boddhisatva is said to have heard ...

> He whose desires have been throttled,
> who is independent of root,
> whose pasture is emptiness—
> signless and free—
> his path is as unknowable
> as that of birds across the heavens.
> *Dhammapada (93)*

HIS FOLLOWERS called him Mahasamatman and said he was a god. He preferred to drop the Maha- and the -atman, however, and called himself Sam. He never claimed to be a god. But then, he never claimed not to be a god. Circumstances being what they were, neither admission could be of any benefit. Silence, though, could.

Therefore, there was mystery about him.

It was in the season of the rains ...

It was well into the time of the great wetness ...

It was in the days of the rains that their prayers went up, not from the fingering of knotted prayer cords or the spinning of prayer wheels, but from the great pray-machine in the monastery of Ratri, goddess of the Night.

9

The high-frequency prayers were directed upward through the atmosphere and out beyond it, passing into that golden cloud called the Bridge of the Gods, which circles the entire world, is seen as a bronze rainbow at night and is the place where the red sun becomes orange at midday.

Some of the monks doubted the orthodoxy of this prayer technique, but the machine had been built and was operated by Yama-Dharma, fallen, of the Celestial City; and, it was told, he had ages ago built the mighty thunder chariot of Lord Shiva: that engine that fled across the heavens belching gouts of fire in its wake.

Despite his fall from favor, Yama was still deemed mightiest of the artificers, though it was not doubted that the Gods of the City would have him to die the real death were they to learn of the pray-machine. For that matter, though, it was not doubted that they would have him to die the real death without the excuse of the pray-machine, also, were he to come into their custody. How he would settle this matter with the Lords of Karma was his own affair, though none doubted that when the time came he would find a way. He was half as old as the Celestial City itself, and not more than ten of the gods remembered the founding of that abode. He was known to be wiser even than the Lord Kubera in the ways of the Universal Fire. But these were his lesser Attributes. He was best known for another thing, though few men spoke of it. Tall, but not overly so; big, but not heavy; his movements, slow and fluent. He wore red and spoke little.

He tended the pray-machine, and the giant metal lotus he had set atop the monastery roof turned and turned in its sockets.

A light rain was falling upon the building, the lotus and the jungle at the foot of the mountains. For six days he had offered many kilowatts of prayer, but the static kept him from being heard On High. Under his breath, he called upon the more notable of the current fertility deities, invoking them in terms of their most prominent Attributes.

A rumble of thunder answered his petition, and the small ape who assisted him chuckled. "Your prayers and your curses come to the same, Lord Yama," commented the ape. "That is to say, nothing."

"It has taken you seventeen incarnations to arrive at this truth?" said Yama. "I can see then why you are still doing time as an ape."

"Not so," said the ape, whose name was Tak. "My fall, while less spectacular than your own, nevertheless involved elements of personal malice on the part of—"

"Enough!" said Yama, turning his back to him.

Tak realized then that he might have touched upon a sore spot. In an attempt to find another subject for conversation, he crossed to the window, leapt onto its wide sill and stared upward.

"There is a break in the cloud cover, to the west," he said.

Yama approached, followed the direction of his gaze, frowned, and nodded.

"Aye," he said. "Stay where you are and advise me."

He moved to a bank of controls.

Overhead, the lotus halted in its turning, then faced the patch of bare sky.

"Very good," he said. "We're getting something."

His hand moved across a separate control panel, throwing a series of switches and adjusting two dials.

Below them, in the cavernous cellars of the monastery, the signal was received and other preparations were begun: the host was made ready.

"The clouds are coming together again!" cried Tak.

"No matter, now," said the other. "We've hooked our fish. Out of Nirvana and into the lotus, he comes."

There was more thunder, and the rain came down with a sound like hail upon the lotus. Snakes of blue lightning coiled, hissing, about the mountaintops.

Yama sealed a final circuit.

"How do you think he will take to wearing the flesh again?" asked Tak.

"Go peel bananas with your feet!"

Tak chose to consider this a dismissal and departed the chamber, leaving Yama to close down the machinery. He made his way along a corridor and down a wide flight of stairs. He reached the landing, and as he stood there he heard the sound of voices and the shuffling of sandals coming in his direction from out a side hall.

Without hesitating, he climbed the wall, using a series of carved panthers and an opposing row of elephants as handholds. Mounting a rafter, he drew back into a well of shadow and waited, unmoving.

Two dark-robed monks entered through the archway.

"So why can she not clear the sky for them?" said the first.

The second, an older, more heavily built man, shrugged. "I am no sage that I can answer such questions. That she is anxious is obvious, or she should never have granted them this sanctuary, nor Yama this usage. But who can mark the limits of night?"

"Or the moods of a woman," said the first. "I have heard that even the priests did not know of her coming."

"That may be. Whatever the case, it would seem a good omen."

"So it would seem."

They passed through another archway, and Tak listened to the sounds of their going until there was only silence.

Still, he did not leave his perch.

The "she" referred to by the monks could only be the goddess Ratri herself, worshiped by the order that had given sanctuary to the followers of Great-Souled Sam, the Enlightened One. Now, Ratri, too, was to be numbered among those fallen from the Celestial City and wearing the skin of a mortal. She had every reason to be bitter over the whole affair; and Tak realized the

chance she was taking in granting sanctuary, let alone
being physically present during this undertaking. It
could jeopardize any possibility of her future reinstate-
ment if word of it got out and reached the proper ears.
Tak recalled her as the dark-haired beauty with silver
eyes, passing in her moon chariot of ebony and chromi-
um, drawn by stallions black and white, tended by her
guard, also black and white, passing up the Avenue of
Heaven, rivaling even Sarasvati in her glory. His heart
leapt within his hairy breast. He had to see her again.
One night, long ago, in happier times and better form,
he had danced with her, on a balcony under the stars.
It had been for only a few moments. But he remembered; and it is a difficult thing to be an ape and to
have such memories.

He climbed down from the rafter.

There was a tower, a high tower rising from the
northeast corner of the monastery. Within that tower
was a chamber. It was said to contain the indwelling
presence of the goddess. It was cleaned daily, the linens
changed, fresh incense burnt and a votive offering laid
just within the door. That door was normally kept
locked.

There were, of course, windows. The question as to
whether a man could have entered by means of any of
these windows must remain academic. Tak proved that
an ape could.

Mounting the monastery roof, he proceeded to scale
the tower, moving from brick to slippery brick, from
projection to irregularity, the heavens growling doglike
above him, until finally he clung to the wall just below
the outer sill. A steady rain fell upon him. He heard a
bird singing within. He saw the edge of a wet, blue
scarf hanging over the sill.

He caught hold of the ledge and raised himself until
he could peer inside.

Her back was to him. She wore a dark blue sari, and
she was seated on a small bench at the opposite end of
the room.

He clambered onto the sill and cleared his throat.

She turned quickly. She wore a veil, so that her features were indistinguishable. She regarded him through it, then rose and crossed the chamber.

He was dismayed. Her figure, once lithe, was wide about the waist; her walk, once the swaying of boughs, was a waddle; her complexion was too dark; even through the veil the lines of her nose and jaw were too pronounced.

He bowed his head.

" 'And so you have drawn near to us, who at your coming have come home,' " he sang, " 'as birds to their nest upon the tree.' "

She stood, still as her statue in the main hall below.

" 'Guard us from the she-wolf and the wolf, and guard us from the thief, oh Night, and so be good for us to pass.' "

She reached out slowly and laid her hand upon his head.

"You have my blessing, little one," she said, after a time. "Unfortunately, that is all I can give. I cannot offer protection or render beauty, who lack these luxuries myself. What is your name?"

"Tak," he told her.

She touched her brow.

"I once knew a Tak," she said, "in a bygone day, a distant place ..."

"I am that Tak, madam."

She seated herself upon the sill. After a time, he realized that she was weeping, within her veil.

"Don't cry, goddess. Tak is here. Remember Tak, of the Archives? Of the Bright Spear? He stands yet ready to do thy bidding."

"Tak ..." she said. "Oh, Tak! You, too? I did not know! I never heard ..."

"Another turning of the wheel, madam, and who knows? Things may yet be better than even once they were."

Her shoulders shook. He reached out, drew back his hand.

She turned and took it.

After an age, she spoke:

"Not by the normal course of events shall we be restored or matters settled, Tak of the Bright Spear. We must beat our own path."

"What mean you?" he inquired; then, "Sam?"

She nodded.

"He is the one. He is our hope against Heaven, dear Tak. If he can be recalled, we have a chance to live again."

"This is why you have taken this chance, why you yourself sit within the jaws of the tiger?"

"Why else? When there is no real hope we must mint our own. If the coin be counterfeit it still may be passed."

"Counterfeit? You do not believe he was the Buddha?"

She laughed, briefly.

"Sam was the greatest charlatan in the memory of god or man. He was also the worthiest opponent Trimurti ever faced. Don't look so shocked at my saying it, Archivist! You know that he stole the fabric of his doctrine, path and attainment, the whole robe, from prehistorical forbidden sources. It was a weapon, nothing more. His greatest strength was his insincerity. If we could have *him* back . . ."

"Lady, saint or charlatan, he *is* returned."

"Do not jest with me, Tak."

"Goddess and Lady, I just left the Lord Yama shutting down the pray-machine, frowning his frown of success."

"The venture was against such mighty odds. . . . Lord Agni once said that no such thing could ever be done."

Tak stood.

"Goddess Ratri," he said, "who, be he god or man,

or anything between, knows more of such matters than
Yama?"

"I have no answer for that question, Tak, because
there is none. But how can you say of a certainty that
he has netted us our fish?"

"Because he is Yama."

"Then take my arm, Tak. Escort me again, as once
you did. Let us view the sleeping Boddhisatva."

He led her out the door, down the stairs, and into the
chambers below.

Light, born not of torches but of the generators of
Yama, filled the cavern. The bed, set upon a platform,
was closed about on three sides by screens. Most of the
machinery was also masked by screens and hangings.
The saffron-robed monks who were in attendance
moved silently about the great chamber. Yama, master
artificer, stood at the bedside.

As they approached, several of the well-disciplined,
imperturbable monks uttered brief exclamations. Tak
then turned to the woman at his side and drew back a
pace, his breath catching in his throat.

She was no longer the dumpy little matron with
whom he had spoken. Once again did he stand at the
side of Night immortal, of whom it has been written,
"The goddess has filled wide space, to its depths and its
heights. Her radiance drives out the dark."

He looked but a moment and covered his eyes. She
still had this trace of her distant Aspect about her.

"Goddess . . ." he began.

"To the sleeper," she stated. "He stirs."

They advanced to the bedstead.

Thereafter to be portrayed in murals at the ends of
countless corridors, carved upon the walls of Temples
and painted onto the ceilings of numerous palaces,
came the awakening of he who was variously known as
Mahasamatman, Kalkin, Manjusri, Siddhartha, Tathagatha, Binder, Maitreya, the Enlightened One, Buddha and Sam. At his left was the goddess of Night; to

his right stood Death; Tak, the ape, was crouched at the foot of the bed, eternal comment upon the coexistence of the animal and the divine.

He wore an ordinary, darkish body of medium height and age; his features were regular and undistinguished; when his eyes opened, they were dark.

"Hail, Lord of Light!" It was Ratri who spoke these words.

The eyes blinked. They did not focus. Nowhere in the chamber was there any movement.

"Hail, Mahasamatman—Buddha!" said Yama.

The eyes stared ahead, unseeing.

"Hello, Sam," said Tak.

The forehead creased slightly, the eyes squinted, fell upon Tak, moved on to the others.

"Where . . . ?" he asked, in a whisper.

"My monastery," answered Ratri.

Without expression, he looked upon her beauty.

Then he shut his eyes and held them tightly closed, wrinkles forming at their corners. A grin of pain made his mouth a bow, his teeth the arrows, clenched.

"Are you truly he whom we have named?" asked Yama.

He did not answer.

"Are you he who fought the army of Heaven to a standstill on the banks of the Vedra?"

The mouth slackened.

"Are you he who loved the goddess of Death?"

The eyes flickered. A faint smile came and went across the lips.

"It is he," said Yama; then, "Who are you, man?"

"I? I am nothing," replied the other. "A leaf caught in a whirlpool, perhaps. A feather in the wind . . ."

"Too bad," said Yama, "for there are leaves and feathers enough in the world for me to have labored so long only to increase their number. I wanted me a man, one who might continue a war interrupted by his absence—a man of power who could oppose with that power the will of gods. I thought you were he."

"I am"—he squinted again—"Sam. I am Sam. Once —long ago . . . I *did* fight, didn't I? Many times . . ."

"You were Great-Souled Sam, the Buddha. Do you remember?"

"Maybe I was . . ." A slow fire was kindled in his eyes.

"Yes," he said then. "Yes, I was. Humblest of the proud, proudest of the humble. I fought. I taught the Way for a time. I fought again, taught again, tried politics, magic, poison . . . I fought one great battle so terrible the sun itself hid its face from the slaughter— with men and gods, with animals and demons, with spirits of the earth and air, of fire and water, with slizzards and horses, swords and chariots—"

"And you lost," said Yama.

"Yes, I did, didn't I? But it was quite a showing we gave them, wasn't it? You, deathgod, were my chario- teer. It all comes back to me now. We were taken prisoner and the Lords of Karma were to be our judges. You escaped them by the will-death and the Way of the Black Wheel. I could not."

"That is correct. Your past was laid out before them. You were judged." Yama regarded the monks who now sat upon the floor, their heads bowed, and he lowered his voice. "To have you to die the real death would have made you a martyr. To have permitted you to walk the world, in any form, would have left the door open for your return. So, as you stole your teachings from the Gottama of another place and time, did they steal the tale of the end of that one's days among men. You were judged worthy of Nirvana. Your *atman* was projected, not into another body, but into the great magnetic cloud that encircles this planet. That was over half a century ago. You are now officially an avatar of Vishnu, whose teachings were misinterpreted by some of his more zealous followers. You, personally, contin- ued to exist only in the form of self-perpetuating wave- lengths, which I succeeded in capturing."

Sam closed his eyes.

"And you *dared* to bring me back?"

"That is correct."

"I was aware of my condition the entire time."

"I suspected as much."

His eyes opened, blazing. "Yet you dared recall me from *that?*"

"Yes."

Sam bowed his head. "Rightly are you called deathgod, Yama-Dharma. You have snatched away from me the ultimate experience. You have broken upon the dark stone of your will that which is beyond all comprehension and mortal splendor. Why could you not have left me as I was, in the sea of being?"

"Because a world has need of your humility, your piety, your great teaching and your Machiavellian scheming."

"Yama, I'm old," he said. "I'm as old as man upon this world. I was one of the First, you know. One of the very first to come here, to build, to settle. All of the others are dead now, or are gods—*dei ex machini*. . . . The chance was mine also, but I let it go by. Many times. I never wanted to be a god, Yama. Not really. It was only later, only when I saw what they were doing, that I began to gather what power I could to me. It was too late, though. They were too strong. Now I just want to sleep the sleep of ages, to know again the Great Rest, the perpetual bliss, to hear the songs the stars sing on the shores of the great sea."

Ratri leaned forward and looked into his eyes. "We need you, Sam," she said.

"I know, I know," he told her. "It's the eternal recurrence of the anecdote. You've a willing horse, so flog him another mile." But he smiled as he said it, and she kissed his brow.

Tak leaped into the air and bounced upon the bed.

"Mankind rejoices," observed the Buddha.

Yama handed him a robe and Ratri fitted him with slippers.

Recovering from the peace which passeth understanding takes time. Sam slept. Sleeping, he dreamed; dreaming, he cried out, or just cried. He had no appetite; but Yama had found him a body both sturdy and in perfect health, one well able to bear the psychosomatic conversion from divine withdrawal.

But he would sit for an hour, unmoving, staring at a pebble or a seed or a leaf. And on these occasions, he could not be aroused.

Yama saw in this a danger, and he spoke of it with Ratri and Tak. "It is not good that he withdraw from the world in this way, now," he said. "I have spoken with him, but it is as if I addressed the wind. He cannot recover that which he has left behind. The very attempt is costing him his strength."

"Perhaps you misread his efforts," said Tak.

"What mean you?"

"See how he regards the seed he has set before him? Consider the wrinkling at the edges of his eyes."

"Yes? What of it?"

"He squints. Is his vision impaired?"

"It is not."

"Then why does he squint?"

"To better study the seed."

"Study? That is not the Way, as once he taught it. Yet he *does* study. He does not meditate, seeking within the object that which leads to release of the subject. No."

"What then does he do?"

"The reverse."

"The reverse?"

"He does study the object, considering its ways, in an effort to bind himself. He seeks within it an excuse to live. He tries once more to wrap himself within the fabric of Maya, the illusion of the world."

"I believe you are right, Tak!" It was Ratri who had spoken. "How can we assist him in his efforts?"

"I am not certain, mistress."

Yama nodded, his dark hair glistening in a bar of sunlight that fell across the narrow porch.

"You have set your finger upon the thing I could not see," he acknowledged. "He has not yet fully returned, though he wears a body, walks upon human feet, talks as we do. His thought is still beyond our ken."

"What then shall we do?" repeated Ratri.

"Take him on long walks through the countryside," said Yama. "Feed him delicacies. Stir his soul with poetry and song. Find him strong drink to drink—there is none here in the monastery. Garb him in bright-hued silks. Fetch him a courtesan or three. Submerge him in living again. It is only thus that he may be freed from the chains of God. Stupid of me not to have seen it sooner . . ."

"Not really, deathgod," said Tak.

The flame that is black leapt within Yama's eyes, and then he smiled. "I am repaid, little one," he acknowledged, "for the comments I, perhaps thoughtlessly, let fall upon thy hairy ears. I apologize, ape-one. You are truly a man, and one of wit and perception."

Tak bowed before him.

Ratri chuckled.

"Tell us, clever Tak—for mayhap we have been gods too long, and so lack the proper angle of vision—how shall we proceed in this matter of rehumanizing him, so as to best serve the ends we seek?"

Tak bowed him then to Ratri.

"As Yama has proposed," he stated. "Today, mistress, you take him for a walk in the foothills. Tomorrow, Lord Yama conducts him as far as the edge of the forest. The following day I shall take him amidst the trees and the grasses, the flowers and the vines. And we shall see. We shall."

"So be it," said Yama, and so it was.

In the weeks that followed, Sam came to look forward to these walks with what appeared at first a mild anticipation, then a moderate enthusiasm, and finally a blazing eagerness. He took to going off unaccompanied for longer and longer stretches of time: at first, it was for several hours in the morning; then, morning and evening. Later, he stayed away all day, and on occasion a day and a night.

At the end of the third week, Yama and Ratri discussed it on the porch in the early hours of morning.

"This thing I do not like," said Yama. "We cannot insult him by forcing our company upon him now, when he does not wish it. But there is danger out there, especially for one born again such as he. I would that we knew how he spends his hours."

"But whatever he does, it is helping him to recover," said Ratri, gulping a sweetmeat and waving a fleshy hand. "He is less withdrawn. He speaks more, even jesting. He drinks of the wine we bring him. His appetite is returning."

"Yet, if he should meet with an agent of Trimurti, the final doom may come to pass."

Ratri chewed slowly.

"It is not likely, though, that such should be abroad in this country, in these days," she stated. "The animals will see him as a child and will not harm him. Men would consider him a holy hermit. The demons fear him of old, and so respect him."

But Yama shook his head. "Lady, it is not so simple. Though I have dismantled much of my machinery and hidden it hundreds of leagues from here, such a massive trafficking of energies as I employed cannot have passed unnoticed. Sooner or later this place will be visited. I used screens and baffling devices, but this general area must have appeared in certain quarters as though the Universal Fire did a dance upon the map. Soon we must move on. I should prefer to wait until our charge is fully recovered, but . . ."

"Could not certain natural forces have produced the same energy effects as your workings?"

"Yes, and they do occur in this vicinity, which is why I chose it as our base—so it may well be that

nothing will come of it. Still, I doubt this. My spies in
the villages report no unusual activities now. But on the
day of his return, riding upon the crest of the storm,
some say the thunder chariot passed, hunting through
the heavens and across the countryside. This was far
from here, but I cannot believe that there was no
connection."

"Yet, it has not returned."

"Not that we know of. But I fear . . ."

"Then let us depart at once. I respect your forebod-
ings too well. You have more of the power upon you
than any other among the Fallen. For me, it is a great
strain even to assume a pleasing shape for more than a
few minutes . . ."

"What powers I possess," said Yama, refilling her
teacup, "are intact because they were not of the same
order as yours."

He smiled then, showing even rows of long, brilliant
teeth. This smile caught at the edge of a scar upon his
left cheek and reached up to the corner of his eye. He
winked to put a period to it and continued, "Much of
my power is in the form of knowledge, which even the
Lords of Karma could not have wrested from me. The
power of most of the gods, however, is predicated upon
a special physiology, which they lose in part when
incarnated into a new body. The mind, somehow
remembering, after a time alters any body to a certain
extent, engendering a new homeostasis, permitting a
gradual return of power. Mine does return quickly,
though, and it is with me fully now. But even if it were
not, I have my knowledge to use as a weapon—and
that is a power."

Ratri sipped her tea. "Whatever its source, if your
power says move, then move we must. How soon?"

Yama opened a pouch of tobacco and rolled a cigarette as he spoke. His dark, supple fingers, she noted,
always had about their movement that which was like
the movements of one who played upon an instrument
of music.

"I should say let us not tarry here more than another week or ten days. We must wean him from this countryside by then."

She nodded. "Where to then?"

"Some small southern kingdom, perhaps, where we may come and go undisturbed."

He lit the cigarette, breathed smoke.

"I've a better idea," said she. "Know that under a mortal name am I mistress of the Palace of Kama in Khaipur."

"The Fornicatorium, madam?"

She frowned. "As such is it often known to the vulgar, and do not call me 'madam' in the same breath— it smacks of an ancient jest. It is a place of rest, pleasure, holiness and much of my revenue. There, I feel, would be a good hiding place for our charge while he makes his recovery and we our plans."

Yama slapped his thigh. "Aye! Aye! Who would think to look for the Buddha in a whorehouse? Good! Excellent! To Khaipur, then, dear goddess—to Khaipur and the Palace of Love!"

She stood and stamped her sandal upon the flagstones. "I will not have you speak that way of my establishment!"

He dropped his eyes, and with pain dropped the grin from his face. He stood then and bowed. "I apologize, dear Ratri, but the revelation came so sudden—" He choked then and looked away. When he looked back, he was full of sobriety and decorum. He continued, "That I was taken aback by the apparent incongruity. Now, though, I do see the wisdom of the thing. It is a most perfect cover-up, and it provides you both with wealth and, what is more important, with a source of privy information among the merchants, warriors and priests. It is an indispensable part of the community. It gives you status and a voice in civil affairs. Being a god is one of the oldest professions in the world. It is only fitting, therefore, that we fallen ones take umbrage within the pale of another venerable tradition. I salute you. I give thanks for your wisdom and forethought. I do not slander the enterprises of a benefactor and co-conspirator. In fact, I look forward to the visit."

She smiled and seated herself once more. "I accept your well-oiled apology, oh son of the serpent. In any event, it is too difficult to remain angry with you. Pour me some more tea, please."

They reclined, Ratri sipping her tea, Yama smoking. In the distance, a storm front drew a curtain across half the prospect. The sun still shone upon them, however, and a cool breeze visited the porch.

"You have seen the ring, the ring of iron which he wears?" asked Ratri, eating another sweetmeat.

"Yes."

"Know you where he obtained it?"

"I do not."

"Nor I. But I feel we should learn its origin."

"Aye."

"How shall we essay this thing?"

"I have assigned the chore to Tak, who is better suited to the ways of the forest than we. Even now he follows the trail."

Ratri nodded. "Good," she said.

"I have heard," said Yama, "that the gods do still occasionally visit the more notable palaces of Kama throughout the land, generally in disguise, but sometimes in full power. Is this true?"

"Yes. But a year ago did Lord Indra come to Khaipur. Some three years back, the false Krishna made a visit. Of all the Celestial party, Krishna the Tireless does cause the greatest consternation among the staff. He stayed for a month of riot, which involved much broken furniture and the services of many physicians. He did near empty the wine cellar and the larder. He played then upon his pipes one night, however, the hearing of which would have been enough to gain the old Krishna forgiveness for near anything. But it was not the true magic we heard that night, for there is only one true Krishna—swart and hairy, his eyes so red and blazing. This one did dance upon the tables, causing much havoc, and his musical accompaniment was insufficient."

"Paid he for this carnage with other than a song?"

She laughed. "Come now, Yama. Let there be no rhetorical questions between us."

He snorted smoke.

"Surya, the sun, is now about to be encompassed," said Ratri, staring out and upward, "and Indra slays the dragon. At any moment, the rains will arrive."

A wave of grayness covered over the monastery. The breeze grew stronger, and the dance of the waters began upon the walls. Like a beaded curtain, the rain covered that open end of the porch at which they stared.

Yama poured more tea. Ratri ate another sweetmeat.

Tak made his way through the forest. He moved from tree to tree, branch to branch, watching the trail below him. His fur was moist, for the leaves shook small showers down upon him as he passed. Clouds mounted at his back, but the sun of early morning still shone in the eastern sky and the forest was a swarm of colors in its red-gold light. About him, birds were singing from within the tangle of branches, vines, leaves and grasses that stood like a wall upon either side of the trail. The birds made their music, insects hummed and occasionally there was a growl or bark. The foliage was stirred by the wind. Below him, the trail bent sharply, entering a clearing. Tak dropped to the ground, proceeded on foot. At the other side of the clearing he took to the trees again. Now, he noticed, the trail was running parallel to the mountains, even inclining slightly back in their direction. There was a distant rattle of thunder and after a time a new breeze came up, cool. He swung on, breaking through moist spider webs, frightening birds into shrieking flurries of bright plumage. The trail continued to move in the direction of the mountains, slowly doubling back upon itself. At times, it met with other hard-packed, yellow trails, dividing, crossing, parting. On these occasions, he descended to the ground and studied the surface markings. Yes, Sam had turned *here;* Sam had stopped beside *this* pool to drink—here, where the orange mushrooms grew taller than a tall man, and wide enough to shelter several from the rains; now, Sam had taken *that* branch of the roadway; here, he had stopped to fix a sandal strap; at this point, he had leaned upon a tree, which showed indications of housing a dryad. . . .

Tak moved on, about half an hour behind his quarry, as he judged it—so giving him plenty of time to get to wherever he was going and to begin whatever activity so engaged his enthusiasms. A halo of heat lightning reached above the mountains he was now facing. There was another rumble of thunder. The trail headed on up into the foothills, where the forest thinned, and Tak moved on all fours amid tall grasses. It headed steadily upward, and rocky outcroppings became more and more prominent. Still, Sam had passed this way, so Tak followed.

Overhead, the pollen-colored Bridge of the Gods vanished as the clouds rolled steadily eastward. Lightning flashed, and now the thunder followed quickly. The wind came faster here in the open; the grasses bent down before it; the temperature seemed suddenly to plummet.

Tak felt the first drops of rain and dashed for the shelter of one of the stands of stone. It ran like a narrow hedge, slightly slanted against the rain. Tak moved along its base as the waters were unleashed and color deserted the world along with the last bit of blue in the sky.

A sea of turbulent light appeared overhead, and three times spilled streams that rode crazy crescendo down to splash upon the stone fang curving blackly into the wind, about a quarter mile up the slope.

When Tak's vision cleared, he saw that which he did now understand. It was as though each bolt that had fallen had left a part of itself, standing, swaying in the gray air, pulsing fires, despite the wetness that came steadily down upon the ground.

Then Tak heard the laughter—or was it a ghost sound left in his ears by the recent thunder?

No, it was laughter—gigantic, unhuman!

After a time, there came a howl of rage. Then there was another flash, another rumble.

Another funnel of fire swayed beside the stone fang.

Tak lay still for about five minutes. Then it came again—the howl, followed by three bright flashes and the crash.

Now there were seven pillars of fire.

Dared he approach, skirting these things, spying upon the fang peak from its opposite side?

And if he did, and if—as he felt—Sam was somehow involved, what good could he do if the Enlightened One himself could not handle the situation?

He had no answer, but he found himself moving forward, crouched low in the damp grass, swinging far to his left.

When he was halfway there it happened again, and ten of the things towered, red and gold and yellow, drifting and returning, drifting and returning, as though their bases were rooted to the ground.

He crouched there wet and shivering, examined his courage and found it to be a small thing indeed. Yet, he pushed on until he was parallel to the strange place, then past it.

He drew up behind it, finding himself in the midst of many large stones. Grateful for their shelter and the cover they provided against observation from below, he inched forward, never taking his eyes from the fang.

He could see now that it was partly hollow. There was a dry, shallow cave at its base, and two figures knelt within it. Holy men at prayer? He wondered.

Then it happened. The most frightful flashing he had ever seen came down upon the stones—not once, or for a mere instant. It was as if a fire-tongued beast licked and licked about the stone, growling as it did so, for perhaps a quarter of a minute.

When Tak opened his eyes, he counted twenty of the blazing towers.

One of the holy men leaned forward, gestured. The other laughed. The sound carried to where Tak lay, and the words: "Eyes of the serpent! Mine now!"

"What is the quantity?" asked the second, and Tak knew it to be the voice of Great-Souled Sam.

"Twice, or none at all!" roared the other, and he leaned forward, rocked back, then gestured as Sam had done.

"Nina from Srinagina!" he chanted, and leaned, rocked, and gestured once more.

"Sacred seven," Sam said softly.

The other howled.

Tak closed his eyes and covered his ears, expecting what might come after that howl.

Nor was he mistaken.

When the blaze and the tumult had passed, he looked down upon an eerily illuminated scene. He did not bother counting. It was apparent that forty of the flamelike things now hung about the place, casting their weird glow: their number had doubled.

The ritual continued. On the left hand of the Buddha, the iron ring glowed with a pale, greenish light all its own.

He heard the words "Twice, or none at all" repeated again, and he heard the Buddha say "Sacred seven" once more, in reply.

This time he thought the mountainside would come apart beneath him. This time he thought the brightness was an afterimage, tattooed upon his retina through closed eyelids. But he was wrong.

When he opened his eyes it was to look upon a veritable army of shifting thunderbolts. Their blaze jabbed into his brain, and he shaded his eyes to stare down below.

"Well, Raltariki?" asked Sam, and a bright emerald light played about his left hand.

"One time again, Siddhartha. Twice, or not at all."

The rains let up for a moment, and, in the great blaze from the host on the hillside, Tak saw that the one called Raltariki had the head of a water buffalo and an extra pair of arms.

He shivered.

He covered his eyes and ears and clenched his teeth, waiting.

After a time, it happened. It roared and blazed, going on and on until finally he lost consciousness.

When he recovered his senses, there was only a grayness and a gentle rain between himself and the sheltering rock. At its base only one figure sat, and it did not wear horns or appear to possess more arms than the customary two.

Tak did not move. He waited.

"This," said Yama, handing him an aerosol, "is demon repellent. In the future, I suggest you annoint yourself thoroughly if you intend venturing very far from the monastery. I had thought this region free of the Rakasha, or I would have given it to you sooner."

Tak accepted the container, placed it on the table before him.

They sat in Yama's chambers, having taken a light meal there. Yama leaned back in his chair, a glass of the Buddha's wine in his left hand, a half-filled decanter in his right.

"Then the one called Raltariki is really a demon?" asked Tak.

"Yes—and no," said Yama. "If by 'demon' you mean a malefic, supernatural creature, possessed of great powers, life span and the ability to temporarily assume virtually any shape—then the answer is no. This is the generally accepted definition, but it is untrue in one respect."

"Oh? And what may that be?"

"It is not a supernatural creature."

"But it is all those other things?"

"Yes."

"Then I fail to see what difference it makes whether it be supernatural or not—so long as it is malefic, possesses great powers and life span and has the ability to change its shape at will."

"Ah, but it makes a great deal of difference, you see. It is the difference between the unknown and the unknowable, between science and fantasy—it is a matter of essence. The four points of the compass be logic, knowledge, wisdom and the unknown. Some do bow in that final direction. Others advance upon it. To bow before the one is to lose sight of the three. I may submit to the unknown, but never to the unknowable. The man who bows in that final direction is either a saint or a fool. I have no use for either."

Tak shrugged and sipped his wine. "But of the demons . . . ?"

"Knowable. I did experiment with them for many years, and I was one of the Four who descended into Hellwell, if you recall, after Taraka fled Lord Agni at Palamaidsu. Are you not Tak of the Archives?"

"I was."

"Did you read then of the earliest recorded contacts with the Rakasha?"

"I read the accounts of the days of their binding . . ."

"Then you know that they are the native inhabitants of this world, that they were present here before the arrival of Man from vanished Urath."

"Yes."

"They are creatures of energy, rather than matter. Their own traditions have it that once they wore bodies, lived in cities. Their quest for personal immortality, however, led them along a different path from that which Man followed. They found a way to perpetuate themselves as stable fields of energy. They abandoned their bodies to live forever as vortices of force.

But pure intellect they are not. They carried with them their complete egos, and born of matter they do ever lust after the flesh. Though they can assume its appearance for a time, they cannot return to it unassisted. For ages they did drift aimlessly about this world. Then the arrival of Man stirred them from their quiescence. They took on the shapes of his nightmares to devil him. This is why they had to be defeated and bound, far beneath the Ratnagaris. We could not destroy them all. We could not permit them to continue their attempts to possess the machines of incarnation and the bodies of men. So they were trapped and contained in great magnetic bottles."

"Yet Sam freed many to do his will," said Tak.

"Aye. He made and kept a nightmare pact, so that some of them do still walk the world. Of all men, they respect perhaps only Siddhartha. And *with* all men do they share one great vice."

"That being . . . ?"

"They do dearly love to gamble. . . . They will make game for any stakes, and gambling debts are their only point of honor. This must be so, or they would not hold the confidence of other gamesters and would so lose that which is perhaps their only pleasure. Their powers being great, even princes will make game with them, hoping to win their services. Kingdoms have been lost in this fashion."

"If," said Tak, "as you feel, Sam was playing one of the ancient games with Raltariki, what could the stakes have been?"

Yama finished his wine, refilled the glass. "Sam is a fool. No, he is not. He is a gambler. There *is* a difference. The Rakasha do control lesser orders of energy— Sam, through that ring he wears, does now command a guard of fire elementals, which he won from Raltariki. These are deadly, mindless creatures— and each bears the force of a thunderbolt."

Tak finished his wine. "But what stakes could Sam have brought to the game?"

Yama sighed. "All my work, all our efforts for over half a century."

"You mean—his body?"

Yama nodded. "A human body is the highest inducement any demon might be offered."

"Why should Sam risk such a venture?"

Yama stared at Tak, not seeing him. "It must have been the only way he could call upon his life-will, to bind him again to his task—by placing himself in jeopardy, by casting his very existence with each roll of the dice."

Tak poured himself another glass of wine and gulped it. *"That* is unknowable to me," he said.

But Yama shook his head. "Unknown, only," he told him. "Sam is not quite a saint, nor is he a fool."

"Almost, though," Yama decided, and that night he squirted demon repellent about the monastery.

The following morning, a small man approached the monastery and seated himself before its front entrance, placing a begging bowl on the ground at his feet. He wore a single, threadbare garment of coarse, brown cloth, which reached to his ankles. A black patch covered his left eye. What remained of his hair was dark and very long. His sharp nose, small chin, and high, flat ears gave to his face a foxlike appearance. His skin was tight-drawn and well-weathered. His single, green eye seemed never to blink.

He sat there for perhaps twenty minutes before one of Sam's monks noticed him and mentioned the fact to one of Ratri's dark-robed Order. This monk located a priest and passed the information to him. The priest, anxious to impress the goddess with the virtues of her followers, sent for the beggar to be brought in and fed, offered new garments and given a cell in which to sleep for as long as he chose to remain.

The beggar accepted the food with the courtesies of a Brahmin, but declined to eat anything other than bread and fruit. He accepted, too, the dark garment of Ratri's Order, casting aside his begrimed smock. Then he

looked upon the cell and the fresh sleeping mat that
had been laid for him.

"I do thank you, worthy priest," he said, in a voice
rich and resonant, and altogether larger than his person. "I do thank you, and pray your goddess smile
upon you for your kindness and generosity in her
name."

The priest smiled at this himself, and still hoped that
Ratri might pass along the hall at that moment, to
witness his kindness and generosity in her name. She
did not, however. Few of her Order had actually seen
her, even on the night when she put on her power and
walked among them: for only those of the saffron robe
had attended Sam's awakening and were certain as to
his identity. She generally moved about the monastery
while her followers were at prayer or after they had
retired for the evening. She slept mainly during the
day; when she did cross their sight she was well-muffled
and cloaked; her wishes and orders she communicated
directly to Gandhiji, the head of the Order, who was
ninety-three years old this cycle, and more than half
blind.

Consequently, both her monks and those of the
saffron robe wondered as to her appearance and sought
to gain possible favor in her eyes. It was said that her
blessing would ensure one's being incarnated as a Brahmin. Only Gandhiji did not care, for he had accepted
the way of the real death.

Since she did not pass along the hall as they stood
there, the priest prolonged the conversation.

"I am Balarma," he stated. "May I inquire as to
your name, good sir, and perhaps your destination?"

"I am Aram," said the beggar, "who has taken upon
himself a ten-year vow of poverty, and of silence for
seven. Fortunately, the seven have elapsed, that I may
now speak to thank my benefactors and answer their
questions. I am heading up into the mountains to find
me a cave where I may meditate and pray. I may,

perhaps, accept your kindly hospitality for a few days, before proceeding on with my journey."

"Indeed," said Balarma, "we should be honored if a holy one were to see fit to bless our monastery with his presence. We will make you welcome. If there is anything you wish to assist you along your path, and we may be able to grant this thing, please name it to us."

Aram fixed him with his unblinking green eye and said, "The monk who first observed me did not wear the robe of your Order." He touched the dark garment as he said it. "Instead, I believe my poor eye did behold one of another color."

"Yes," said Balarma, "for the followers of the Buddha do shelter here among us, resting awhile from their wanderings."

"That is truly interesting," said Aram, "for I should like to speak with them and perhaps learn more of their Way."

"You should have ample opportunity if you choose to remain among us for a time."

"This then shall I do. For how long will they remain?"

"I do not know."

Aram nodded. "When might I speak with them?"

"This evening there will be an hour when all the monks are gathered together and free to speak as they would, save for those who have taken vows of silence."

"I shall pass the interval till then in prayer," said Aram. "Thank you."

Each bowed slightly, and Aram entered his room.

That evening, Aram attended the community hour of the monks. Those of both Orders did mingle at this time and engage in conversation. Sam did not attend it himself, nor did Tak; and Yama never attended it in person.

Aram seated himself at the long table in the refectory, across from several of the Buddha's monks. He talked for some time with these, discoursing on doctrine and practice, caste and creed, weather and the affairs of the day.

"It seems strange," he said after a while, "that those of your Order have come so far to the south and the west so suddenly."

"We are a wandering Order," replied the monk to whom he had spoken. "We follow the wind. We follow our hearts."

"To the land of rusted soil in the season of lightnings? Is there perhaps some revelation to occur hereabout, which might be enlarging to my spirit were I to behold it?"

"The entire universe is a revelation," said the monk. "All things change, yet all things remain. Day follows night . . . each day is different, yet each is day. Much of the world is illusion, yet the forms of that illusion follow a pattern which is a part of divine reality."

"Yes, yes," said Aram. "In the ways of illusion and reality am I well-versed, but by my inquiry I did mean to know whether perhaps a new teacher had arisen in this vicinity, or some old one returned, or mayhap a divine manifestation, the presence of which it might profit my soul to be aware."

As he spoke, the beggar brushed from the table before him a red, crawling beetle, the size of a thumbnail, and he moved his sandal as if to crush it.

"Pray, brother, do not harm it," said the monk.

"But they are all over the place, and the Masters of Karma have stated that a man cannot be made to return as an insect, and the killing of an insect is a karmically inoperative act."

"Nevertheless," said the monk, "all life being one, in this monastery all do practice the doctrine of *ahimsa* and refrain from taking life of any sort."

"Yet," said Aram, "Patanjali does state that it is the *intention* rather than the act which governs. Therefore, if I killed with love rather than malice, it would be as if I had not killed. I confess that this was not the case and that malice was present—therefore, even if I did not kill I do bear the burden of the guilt because of the presence of that intention. So I could step upon it now and be none the worse for it, according to the principle of *ahimsa*. Since I am a guest, however, I of course respect the practice and do not do this thing." With this, he moved his sandal away from the insect, which stood immobile, reddish antennae pricked upward.

"Indeed, he is a scholar," said one of the Order of Ratri.

Aram smiled. "Thank you, but it is not so," he stated. "I am only a humble seeker of truth, and on occasion in the past have I been privileged to overhear the discourses of the learned. Would that I might be so privileged again! If there were some great teacher or scholar in the vicinity, then I would most surely walk his words or observe his example. It his feet and to hear

He stopped then, for all eyes had suddenly turned upon the doorway at his back. He did not move his head, but reached out to crush a beetle that stood near his hand. The tip of a small crystal and two tiny wires protruded through the broken chitin of its back.

Then he turned, his green eye sweeping across the row of monks seated between himself and the doorway, and he looked upon Yama, who wore breeches, boots, shirt, sash, cloak and gloves all of red, and about whose head was twisted a turban the color of blood.

" 'If?' " said Yama. "You were saying 'if'? If some sage or some avatar of the godhead resided in the vicinity, you should like to make his acquaintance? Is that what you were saying, stranger?"

The beggar rose from the table. He bowed. "I am Aram," he stated, "a fellow seeker and traveler with all who wish enlightenmnt."

Yama did not return the salute. "Why do you spell your name backward, Lord of Illusion, when all your words and actions herald it before you?"

The beggar shrugged. "I do not understand what you say."

But the smile came again to his lips. "I am one who seeks the Path and the Right," he added.

"I find that hard to believe, after witnessing at least a thousand years of your treachery."

"You speak of the lifetime of gods."

"Unfortunately, I do. You have made a serious mistake, Mara."

"What may that be?"

"You feel that you must be permitted to leave here alive."

"I admit that I anticipate doing so."

"Not considering the numerous accidents which might befall a lone traveler in this wild region."

"I have been a lone traveler for many years. Accidents always happen to other people."

"You might believe that ~~~~~~~~~~~ body were destroyed here, your *atman* would be transferred remotely to another body located elsewhere. I understand that someone has deciphered my notes, and the trick is now possible."

· The beggar's brows moved a quarter of an inch lower and closer together.

"You do not realize the forces which even now contain this building, defending against any such transfer."

The beggar stepped to the center of the room. "Yama," he stated, "you are a fool if you think to match your puny fallen powers against those of the Dreamer."

"Perhaps this is so, Lord Mara," Yama replied, "but I have waited too long for this opportunity to postpone it further. Remember my promise at Keenset? If you wish to continue your chain of existence you will have to pass through this, the only door to this room, which I bar. Nothing beyond this room can help you now."

Mara then raised his hands, and the fires were born.

Everything was flaming. Flames leapt from the stone walls, the tables, the robes of the monks. Smoke billowed and curled about the room. Yama stood in the midst of a conflagration, but he did not move.

"Is that the best you can do?" he asked. "Your flames are everywhere, but nothing burns."

Mara clapped his hands and the flames vanished.

In their place, its swaying head held at almost twice the height of a man, its silver hood fanned, the mechobra drew into its S-shaped strike position.

Yama ignored it, his shadowy gaze reaching now like the probe of a dark insect, boring into Mara's single eye.

The mechobra faded in mid-strike. Yama strode forward.

Mara fell back a pace.

They stood thus for perhaps three heartbeats, then Yama moved forward two paces farther and Mara backed away again. Perspiration blistered upon both their brows.

The beggar now stood taller and his hair was heavier; he was thicker about the waist and broader across the shoulders. A certain grace, not previously apparent, accompanied all his movements.

He fell back another step.

"Yes, Mara, there is a deathgod," said Yama between clenched teeth. "Fallen or no, the real death dwells in my eyes. You must meet them. When you reach the wall you can back no farther. Feel the strength go out of your limbs. Feel the coldness begin in your hands and your feet."

Mara's teeth bared in a snarl. His neck was as thick as a bull's. His biceps were as big about as a man's thighs. His chest was a barrel of strength and his legs were like great trees of the forest.

"Coldness?" he asked, extending his arms. "I can break a giant with these hands, Yama. What are you but a banished carrion god? Your frown may claim the aged and the infirm. Your eyes may chill dumb animals and those of the lower classes of men. I stand as high above you as a star above the ocean's bottom."

Yama's red-gloved hands fell like a pair of cobras upon his throat. "Then try that strength which you so mock, Dreamer. You have taken on the appearance of power. Use it! Best me not with words!"

His cheeks and forehead bloomed scarlet as Yama's hands tightened upon his throat. His eye seemed to leap, a green search-light sweeping the world.

Mara fell to his knees. "Enough, Lord Yama!" he gasped. "Wouldst slay thyself?"

He changed. His features flowed, as though he lay beneath restless waters.

Yama looked down upon his own face, saw his own red hands plucking at his wrists.

"You grow desperate now, Mara, as the life leaves you. But Yama is no child, that he fears breaking the mirror you have become. Try your last, or die like a man, it is all the same in the end."

But once more there was a flowing and a change.

This time Yama hesitated, breaking his strength.

Her bronze hair fell upon his hands. Her pale eyes pleaded with him. Caught about her throat was a necklace of ivory skulls, but slightly paler than her flesh. Her sari was the color of blood. Her hands rested upon his own, almost caressing . . .

"Goddess!" he hissed.

"You would not slay Kali . . . ? Durga . . . ?" she choked.

"Wrong again, Mara," he whispered. "Did you not know that each man kills the thing he loved?" and with this his hands twisted, and there was a sound of breaking bones.

"Tenfold be your damnation," he said, his eyes tightly closed. "There shall be no rebirth."

His hands came open then.

A tall, nobly proportioned man lay upon the floor at his feet, his head resting upon his right shoulder.

His eye had finally closed.

Yama turned the corpse with the toe of his boot. "Build a pyre and burn this body," he said to the monks, not turning toward them. "Spare none of the rites. One of the highest has died this day."

Then he removed his eyes from this work of his hands, turned upon his heel and left the room.

That evening the lightnings fled across the skies and the rain came down like bullets from Heaven.

The four of them sat in the chamber in the high tower that rose from the northeast corner of the monastery.

Yama paced the room, stopping at the window each time he came to it.

The others sat watching him, listening.

"They suspect," he told them, "but they do not know. They would not ravage the monastery of a fellow god, displaying before men the division of their ranks—not unless they were certain. They were not certain, so they investigated. This means that time is still with us."

They nodded.

"A Brahmin who renounced the world to find his soul passed this way, suffered an accident, died here the real death. His body was burnt and his ashes cast into the river that leads to the sea. This is what occurred. . . . The wandering monks of the Enlightened One were visiting at the time. They moved on shortly after this occurrence. Who knows where they went?"

Tak stood as nearly erect as he could.

"Lord Yama," he stated, "while it may hold for a week, a month—possibly even longer—this story will come apart in the hands of the Master to judge the first of any of those here present in this monastery who pass within the Halls of Karma. Under the circumstances, I believe some of them may achieve early judgment for just this reason. What then?"

Yama rolled a cigarette with care and precision. "It must be arranged that what I said is what actually occurred."

"How can that be? When a man's brain is subject to karmic play-back, all the events he has witnessed in his most recent cycle of life are laid out before his judge and the machine, like a scroll."

"That is correct," said Yama. "And have you, Tak of the Archives, never heard of a palimpsest—a scroll which has been used previously, cleaned, and then used again?"

"Of course, but the mind is not a scroll."

"No?" Yama smiled. "Well, it was your simile to begin with, not mine. What's truth, anyway? Truth is what you make it."

He lit his cigarette. "These monks have witnessed a strange and terrible thing," he continued. "They saw me take on my Aspect and wield an Attribute. They saw Mara do the same—here, in this monastery where we have revived the principle of *ahimsa*. They are aware that a god may do such things without karmic burden, but the shock was great and the impression vivid. And the final burning is still to come. By the time of that burning, the tale I have told you must be true in their minds."

"How?" asked Ratri.

"This very night, this very hour," he said, "while the image of the act flames within their consciousness and their thoughts are troubled, the new truth will be forged and nailed into place. . . . Sam, you have rested long enough. This thing is now yours to do. You must preach them a sermon. You must call forth within them those nobler sentiments and higher qualities of spirit which make men subject to divine meddling. Ratri and I will then combine our powers and a new truth will be born."

Sam shifted and dropped his eyes. "I don't know if I can do it. It's been so long . . ."

"Once a Buddha, always a Buddha, Sam. Dust off some of your old parables. You have about fifteen minutes."

Sam held out his hand. "Give me some tobacco and a paper."

He accepted the package, rolled himself a cigarette. "Light? . . . Thanks."

He drew in deeply, exhaled, coughed. "I'm tired of

lying to them," he finally said. "I guess that's what it really is."

"Lying?" asked Yama. "Who asked you to lie about anything? Quote them the Sermon on the Mount, if you want. Or something from the Popul Voh, or the *Iliad*. I don't care what you say. Just stir them a bit, soothe them a little. That's all I ask."

"Then what?"

"Then? Then I shall proceed to save them—and us!"

Sam nodded slowly. "When you put it that way ... but I'm a little out of shape when it comes to this sort of thing. Sure, I'll find me a couple truths and throw in a few pieties, but make it twenty minutes."

"Twenty minutes, then. And afterward we pack. Tomorrow we leave for Khaipur."

"So soon?" asked Tak.

Yama shook his head. "So late," he said.

The monks were seated upon the floor of the refectory. The tables had been moved back against the walls. The insects had vanished. Outside, the rain continued to fall.

Great-Souled Sam, the Enlightened One, entered and seated himself before them.

Ratri came in dressed as a Buddhist nun, and veiled.

Yama and Ratri moved to the back of the room and settled to the floor. Somewhere, Tak too, was listening.

Sam sat with his eyes closed for several minutes, then said softly:

"I have many names, and none of them matter." He opened his eyes slightly then, but he did not move his head. He looked upon nothing in particular.

"Names are not important," he said. "To speak is to name names, but to speak is not important. A thing happens once that has never happened before. Seeing it, a man looks upon reality. He cannot tell others what he has seen. Others wish to know, however, so they question him saying, 'What is it like, this thing you have seen?' So he tries to tell them. Perhaps he has seen the very first fire in the world. He tells them, 'It is red, like a poppy, but through it dance other colors. It has no form, like water, flowing everywhere. It is warm, like the sun of summer, only warmer. It exists for a time upon a piece of wood, and then the wood is gone, as though it were eaten, leaving behind that which is black and can be sifted like sand. When the wood is gone, it too is gone.' Therefore, the hearers must think reality is like a poppy, like water, like the sun, like that which eats and excretes. They think it is like to anything that they are told it is like by the man who has known it. But they have not looked upon fire. They cannot really know it. They can only know of it. But fire comes again into the world, many times. More men look upon fire. After a time, fire is as common as grass and clouds and the air they breathe. They see that, while it is like a poppy, it is not a poppy, while it is like water, it is not water, while it is like the sun, it is not the sun, and while it is like that which eats and passes wastes, it is not that which eats and passes wastes, but something different from each of these apart or all of these together. So they look upon this new thing and they make a new word to call it. They call it 'fire.'

"If they come upon one who still has not seen it and they speak to him of fire, he does not know what they mean. So they, in turn, fall back upon telling him what fire is like. As they do so, they know from their own experience that what they are telling him is not the truth, but only a part of it. They know that this man will never know reality from their words, though all the words in the world are theirs to use. He must look upon the fire, smell of it, warm his hands by it, stare into its heart, or remain forever ignorant. Therefore, 'fire' does not matter, 'earth' and 'air' and 'water' do not matter. 'I' do not matter. No word matters. But man forgets reality and remembers words. The more words he remembers, the cleverer do his fellows esteem him. He looks upon the great transformations of the world, but he does not see them as they were seen when man

looked upon reality for the first time. Their names
come to his lips and he smiles as he tastes them,
thinking he knows them in the naming. The thing that
has never happened before is still happening. It is still a
miracle. The great burning blossom squats, flowing,
upon the limb of the world, excreting the ash of the
world, and being none of these things I have named
and at the same time all of them, and *this* is reality—
the Nameless.

"Therefore, I charge you—forget the names you
bear, forget the words I speak as soon as they are
uttered. Look, rather, upon the Nameless within yourselves, which arises as I address it. It hearkens not to
my words, but to the reality within me, of which it is
part. This is the *atman,* which hears *me* rather than my
words. All else is unreal. To define is to lose. The
essence of all things is the Nameless. The Nameless is
unknowable, mightier even than Brahma. Things pass,
but the essence remains. You sit, therefore, in the midst
of a dream.

"Essence dreams it a dream of form. Forms pass, but
the essence remains, dreaming new dreams. Man names
these dreams and thinks to have captured the essence,
not knowing that he invokes the unreal. These stones,
these walls, these bodies you see seated about you are
poppies and water and the sun. They are the dreams of
the Nameless. They are fire, if you like.

"Occasionally, there may come a dreamer who is
aware that he is dreaming. He may control something
of the dream-stuff, bending it to his will, or he may
awaken into greater self-knowledge. If he chooses the
path of self-knowledge, his glory is great and he shall
be for all ages like unto a star. If he chooses instead the
way of the Tantras, combining Samsara and Nirvana,
comprehending the world and continuing to live in it,
this one is mighty among dreamers. He may be mighty
for good or for ill, as we look upon him—though these
terms, too, are meaningless, outside of the namings of
Samsara.

"To dwell within Samsara, however, is to be subject to the works of those who are mighty among dreamers. If they be mighty for good, it is a golden time. If they be mighty for ill, it is a time of darkness. The dream may turn to nightmare.

"It is written that to live is to suffer. This is so, say the sages, for man must work off his burden of Karma if he is to achieve enlightenment. For this reason, say the sages, what does it profit a man to struggle within a dream against that which is his lot, which is the path he must follow to attain liberation? In the light of eternal values, say the sages, the suffering is as nothing; in the terms of Samsara, say the sages, it leads to that which is good. What justification, then, has a man to struggle against those who be mighty for ill?"

He paused for a moment, raised his head higher.

"This night the Lord of Illusion passed among you— Mara, mighty among dreamers—mighty for ill. He did come upon another who may work with the stuff of dreams in a different way. He did meet with Dharma, who may expel a dreamer from his dream. They did struggle, and the Lord Mara is no more. Why did they struggle, deathgod against illusionist? You say their ways are incomprehensible, being the ways of gods. This is not the answer.

"The answer, the justification, is the same for men as it is for gods. Good or ill, say the sages, mean nothing for they are of Samsara. Agree with the sages, who have taught our people for as far as the memory of man may reach. Agree, but consider also a thing of which the sages do not speak. This thing is 'beauty,' which is a word—but look behind the word and consider the Way of the Nameless. And what is the way of the Nameless? It is the Way of Dream. And why does the Nameless dream? This thing is not known to any dweller within Samsara. So ask, rather, *what* does the Nameless dream?

"The Nameless, of which we are all a part, does dream form. And what is the highest attribute any form may possess? It is beauty. The Nameless, then, is an artist. The problem, therefore, is not one of good or evil, but one of esthetics. To struggle against those who are mighty among dreamers and are mighty for ill, or ugliness, is not to struggle for that which the sages have taught us to be meaningless in terms of Samsara or Nirvana, but rather it is to struggle for the symmetrical dreaming of a dream, in terms of the rhythm and the point, the balance and the antithesis which will make it a thing of beauty. Of this, the sages say nothing. This truth is so simple that they have obviously overlooked it. For this reason, I am bound by the esthetics of the situation to call it to your attention. To struggle against the dreamers who dream ugliness, be they men or gods, cannot but be the will of the Nameless. This struggle will also bear suffering, and so one's karmic burden will be lightened thereby, just as it would be by enduring the ugliness; but *this* suffering is productive of a higher end in the light of the eternal values of which the sages so often speak.

"Therefore, I say unto you, the esthetics of what you have witnessed this evening were of a high order. You may ask me, then, 'How am I to know that which is beautiful and that which is ugly, and be moved to act thereby?' This question, I say, you must answer for yourself. To do this, first forget what I have spoken, for I have said nothing. Dwell now upon the Nameless."

He raised his right hand and bowed his head.

Yama stood, Ratri stood, Tak appeared upon a table.

The four of them left together, knowing the machineries of Karma to have been defeated for a time.

They walked through the jagged brilliance of the morning, beneath the Bridge of the Gods. Tall fronds, still wet with the night's rain, glistened at the sides of the trail. The tops of trees and the peaks of the distant mountains rippled beyond the rising vapors. The day was cloudless. The faint breezes of morning still bore a trace of the night's cold. The clicking and buzzing and chirping of the jungle accompanied the monks as they walked. The monastery from which they had departed was only partly visible above the upper reaches of the treetops; high in the air above it, a twisting line of smoke endorsed the heavens.

Ratri's servitors bore her litter in the midst of the moving party of monks, servants and her small guard of warriors. Sam and Yama walked near the head of the band. Silent overhead, Tak followed, passing among leaves and branches, unseen.

"The pyre still blazes," said Yama.

"Yes."

"They burn the wanderer who suffered a heart attack as he took his rest among them."

"This is true."

"For a spur of the moment thing, you came up with a fairly engaging sermon."

"Thanks."

"Do you really believe what you preached?"

Sam laughed. "I'm very gullible when it comes to my own words. I believe everything I say, though I know I'm a liar."

Yama snorted. "The rod of Trimurti still falls upon the backs of men. Nirriti stirs within his dark lair; he harasses the seaways of the south. Do you plan on spending another lifetime indulging in metaphysics—to find new justification for opposing your enemies? Your talk last night sounded as if you have reverted to considering *why* again, rather than *how*."

"No," said Sam, "I just wanted to try another line on the audience. It is difficult to stir rebellion among those to whom all things are good. There is no room for evil in their minds, despite the fact that they suffer it constantly. The slave upon the rack who knows that he will be born again—perhaps as a fat merchant—if he suffers willingly—his outlook is not the same as that of a man with but one life to live. He can bear anything, knowing that great as his present pain may be, his future pleasure will rise higher. If such a one does not choose to believe in good or evil, perhaps then beauty and ugliness can be made to serve him as well. Only the names have been changed."

"This, then, is the new, official party line?" asked Yama.

"It is," said Sam.

Yama's hand passed through an invisible slit in his robe and emerged with a dagger, which he raised in salute.

"To beauty," he said. "Down with ugliness!"

A wave of silence passed across the jungle. All the life-sounds about them ceased.

Yama raised one hand, returning the dagger to its hidden sheath with the other.

"Halt!" he cried out.

He looked upward, squinting against the sun, head cocked to his right.

"Off the trail! Into the brush!" he called.

They moved. Saffron-cloaked bodies flashed from off the trail. Ratri's litter was borne in among the trees. She now stood at Yama's side.

"What is it?" she asked.

"Listen!"

It came then, riding down the sky on a blast of sound. It flashed above the peaks of the mountains, crossed over the monastery, whipping the smokes into invisibility. Explosions of sound trumpeted its coming, and the air quaked as it cut its way through the wind and the light.

It was a great-looped tau cross, a tail of fire streaming behind it.

"Destroyer come a-hunting," said Yama.

"Thunder chariot!" cried one of the mercenaries, making a sign with his hand.

"Shiva passes," said a monk, eyes wide with fear. "The Destroyer . . ."

"Had I known at the time how well I wrought," said Yama, "I might have numbered its days intentionally. Occasionally, do I regret my genius."

It passed beneath the Bridge of the Gods, swung above the jungle, fell away to the south. Its roar gradually diminished as it departed in that direction. Then there was silence.

A bird made a brief piping noise. Another replied to it. Then all the sounds of life began again and the travelers returned to their trail.

"He will be back," said Yama, and this was true.

Twice more that day did they have to leave the trail as the thunder chariot passed above their heads. On the last occasion, it circled the monastery, possibly observing the funeral rites being conducted there. Then it crossed over the mountains and was gone.

That night they made camp under the stars, and on the second night they did the same.

The third day brought them to the river Deeva and the small port city of Koona. It was there that they found the transportation they wished, and they set forth that same evening, heading south by bark to where the Deeva joined with the mighty Vedra, and then proceeded onward to pass at last the wharves of Khaipur, their destination.

As they flowed with the river, Sam listened to its sounds. He stood upon the dark deck, his hands resting on the rail. He stared out across the waters where the bright heavens rose and fell, star bending back upon star. It was then that the night addressed him in the voice of Ratri, from somewhere nearby.

"You have passed this way before, Tathagatha."

"Many times," he replied.

"The Deeva is a thing of beauty under the stars, in its rippling and its folding."

"Indeed."

"We go now to Khaipur and the Palace of Kama. What will you do when we arrive?"

"I will spend some time in meditation, goddess."

"Upon what shall you meditate?"

"Upon my past lives and the mistakes they each

contained. I must review my own tactics as well as those of the enemy."

"Yama thinks the Golden Cloud to have changed you."

"Perhaps it has."

"He believes it to have softened you, weakened you. You have always posed as a mystic, but now he believes you have become one—to your own undoing, to our undoing."

He shook his head, turned around. But he did not see her. Stood she there invisible, or had she withdrawn? He spoke softly and without inflection:

"I shall tear these stars from out the heavens," he stated, "and hurl them in the faces of the gods, if this be necessary. I shall blaspheme in every Temple throughout the land. I shall take lives as a fisherman takes fish, by the net, if this be necessary. I shall mount me again up to the Celestial City, though every step be a flame or a naked sword and the way be guarded by tigers. One day will the gods look down from Heaven and see me upon the stair, bringing them the gift they fear most. That day will the new Yuga begin.

"But first I must meditate for a time," he finished.

He turned back again and stared out over the waters.

A shooting star burnt its way across the heavens. The ship moved on. The night sighed about him.

Sam stared ahead, remembering.

ii

*One time a minor rajah from a minor principality
came with his retinue into Mahartha, the city that is
called Gateway of the South and Capital of the Dawn,
there to purchase him a new body. This was in the days
when the thread of destiny might yet be plucked from
out a gutter, the gods were less formal, the demons still
bound, and the Celestial City yet occasionally open to
men. This is the story of how the prince did bait the
one-armed receiver of devotions before the Temple,
incurring the disfavor of Heaven for his presumption.*

. . .

> Few are the beings born again among men; more
> numerous are those born again elsewhere.
> *Anguttara-nikaya (I, 35)*

RIDING into the capital of dawn at midafternoon, the
prince, mounted upon a white mare, passed up the
broad avenue of Surya, his hundred retainers massed at
his back, his adviser Strake at his left hand, his scimitar
in his sash, and a portion of his wealth in the bags his
pack horses bore.

The heat crashed down upon the turbans of the men,
washed past them, came up again from the roadway.

A chariot moved slowly by, headed in the opposite
direction, its driver squinting up at the banner the chief
retainer bore; a courtesan stood at the gateway to her
pavilion, studying the traffic; and a pack of mongrel
dogs followed at the heels of the horses, barking.

The prince was tall, and his mustaches were the color
of smoke. His hands, dark as coffee, were marked with
the stiff ridges of his veins. Still, his posture was erect,

and his eyes were like the eyes of an ancient bird, electric and clear.

Ahead, a crowd gathered to watch the passing troop. Horses were ridden only by those who could afford them, and few were that wealthy. The slizzard was the common mount—a scaled creature with snakelike neck, many teeth, dubious lineage, brief life span and a vicious temperament; the horse, for some reason, having grown barren in recent generations.

The prince rode on, into the capital of dawn, the watchers watching.

Passing, they turned off the avenue of the sun and headed up a narrow thoroughfare. They passed the low buildings of commerce, the great shops of the great merchants, the banks, the Temples, the inns, the brothels. They passed on, until at the fringe of the business district they came upon the princely hostel of Hawkana, the Most Perfect Host. They drew rein at the gate, for Hawkana himself stood outside the walls, simply dressed, fashionably corpulent and smiling, waiting to personally conduct the white mare within.

"Welcome, Lord Siddhartha!" he called in a loud voice, so that all within earshot might know the identity of his guest. "Welcome to this well-nightingaled vicinity, and to the perfumed gardens and marble halls of this humble establishment! To your riders welcome also, who have ridden a goodly ride with you and no doubt seek subtle refreshment and dignified ease as well as yourself. Within, you will find all things to your liking, I trust, as you have upon the many occasions in the past when you have tarried within these halls in the company of other princely guests and noble visitors, too numerous to mention, such as—"

"And a good afternoon to you also, Hawkana!" cried the prince, for the day was hot and the innkeeper's speeches, like rivers, always threatened to flow on forever. "Let us enter quickly within your walls, where, among their other virtues too numerous to mention, it is also cool."

Hawkana nodded briskly, and taking the mare by the bridle led her through the gateway and into his courtyard; there, he held the stirrup while the prince dismounted, then gave the horses into the keeping of his stable hands and dispatched a small boy through the gateway to clean the street where they had waited.

Within the hostel, the men were bathed, standing in the marble bath hall while servants poured water over their shoulders. Then did they annoint themselves after the custom of the warrior caste, put on fresh garments and passed into the hall of dining.

The meal lasted the entire afternoon, until the warriors who sat at the head of the long, low, serving board, three dancers wove their way through an intricate pattern, finger cymbals clicking, faces bearing the proper expressions for the proper moments of the dance, as four veiled musicians played the traditional music of the hours. The table was covered with a richly woven tapestry of blue, brown, yellow, red and green, wherein was worked a series of hunting and battle scenes: riders mounted on slizzard and horse met with lance and bow the charges of feather-panda, fire-rooster and jewel-podded command plant; green apes wrestled in the tops of trees; the Garuda Bird clutched a sky demon in its talons, assailing it with beak and pinions; from the depths of the sea crawled an army of horned fish, clutching spikes of pink coral in their jointed fins, facing a row of kirtled and helmeted men who bore lances and torches to oppose their way upon the land.

The prince ate but sparingly. He toyed with his food, listened to the music, laughed occasionally at the jesting of one of his men.

He sipped a sherbet, his rings clicking against the sides of the glass.

Hawkana appeared beside him. "Goes all well with you, Lord?" he inquired.

"Yes, good Hawkana, all is well," he replied.

"You do not eat as do your men. Does the meal displease you?"

"It is not the food, which is excellent, nor its preparation, which is faultless, worthy Hawkana. Rather, it is my appetite, which has not been high of late."

"Ah!" said Hawkana, knowingly. "I have the thing, the very thing! Only one such as yourself may truly appreciate it. Long has it rested upon the special shelf of my cellar. The god Krishna had somehow preserved it against the ages. He gave it to me many years ago because the accommodations here did not displease him. I shall fetch it for you."

He bowed then, and backed from the hall.

When he returned he bore a bottle. Before he saw the paper upon its side, the prince recognized the shape of that bottle.

"Burgundy!" he exclaimed.

"Just so," said Hawkana. "Brought from vanished Uratha, long ago."

He sniffed at it and smiled. Then he poured a small quantity into a pear-shaped goblet and set it before his guest.

The prince raised it and inhaled of its bouquet. He took a slow sip. He closed his eyes.

There was a silence in the room, in respect of his pleasure.

Then he lowered the glass, and Hawkana poured into it once again the product of the *pinot noir* grape, which could not be cultivated in this land.

The prince did not touch the glass. Instead, he turned to Hawkana, saying, "Who is the oldest musician in this house?"

"Mankara, here," said his host, gesturing toward the white-haired man who took his rest at the serving table in the corner.

"Old not in body, but in years," said the prince.

"Oh, that would be Dele," said Hawkana, "if he is to be counted as a musician at all. He says that once he was such a one."

"Dele?"

"The boy who keeps the stables."

"Ah, I see. . . . Send for him." Hawkana clapped his hands and ordered the servant who appeared to go into the stables, make the horse-boy presentable and fetch him with dispatch into the presence of the diners.

"Pray, do not bother making him presentable, but simply bring him here," said the prince.

He leaned back and waited then, his eyes closed. When the horse-boy stood before him, he asked:

"Tell me, Dele, what music do you play?"

"That which no longer finds favor in the hearing of Brahmins," said the boy.

"What was your instrument?"

"Piano," said Dele.

"Can you play upon any of these?" He gestured at those instruments that stood, unused now, upon the small platform beside the wall.

The boy cocked his head at them. "I suppose I could manage on the flute, if I had to."

"Do you know any waltzes?"

"Yes."

"Will you play me 'The Blue Danube'?"

The boy's sullen expression vanished, to be replaced by one of uneasiness. He cast a quick glance back at Hawkana, who nodded.

"Siddhartha is a prince among men, being of the First," stated the host.

" 'The Blue Danube,' on one of these flutes?"

"If you please."

The boy shrugged. "I'll try," he said. "It's been an awfully long time. . . . Bear with me."

He crossed to where the instruments lay and muttered something to the owner of the flute he selected. The man nodded his head. Then he raised it to his lips and blew a few tentative notes. He paused, repeated the trial, then turned about.

He raised it once more and began the quivering

movement of the waltz. As he played, the prince sipped his wine.

When he paused for breath, the prince motioned him to continue. He played tune after forbidden tune, and the professional musicians put professional expressions of scorn upon their faces; but beneath their table several feet were tapping in slow time with the music.

Finally, the prince had finished his wine. Evening was near to the city of Mahartha. He tossed the boy a purse of coins and did not look into his tears as he departed from the hall. He rose then and stretched, smothering a yawn with the back of his hand.

"I retire to my chambers," he said to his men. "Do not gamble away your inheritances in my absence."

They laughed then and bade him good night, calling for strong drink and salted biscuits. He heard the rattle of dice as he departed.

The prince retired early so that he might arise before daybreak. He instructed a servant to remain outside his door all the following day and to refuse admission to any who sought it, saying that he was indisposed.

Before the first flowers had opened to the first insects of morning, he had gone from the hostel, only an ancient green parrot witnessing his departure. Not in silks sewn with pearls did he go, but in tatters, as was his custom on these occasions. Not preceded by conch and drum did he move, but by silence, as he passed along the dim streets of the city. These streets were deserted, save for an occasional doctor or prostitute returning from a late call. A stray dog followed him as he passed through the business district, heading in the direction of the harbor.

He seated himself upon a crate at the foot of a pier. The dawn came to lift the darkness from the world; and he watched the ships stirring with the tide, empty of sail, webbed with cables, prows carved with monster or maiden. His every visit to Mahartha brought him again to the harbor for a little while.

Morning's pink parasol opened above the tangled hair of the clouds, and cool breezes crossed the docks. Scavenger birds uttered hoarse cries as they darted about loop-windowed towers, then swooped across the waters of the bay.

He watched a ship put out to sea, tentlike vanes of canvas growing to high peaks and swelling in the salt air. Aboard other ships, secure in their anchorage, there was movement now, as crews made ready to load or unload cargoes of incense, coral, oil and all kinds of fabrics, as well as metals, cattle, hardwoods and spices. He smelled the smells of commerce and listened to the cursing of the sailors, both of which he admired: the former, as it reeked of wealth, and the latter because it combined his two other chief preoccupations, these being theology and anatomy.

After a time, he spoke with a foreign sea captain who had overseen the unloading of sacks of grain, and now took his rest in the shade of the crates.

"Good morning," he said. "May your passages be free of storm and shipwreck, and the gods grant you safe harbor and a good market for your cargoes."

The other nodded, seated himself upon a crate and proceeded to fill a small clay pipe.

"Thank you, old one," he said. "Though I do pray to the gods of the Temples of my own choosing, I accept the blessings of any and all. One can always use blessings, especially a seaman."

"Had you a difficult voyage?"

"Less difficult than it might have been," said the sea captain. "That smouldering sea mountain, the Cannon of Nirriti, discharges its bolts against heaven once again."

"Ah, you sailed from the southwest!"

"Yes. Chatisthan, from Ispar-by-the-Sea. The winds are good in this season of the year, but for this reason they also carried the ash of the Cannon much farther than any would think. For six days this black snow fell upon us, and the odors of the underworld pursued us, fouling food and water, making the eyes to weep and the throat to burn. We offered much thanksgiving when we finally outran it. See how the hull is smeared? You should have seen the sails—black as the hair of Ratri!"

The prince leaned forward to better regard the vessel. "But the waters were not especially troubled?" he asked.

The sailor shook his head. "We hailed a cruiser near the Isle of Salt, and we learned of it that we had missed by six days the worst dischargings of the Cannon. At that time, it burnt the clouds and raised great waves, sinking two ships the cruiser did know of, and possibly a third." The sailor leaned back, stoking his pipe. "So, as I say, a seaman of the sea," said the prince. "A captain. His name is Jan Olvegg, or perhaps he is now known as Olvagga. Do you know him?"

"I knew him," said the other, "but it has been long since he sailed."

"Oh? What has become of him?"

The sailor turned his head to better study him. "Who are you to ask?" he finally inquired.

"My name is Sam. Jan is a very old friend of mine."

"How old is 'very old'?"

"Many, many years ago, in another place, I knew him when he was captain of a ship which did not sail these oceans."

The sea captain leaned forward suddenly and picked up a piece of wood, which he hurled at the dog who had rounded a piling at the other side of the pier. It yelped once and dashed off toward the shelter of a warehouse. It was the same dog who had followed the prince from the hostel of Hawkana.

"Beware the hounds of hell," said the captain. "There are dogs and there are dogs—and there are dogs. Three different kinds, and in this port drive them all from your presence." Then he appraised the other once again. "Your hands," he said, gesturing with his pipe, "have recently worn many rings. Their impressions yet remain."

Sam glanced at his hands and smiled. "Your eyes miss nothing, sailor," he replied. "So I admit to the obvious. I have recently worn rings."

"So, like the dogs, you are not what you appear to be—and you come asking after Olvagga, by his most ancient name. Your name, you say, is Sam. Are you, perchance, one of the First?"

Sam did not reply immediately, but studied the other as though waiting for him to say more.

Perhaps realizing this, the captain continued:

"Olvagga, I know, was numbered among the First, among the First, or are one of them. Whether you are yourself aware of this. So I do not betray him by so speaking. I do wish to know whether I speak to a friend or an enemy, however."

Sam frowned. "Jan was never known for the making of enemies," he said. "You speak as if he has them now, among those whom you call the Masters."

The seaman continued to stare at him. "You are not a Master," he finally said, "and you come from afar."

"You are correct," said Sam, "but tell me how you know these things."

"First," said the other, "you are an old man. A Master, too, *could* have upon him an old body, but he would not—any more than he would remain a dog for very long. His fear of dying the real death, suddenly, in the manner of the old, would be too great. So he would not remain so long as to leave the marks of rings deeply imprinted upon the fingers. The wealthy are never despoiled of their bodies. If they are refused rebirth, they live out the full span of their days. The Masters would fear a rising up in arms among the followers of such a one, were he to meet with other than a natural passing. So a body such as yours could not be obtained in this manner. A body from the life tanks would not have marked fingers either.

"Therefore," he concluded, "I take you to be a man of importance other than a Master. If you knew Olvagga of old, then you are also one of the Firstlings, such as he. Because of the sort of information which you seek, I take you to be one from afar. Were you a man of Mahartha you would know of the Masters, and knowing of the Masters you would know why Olvagga cannot sail."

"Your knowledge of matters in Mahartha seems greater than my own—oh, newly arrived sailor."

"I, too, come from a distant place," acknowledged the captain, smiling faintly, "but in the space of a dozen months I may visit twice as many ports. I hear news—news and gossip and tales from all over—from more than a double dozen ports. I hear of the intrigues of the palace and the affairs of the Temple. I hear the secrets whispered at night to the golden girls beneath the sugar-cane bow of Kama. I hear of the campaigns of the Khshatriya and the dealings of the great merchants in the futures of grains and spices, jewels and silk. I drink with the bards and the astrologers, with the actors and the servants, the coachmen and the tailors. Sometimes, perhaps, I may strike the port where freebooters have haven and learn there the faring of those they hold to ransom. So do not think it strange that I, who come from afar, may know more of Mahartha than you, who may dwell perhaps a week's faring hence. Occasionally, I may even hear of the doings of the gods."

"Then you can tell me of the Masters, and why they are to be numbered as enemies?" asked Sam.

"I can tell you something of them," replied the captain, "since you should not go unwarned. The body merchants are now the Masters of Karma. Their individual names are now kept secret, after the manner of the gods, so that they seem as impersonal as the Great Wheel, which they claim to represent. They are no longer merely body merchants, but are allied with the Temples. These, too, are changed, for your kinsmen of the First who are now gods do commune with them from Heaven. If you are indeed of the First, Sam, your way must lead you either to deification or extinction, when you face these new Masters of Karma."

"How?" asked Sam.

"Details you must seek elsewhere," said the other. "I do not know the processes whereby these things are achieved. Ask after Jannaveg the sailmaker on the Street of the Weavers."

"This is how Jan is now known?"

The other nodded.

"And beware the dogs," he said, "or, for that matter, anything else which is alive and may harbor intelligence."

"What is your name, captain?" asked Sam.

"In this port, I have no name at all or a false one, and I see no reason for lying to you. Good day, Sam."

"Good day, captain. Thank you for your words."

Sam rose and departed the harbor, heading back toward the business district and the streets of the trades.

The sun was a red discus in the heavens, rising to meet the Bridge of the Gods. The prince walked through the awakened city, threading his way among the stalls displaying the skills of the workmen in the small crafts. Hawkers of unguents and powders, perfumes and oils, moved about him. Florists waved their garlands and corsages at the passer-by; and the vintners said nothing, sitting with their wineskins on rows of shaded benches, waiting for their customers to come to them as they always did. The morning smelled of cooking food, musk, flesh, excrement, oils and incense all churned up together and turned loose to wander like an invisible cloud.

Dressed as a beggar himself, it did not seem out of place for him to stop and speak to the hunchback with the begging bowl.

"Greetings, brother," he stated. "I am far from my

quarter on an errand. Can you direct me to the Street of the Weavers?"

The hunchback nodded and shook his bowl suggestively.

He withdrew a small coin from the pouch concealed beneath his tattered garments. He dropped it into the hunchback's bowl and it quickly vanished.

"That way." The man gestured with his head. "The third street you come upon, turn there to the left. Then follow it past two streets more, and you will be at the Circle of the Fountain before the Temple of Varuna. Coming into that Circle, the Street of the Weavers is marked by the Sign of the Awl."

He nodded to the hunchback, patted his hump and continued on his way.

When he reached the Circle of the Fountain, the prince halted. Several dozen people stood in a shifting line before the Temple of Varuna, most stern and august of all the deities. These people were not preparing to enter the Temple, but rather were engaged in some occupation that required waiting and taking turns. He heard the rattling of coins and he wandered nearer.

It was a machine, gleaming and metallic, before which they moved.

A man inserted a coin into the mouth of a steel tiger. The machine began to purr. He pressed buttons cast in the likenesses of animals and demons. There came then a flashing of lights along the lengths of the Nagas, the two holy serpents who twisted about the transparent face of the machine.

He edged closer.

The man drew down upon the lever that grew from the side of the machine cast in the likeness of the tail of a fish.

A holy blue light filled the interior of the machine; the serpents pulsed redly; and there, in the midst of the light and a soft music that had begun to play, a prayer wheel swung into view and began spinning at a furious pace.

The man wore a beatific expression. After several minutes, the machine shut itself off. He inserted another coin and pulled the lever once more, causing several of those nearer to the end of the line to grumble audibly, remarking to the effect that that was his seventh coin, it was a warm day, there were other people waiting to get some praying done and why did he not go inside and render such a large donation directly to the priests? Someone replied that the little man obviously had much atoning to do. There then began some speculation as to the possible nature of his sins. This was accompanied by considerable laughter.

Seeing that there were several beggars waiting their turn in line, the prince moved to its end and stood there.

As the line advanced, he noted that, while some of those who passed before the machine pushed its buttons, others merely inserted a flat metal disc into the mouth of the second tiger on the opposite side of the chassis. After the machine had ceased to function, the disc fell into a cup and was retrieved by its owner. The prince decided to venture an inquiry.

He addressed the man who stood before him in line:

"Why is it," he asked, "that some men do have discs of their own?"

"It is because they have registered," said the other, without turning his head.

"In the Temple?"

"Yes."

"Oh."

He waited half a minute, then inquired, "Those who are unregistered, and wish to use it—they push the buttons?"

"Yes," said the other, "spelling out their name, occupation, and address."

"Supposing one be a visitor here, such as myself?"

"You should add the name of your city."

"Supposing one is unlettered, such as myself—what then?"

The other turned to him. "Perhaps 'twere better," he said, "that you make prayer in the old way, and give the donation directly into the hands of the priests. Or else register and obtain a disc of your own."

"I see," said the prince. "Yes, you are right. I must think of this more. Thank you."

He left the line and circled the fountain to where the Sign of the Awl hung upon a pillar. He moved up the Street of the Weavers.

Three times did he ask after Janagga the sailmaker, the third time of a short woman with powerful arms and a small mustache, who sat cross-legged, plaiting a rug, in her stall beneath the low eave of what once might have been a stable and still smelled as if it were.

She growled him directions, after raking him upward and down again with oddly lovely brown-velvet eyes. He followed her directions, taking his way up a zigzagging alley and down an outer stair, which ran along the wall of a five-story building, ending at a door that opened upon a basement hallway. It was damp and dark within.

He knocked upon the third door to his left, and after a time it opened.

The man stared at him. "Yes?"

"May I come in? It is a matter of some urgency . . ."

The man hesitated a moment, then nodded abruptly and stepped aside.

The prince moved past him and into his chamber. A great sheet of canvas was spread out over the floor, before the stool upon which the man reseated himself. He motioned the prince into the only other chair in the room.

He was short and big in the shoulders; his hair was pure white, and the pupils of his eyes bore the smoky beginnings of cataract invasion. His hands were brown and hard, the joints of his fingers knotted.

"Yes?" he repeated.

"Jan Olvegg," said the other.

"The old man's eyes widened, then narrowed to slits. He weighed a pair of scissors in his hand.

" 'It's a long way to Tipperary,' " said the prince.

The man stared, then smiled suddenly. " 'If your heart's not here,' " he said, placing the scissors on his workstand. "How long has it been, Sam?" he asked.

"I've lost count of the years."

"Me too. But it must be forty—forty-five?—since I've seen you. Much beer over the damn dam since then, I daresay?"

Sam nodded.

"I don't really know where to begin . . ." said the man.

"For a start, tell me—why 'Janagga'?"

"Why not?" asked the other. "It has a certain earnest, working-class sound about it. How about yourself? Still in the prince business?"

"I'm still me," said Sam, "and they still call me Siddhartha when they come to call."

The other chuckled. "And 'Binder of the Demons,' " he recited. "Very good. I take it, then, since your fortunes do not match your garb, that you are casing the scene, as is your wont."

Sam nodded. "And I have come upon much which I do not understand."

"Aye," sighed Jan. "Aye. How shall I begin? How? I shall tell you of myself, that's how. . . . I have accumulated too much bad karma to warrant a current transfer."

"What?"

"Bad karma, that's what I said. The old religion is not only *the* religion—it is the revealed, enforced and frighteningly demonstrable religion. But don't think that last part too loudly. About a dozen years ago the Council authorized the use of psych-probes on those who were up for renewal. This was right after the Accelerationist-Deicrat split, when the Holy Coalition squeezed out the tech boys and kept right on squeezing.

The simplest solution was to outlive the problem. The Temple crowd then made a deal with the body sellers, customers were brain-probed and Accelerationists were refused renewal, or ... well ... simple as that. There aren't too many Accelerationists now. But that was only the beginning. The god party was quick to realize that therein lay the way of power. Having your brains scanned has become a standard procedure, just prior to a transfer. The body merchants are become the Masters of Karma, and a part of the Temple structure. They read over your past life, weigh the karma, and determine your life that is yet to come. It's a perfect way of maintaining the caste system and ensuring Deicratic control. By the way, most of our old acquaintances are in it up to their halos."

"God!" said Sam.

"Plural," Jan corrected. "They've always been considered gods, with their Aspects and Attributes, but they've made it awfully official now. And anyone who happens to be among the First had bloody well better be sure whether he wants quick deification or the pyre when he walks into the Hall of Karma these days.

"When's your appointment?" he finished.

"Tomorrow," said Sam, "in the afternoon. . . . Why are you still walking around, if you don't have a halo or a handful of thunderbolts?"

"Because I do have a couple friends, both of whom suggested I continue living—quietly—rather than face the probe. I took their sage advice to heart and consequently am still around to mend sails and raise occasional hell in the local bistros. Else"—he raised a callused hand, snapped his fingers—"else, if not the real death, then perhaps a body shot full with cancer, or the interesting life of a gelded water buffalo, or . . ."

"A dog?" asked Sam.

- "Just so," Jan replied.

Jan filled the silence and two glasses with a splashing of alcohol.

"Thanks."

"Happy hellfire." He replaced the bottle on his workstand.

"On an empty stomach yet. . . . You make that yourself?"

"Yep. Got a still in the next room."

"Congratulations, I guess. If I had any bad karma, it should all be dissolved by now."

"The definition of bad karma is anything our friends the gods don't like."

"What made you think you had some?"

"I wanted to start passing out machines among our descendants here. Got batted down at Council for it. Recanted, and hoped they'd forget. But Accelerationism is so far out now that it'll never make it back in during my lifetime. Pity, too. I'd like to lift sail again, head off toward another horizon. Or lift ship . . ."

"The probe is actually sensitive enough to spot something as intangible as an Accelerationist attitude?"

"The probe," said Jan, "is sensitive enough to tell what you had for breakfast eleven years ago yesterday and where you cut yourself shaving that morning, while humming the Andorran national anthem."

"They were experimental things when we left—home," said Sam. "The two we brought along were very basic brain-wave translators. When did the breakthrough occur?"

"Hear me, country cousin," said Jan. "Do you remember a snot-nosed brat of dubious parentage, third generation, named Yama? The kid who was always souping up generators, until one day one blew and he was so badly burned that he got his second body—one over fifty years old—when he was only sixteen? The kid who loved weapons? The fellow who anesthetized one of everything that moves out there and dissected it, taking such pleasure in his studies that we called him deathgod?"

"Yes, I recall him. Is he still alive?"

"If you want to call it that. He now *is* deathgod—not by nickname, but by title. He perfected the probe about forty years ago, but the Deicrats kept it under wraps until fairly recently. I hear he's dreamed up some other little jewels, too, to serve the will of the gods ... like a mechanical cobra capable of registering encephalogram readings from a mile away, when it rears and spreads its fan. It can pick one man out of a crowd, regardless of the body he wears. There is no known antidote for its venom. Four seconds, no more. ... Or the fire wand, which is said to have scored the surfaces of all three moons while Lord Agni stood upon the seashore and waved it. And I understand that he is designing some sort of jet-propeled juggernaut for Lord Shiva at this moment ... things like that."

"Oh," said Sam.

"Will you pass the probe?" Jan asked.

"I'm afraid not," he replied. "Tell me, I saw a machine this morning which I think may best be described as a pray-o-mat—are they very common?"

"Yes," said Jan. "They appeared about two years ago—dreamed up by young Leonardo over a short glass of soma one night. Now that the karma idea has caught on, the things are better than tax collectors. When mister citizen presents himself at the clinic of the god of the church of his choice on the eve of his sixtieth year, his prayer account is said to be considered along with his sin account, in deciding the caste he will enter—as well as the age, sex and health of the body he will receive. Nice. Neat."

"I will not pass the probe," said Sam, "even if I build up a mighty prayer account. They'll snare me when it comes to sin."

"What sort of sin?"

"Sins I have yet to commit, but which are being written in my mind as I consider them now."

"You plan to oppose the gods?"

"Yes."

"How?"

"I do not yet know. I shall begin, however, by contacting them. Who is their chief?"

"I can name you no one. Trimurti rules—that is, Brahma, Vishnu and Shiva. Which of these three be chiefest at any one time, I cannot say. Some say Brahma—"

"Who are they—really?" asked Sam.

Jan shook his head. "I do not know. They all wear different bodies than they did a generation ago. They all use god names."

Sam stood. "I will return later, or send for you."

"I hope so. . . . Another drink?"

Sam shook his head. "I go to become Siddhartha once more, to break my fast at the hostel of Hawkana and announce there my intent to visit the Temples. If our friends are now gods then they must commune with their priests. Siddhartha goes to pray."

"Then put in no words for me," said Jan, as he poured out another drink. "I do not know whether I would live through a divine visitation."

Sam smiled. "They are not omnipotent."

"I sincerely hope not," replied the other, "but I fear that day is not far off."

"Good sailing, Jan."

"*Skaal.*"

Prince Siddhartha stopped on the Street of the Smiths, on his way to the Temple of Brahma. Half an hour later he emerged from a shop, accompanied by Strake and three of his retainers. Smiling, as though he had received a vision of what was to come, he passed through the center of Mahartha, coming at last to the high, wide Temple of the Creator.

Ignoring the stares of those who stood before the pray-o-mat, he mounted the long, shallow stairway, meeting at the Temple entrance with the high priest, whom he had advised earlier of his coming.

Siddhartha and his men entered the Temple, disarming themselves and paying preliminary obeisances toward its central chamber before addressing the priest.

Strake and the others drew back a respectful distance

as the prince placed a heavy purse in the priest's hands
and said, in a low voice:

"I'd like to speak with God."

The priest studied his face as he replied, "The Temple is open to all, Lord Siddhartha, where one may
commune with Heaven for so long as one wishes."

"That is not exactly what I had in mind," said
Siddhartha. "I was thinking of something more personal than a sacrifice and a long litany."

"I do not quite follow you . . ."

"But you understand the weight of that purse, do
you not? It contains silver. Another which I bear is
filled with gold—payable upon delivery. I want to use
your telephone."

"Tele . . . ?"

"Communication system. If you were of the First,
such as I, you would understand my reference."

"I do not . . ."

"I assure you my call will not reflect adversely upon
your wardenship here. I am aware of these matters and
my discretion has always been a byword among the
First. Call First Base yourself and inquire, if it will put
you at ease. I'll wait here in the outer chamber. Tell
them Sam would have words with Trimurti. They will
take the call."

"I do not know . . ."

Sam withdrew the second purse and weighed it in the
palm of his hand. The priest's eyes fell upon it and he
licked his lips.

"Wait here," he ordered, and he turned on his heel
and left the chamber.

Ili, the fifth note of the harp, buzzed within the
Garden of the Purple Lotus.

Brahma loafed upon the edge of the heated pool,
where he bathed with his harem. His eyes appeared
closed, as he leaned there upon his elbows, his feet
dangling in the water.

But he stared out from beneath his long lashes,

watching the dozen girls at sport in the pool, hoping to
see one or more cast an appreciative glance upon the
dark, heavily muscled length of his body. Black upon
brown, his mustaches glistened in moist disarray and
his hair was a black wing upon his back. He smiled a
bright smile in the filtered sunlight.

But none of them appeared to notice, so he refolded
his smile and put it away. All their attention lay with
the game of water polo in which they were engaged.

Ili, the bell of communication, buzzed once more, as
an artificial breeze wafted the odor of garden jasmine to
his nostrils. He sighed. He wanted so for them to
worship him—his powerful physique, his carefully
molded features. To worship him as a man, not as a
god.

But though his special and improved body permitted
feats no mortal man could duplicate, still he felt uneasy
in the presence of an old war horse like Lord Shiva—
who, despite his adherence to the normal body matrix,
seemed to hold far more attraction for women. It was
almost as if sex were a thing that transcended biology;
and no matter how hard he tried to suppress the memory and destroy that segment of spirit, Brahma had been
born a woman and somehow was woman still. Hating
this thing, he had elected to incarnate time after time as
an eminently masculine man, did so, and still felt somehow inadequate, as though the mark of his true sex
were branded upon his brow. It made him want to
stamp his foot and grimace.

He rose and stalked off toward his pavilion, past
stunted trees that twisted with a certain grotesque beauty, past trellises woven with morning glory, pools of
blue water lilies, strings of pearls swinging from rings
all wrought of white gold, past lamps shaped like girls,
tripods wherein pungent incenses burnt and an eight-
armed statue of a blue goddess who played upon the
veena when properly addressed.

Brahma entered the pavilion and crossed to the

screen of crystal, about which a bronze Naga twisted, tail in teeth. He activated the answering mechanism.

There was a static snowfall, and then he faced the high priest of his Temple in Mahartha. The priest dropped to his knees and touched his caste mark three times upon the floor.

"♪Of the four orders of gods and the eighteen hosts of Paradise, mightiest is Brahma," said the priest. "♪Creator of all, Lord of high Heaven and everything beneath it. ♪A lotus springs forth from your navel, your hands churn the oceans, in three strides your feet encompass all the worlds. ♪The drum of your glory strikes terror in the hearts of your enemies. ♪Upon your right hand is the wheel of the law. ♪You tether catastrophes, using a snake for rope. ♪Hail! ♪See fit to accept the prayer of your priest. ♪Bless me and hear me, Brahma!♪"

"Arise . . . priest," said Brahma, having forgotten his name. "What thing of mighty importance moved you to call me thus?"

The priest arose, cast a quick glance upon Brahma's dripping person and looked away again.

"Lord," said the priest, "I did not mean to call while you were at bath, but there is one among your worshipers here now who would speak with you, on a matter which I take to be of mighty importance."

"One of my worshipers! Tell him that all-hearing Brahma hears all, and direct him to pray to me in the ordinary manner, in the Temple proper!"

Brahma's hand moved toward the shutoff switch, then paused. "How came he to know of the Temple-to-Heaven line?" he inquired. "And of the direct communion of saints and gods?"

"He says," replied the priest, "that he is of the First, and that I should relay the message that Sam would have words with Trimurti."

"Sam?" said Brahma. "Sam? Surely it cannot be . . . *that* Sam?"

"He is the one known hereabouts as Siddhartha, Binder of the Demons."

"Await my pleasure," said Brahma, "singing the while various appropriate verses from the Vedas."

"I hear, my Lord," said the priest, and he commenced singing.

Brahma moved to another part of the pavilion and stood awhile before his wardrobe, deciding what to wear.

The prince, hearing his name called, turned from the contemplation of the Temple's interior. The priest, whose name he had forgotten, beckoned him along a corridor. He followed, and the passage led into a storage chamber. The priest fumbled after a hidden catch, then drew upon a row of shelves that opened outward, doorlike.

The prince passed through this doorway. He found himself within a richly decorated shrine. A glowing view-screen hung above its altar/control-panel, encircled by a bronze Naga, which held its tail in its teeth.

The priest bowed three times.

"♪Hail, ruler of the universe, mightiest of the four orders of gods and the eighteen hosts of paradise. ♪From your navel springs forth the lotus, your hands churn the oceans, in three strides—♪"

"I acknowledge the truth of what you say," replied Brahma. "You are blessed and heard. You may leave us now."

"♪?"

"That is correct. Sam is doubtless paying you for a private line, is he not?"

"Lord . . . !"

"Enough! Depart!"

The priest bowed quickly and left, closing the shelves behind him.

Brahma studied Sam, who was wearing dark jodhpurs, a sky-blue *khameez*, the blue-green turban of

Urath and an empty scabbard upon a chain belt of dark iron.

Sam, in turn, studied the other, who stood with blackness at his back, wearing a feather cloak over a suit of light mail. It was caught at the throat with a clasp of fire opal. Brahma wore a purple crown, studded with pulsating amethysts, and he bore in his right hand a scepter mounted with the nine auspicious gems. His eyes were two dark stains upon his dark face. The gentle strumming of a *veena* occurred about him.

"Sam?" he said.

Sam nodded.

"I am trying to guess your true identity, Lord Brahma. I confess that I cannot."

"This is as it should be," said Brahma, "if one is to be a god who was, is and always shall be."

"Fine garments, those you wear," said Sam. "Quite fetching."

"Thank you. I find it hard to believe that you still exist. Checking, I note that you have not sought a new body for half a century. That is taking quite a chance."

Sam shrugged. "Life is full of chances, gambles, uncertainties . . ."

"True," said Brahma. "Pray, draw up a chair and sit down. Make yourself comfortable."

Sam did this, and when he looked up again, Brahma was seated upon a high throne carved of red marble, with a matching parasol flared above it.

"That looks a bit uncomfortable," he remarked.

"Foam-rubber cushion," replied the god, smiling. "You may smoke, if you wish."

"Thanks." Sam drew his pipe from the pouch at his belt, filled it, tamped it carefully and struck it to fire.

"What have you been doing all this time," asked the god, "since you left the roost of Heaven?"

"Cultivating my own gardens," said Sam.

"We could have used you here," said Brahma, "in

our hydroponics section. For that matter, perhaps we still could. Tell me more of your stay among men."

"Tiger hunts, border disputes with neighboring kingdoms, keeping up the morale of the harem, a bit of botanical research—things like that—the stuff of life," said Sam. "Now my powers slacken, and I seek once more my youth. But to obtain it again, I understand that I must have my brains strained. Is that true?"

"After a fashion," said Brahma.

"To what end, may I ask?"

"That wrong shall fail and right prevail," said the god, smiling.

"Supposing I'm wrong," asked Sam, "how shall I fail?"

"You shall be required to work off your karmic burden in a lesser form."

"Have you any figures readily available as to the percentage that fails, vis-à-vis that which prevails?"

"Think not less of me in my omniscience," said Brahma, stifling a yawn with his scepter, "if I admit to having, for the moment, forgotten these figures."

Sam chuckled. "You say you have need of a gardener there in the Celestial City?"

"Yes," said Brahma. "Would you like to apply for the job?"

"I don't know," said Sam. "Perhaps."

"And then again, perhaps not?" said the other.

"Perhaps not, also," he acknowledged. "In the old days there was none of this shillyshallying with a man's mind. If one of the First sought renewal, he paid the body price and was served."

"We no longer dwell in the old days, Sam. The new age is at hand."

"One would almost think that you sought the removal of all of the First who are not marshaled at your back."

"A pantheon has room for many, Sam. There is a niche for you, if you choose to claim it."

"If I do not?"

"Then inquire in the Hall of Karma after your body."

"And if I elect godhood?"

"Your brains will not be probed. The Masters will be advised to serve you quickly and well. A flying machine will be dispatched to convey you to Heaven."

"It bears a bit of thinking," said Sam. "I'm quite fond of *this* world, though it wallows in an age of darkness. On the other hand, such fondness will not serve me to enjoy the things I desire, if it is decreed that I die the real death or take on the form of an ape and wander about the jungles. But I am not overly fond of artificial perfection either, such as existed in Heaven when last I visited there. Bide with me a moment while I meditate."

"I consider such indecision presumptuous," said Brahma, "when one has just been made such an offer."

"I know, and perhaps I should also, were our positions reversed. But if I were God and you were me, I do believe I would extend a moment's merciful silence while a man makes a major decision regarding his life."

"Sam, you are an impossible haggler! Who else would keep me waiting while his immortality hangs in the balance? Surely you do not seek to bargain with *me?*"

"Well, I do come from a long line of slizzard traders —and I do very badly want something."

"And what may that be?"

"Answers to a few questions which have plagued me for a while now."

"These being ... ?"

"As you are aware, I stopped attending the old Council meetings over a century ago, for they had become lengthy sessions calculated to postpone decision-making, and were primarily an excuse for a Festival of the First. Now, I have nothing against festivals. In fact, for a century and a half I went to them only to drink good Earth booze once more. But, I felt that we should be doing something about the passengers, as well as the offspring of our many bodies, rather than letting them wander a vicious world, reverting to savagery. I felt that we of the crew should be assisting them, granting them the benefits of the technology we had preserved, rather than building ourselves an impregnable paradise and treating the world as a combination game preserve and whorehouse. So, I have wondered long why this thing was not done. It would seem a fair and equitable way to run a world."

"I take it from this that you are an Accelerationist?"

"No," said Sam, "simply an inquirer. I am curious, that's all, as to the reasons."

"Then, to answer your questions," said Brahma, "it is because they are not ready for it. Had we acted immediately—yes, this thing could have been done. But we were indifferent at first. Then, when the question arose, we were divided. Too much time passed. They are not ready, and will not be for many centuries. If they were to be exposed to an advanced technology at this point, the wars which would ensue would result in the destruction of the beginnings they have already made. They have come far. They have begun a civilization after the manner of their fathers of old. But they are still children, and like children would they play with our gifts and be burnt by them. They *are* our children, by our long-dead First bodies, and second, and third and many after—and so, ours is the parents' responsibility toward them. We must not permit them to be accelerated into an industrial revolution and so destroy the first stable society on this planet. Our parental functions can best be performed by guiding them as we do, through the Temples. Gods and goddesses are basically parent figures, so what could be truer and more just than that we assume these roles and play them thoroughly?"

"Why then do you destroy their own infant technology? The printing press has been rediscovered on three occasions that I can remember, and suppressed each time."

"This was done for the same reason—they were not yet ready for it. And it was not truly discovered, but rather it was remembered. It was a thing out of legend which someone set about duplicating. If a thing is to come, it must come as a result of factors already present in the culture, and not be pulled from out of the past like a rabbit from a hat."

"It seems you are drawing a mighty fine line at that point, Brahma. I take it from this that your minions go to and fro in the world, destroying all signs of progress they come upon?"

"This is not true," said the god. "You talk as if we desire perpetually this burden of godhood, as if we seek to maintain a dark age that we may know forever the wearisome condition of our enforced divinity!"

"In a word," said Sam, "yes. What of the pray-o-mat which squats before this very Temple? Is it on par, culturally, with a chariot?"

"That is different," said Brahma. "As a divine manifestation, it is held in awe by the citizens and is not questioned, for religious reasons. It is hardly the same as if gunpowder were to be introduced."

"Supposing some local atheist hijacks one and picks it apart? And supposing he happens to be a Thomas Edison? What then?"

"They have tricky combination locks on them. If anyone other than a priest opens one, it will blow up and take him along with it."

"And I notice you were unable to suppress the rediscovery of the still, though you tried. So you slapped on an alcohol tax, payable to the Temples."

"Mankind has always sought release through drink," said Brahma. "It has generally figured in somewhere in his religious ceremonies. Less guilt involved that way. True, we tried suppressing it at first, but we quickly saw we could not. So, in return for our tax, they receive here a blessing upon their booze. Less guilt, less of a hangover, fewer recriminations—it *is* psychosomatic, you know—and the tax isn't that high."

"Funny, though, how many prefer the profane brew."

"You came to pray and you are staying to scoff, is that what you're saying, Sam? I offered to answer your questions, not debate Deicrat policies with you. Have you made up your mind yet regarding my offer?"

"Yes, Madeleine," said Sam, "and did anyone ever tell you how lovely you are when you're angry?"

Brahma sprang forward off the throne. *"How could you? How could you tell?"* screamed the god.

"I couldn't, really," said Sam. "Until now. It was just a guess, based upon some of your mannerisms of speech and gesture which I remembered. So you've finally achieved your lifelong ambition, eh? I'll bet you've got a harem, too. What's it feel like, madam, to be a real stud after having been a gal to start out with? Bet every Lizzie in the world would envy you if she knew. Congratulations."

Brahma drew himself up to full height and glared. The thone was a flame at his back. The *veena* thrummed on, dispassionately. He raised his scepter then and spoke:

"Prepare yourself to receive the curse of Brahma . . ." he began.

"Whatever for?" asked Sam. "Because I guessed your secret? If I am to be a god, what difference does it make? Others must know of it. Are you angry because the only way I could learn your true identity was by baiting you a little? I had assumed you would appreciate me the more if I demonstrated my worth by displaying my wit in this manner. If I have offended you, I do apologize."

"It is not because you guessed—or even because of the manner in which you guessed—but because you mocked me, that I curse you."

"Mocked you?" said Sam. "I do not understand. I intended no disrespect. I was always on good terms with you in the old days. If you will but think back over them, you will recall that this is true. Why should I jeopardize my position by mocking you now?"

"Because you said what you thought too quickly, without thinking a second time."

"Nay, my Lord. I did but jest with you as any one man might with another when discussing these matters. I am sorry if you took it amiss. I'll warrant you've a harem I'd envy, and which I'll doubtless try to sneak into some night. If you'd curse me for being surprised, then curse away." He drew upon his pipe and wreathed his grin in smoke.

Finally, Brahma chuckled. "I'm a bit quick-tempered, 'tis true," he explained, "and perhaps too touchy about my past. Of course, I've often jested so with other men. You are forgiven. I withdraw my beginning curse.

"And your decision, I take it, is to accept my offer?" he inquired.

"That is correct," said Sam.

"Good. I've always felt a brotherly affection for you. Go now and summon my priest, that I may instruct him concerning your incarnation. I'll see you soon."

"Sure thing, Lord Brahma." Sam nodded and raised his pipe. Then he pushed back the row of shelves and sought the priest in the hall without. Various thoughts passed through his mind, but this time he let them remain unspoken.

That evening, the prince held council with those of his retainers who had visited kinsmen and friends within Mahartha, and with those who had gone about through the town obtaining news and gossip. From these he learned that there were only ten Masters of Karma in Mahartha and that they kept their lodgings in a palace on the southeastern slopes above the city. They made scheduled visits to the clinics, or reading rooms, of the Temples, where the citizens presented themselves for judgment when they applied for renewal. The Hall of Karma itself was a massive black structure within the

courtyard of their palace, where a person applied shortly after judgment to have his transfer made into his new
body. Strake, along with two of his advisers, departed
while daylight yet remained to make sketches of the
palace fortifications. Two of the prince's courtiers were
dispatched across town to deliver an invitation to late
dining and revelry to the Shan of Irabek, an old man
and distant neighbor of Siddhartha's with whom he had
fought three bloody border skirmishes and occasionally
hunted tiger. The Shan was visiting with relatives while
waiting his appointment with the Masters of Karma.
Another man was sent to the Street of the Smiths,
where he requested of the metal workers that they
double the prince's order and have it ready by early
morning. He took along additional money to ensure
their cooperation.

Later, the Shan of Irabek arrived at the Hostel of
Hawkana, accompanied by six of his relatives, who
were of the merchant caste but came armed as if they
were warriors. Seeing that the hostel was a peaceable
abode, however, and that none of the other guests or
visitors bore arms, they put aside their weapons and
seated themselves near the head of the table, beside the
prince.

The Shan was a tall man, but his posture was considerably hunched. He wore maroon robes and a dark
turban reaching down almost to his great, caterpillar-
like eyebrows, which were the color of milk. His beard
was a snowy bush, his teeth shown as dark stumps
when he laughed and his lower eyelids jutted redly, as
though sore and weary after so many years of holding
back his bloodshot orbs in their obvious attempt to
push themselves forward out of their sockets. He
laughed a phlegmy laugh and pounded the table, re-
peating, "Elephants are too expensive these days, and
no damn good at all in mud!" for the sixth time; this
being in reference to their conversation as to the best
time of year to fight a war. Only one very new in the
business would be so boorish as to insult a neighbor's

ambassador during the rainy season, it was decided, and that one would thereafter be marked as a *nouveau roi*.

As the evening wore on, the prince's physician excused himself so as to superintend the preparation of the dessert and introduce a narcotic into the sweetcakes being served up to the Shan. As the evening wore further on, subsequent to the dessert, the Shan grew more and more inclined to close his eyes and let his head slump forward for longer and longer periods of time. "Good party," he muttered, between snores, and finally, "Elephants are no damn good at all . . ." and so passed to sleep and could not be awakened. His kinsmen did not see fit to escort him home at this time, because of the fact that the prince's physician had added chloral hydrate to their wine, and they were at that moment sprawled upon the floor, snoring. The prince's chief courtier arranged with Hawkana for their accommodation, and the Shan himself was taken to Siddhartha's suite, where he was shortly visited by the physician, who loosened his garments and spoke to him in a soft, persuasive voice:

"Tomorrow afternoon," he was saying, "you will be Prince Siddhartha and these will be your retainers. You will report to the Hall of Karma in their company, to claim there the body which Brahma has promised you without the necessity of prior judgment. You will remain Siddhartha throughout the transfer, and you will return here in the company of your retainers, to be examined by me. Do you understand?"

"Yes," whispered the Shan.

"Then repeat what I have told you."

"Tomorrow afternoon," said the Shan, "I will be Siddhartha, commanding these retainers . . ."

Bright bloomed the morning, and debts were settled beneath it. Half of the prince's men rode out of the city, heading north. When they were out of sight of Mahartha they began circling to the southeast, working

their way through the hills, stopping only to don their
battle gear.

Half a dozen men were dispatched to the Street of
the Smiths, whence they returned bearing heavy canvas
bags, the contents of which were divided into the
pouches of three dozen men who departed after breakfast into the city.

The prince took counsel with his physician, Narada,
saying, "If I have misjudged the clemency of Heaven,
then am I cursed indeed."

But the doctor smiled and replied, "I doubt you
misjudged."

And so they passed from morning into the still center
of day, the Ridge of the Gods golden above them.

When their charges awakened, they ministered to
their hangovers. The Shan was given a posthypnotic
and sent with six of Siddhartha's retainers to the Palace
of the Masters. His kinsmen were assured that he remained sleeping in the prince's quarters.

"Our major risk at this point," said the physician, "is
the Shan. Will he be recognized? The factors in our
favor are that he is a minor potentate from a distant
kingdom, he has only been in town for a short period
of time, has spent most of that time with his kinsmen
and he has not yet presented himself for judgment. The
Masters should still be unaware of your own physical
appearance—"

"Unless I have been described to them by Brahma or
his priest," said the prince. "For all I know, my communication may have been taped and the tape relayed
to them for identification purposes."

"Why, though, should this have been done?" inquired Narada. "They should hardly expect stealth and
elaborate precautions of one for whom they are doing a
favor. No, I think we should be able to pull it off. The
Shan would not be able to pass a probe, of course, but
he should pass surface scrutiny, accompanied as he is
by your retainers. At the moment, he *does* believe he is
Siddhartha, and he could pass any simple lie-detection

test in that regard—which I feel is the most serious obstacle he might encounter."

So they waited, and the three dozen men returned with empty pouches, gathered their belongings, mounted their horses and one by one drifted off through the town, as though in search of revelry, but actually drifting slowly in a southeasterly direction.

"Good-bye, good Hawkana," said the prince, as the remainder of his men packed and mounted. "I shall bear, as always, good report of your lodgings to all whom I meet about the land. I regret that my stay here must be so unexpectedly terminated, but I must ride to put down an uprising in the provinces as soon as I leave the Hall of Karma. You are aware of how these things spring up the moment a ruler's back is turned. So, while I should have liked to spend another week beneath your roof, I fear that this pleasure must be postponed until another time. If any ask after me, tell them to seek me in Hades."

"Hades, my Lord?"

"It is the southernmost province of my kingdom, noted for its excessively warm weather. Be sure to phrase it just so, especially to the priests of Brahma, who may become concerned as to my whereabouts in days to come."

"I'll do that, my Lord."

"And take especial care of the boy Dele. I expect to hear him play again on my next visit."

Hawkana bowed low and was about to begin a speech, so the prince decided upon that moment to toss him the final bag of coins and make an additional comment as to the wines of Urath—before mounting quickly and shouting orders to his men, in such a manner as to drown out any further conversation.

Then they rode through the gateway and were gone, leaving behind only the physician and three warriors, whom he was to treat an additional day for an obscure condition having to do with the change of climate, before they rode on to catch up with the others.

They passed through the town, using side streets, and came after a time to the roadway that led up toward the Palace of the Masters of Karma. As they passed along its length, Siddhartha exchanged secret signs with those three dozen of his warriors who lay in hiding at various points off in the woods.

When they had gone half the distance to the palace, the prince and the eight men who accompanied him drew rein and made as if to rest, waiting the while for the others to move abreast of them, passing carefully among the trees.

Before long, however, they saw movement on the trail ahead. Seven riders were advancing on horseback, and the prince guessed them to be his six lancers and the Shan. When they came within hailing distance, they advanced to meet them.

"Who are you?" inquired the tall, sharp-eyed rider mounted upon the white mare. "Who are you that dares block the passage of Prince Siddhartha, Binder of Demons?"

The prince looked upon him—muscular and tanned, in his mid-twenties, possessed of hawklike features and a powerful bearing—and he felt suddenly that his doubts had been unfounded and that he had betrayed himself by his suspicion and mistrust. It appeared from the lithe physical specimen seated upon his own mount that Brahma had bargained in good faith, authorizing for his use an excellent and sturdy body, which was now possessed by the ancient Shan.

"Lord Siddhartha," said his man, who had ridden at the side of the Lord of Irabek, "it appears that they dealt fairly. I see naught amiss about him."

"Siddhartha!" cried the Shan. "Who is this one you dare address with the name of your master? *I* am Siddhartha, Binder of—" With that he threw his head back and his words gurgled in his throat.

Then the fit hit the Shan. He stiffened, lost his seating and fell from the saddle. Siddhartha ran to his side. There were little flecks of foam at the corners of his mouth, and his eyes were rolled upward.

"Epileptic!" cried the prince. "They meant me to have a brain which had been damaged."

The others gathered around and helped the prince minister to the Shan until the seizure passed and his wits had returned to his body.

"Wh-what happened?" he asked.

"Treachery," said Siddhartha. "Treachery, oh Shan of Irabek! One of my men will convey you now to my personal physician, for an examination. After you have rested, I suggest you lodge a protest at Brahma's reading room. My physician will treat you at Hawkana's, and then you will be released. I am sorry this thing happened. It will probably be set aright. But if not, remember the last siege of Kapil and consider us even on all scores. Good afternoon, brother prince." He bowed to the other, and his men helped the Shan to mount Hawkana's bay, which Siddhartha had borrowed earlier.

Mounting the mare, the prince observed their departure, then turned to the men who stood about him, and he spoke in a voice sufficiently loud to be heard by those who waited off the road:

"The nine of us will enter. Two blasts upon the horn, and you others follow. If they resist, make them wish they had been more prudent, for three more blasts upon the horn will bring the fifty lancers down from the hills, if they be needed. It is a palace of ease, and not a fort where battles would be fought. Take the Masters prisoner. Do not harm their machineries or allow others to do so. If they do not resist us, all well and good. If they do, we shall walk through the Palace and Hall of the Masters of Karma like a small boy across an extensive and excessively elaborate ant hill. Good luck. No gods be with you!"

And turning his horse, he headed on up the road, the eight lancers singing softly at his back.

The prince rode through the wide double gate, which stood open and unguarded. He set immediately to wondering concerning secret defenses that Strake might have missed.

The courtyard was landscaped and partly paved. In a large garden area, servants were at work pruning, trimming and cultivating. The prince sought after weapon emplacements and saw none. The servants glanced up as he entered, but did not halt their labors.

At the far end of the courtyard was the black stone Hall. He advanced in that direction, his horsemen following, until he was hailed from the steps of the palace itself, which lay to his right.

He drew rein and turned to look in that direction. The man wore black livery, a yellow circle on his breast, and he carried an ebony staff. He was tall, heavy and muffled to the eyes. He did not repeat his salutation, but stood waiting.

The prince guided his mount to the foot of the wide stairway. "I must speak to the Masters of Karma," he stated.

"Have you an appointment?" inquired the man.

"No," said the prince, "but it is a matter of importance."

"Then I regret that you have made this trip for nothing," replied the other. "An appointment is necessary. You may make arrangements at any Temple in Mahartha."

He then struck upon the stair with his staff, turned his back and began to move away.

"Uproot that garden," said the prince to his men, "cut down yonder trees, heap everything together and set a torch to it."

The man in black halted, turned again.

Only the prince waited at the foot of the stair. His men were already moving off in the direction of the garden.

"You can't do that," said the man.

The prince smiled.

His men dismounted and began hacking at the shrubbery, kicking their way through the flower beds.

"Tell them to stop!"

"Why should I? I have come to speak with the Masters of Karma, and you tell me that I cannot. I tell you that I can, and will. Let us see which of us is correct."

"Order them to stop," said the other, "and I will bear your message to the Masters."

"Halt!" cried the prince. "But be ready to begin again."

The man in black mounted the stairs, vanished into the palace. The prince fingered the horn that hung on a cord about his neck.

In a short while there was movement, and armed men began to emerge from the doorway. The prince raised his horn and gave wind to it twice.

The men wore leather armor—some still buckling it hastily into place—and caps of the same material. Their sword arms were padded to the elbow, and they wore small, oval-shaped metal shields, bearing as device a yellow wheel upon a black field. They carried long, curved blades. They filled the stairway completely and stood as if waiting orders.

The man in black emerged again, and he stood at the head of the stair. "Very well," he stated, "if you have a message for the Masters, say it!"

"Are you a Master?" inquired the prince.

"I am."

"Then must your rank be lowest of them all, if you must also do duty as doorman. Let me speak to the Master in charge here."

"Your insolence will be repaid both now and in a life yet to come," observed the Master.

Then three dozen lancers rode through the gate and arrayed themselves at the sides of the prince. The eight who had begun the deflowering of the garden remounted their horses and moved to join the formation, blades laid bare across their laps.

"Must we enter your palace on horseback?" inquired the prince. "Or will you now summon the other Masters, with whom I wish to hold conversation?"

Close to eighty men stood upon the stair facing them, blades in hand. The Master seemed to weigh the balance of forces. He decided in favor of maintaining things as they were.

"Do nothing rash," he stated, "for my men will defend themselves in a particularly vicious fashion. Wait upon my return. I shall summon the others."

The prince filled his pipe and lit it. His men sat like statues, lances ready. Perspiration was most evident upon the faces of the foot soldiers who held the first rank on the stairway.

The prince, to pass the time, observed to his lancers, "Do not think to display your skill as you did at the last siege of Kapil. Make target of the breast, rather than the head.

"Also," he continued, "think not to engage in the customary mutilation of the wounded and the slain— for this is a holy place and should not be profaned in such a manner.

"On the other hand," he added, "I shall take it as a personal affront if there are not ten prisoners for sacrifice to Nirriti the Black, my personal patron—outside these walls, of course, where observance of the Dark Feast will not be held so heavily against us . . ."

There was a clatter to the right, as a foot soldier who had been staring up the length of Strake's lance passed out and fell from the bottom stair.

"Stop!" cried the figure in black, who emerged with six others—similarly garbed—at the head of the stairway. "Do not profane the Palace of Karma with bloodshed. Already that fallen warrior's blood is—"

"Rising to his cheeks," finished the prince, "if he be conscious—for he is not slain."

"What is it you want?" The figure in black who was addressing him was of medium height, but of enormous girth. He stood like a huge, dark barrel, his staff a sable thunderbolt.

"I count seven," replied the prince. "I understand that ten Masters reside here. Where are the other three?"

"Those others are presently in attendance at three reading rooms in Mahartha. What is it you want of us?"

"You are in charge here?"

"Only the Great Wheel of the Law is in charge here."

"Are you the senior representative of the Great Wheel within these walls?"

"I am."

"Very well. I wish to speak with you in private—over there," said the prince, gesturing toward the black Hall.

"Impossible!"

The prince knocked his pipe empty against his heel, scraped its bowl with the point of his dagger, replaced it in his pouch. Then he sat very erect upon the white mare and clasped the horn in his left hand. He met the Master's eyes.

"Are you absolutely certain of that?" he asked.

The Master's mouth, small and bright, twisted around words he did not speak. Then:

"As you say," he finally acknowledged. "Make way for me here!" and he passed down through the ranks of the warriors and stood before the white mare.

The prince guided the horse with his knees, turning her in the direction of the dark Hall.

"Hold ranks, for now!" called out the Master.

"The same applies," said the prince to his men.

The two of them crossed the courtyard, and the prince dismounted before the Hall.

"You owe me a body," he said in a soft voice.

"What talk is this?" said the Master.

"I am Prince Siddhartha of Kapil, Binder of Demons."

"Siddhartha has already been served," said the other.

"So you think," said the prince, "served up as an epileptic, by order of Brahma. This is not so, however. The man you treated earlier today was an unwilling impostor. I am the real Siddhartha, oh nameless priest, and I have come to claim my body—one that is whole and strong, and without hidden disease. You will serve me in this matter. You will serve me willingly or unwillingly, but you will serve me."

"You think so?"

"I think so," replied the prince.

"Attack!" cried the Master, and he swung his dark staff at the prince's head.

The prince ducked the blow and retreated, drawing his blade. Twice, he parried the staff. Then it fell upon his shoulder, a glancing blow, but sufficient to stagger him. He circled around the white mare, pursued by the Master. Dodging, keeping the horse between himself and his opponent, he raised the horn to his lips and sounded it three times. Its notes rose above the fierce noises of the combat on the palace stair. Panting, he turned and raised his guard in time to ward off a temple blow that would surely have slain him had it landed.

"It is written," said the Master, almost sobbing out the words, "that he who gives orders without having the power to enforce them, that man is a fool."

"Even ten years ago," panted the prince, "you'd never have laid that staff on me."

He hacked at it, hoping to split the wood, but the other always managed to turn the edge of his blade, so that while he nicked it and shaved it in places, the grain held and the staff remained of a piece.

Using it as a singlestick, the Master laid a solid blow across the prince's left side, and he felt his ribs break within him. . . . He fell.

It was not by design that it happened, for the blade spun from out his hands as he collapsed; but the weapon caught the Master across the shins and he dropped to his knees, howling.

"We're evenly matched, at that," gasped the prince. "My age against your fat . . ."

He drew his dagger as he lay there, but could not hold it steady. He rested his elbow on the ground. The Master, tears in his eyes, attempted to rise and fell again to his knees.

There came the sound of many hooves.

"I am not a fool," said the prince, "and now I have the power to enforce my orders."

"What is happening?"

"The rest of my lancers are arrived. Had I entered in full force, you'd have holed up like a *gekk* in a wood-pile, and it might have taken days to pull your palace apart and fetch you out. Now I have you in the palm of my hand."

The Master raised his staff.

The prince drew back his arm.

"Lower it," he said, "or I'll throw the dagger. I don't know myself whether I'll miss or hit, but I may hit. You're not anxious to gamble against the real death, are you?"

The Master lowered his staff.

"You will know the real death," said the Master, "when the wardens of Karma have made dog meat of your horse soldiers."

The prince coughed, stared disinterestedly at his bloody spittle. "In the meantime, let's discuss politics," he suggested.

After the sounds of battle had ended, it was Strake—tall, dusty, his hair near matching the gore that dried on his blade—Strake, who was nuzzled by the white mare as he saluted his prince and said, "It is over."

"Do you hear that, Master of Karma?" asked the prince. "Your wardens are dog meat."

The Master did not answer.

"Serve me now and you may have your life," said the prince. "Refuse, and I'll have it."

"I will serve you," said the Master.

"Strake," ordered the prince, "send two men down into the town—one to fetch back Narada, my physician, and the other to go to the Street of the Weavers and bring here Jannaveg the sailmaker. Of the three lancers who remain at Hawkana's, leave but one to hold the Shan of Irabek till sundown. He is then to bind him and leave him, joining us here himself."

Strake smiled and saluted.

"Now bring men to bear me within the Hall, and to keep an eye on this Master."

He burned his old body, along with all the others. The wardens of Karma, to a man, had passed in battle. Of the seven nameless Masters, only the one who had been fat survived. While the banks of sperm and ova, the growth tanks and the body lockers could not be transported, the transfer equipment itself was dismantled under the direction of Dr. Narada, and its components were loaded onto the horses of those who had fallen in the battle. The young prince sat upon the white mare and watched the jaws of flame close upon the bodies. Eight pyres blazed against the predawn sky. The one who had been a sailmaker turned his eyes to the pyre nearest the gate—the last to be ignited, its flames were only just now reaching the top, where lay the gross bulk of one who wore a robe of black, a circle of yellow on the breast. When the flames touched it and the robe began to smoulder, the dog who cowered in the ruined garden raised his head in a howl that was near to a sob.

"This day your sin account is filled to overflowing," said the sailmaker.

"But, ah, my prayer account!" replied the prince. "I'll stand on that for the time being. Future theologians will have to make the final decision, though, as to the acceptability of all those slugs in the pray-o-mats. Let Heaven wonder now what happened here this day— where I am, if I am, and who. The time has come to ride, my captain. Into the mountains for a while, and then our separate ways, for safety's sake. I am not sure as to the road I will follow, save that it leads to Heaven's gate and I must go armed."

"Binder of Demons," said the other, and he smiled.

The lancer chief approached. The prince nodded to him. Orders were shouted.

The columns of mounted men moved forward, passed out through the gates of the Palace of Karma, turned off the roadway and headed up the slope that lay to the southeast of the city of Mahartha, comrades blazing like the dawn at their back.

iii

It is said that, when the Teacher appeared, those of all castes went to hear his teachings, as well as animals, gods and an occasional saint, to come away improved and uplifted. It was generally conceded that he had received enlightenment, except by those who believed him to be a fraud, sinner, criminal or practical joker. These latter ones were not all to be numbered as his enemies; but, on the other hand, not all of those improved and uplifted could be counted as his friends and supporters. His followers called him Mahasamatman and some said he was a god. So, after it was seen that he had been accepted as a teacher, was looked upon with respect, had many of the wealthy numbered as his supporters and had gained a reputation reaching far across the land, he was referred to as Tathagatha, meaning He Who Has Achieved. It must be noted that while the goddess Kali (sometimes known as Durga in her softer moments) never voiced a formal opinion as to his buddhahood, she did render him the singular honor of dispatching her holy executioner to pay him her tribute, rather than a mere hired assassin. . . .

There is no disappearing of the true Dhamma
until a false Dhamma arises in the world.
When the false Dhamma arises, he makes the
true Dhamma to disappear.
Samyutta-nikaya (II, 224)

NEAR the city of Alundil there was a rich grove of blue-barked trees, having purple foliage like feathers. It was famous for its beauty and the shrinelike peace of its shade. It had been the property of the merchant

Vasu until his conversion, at which time he had
presented it to the teacher variously known as Mahasamatman, Tathagatha and the Enlightened One. In that
wood did this teacher abide with his followers, and
when they walked forth into the town at midday their
begging bowls never went unfilled.

There was always a large number of pilgrims about
the grove. The believers, the curious and those who
preyed upon the others were constantly passing through
it. They came by horseback, they came by boat, they
came on foot.

Alundil was not an overly large city. It had its share
of thatched huts, as well as wooden bungalows; its main
roadway was unpaved and rutted; it had two large
bazaars and many small ones; there were wide fields of
grain, owned by the Vaisyas, tended by the Sudras,
which flowed and rippled, blue-green, about the city; it
had many hostels (though none so fine as the legendary
hostel of Hawkana, in far Mahartha), because of the
constant passage of travelers; it had its holy men and its
storytellers; and it had its Temple.

The Temple was located on a low hill near the center
of town, enormous gates on each of its four sides. These
gates, and the walls about them, were filled with layer
upon layer of decorative carvings, showing musicians
and dancers, warriors and demons, gods and goddesses,
animals and artists, lovemakers and half-people,
guardians and devas. These gates led into the first
courtyard, which held more walls and more gates, lead-
ing in turn into the second courtyard. The first courtyard contained a little bazaar, where offerings to the
gods were sold. It also housed numerous small shrines
dedicated to the lesser deities. There were begging beggars, meditating holy men, laughing children, gossiping
women, burning incenses, singing birds, gurgling purifi-
cation tanks and humming pray-o-mats to be found in
this courtyard at any hour of the day.

The inner courtyard, though, with its massive shrines
dedicated to the major deities, was a focal point of

religious intensity. People chanted or shouted prayers, mumbled verses from the Vedas, or stood, or knelt, or lay prostrate before huge stone images, which often were so heavily garlanded with flowers, smeared with red *kumkum* paste and surrounded by heaps of offerings that it was impossible to tell which deity was so immersed in tangible adoration. Periodically, the horns of the Temple were blown, there was a moment's hushed appraisal of their echo and the clamor began again.

And none would dispute the fact that Kali was queen of this Temple. Her tall, white-stone statue, within its gigantic shrine, dominated the inner courtyard. Her faint smile, perhaps contemptuous of the other gods and their worshipers, was, in its way, as arresting as the chained grins of the skulls she wore for a necklace. She held daggers in her hands; and poised in mid-step she stood, as though deciding whether to dance before or slay those who came to her shrine. Her lips were full, her eyes were wide. Seen by torchlight, she seemed to move.

It was fitting, therefore, that her shrine faced upon that of Yama, god of Death. It had been decided, logically enough, by the priests and architects, that he was best suited of all the deities to spend every minute of the day facing her, matching his unfaltering death-gaze against her own, returning her half smile with his twisted one. Even the most devout generally made a detour rather than pass between the two shrines; and after dark their section of the courtyard was always the abode of silence and stillness, being untroubled by late worshipers.

From out of the north, as the winds of spring blew across the land, there came the one called Rild. A small man, whose hair was white, though his years were few—Rild, who wore the dark trappings of a pilgrim, but about whose forearm, when they found him lying in a ditch with the fever, was wound the crimson strangling cord of his true profession: Rild.

Rild came in the spring, at festival-time, to Alundil of the blue-green fields, of the thatched huts and the bungalows of wood, of unpaved roadways and many hostels, of bazaars and holy men and storytellers, of the great religious revival and its Teacher, whose reputation had spread far across the land—to Alundil of the Temple, where his patron goddess was queen.

Festival-time.

Twenty years earlier, Alundil's small festival had been an almost exclusively local affair. Now, though, with the passage of countless travelers, caused by the presence of the Enlightened One, who taught the Way of the Eightfold Path, the Festival of Alundil attracted so many pilgrims that local accommodations were filled to overflowing. Those who possessed tents could charge a high fee for their rental. Stables were rented out for human occupancy. Even bare pieces of land were let as camping sites.

Alundil loved its Buddha. Many other towns had tried to entice him away from his purple grove: Shengodu, Flower of the Mountains, had offered him a palace and harem to come bring his teaching to the slopes. But the Enlightened One did not go to the mountain. Kannaka, of the Serpent River, had offered him elephants and ships, a town house and a country villa, horses and servants, to come and preach from its wharves. But the Enlightened One did not go to the river.

The Buddha remained in his grove and all things came to him. With the passage of years the festival grew larger and longer and more elaborate, like a well-fed dragon, scales all a-shimmer. The local Brahmins did not approve of the antiritualistic teachings of the Buddha, but his presence filled their coffers to overflowing; so they learned to live in his squat shadow, never voicing the word *tirthika*—heretic.

So the Buddha remained in his grove and all things came to him, including Rild.

Festival-time.

The drums began in the evening on the third day.

On the third day, the massive drums of the *kathakali* began their rapid thunder. The miles-striding staccato of the drums carried across the fields to the town, across the town, across the purple grove and across the wastes of marshland that lay behind it. The drummers, wearing white *mundus,* bare to the waist, their dark flesh glistening with perspiration, worked in shifts, so strenuous was the mighty beating they set up; and never was the flow of sound broken, even as the new relay of drummers moved into position before the tightly stretched heads of the instruments.

As darkness arrived in the world, the travelers and townsmen who had begun walking as soon as they heard the chatter of the drums began to arrive at the festival field, large as a battlefield of old. There they found places and waited for the night to deepen and the drama to begin, sipping the sweet-smelling tea that they purchased at the stalls beneath the trees.

A great brass bowl of oil, tall as a man, wicks hanging down over its edges, stood in the center of the field. These wicks were lighted, and torches flickered beside the tents of the actors.

The drumming, at close range, was deafening and hypnotic, the rhythms complicated, syncopated, insidious. As midnight approached, the devotional chanting began, rising and falling with the drumbeat, working a net about the senses.

There was a brief lull as the Enlightened One and his monks arrived, their yellow robes near-orange in the flamelight. But they threw back their cowls and seated themselves cross-legged upon the ground. After a time, it was only the chanting and the voices of the drums that filled the minds of the spectators.

When the actors appeared, gigantic in their makeup, ankle bells jangling as their feet beat the ground, there was no applause, only rapt attention. The *kathakali* dancers were famous, trained from their youth in acro-

batics as well as the ages-old patterns of the classical
dance, knowing the nine distinct movements of the
neck and of the eyeballs and the hundreds of hand
positions required to re-enact the ancient epics of love
and battle, of the encounters of gods and demons, of
the valiant fights and bloody treacheries of tradition.
The musicians shouted out the words of the stories as
the actors, who never spoke, portrayed the awesome
exploits of Rama and of the Pandava brothers. Wearing
makeup of green and red, or black and stark white,
they stalked across the field, skirts billowing, their mir-
ror-sprinkled halos glittering in the light of the lamp.
Occasionally, the lamp would flare or sputter, and it
was as if a nimbus of holy or unholy light played about
their heads, erasing entirely the sense of the event,
causing the spectators to feel for a moment that they
themselves were the illusion, and that the great-bodied
figures of the cyclopean dance were the only real things
in the world.

The dance would continue until daybreak, to end
with the rising of the sun. Before daybreak, however,
one of the wearers of the saffron robe arrived from the
direction of town, made his way through the crowd and
spoke into the ear of the Enlightened One.

The Buddha began to rise, appeared to think better
of it and reseated himself. He gave a message to the
monk, who nodded and departed from the field of the
festival.

The Buddha, looking imperturbable, returned his attention to the drama. A monk seated nearby noted that
he was tapping his fingers upon the ground, and he
decided that the Enlightened One must be keeping time
with the drumbeats, for it was common knowledge that
he was above such things as impatience.

When the drama had ended and Surya the sun
pinked the skirts of Heaven above the eastern rim of
the world, it was as if the night just passed had held the
crowd prisoner within a tense and frightening dream,

from which they were just now released, weary, to wander this day.

The Buddha and his followers set off walking immediately, in the direction of the town. They did not pause to rest along the way, but passed through Alundil at a rapid but dignified gait.

When they came again to the purple grove, the Enlightened One instructed his monks to take rest, and he moved off in the direction of a small pavilion located deep within the wood.

The monk who had brought the message during the drama sat within the pavilion. There he tended the fever of the traveler he had come upon in the marshes, where he walked often to better meditate upon the putrid condition his body would assume after death.

Tathagatha studied the man who lay upon the sleeping mat. His lips were thin and pale; he had a high forehead, high cheekbones, frosty eyebrows, pointed ears; and Tathagatha guessed that when those eyelids rose, the eyes revealed would be of a faded blue or gray. There was a quality of—translucency?—fragility perhaps, about his unconscious form, which might have been caused partly by the fevers that racked his body, but which could not be attributed entirely to them. The small man did not give the impression of being one who would bear the thing that Tathagatha now raised in his hands. Rather, on first viewing, he might seem to be a very old man. If one granted him a second look, and realized then that his colorless hair and his slight frame did not signify advanced age, one might then be struck by something childlike about his appearance. From the condition of his complexion, Tathagatha doubted that he need shave very often. Perhaps a slightly mischievous pucker was now hidden somewhere between his cheeks and the corners of his mouth. Perhaps not, also.

The Buddha raised the crimson strangling cord, which was a thing borne only by the holy executioners of the goddess Kali. He fingered its silken length, and it passed like a serpent through his hand, clinging slightly. He did not doubt but that it was intended to move in such a manner about his throat. Almost unconsciously, he held it and twisted his hands through the necessary movements.

Then he looked up at the wide-eyed monk who had watched him, smiled his imperturbable smile and laid the cord aside. With a damp cloth, the monk wiped the perspiration from the pale brow.

The man on the sleeping mat shuddered at the contact, and his eyes snapped open. The madness of the fever was in them and they did not truly see, but Tathagatha felt a sudden jolt at their contact.

Dark, so dark they were almost jet, and it was impossible to tell where the pupil ended and the iris began. There was something extremely unsettling about eyes of such power in a body so frail and effete.

He reached out and stroked the man's hands, and it was like touching steel, cold and impervious. He drew his fingernail sharply across the back of the right hand. No scratch or indentation marked its passage, and his nail fairly slid, as though across a pane of glass. He squeezed the man's thumbnail and released it. There was no sudden change of color. It was as though these hands were dead or mechanical things.

He continued his examination. The phenomenon ended somewhat above the wrists, occurred again in other places. His hands, breast, abdomen, neck and portions of his back had soaked within the death bath, which gave this special unyielding power. Total immersion would, of course, have proved fatal; but as it was, the man had traded some of his tactile sensitivity for the equivalent of invisible gauntlets, breastplate, neckpiece and back armor of steel. He was indeed one of the select assassins of the terrible goddess.

"Who else knows of this man?" asked the Buddha.

"The monk Simha," replied the other, "who helped me bear him here."

"Did he see"—Tathagatha gestured with his eyes toward the crimson cord—"that?" he inquired.

The monk nodded.

"Then go fetch him. Bring him to me at once. Do not mention anything of this to anyone, other than that a pilgrim was taken ill and we are tending him here. I will personally take over his care and minister to his illness."

"Yes, Illustrious One."

The monk hurried forth from the pavilion.

Tathagatha seated himself beside the sleeping mat and waited.

It was two days before the fever broke and intelligence returned to those dark eyes. But during those two days, anyone who passed by the pavilion might have heard the voice of the Enlightened One droning on and on, as though he addressed his sleeping charge. Occasionally, the man himself mumbled and spoke loudly, as those in a fever often do.

On the second day, the man opened his eyes suddenly and stared upward. Then he frowned and turned his head.

"Good morning, Rild," said Tathagatha.

"You are ... ?" asked the other, in an unexpected baritone.

"One who teaches the way of liberation," he replied.

"The Buddha?"

"I have been called such."

"Tathagatha?"

"This name, too, have I been given."

The other attempted to rise, failed, settled back. His eyes never left the placid countenance. "How is it that you know my name?" he finally asked.

"In your fever you spoke considerably."

"Yes, I was very sick, and doubtless babbling. It was in that cursed swamp that I took the chill."

Tathagatha smiled. "One of the disadvantages of

traveling alone is that when you fall there is none to assist you."

"True," acknowledged the other, and his eyes closed once more and his breathing deepened.

Tathagatha remained in the lotus posture, waiting.

When Rild awakened again, it was evening. "Thirsty," he said.

Tathagatha gave him water. "Hungry?" he asked.

"No, not yet. My stomach would rebel."

He raised himself up onto his elbows and stared at his attendant. Then he sank back upon the mat. "You are the one," he announced.

"Yes," replied the other.

"What are you going to do?"

"Feed you, when you say you are hungry."

"I mean, after that."

"Watch as you sleep, lest you lapse again into the fever."

"That is not what I meant."

"I know."

"After I have eaten and rested and recovered my strength—what then?"

Tathagatha smiled as he drew the silken cord from somewhere beneath his robe. "Nothing," he replied, "nothing at all," and he draped the cord across Rild's shoulder and withdrew his hand.

The other shook his head and leaned back. He reached up and fingered the length of crimson. He twined it about his fingers and then about his wrist. He stroked it.

"It is holy," he said, after a time.

"So it would seem."

"You know its use, and its purpose?"

"Of course."

"Why then will you do nothing at all?"

"I have no need to move or to act. All things come to me. If anything is to be done, it is you who will do it."

"I do not understand."

"I know that, too."

The man stared into the shadows overhead. "I will attempt to eat now," he announced.

Tathagatha gave him broth and bread, which he managed to keep down. Then he drank more water, and when he had finished he was breathing heavily.

"You have offended Heaven," he stated.

"Of that, I am aware."

"And you have detracted from the glory of a goddess, whose supremacy here has always been undisputed."

"I know."

"But I owe you my life, and I have eaten your bread . . ."

There was no reply.

"Because of this, I must break a most holy vow," finished Rild. "I cannot kill you, Tathagatha."

"Then I owe my life to the fact that you owe me yours. Let us consider the life-owing balanced."

Rild uttered a short chuckle. "So be it," he said.

"What will you do, now that you have abandoned your mission?"

"I do not know. My sin is too great to permit me to return. Now I, too, have offended against Heaven, and the goddess will turn away her face from my prayers. I have failed her."

"Such being the case, remain here. You will at least have company in damnation."

"Very well," agreed Rild. "There is nothing else left to me."

He slept once again, and the Buddha smiled.

In the days that followed, as the festival wore on, the Enlightened One preached to the crowds who passed through the purple grove. He spoke of the unity of all things, great and small, of the law of cause, of becoming and dying, of the illusion of the world, of the spark of the *atman,* of the way of salvation through renunciation of the self and union with the whole; he spoke of realization and enlightenment, of the meaninglessness of the Brahmins' rituals, comparing their forms to vessels empty of content. Many listened, a few heard and some remained in the purple grove to take up the saffron robe of the seeker.

And each time he taught, the man Rild sat nearby, wearing his black garments and leather harness, his strange dark eyes ever upon the Enlightened One.

Two weeks after his recovery, Rild came upon the teacher as he walked through the grove in meditation. He fell into step beside him, and after a time he spoke.

"Enlightened One, I have listened to your teachings, and I have listened well. Much have I thought upon your words."

The other nodded.

"I have always been a religious man," he stated, "or I would not have been selected for the post I once occupied. After it became impossible for me to fulfill my mission, I felt a great emptiness. I had failed my goddess, and life was without meaning for me."

The other listened, silently.

"But I have heard your words," he said, "and they have filled me with a kind of joy. They have shown me another way to salvation, a way which I feel to be superior to the one I previously followed."

The Buddha studied his face as he spoke.

"Your way of renunciation is a strict one, which I feel to be good. It suits my needs. Therefore, I request permission to be taken into your community of seekers, and to follow your path."

"Are you certain," asked the Enlightened One, "that you do not seek merely to punish yourself for what has been weighing upon your conscience as a failure, or a sin?"

"Of that I am certain," said Rild. "I have held your words within me and felt the truth which they contain. In the service of the goddess have I slain more men than purple fronds upon yonder bough. I am not even

counting women and children. So I am not easily taken
in by words, having heard too many, voiced in all tones
of speech—words pleading, arguing, cursing. But your
words move me, and they are superior to the teachings
of the Brahmins. Gladly would I become your executioner, dispatching for you your enemies with a saffron
cord—or with a blade, or pike, or with my hands, for I
am proficient with all weapons, having spent three lifetimes learning their use—but I know that such is not
your way. Death and life are as one to you, and you do
not seek the destruction of your enemies. So I request
entrance to your Order. For me, it is not so difficult a
thing as it would be for another. One must renounce
home and family, origin and property. I lack these
things. One must renounce one's own will, which I have
already done. All I need now is the yellow robe."

"It is yours," said Tathagatha, "with my blessing."

Rild donned the robe of a buddhist monk and took
to fasting and meditating. After a week, when the
festival was near to its close, he departed into the town
with his begging bowl, in the company of the other
monks. He did not return with them, however. The day
wore on into evening, the evening into darkness. The
horns of the Temple had already sounded the last notes
of the *nagaswaram,* and many of the travelers had since
departed the festival.

For a long while, the Enlightened One walked the
woods, meditating. Then he, too, vanished.

Down from the grove, with the marshes at its back,
toward the town of Alundil, above which lurked the
hills of rock and around which lay the blue-green
fields, into the town of Alundil, still astir with travelers,
many of them at the height of their revelry, up the
streets of Alundil toward the hill with its Temple,
walked the Buddha.

He entered the first courtyard, and it was quiet there.
The dogs and children and beggars had gone away. The
priests slept. One drowsing attendant sat behind a

bench at the bazaar. Many of the shrines were now empty, the statues having been borne within. Before several of the others, worshipers knelt in late prayer.

He entered the inner courtyard. An ascetic was seated on a prayer mat before the statue of Ganesha. He, too, seemed to qualify as a statue, making no visible movements. Four oil lamps flickered about the yard, their dancing light serving primarily to accentuate the shadows that lay upon most of the shrines. Small votive lights cast a faint illumination upon some of the statues.

Tathagatha crossed the yard and stood facing the towering figure of Kali, at whose feet a tiny lamp blinked. Her smile seemed a plastic and moving thing, as she regarded the man before her.

Draped across her outstretched hand, looped once about the point of her dagger, lay a crimson strangling cord.

Tathagatha smiled back at her, and she seemed almost to frown at that moment.

"It is a resignation, my dear," he stated. "You have lost this round."

She seemed to nod in agreement.

"I am pleased to have achieved such a height of recognition in so short a period of time," he continued. "But even if you had succeeded, old girl, it would have done you little good. It is too late now. I have started something which you cannot undo. Too many have heard the ancient words. You had thought they were lost, and so did I. But we were both wrong. The religion by which you rule is very ancient, goddess, but my protest is also that of a venerable tradition. So call me a protestant, and remember—now I am more than a man. Good night."

He left the Temple and the shrine of Kali, where the eyes of Yama had been fixed upon his back.

It was many months before the miracle occurred,

and when it did, it did not seem a miracle, for it had grown up slowly about them.

Rild, who had come out of the north as the winds of spring blew across the land, wearing death upon his arm and the black fire within his eyes—Rild, of the white brows and pointed ears—spoke one afternoon, after the spring had passed, when the long days of summer hung warm beneath the Bridge of the Gods. He spoke, in that unexpected baritone, to answer a question asked him by a traveler.

The man asked him a second question, and then a third.

He continued to speak, and some of the other monks and several pilgrims gathered about him. The answers following the questions, which now came from all of them, grew longer and longer, for they became parables, examples, allegories.

Then they were seated at his feet, and his dark eyes became strange pools, and his voice came down as from Heaven, clear and soft, melodic and persuasive.

They listened, and then the travelers went their way. But they met and spoke with other travelers upon the road, so that, before the summer had passed, pilgrims coming to the purple grove were asking to meet this disciple of the Buddha's, and to hear his words also.

Tathagatha shared the preaching with him. Together, they taught of the Way of the Eightfold Path, the glory of Nirvana, the illusion of the world and the chains that the world lays upon a man.

And then there were times when even the soft-spoken Tathagatha listened to the words of his disciple, who had digested all of the things he had preached, had meditated long and fully upon them and now, as though he had found entrance to a secret sea, dipped with his steel-hard hand into places of hidden waters, and then sprinkled a thing of truth and beauty upon the heads of the hearers.

Summer passed. There was no doubt now that there were two who had received enlightenment: Tathagatha and his small disciple, whom they called Sugata. It was even said that Sugata was a healer, and that when his eyes shone strangely and the icy touch of his hands came upon a twisted limb, that limb grew straight again. It was said that a blind man's vision had suddenly returned to him during one of Sugata's sermons.

There were two things in which Sugata believed: the Way of Salvation and Tathagatha, the Buddha.

"Illustrious One," he said to him one day, "my life was empty until you revealed to me the True Path. When you received your enlightenment, before you began your teaching, was it like a rush of fire and the roaring of water and you everywhere and a part of everything—the clouds and the trees, the animals in the forest, all people, the snow on the mountaintop and the bones in the field?"

"Yes," said Tathagatha.

"I, also, know the joy of all things," said Sugata.

"Yes, I know," said Tathagatha.

"I see now why once you said that all things come to you. To have brought such a doctrine into the world—I can see why the gods were envious. Poor gods! They are to be pitied. But you know. You know all things."

Tathagatha did not reply.

When the winds of spring blew again across the land, the year having gone full cycle since the arrival of the second Buddha, there came one day from out of the heavens a fearful shrieking.

The citizens of Alundil turned out into their streets to stare up at the sky. The Sudras in the fields put by their work and looked upward. In the great Temple on the hill there was a sudden silence. In the purple grove beyond the town, the monks turned their heads.

It paced the heavens, the one who was born to rule the wind. . . . From out of the north it came—green and red, yellow and brown. . . . Its glide was a dance, its way was the air. . . .

There came another shriek, and then the beating of

mighty pinions as it climbed past clouds to become a tiny dot of black.

And then it fell, like a meteor, bursting into flame, all of its colors blazing and burning bright, as it grew and grew, beyond all belief that anything could live at that size, that pace, that magnificence. . . .

Half spirit, half bird, legend darkening the sky.

Mount of Vishnu, whose beak smashes chariots.

The Garuda Bird circled above Alundil.

Circled, and passed beyond the hills of rock that stood behind the city.

"Garuda!" The word ran through the town, the fields, the Temple, the grove.

If he did not fly alone; it was known that only a god could use the Garuda Bird for a mount.

There was silence. After those shrieks and that thunder of pinions, voices seemed naturally to drop to a whisper.

The Enlightened One stood upon the road before the grove, his monks moving about him, facing in the direction of the hills of rock.

Sugata came to his side and stood there. "It was but a spring ago . . ." he said.

Tathagatha nodded.

"Rild failed," said Sugata. "What new thing comes from Heaven?"

The Buddha shrugged.

"I fear for you, my teacher," he said. "In all my lifetimes, you have been my only friend. Your teaching has given me peace. Why can they not leave you alone? You are the most harmless of men, and your doctrine the gentlest. What ill could you possibly bear them?"

The other turned away.

At that moment, with a mighty beating of the air and a jagged cry from its opened beak, the Garuda Bird rose once more above the hills. This time, it did not circle over the town, but climbed to a great height in the heavens and swept off to the north. Such was the speed of its passing that it was gone in a matter of moments.

"Its passenger has dismounted and remains behind," suggested Sugata.

The Buddha walked within the purple grove.

He came from beyond the hills of stone, walking.

He came to a passing place through stone, and he followed this trail, his red leather boots silent on the rocky path.

Ahead, there was a sound of running water, from where a small stream cut across his way. Shrugging his blood-bright cloak back over his shoulders, he advanced upon a bend in the trail, the ruby head of his scimitar gleaming in his crimson sash.

Rounding a corner of stone, he came to a halt.

One waited ahead, standing beside the log that led across the stream.

His eyes narrowed for an instant, then he moved forward again.

It was a small man who stood there, wearing the dark garments of a pilgrim, caught about with a leather harness from which was suspended a short, curved blade of bright steel. This man's head was closely shaven, save for a small lock of white hair. His eyebrows were white above eyes that were dark, and his skin was pale; his ears appeared to be pointed.

The traveler raised his hand and spoke to this man, saying, "Good afternoon, pilgrim."

The man did not reply, but moved to bar his way, positioning himself before the log that led across the stream.

"Pardon me, good pilgrim, but I am about to cross here and you are making my passage difficult," he stated.

"You are mistaken, Lord Yama, if you think you are about to pass here," replied the other.

The One in Red smiled, showing a long row of even, white teeth. "It is always a pleasure to be recognized," he acknowledged, "even by one who conveys misinformation concerning other matters."

"I do not fence with words," said the man in black.

"Oh?" The other raised his eyebrows in an expression of exaggerated inquiry. "With what then do you fence, sir? Surely not that piece of bent metal you bear."

"None other."

"I took it for some barbarous prayer-stick at first. I understand that this is a region fraught with strange cults and primitive sects. For a moment, I took you to be a devotee of some such superstition. But if, as you say, it is indeed a weapon, then I trust you are familiar with its use?"

"Somewhat," replied the man in black.

"Good, then," said Yama, "for I dislike having to kill a man who does not know what he is about. I feel obligated to point out to you, however, that when you stand before the Highest for judgment, you will be accounted a suicide."

The other smiled faintly.

"Any time that you are ready, deathgod, I will facilitate the passage of your spirit from out its fleshy envelope."

"One more item only, then," said Yama, "and I shall put a quick end to conversation. Give me a name to tell the priests, so that they shall know for whom they offer the rites."

"I renounced my final name but a short while back," answered the other. "For this reason, Kali's consort must take his death of one who is nameless."

"Rild, you are a fool," said Yama, and drew his blade.

The man in black drew his.

"And it is fitting that you go unnamed to your doom. You betrayed your goddess."

"Life is full of betrayals," replied the other, before he struck. "By opposing you now and in this manner, I also betray the teachings of my new master. But I must follow the dictates of my heart. Neither my old name nor my new do therefore fit me, nor are they deserved—so call me by no name!"

Then his blade was fire, leaping everywhere, clicking, blazing.

Yama fell back before this onslaught, giving ground foot by foot, moving only his wrist as he parried the blows that fell about him.

Then, after he had retreated ten paces, he stood his ground and would not be moved. His parries widened slightly, but his ripostes became more sudden now, and were interspersed with feints and unexpected attacks.

They swaggered blades till their perspiration fell upon the ground in showers; and then Yama began to press the attack, slowly, forcing his opponent into a retreat. Step by step, he recovered the ten paces he had given.

When they stood again upon the ground where the first blow had been struck, Yama acknowledged, over the clashing of steel, "Well have you learned your lessons, Rild! Better even than I had thought! Congratulations!"

As he spoke, his opponent wove his blade through an elaborate double feint and scored a light touch that cut his shoulder, drawing blood that immediately merged with the color of his garment.

At this, Yama sprang forward, beating down the other's guard, and delivered a blow to the side of his neck that might have decapitated him.

The man in black raised his guard, shaking his head, parried another attack and thrust forward, to be parried again himself.

"So, the death bath collars your throat," said Yama. "I'll seek entrance elsewhere, then," and his blade sang a faster song, as he tried for a low-line thrust.

Yama unleashed the full fury of that blade, backed by the centuries and the masters of many ages. Yet, the other met his attacks, parrying wider and wider, retreating faster and faster now, but still managing to hold him off as he backed away, counterthrusting as he went.

He retreated until his back was to the stream. Then Yama slowed and made comment:

"Half a century ago," he stated, "when you were my pupil for a brief time, I said to myself, 'This one has within him the makings of a master.' Nor was I wrong, Rild. You are perhaps the greatest swordsman raised up in all the ages I can remember. I can almost forgive apostasy when I witness your skill. It is indeed a pity . . ."

He feinted then a chest cut, and at the last instant moved around the parry so that he lay the edge of his weapon high upon the other's wrist.

Leaping backward, parrying wildly and cutting at Yama's head, the man in black came into a position at the head of the log that lay above the crevice that led down to the stream.

"Your hand, too, Rild! Indeed, the goddess is lavish with her protection. Try this!"

The steel screeched as he caught it in a bind, nicking the other's bicep as he passed about the blade.

"Aha! There's a place she missed!" he cried. "Let's try for another!"

Their blades bound and disengaged, feinted, thrust, parried, riposted.

Yama met an elaborate attack with a stop-thrust, his longer blade again drawing blood from his opponent's upper arm.

Yama met an elaborate attack with a stop-thrust, his longer blade again drawing blood from his opponent's upper arm.

The man in black stepped up upon the log, swinging a vicious head cut, which Yama beat away. Pressing the attack then even harder, Yama forced him to back out upon the log and then he kicked at its side.

The other jumped backward, landing upon the opposite bank. As soon as his feet touched ground, he, too, kicked out, causing the log to move.

It rolled, before Yama could mount it, slipping free of the banks, crashing down into the stream, bobbing about for a moment, and then following the water trail westward.

"I'd say it is only a seven- or eight-foot jump, Yama! Come on across!" cried the other.

The deathgod smiled. "Catch your breath quickly now, while you may," he stated. "Breath is the least appreciated gift of the gods. None sing hymns to it, praising the good air, breathed by king and beggar, master and dog alike. But, oh to be without it! Appreciate each breath, Rild, as though it were your last—for that one, too, is near at hand!"

"You are said to be wise in these matters, Yama," said the one who had been called Rild and Sugata. "You are said to be a god, whose kingdom is death and whose knowledge extends beyond the ken of mortals. I would question you, therefore, while we are standing idle."

Yama did not smile his mocking smile, as he had to all his opponent's previous statements. This one had a touch of ritual about it.

"What is it that you wish to know? I grant you the death-boon of a question."

Then, in the ancient words of the *Katha Upanishad*, the one who had been called Rild and Sugata chanted:

" 'There is doubt concerning a man when he is dead. Some say he still exists. Others say he does not. This thing I should like to know, taught by you.' "

Yama replied with the ancient words, " 'On this subject even the gods have their doubts. It is not easy to understand, for the nature of the *atman* is a subtle thing. Ask me another question. Release me from this boon!' "

" 'Forgive me if it is foremost in my mind, oh Death, but another teacher such as yourself cannot be found, and surely there is no other boon which I crave more at this moment.' "

" 'Keep your life and go your way,' " said Yama, plunging his blade again into his sash. " 'I release you from your doom. Choose sons and grandsons; choose elephants, horses, herds of cattle and gold. Choose any other boon—fair maidens, chariots, musical instruments. I shall give them unto you and they shall wait upon you. But ask me not of death.' "

" 'Oh Death,' " sang the other, " 'these endure only till tomorrow. Keep your maidens, horses, dances and songs for yourself. No boon will I accept but the one which I have asked—tell me, oh Death, of that which lies beyond life, of which men and the gods have their doubts.' "

Yama stood very still and he did not continue the poem. "Very well, Rild," he said, his eyes locking with the other's, "but it is not a kingdom subject to words. I must show you."

They stood, so, for a moment; and then the man in black swayed. He threw his arm across his face, covering his eyes, and a single sob escaped his throat.

When this occurred, Yama drew his cloak from his shoulders and cast it like a net across the stream.

Weighted at the hems for such a maneuver, it fell, netlike, upon his opponent.

As he struggled to free himself, the man in black heard rapid footfalls and then a crash, as Yama's blood-red boots struck upon his side of the stream. Casting aside the cloak and raising his guard, he parried Yama's new attack. The ground behind him sloped upward, and he backed farther and farther, to where it steepened, so that Yama's head was no higher than his belt. He then struck down at his opponent. Yama slowly fought his way uphill.

"Deathgod, deathgod," he chanted, "forgive my presumptuous question, and tell me you did not lie."

"Soon you shall know," said Yama, cutting at his legs.

Yama struck a blow that would have run another

man through, cleaving his heart. But it glanced off his opponent's breast.

When he came to a place where the ground was broken, the small man kicked, again and again, sending showers of dirt and gravel down upon his opponent. Yama shielded his eyes with his left hand, but then larger pieces of stone began to rain down upon him. These rolled on the ground, and, as several came beneath his boots, he lost his footing and fell, slipping backward down the slope. The other kicked at heavy rocks then, even dislodging a boulder and following it downhill, his blade held high.

Unable to gain his footing in time to meet the attack, Yama rolled and slid back toward the stream. He managed to brake himself at the edge of the crevice, but he saw the boulder coming and tried to draw back out of its way. As he pushed at the ground with both hands, his blade fell into the waters below.

With his dagger, which he drew as he sprang into a stumbling crouch, he managed to parry the high cut of the other's blade. The boulder splashed into the stream.

Then his left hand shot forward, seizing the wrist that had guided the blade. He slashed upward with the dagger and felt his own wrist taken.

They stood then, locking their strength, until Yama sat down and rolled to his side, thrusting the other from him.

Still, both locks held, and they continued to roll from the force of that thrust. Then the edge of the crevice was beside them, beneath them, above them. He felt the blade go out of his hand as it struck the stream bed.

When they came again above the surface of the water, gasping for breath, each held only water in his hands.

"Time for the final baptism," said Yama, and he lashed out with his left hand.

The other blocked the punch, throwing one of his own.

They moved to the left with the waters, until their

feet struck upon rock and they fought, wading, along the length of the stream.

It widened and grew more shallow as they moved, until the waters swirled about their waists. In places, the banks began to fall nearer the surface of the water.

Yama landed blow after blow, both with his fists and the edges of his hands; but it was as if he assailed a statue, for the one who had been Kali's holy executioner took each blow without changing his expression, and he returned them with twisting punches of bone-breaking force. Most of these blows were slowed by the water or blocked by Yama's guard, but one landed between his rib cage and hipbone and another glanced off his left shoulder and rebounded from his cheek.

Yama cast himself into a backstroke and made for shallower water.

The other followed and sprang upon him, to be caught in his impervious midsection by a red boot, as the front of his garment was jerked forward and down. He continued on, passing over Yama's head, to land upon his back on a section of shale.

Yama rose to his knees and turned, as the other found his footing and drew a dagger from his belt. His face was still impassive as he dropped into a crouch.

For a moment their eyes met, but the other did not waver this time.

"Now can I meet your death-gaze, Yama," he stated, "and not be stopped by it. You have taught me too well!"

And as he lunged, Yama's hands came away from his waist, snapping his wet sash like a whip about the other's thighs.

He caught him and locked him to him as he fell forward, dropping the blade; and with a kick he bore them both back into deeper water.

"None sing hymns to breath," said Yama. "But, oh to be without it!"

Then he plunged downward, bearing the other with him, his arms like steel loops about his body.

Later, much later, as the wet figure stood beside the stream, he spoke softly and his breath came in gasps:

"You were—the greatest—to be raised up against me—in all the ages I can remember. . . . It is indeed a pity . . ."

Then, having crossed the stream, he continued on his way through the hills of stone, walking.

Entering the town of Alundil, the traveler stopped at the first inn he came to. He took a room and ordered a tub of water. He bathed while a servant cleaned his garments.

Before he had his dinner, he moved to the window and looked down into the street. The smell of slizzard was strong upon the air, and the babble of many voices arose from below.

People were leaving the town. In the courtyard at his back, preparations for the departure of a morning caravan were being made. This night marked the end of the spring festival. Below him in the street, businessmen were still trading, mothers were soothing tired children and a local prince was returning with his men from the hunt, two fire-roosters strapped to the back of a skittering slizzard. He watched a tired prostitute discussing something with a priest, who appeared to be even more tired, as he kept shaking his head and finally walked away. One moon was already high in the heavens— seen as golden through the Bridge of the Gods—and a second, smaller moon had just appeared above the horizon. There was a cool tingle in the evening air, bearing to him, above the smells of the city, the scents of the growing things of spring: the small shoots and the tender grasses, the clean smell of the blue-green spring wheat, the moist ground, the roiling freshet. Leaning forward, he could see the Temple that stood upon the hill.

He summoned a servant to bring his dinner in his chamber and to send for a local merchant.

He ate slowly, not paying especial attention to his

food, and when he had finished, the merchant was shown in.

The man bore a cloak full of samples, and of these he finally decided upon a long, curved blade and a short, straight dagger, both of which he thrust into his sash.

Then he went out into the evening and walked along the rutted main street of the town. Lovers embraced in doorways. He passed a house where mourners were wailing for one dead. A beggar limped after him for half a block, until he turned and glanced into his eyes, saying, "You are not lame," and then the man hurried away, losing himself in a crowd that was passing. Overhead, the fireworks began to burst against the sky, sending long, cherry-colored streamers down toward the ground. From the Temple came the sound of the gourd horns playing the *nagaswaram* music. A man stumbled from out a doorway, brushing against him, and he broke the man's wrist as he felt his hand fall upon his purse. The man uttered a curse and called for help, but he pushed him into the drainage ditch and walked on, turning away his two companions with one dark look.

At last, he came to the Temple, hesitated a moment and passed within.

He entered the inner courtyard behind a priest who was carrying in a small statue from an outer niche.

He surveyed the courtyard, then quickly moved to the place occupied by the statue of the goddess Kali. He studied her for a long while, drawing his blade and placing it at her feet. When he picked it up and turned away, he saw that the priest was watching him. He nodded to the man, who immediately approached and bade him a good evening.

"Good evening, priest," he replied.

"May Kali sanctify your blade, warrior."

"Thank you. She has."

The priest smiled. "You speak as if you knew that for certain."

"And that is presumptuous of me, eh?"

"Well, it may not be in the best of taste."

"Nevertheless, I felt her power come over me as I gazed upon her shrine."

The priest shuddered. "Despite my office," he stated, "that is a feeling of power I can do without."

"You fear her power?"

"Let us say," said the priest, "that despite its magnificence, the shrine of Kali is not so frequently visited as are those of Lakshmi, Sarasvati, Shakti, Sitala, Ratri and the other less awesome goddesses."

"But she is greater than any of these."

"And more terrible."

"So? Despite her strength, she is not an unjust goddess."

The priest smiled. "What man who has lived for more than a score of years desires justice, warrior? For my part, I find mercy infinitely more attractive. Give me a forgiving deity any day."

"Well taken," said the other, "but I am, as you say, a warrior. My own nature is close to hers. We think alike, the goddess and I. We generally agree on most matters. When we do not, I remember that she is also a woman."

"I live here," said the priest, "and I do not speak that intimately of my charges, the gods."

"In public, that is," said the other. "Tell me not of priests. I have drunk with many of you, and know you to be as blasphemous as the rest of mankind."

"There is a time and place for everything," said the priest, glancing back at Kali's statue.

"Aye, aye. Now tell me why the base of Yama's shrine has not been scrubbed recently. It is dusty."

"It was cleaned but yesterday, but so many have passed before it since then that it has felt considerable usage."

The other smiled. "Why then are there no offerings laid at his feet, no remains of sacrifices?"

"No one gives flowers to Death," said the priest. "They just come to look and go away. We priests have always felt the two statues to be well situated. They make a terrible pair, do they not? Death, and the mistress of destruction?"

"A mighty team," said the other. "But do you mean to tell me that no one makes sacrifice to Yama? No one at all?"

"Other than we priests, when the calendar of devotions requires it, and an occasional townsman, when a loved one is upon the death-bed and has been refused direct incarnation—other than these, no, I have never seen sacrifice made to Yama, simply, sincerely, with good will or affection."

"He must feel offended."

"Not so, warrior. For are not all living things, in themselves, sacrifices to Death?"

"Indeed, you speak truly. What need has he for their good will or affection? Gifts are unnecessary, for he takes what he wants."

"Like Kali," acknowledged the priest. "And in the cases of both deities have I often sought justification for atheism. Unfortunately, they manifest themselves too strongly in the world for their existence to be denied effectively. Pity."

The warrior laughed. "A priest who is an unwilling believer! I like that. It tickles my funny bone! Here, buy yourself a barrel of soma—for sacrificial purposes."

"Thank you, warrior. I shall. Join me in a small libation now—on the Temple?"

"By Kali, I will!" said the other. "But a small one only."

He accompanied the priest into the central building and down a flight of stairs into the cellar, where a barrel of soma was tapped and two beakers drawn.

"To your health and long life," he said, raising it.

"To your morbid patrons—Yama and Kali," said the priest.

"Thank you."

They gulped the potent brew, and the priest drew two more. "To warm your throat against the night."

"Very good."

"It is a good thing to see some of these travelers depart," said the priest. "Their devotions have enriched the Temple, but they have also tired the staff considerably."

"To the departure of the pilgrims!"

"To the departure of the pilgrims!"

They drank again.

"I thought that most of them came to see the Buddha," said Yama.

"That is true," replied the priest, "but on the other hand, they are not anxious to antagonize the gods by this. So, before they visit the purple grove, they generally make sacrifice or donate to the Temple for prayers."

"What do you know of the one called Tathagatha, and of his teachings?"

The other looked away. "I am a priest of the gods and a Brahmin, warrior. I do not wish to speak of this one."

"So, he has gotten to you, too?"

"Enough! I have made my wishes known to you. It is not a subject on which I will discourse."

"It matters not—and will matter less shortly. Thank you for the soma. Good evening, priest."

"Good evening, warrior. May the gods smile upon your path."

"And yours also."

Mounting the stairs, he departed the Temple and continued on his way through the city, walking.

When he came to the purple grove, there were three moons in the heavens, small camplights behind the trees, pale blossoms of fire in the sky above the town, and a breeze with a certain dampness in it stirring the growth about him.

He moved silently ahead, entering the grove.

When he came into the lighted area, he was faced with row upon row of motionless, seated figures. Each wore a yellow robe with a yellow cowl drawn over the head. Hundreds of them were seated so, and not one uttered a sound.

He approached the one nearest him.

"I have come to see Tathagatha, the Buddha," he said.

The man did not seem to hear him.

"Where is he?"

The man did not reply.

He bent forward and stared into the monk's half-closed eyes. For a moment, he glared into them, but it was as though the other was asleep, for the eyes did not even meet with his.

Then he raised his voice, so that all within the grove might hear him:

"I have come to see Tathagatha, the Buddha," he said. "Where is he?"

It was as though he addressed a field of stones.

"Do you think to hide him in this manner?" he called out. "Do you think that because you are many, and all dressed alike, and because you will not answer me, that for these reasons I cannot find him among you?"

There was only the sighing of the wind, passing through from the back of the grove. The light flickered and the purple fronds stirred.

He laughed. "In this, you may be right," he admitted. "But you must move sometime, if you intend to go on living—and I can wait as long as any man."

Then he seated himself upon the ground, his back against the blue bark of a tall tree, his blade across his knees.

Immediately, he was seized with drowsiness. His head nodded and jerked upward several times. Then his chin came to rest upon his breast and he snored.

Was walking, across a blue-green plain, the grasses bending down to form a pathway before him. At the end of this pathway was a massive tree, a tree such as did not grow upon the world, but rather held the world together with its roots, and with its branches reached up to utter leaves among the stars.

At its base sat a man, cross-legged, a faint smile upon his lips. He knew this man to be the Buddha, and he approached and stood before him.

"Greetings, oh Death," said the seated one, crowned with a rose-hued aureole that was bright in the shadow of the tree.

Yama did not reply, but drew his blade.

The Buddha continued to smile, and as Yama moved forward he heard a sound like distant music.

He halted and looked about him, his blade still upraised.

They came from all quarters, the four Regents of the world, come down from Mount Sumernu: the Master of the North advanced, followed by his Yakshas, all in gold, mounted on yellow horses, bearing shields that blazed with golden light; the Angel of the South came on, followed by his hosts, the Kumbhandas, mounted upon blue steeds and bearing sapphire shields; from the East rode the Regent whose horsemen carry shields of pearl, and who are clad all in silver; and from the West there came the One whose Nagas mounted blood-red horses, were clad all in red and held before them shields of coral. Their hooves did not appear to touch the grasses, and the only sound in the air was the music, which grew louder.

"Why do the Regents of the world approach?" Yama found himself saying.

"They come to bear my bones away," replied the Buddha, still smiling.

The four Regents drew rein, their hordes at their backs, and Yama faced them.

"You come to bear his bones away," said Yama, "but who will come for yours?"

The Regents dismounted.

"You may not have this man, oh Death," said the

Master of the North, "for he belongs to the world, and we of the world will defend him."

"Hear me, Regents who dwell upon Sumernu," said Yama, taking his Aspect upon him. "Into your hands is given the keeping of the world, but Death takes whom he will from out the world, and whenever he chooses. It is not given to you to dispute my Attributes, or the ways of their working."

The four Regents moved to a position between Yama and Tathagatha.

"We do dispute your way with this one, Lord Yama. For in his hands he holds the destiny of our world. You may touch him only after having overthrown the four Powers."

"So be it," said Yama. "Which among you will be first to oppose me?"

"I will," said the speaker, drawing his golden blade.

Yama, his Aspect upon him, sheared through the soft metal like butter and laid the flat of his scimitar along the Regent's head, sending him sprawling upon the ground.

A great cry came up from the ranks of the Yakshas, and two of the golden horsemen came forward to bear away their leader. Then they turned their mounts and rode back into the North.

"Who is next?"

The Regent of the East came before him, bearing a straight blade of silver and a net woven of moonbeams. "I," he said, and he cast with the net.

Yama set his foot upon it, caught it in his fingers, jerked the other off balance. As the Regent stumbled forward, he reversed his blade and struck him in the jaw with its pommel.

Two silver warriors glared at him, then dropped their eyes, as they bore their Master away to the East, a discordant music trailing in their wake.

"Next!" said Yama.

Then there came before him the burly leader of the

Nagas, who threw down his weapons and stripped off his tunic, saying, "I will wrestle with you, deathgod."

Yama laid his weapons aside and removed his upper garments.

All the while this was happening, the Buddha sat in the shade of the great tree, smiling, as though the passage of arms meant nothing to him.

The Chief of the Nagas caught Yama behind the neck with his left hand, pulling his head forward. Yama did the same to him; and the other did then twist his body, casting his right arm over Yama's left shoulder and behind his neck, locking it then tight about his head, which he now drew down hard against his hip, turning his body as he dragged the other forward.

Reaching up behind the Naga Chief's back, Yama caught his left shoulder in his left hand and then moved his right hand behind the Regent's knees, so that he lifted both his legs off the ground while drawing back upon his shoulder.

For a moment he held this one cradled in his arms like a child, then raised him up to shoulder level and dropped away his arms.

When the Regent struck the ground, Yama fell upon him with his knees and rose again. The other did not.

When the riders of the West had departed, only the Angel of the South, clad all in blue, stood before the Buddha.

"And you?" asked the deathgod, raising his weapons again.

"I will not take up weapons of steel or leather or stone, as a child takes up toys, to face you, god of death. Nor will I match the strength of my body against yours," said the Angel. "I know I will be bested if I do these things, for none may dispute you with arms."

"Then climb back upon your blue stallion and ride away," said Yama, "if you will not fight."

The Angel did not answer, but cast his blue shield

into the air, so that it spun like a wheel of sapphire, growing larger and larger as it hung above them.

Then it fell to the ground and began to sink into it, without a sound, still growing as it vanished from sight, the grasses coming together again above the spot where it had struck.

"And what does that signify?" asked Yama.

"I do not actively contest. I merely defend. Mine is the power of passive opposition. Mine is the power of life, as yours is the power of death. While you can destroy anything I send against you, you cannot destroy everything, oh Death. Mine is the power of the shield, but not the sword. Life will oppose you, Lord Yama, to defend your victim."

The Blue One turned then, mounted his blue steed and rode into the South, the Kumbhandas at his back. The sound of the music did not go with him, but remained in the air he had occupied.

Yama advanced once more, his blade in his hand. "Their efforts came to naught," he said. "Your time is come."

He struck forward with his blade.

The blow did not land, however, as a branch from the great tree fell between them and struck the scimitar from his grasp.

He reached for it and the grasses bent to cover it over, weaving themselves into a tight, unbreakable net.

Cursing, he drew his dagger and struck again.

One mighty branch bent down, came swaying before his target, so that his blade was imbedded deeply in its fibers. Then the branch lashed again skyward, carrying the weapon with it, high out of reach.

The Buddha's eyes were closed in meditation and his halo glowed in the shadows.

Yama took a step forward, raising his hands, and the grasses knotted themselves about his ankles, holding him where he stood.

He struggled for a moment, tugging at their unyielding roots. Then he stopped and raised both hands high, throwing his head far back, death leaping from his eyes.

"Hear me, oh Powers!" he cried. "From this moment forward, this spot shall bear the curse of Yama! No living thing shall ever stir again upon this ground! No bird shall sing, nor snake slither here! It shall be barren and stark, a place of rocks and shifting sand! Not a spear of grass shall ever be upraised from here against the sky! I speak this curse and lay this doom upon the defenders of my enemy!"

The grasses began to wither, but before they had released him there came a great splintering, cracking noise, as the tree whose roots held together the world and in whose branches the stars were caught, as fish in a net, swayed forward, splitting down its middle, its uppermost limbs tearing apart the sky, its roots opening chasms in the ground, its leaves falling like blue-green rain about him. A massive section of its trunk toppled toward him, casting before it a shadow dark as night.

In the distance, he still saw the Buddha, seated in meditation, as though unaware of the chaos that erupted about him.

Then there was only blackness and a sound like the crashing of thunder.

Yama jerked his head, his eyes springing open.

He sat in the purple grove, his back against the bole of a blue tree, his blade across his knees.

Nothing seemed to have changed.

The rows of monks were seated, as in meditation, before him. The breeze was still cool and moist and the lights still flickered as it passed.

Yama stood, knowing then, somehow, where he must go to find that which he sought.

He moved past the monks, following a well-beaten path that led far into the interior of the wood.

He came upon a purple pavilion, but it was empty.

He moved on, tracing the path back to where the wood became a wilderness. Here, the ground was damp and a faint mist sprang up about him. But the way was still clear before him, illuminated by the light of the three moons.

The trail led downward, the blue and purple trees growing shorter and more twisted here than they did above. Small pools of water, with floating patches of leprous, silver scum, began to appear at the sides of the trail. A marshland smell came to his nostrils, and the wheezing of strange creatures came out of clumps of brush.

He heard the sound of singing, coming from far up behind him, and he realized that the monks he had left were now awake and stirring about the grove. They had finished with the task of combining their thoughts to force upon him the vision of their leader's invincibility. Their chanting was probably a signal, reaching out to—

There!

He was seated upon a rock in the middle of a field, the moonlight falling full upon him.

Yama drew his blade and advanced.

When he was about twenty paces away, the other turned his head.

"Greetings, oh Death," he said.

"Greetings, Tathagatha."

"Tell me why you are here."

"It has been decided that the Buddha must die."

"That does not answer my question, however. Why have you come here?"

"Are you not the Buddha?"

"I have been called Buddha, and Tathagatha, and the Enlightened One, and many other things. But, in answer to your question, no, I am not the Buddha. You have already succeeded in what you set out to do. You slew the real Buddha this day."

"My memory must indeed be growing weak, for I confess that I do not remember doing this thing."

"The real Buddha was named by us Sugata," replied the other. "Before that, he was known as Rild."

"Rild!" Yama chuckled. "You are trying to tell me

that he was more than an executioner whom you talked out of doing his job?"

"Many people are executioners who have been talked out of doing their jobs," replied the one on the rock. "Rild gave up his mission willingly and became a follower of the Way. He was the only man I ever knew to really achieve enlightenment."

"Is this not a pacifistic religion, this thing you have been spreading?"

"Yes."

Yama threw back his head and laughed. "Gods! Then it is well you are not preaching a militant one! Your foremost disciple, enlightenment and all, near had my head this afternoon!"

A tired look came over the Buddha's wide countenance. "Do you think he could actually have beaten you?"

Yama was silent a moment, then, "No," he said.

"Do you think he knew this?"

"Perhaps," Yama replied.

"Did you not know one another prior to this day's meeting? Have you not seen one another at practice?"

"Yes," said Yama. "We were acquainted."

"Then he knew your skill and realized the outcome of the encounter."

Yama was silent.

"He went willingly to his martyrdom, unknown to me at the time. I do not feel that he went with real hope of beating you."

"Why, then?"

"To prove a point."

"What point could he hope to prove in such a manner?"

"I do not know. I only know that it must be as I have said, for I knew him. I have listened too often to his sermons, to his subtle parables, to believe that he would do a thing such as this without a purpose. You have slain the true Buddha, deathgod. You know what *I* am."

"Siddhartha," said Yama, "I know that you are a fraud. I know that you are not an Enlightened One. I realize that your doctrine is a thing which could have been remembered by any among the First. You chose to resurrect it, pretending to be its originator. You decided to spread it, in hopes of raising an opposition to the religion by which the true gods rule. I admire the effort. It was cleverly planned and executed. But your biggest mistake, I feel, is that you picked a pacifistic creed with which to oppose an active one. I am curious why you did this thing, when there were so many more appropriate religions from which to choose."

"Perhaps I was just curious to see how such a countercurrent would flow," replied the other.

"No, Sam, that is not it," answered Yama. "I feel it is only part of a larger plan you have laid, and that for all these years—while you pretended to be a saint and preached sermons in which you did not truly believe yourself—you have been making other plans. An army, great in space, may offer opposition in a brief span of time. One man, brief in space, must spread his opposition across a period of many years if he is to have a chance of succeeding. You are aware of this, and now that you have sown the seeds of this stolen creed, you are planning to move on to another phase of opposition. You are trying to be a one-man antithesis to Heaven, opposing the will of the gods across the years, in many ways and from behind many masks. But it will end here and now, false Buddha."

"Why, Yama?" he asked.

"It was considered quite carefully," said Yama. "We did not want to make you a martyr, encouraging more than ever the growth of this thing you have been teaching. On the other hand, if you were not stopped, it would still continue to grow. It was decided, therefore, that you must meet your end at the hands of an agent of Heaven—thus showing which religion is the stronger. So, martyr or no, Buddhism will be a second-rate religion henceforth. That is why you must now die the real death."

"When I asked 'Why?' I meant something different. You have answered the wrong question. I meant, why have *you* come to do this thing, Yama? Why have you, master of arms, master of sciences, come as lackey to a crew of drunken body-changers, who are not qualified to polish your blade or wash out your test tubes? Why do you, who might be the freest spirit of us all, demean yourself by serving your inferiors?"

"For that, your death shall not be a clean one."

"Why? I did but ask a question, which must have long since passed through more minds than my own. I did not take offense when you called me a false Buddha. I know what I am. Who are you, deathgod?"

Yama placed his blade within his sash and withdrew a pipe, which he had purchased at the inn earlier in the day. He filled its bowl with tobacco, lit it, and smoked.

"It is obvious that we must talk a little longer, if only to clear both our minds of questions," he stated, "so I may as well be comfortable." He seated himself upon a low rock. "First, a man may in some ways be superior to his fellows and still serve them, if together they serve a common cause which is greater than any one man. I believe that I serve such a cause, or I would not be doing it. I take it that you feel the same way concerning what you do, or you would not put up with this life of miserable asceticism—though I note that you are not so gaunt as your followers. You were offered godhood some years ago in Mahartha, as I recall, and you mocked Brahma, raided the Palace of Karma, and filled all the pray-machines of the city with slugs . . ."

The Buddha chuckled. Yama joined him briefly and continued, "There are no Accelerationists remaining in the world, other than yourself. It is a dead issue, which should never have become an issue in the first place. I do have a certain respect for the manner in which you have acquitted yourself over the years. It has even occurred to me that if you could be made to realize the hopelessness of your present position, you might still be persuaded to join the hosts of Heaven. While I did come here to kill you, if you can be convinced of this now and give me your word upon it, promising to end your foolish fight, I will take it upon myself to vouch for you. I will take you back to the Celestial City with me, where you may now accept that which you once refused. They will harken to me, because they need me."

"No," said Sam, "for I am not convinced of the futility of my position, and I fully intend to continue the show."

The chanting came down from the camp in the purple grove. One of the moons disappeared beyond the treetops.

"Why are your followers not beating the bushes, seeking to save you?"

"They would come if I called, but I will not call. I do not need to."

"Why did they cause me to dream that foolish dream?"

The Buddha shrugged.

"Why did they not arise and slay me as I slept?"

"It is not their way."

"You might have, though, eh? If you could get away with it? If none would know the Buddha did it?"

"Perhaps," said the other. "As you know, the personal strengths and weaknesses of a leader are no true indication of the merits of his cause."

Yama drew upon his pipe. The smoke wreathed his head and eddied away to join the fogs, which were now becoming more heavy upon the land.

"I know we are alone here, and you are unarmed," said Yama.

"We are alone here. My traveling gear is hidden farther along my route."

"Your traveling gear?"

"I have finished here. You guessed correctly. I have

begun what I set out to begin. After we have finished our conversation, I will depart."

Yama chuckled. "The optimism of a revolutionary always gives rise to a sense of wonder. How do you propose to depart? On a magic carpet?"

"I shall go as other men go."

"That is rather condescending of you. Will the powers of the world rise up to defend you? I see no great tree to shelter you with its branches. There is no clever grass to seize at my feet. Tell me how you will achieve your departure?"

"I'd rather surprise you."

"What say we fight? I do not like to slaughter an unarmed man. If you actually do have supplies cached somewhere nearby, go fetch your blade. It is better than no chance at all. I've even heard it said that Lord Siddhartha was, in his day, a formidable swordsman."

"Thank you, no. Another time, perhaps. But not this time."

Yama drew once more upon his pipe, stretched, and yawned. "I can think of no more questions then, which I wish to ask you. It is futile to argue with you. I have nothing more to say. Is there anything else that you would care to add to the conversation?"

"Yes," said Sam. "What's she like, that bitch Kali? There are so many different reports that I'm beginning to believe she is all things to all men—"

Yama hurled the pipe, which struck him upon the shoulder and sent a shower of sparks down his arm. His scimitar was a bright flash about his head as he leapt forward.

When he struck the sandy stretch before the rock, his motion was arrested. He almost fell, twisted himself perpendicularly and remained standing. He struggled, but could not move.

"Some quicksand," said Sam, "is quicker than other quicksand. Fortunately, you are settling into that of the slower sort. So you have considerable time yet remaining at your disposal. I would like to prolong the conversation, if I thought I had a chance of persuading you to join with me. But I know that I do not—no more than you could persuade me to go to Heaven."

"I will get free," said Yama softly, not struggling. "I will get free somehow, and I will come after you again."

"Yes," said Sam, "I feel this to be true. In fact, in a short while I will instruct you how to go about it. For the moment, however, you are something every preacher longs for—a captive audience, representing the opposition. So, I have a brief sermon for you, Lord Yama."

Yama hefted his blade, decided against throwing it, thrust it again into his sash.

"Preach on," he said, and he succeeded in catching the other's eyes.

Sam swayed where he sat, but he spoke again:

"It is amazing," he said, "how that mutant brain of yours generated a mind capable of transferring its powers to any new brain you choose to occupy. It has been years since I last exercised my one ability, as I am at this moment—but it, too, behaves in a similar manner. No matter what body I inhabit, it appears that my power follows me into it also. I understand it is still that way with most of us. Sitala, I hear, can control temperatures for a great distance about her. When she assumes a new body, the power accompanies her into her new nervous system, though it comes only weakly at first. Agni, I know, can set fire to objects by staring at them for a period of time and willing that they burn. Now, take for example the death-gaze you are at this moment turning upon me. Is it not amazing how you keep this gift about you in all times and places, over the centuries? I have often wondered as to the physiological basis for the phenomenon. Have you ever researched the area?"

"Yes," said Yama, his eyes burning beneath his dark brows.

"And what is the explanation? A person is born with

an abnormal brain, his psyche is later transferred to a normal one and yet his abnormal abilities are not destroyed in the transfer. Why does this thing happen?"

"Because you really have only one body-image, which is electrical as well as chemical in nature. It begins immediately to modify its new physiological environment. The new body has much about it which it treats rather like a disease, attempting to cure it into being the old body. If the body which you now inhabit were to be made physically immortal, it would someday come to resemble your original body."

"How interesting."

"That is why the transferred power is weak at first, but grows stronger as you continue occupancy. That is why it is best to cultivate an Attribute, and perhaps to employ mechanical aids, also."

"Well. That is something I have often wondered about. Thank you. By the way, keep trying with your death-gaze—it is painful, you know. So that is something, anyway. Now, as to the sermon—a proud and arrogant man, such as yourself—with an admittedly admirable quality of didacticism about him—was given to doing research in the area of a certain disfiguring and degenerative disease. One day he contracted it himself. Since he had not yet developed a cure for the condition, he did take time out to regard himself in a mirror and say, 'But on *me* it does look good.' You are such a man, Yama. You will not attempt to fight your condition. Rather, you are proud of it. You betrayed yourself in your fury, so I know that I speak the truth when I say that the name of your disease is Kali. You would not give power into the hands of the unworthy if that woman did not bid you do it. I knew her of old, and I am certain that she has not changed. She cannot love a man. She cares only for those who bring her gifts of chaos. If ever you cease to suit her purposes, she will put you aside, deathgod. I do not say this because we are enemies, but rather as one man to another. I know. Believe me, I do. Perhaps it is unfortunate that you were never really young, Yama, and did not know your first love in the days of spring. . . . The moral, therefore, of my sermon on this small mount is this—even a mirror will not show you yourself, if you do not wish to see. Cross her once to try the truth of my words, even in a small matter, and see how quickly she responds, and in what fashion. What will you do if your own weapons are turned against you, Death?"

"You have finished speaking now?" asked Yama.

"That's about it. A sermon is a warning, and you have been warned."

"Whatever your power, Sam, I see that it is at this moment proof against my death-gaze. Consider yourself fortunate that I am weakened—"

"I do indeed, for my head is about to split. Damn your eyes!"

"One day I will try your power again, and even if it should still be proof against my own, you will fall on that day. If not by my Attribute, then by my blade."

"If that is a challenge, I choose to defer acceptance. I suggest that you do try my words before you attempt to make it good."

At this point, the sand was halfway up Yama's thighs.

Sam sighed and climbed down from his perch.

"There is only one clear path to this rock, and I am about to follow it away from here. Now, I will tell you how to gain your life, if you are not too proud. I have instructed the monks to come to my aid, here at this place, if they hear a cry for help. I told you earlier that I was not going to call for help, and that is true. If, however, you begin calling out for aid with that powerful voice of yours, they shall be here before you sink too much farther. They will bring you safely to firm ground and will not try to harm you, for such is their way. I like the thought of the god of death being saved by the monks of Buddha. Good night, Yama, I'm going to leave you now."

Yama smiled. "There will be another day, oh Buddha," he stated. "I can wait for it. Flee now as far and as fast as you can. The world is not large enough to hide you from my wrath. I will follow you, and I will teach you of the enlightenment that is pure hellfire."

"In the meantime," said Sam, "I suggest you solicit aid of my followers or learn the difficult art of mud-breathing."

He picked his way across the field, Yama's eyes burning into his back.

When he reached the trail, he turned. "And you may want to mention in Heaven," he said, "that I was called out of town on a business deal."

Yama did not reply.

"I think I am going to make a deal for some weapons," he finished, "some rather special weapons. So when you come after me, bring your girl friend along. If she likes what she sees, she may persuade you to switch sides."

Then he struck the trail and moved away through the night, whistling, beneath a moon that was white and a moon that was golden.

iv

*It is told how the Lord of Light descended into the
Well of the Demons, to make there a bargain with the
chief of the Rakasha. He dealt in good faith, but the
Rakasha are the Rakasha. That is to say, they are
malefic creatures, possessed of great powers, life-span
and the ability to assume nearly any shape. The Rakasha are almost indestructible. Their chiefest lack is a
true body; their chiefest virtue, their honor toward their
gambling debts. That the Lord of Light went to Hellwell at all serves to show that perhaps he was somewhat distraught concerning the state of the world. . . .*

When the gods and the demons, both offspring
of Prajapati, did battle with one another, the
gods seized upon the life-principle of the Udgitha, thinking that with this would they vanquish
the demons.

They meditated upon the Udgitha which functions through the nose, but the demons pierced
it through with evil. Therefore, with the breath
one smells both that which is pleasant and that
which is foul. Thus the breath is touched by evil.

They meditated upon the Udgitha as words,
but the demons pierced it through with evil.
Therefore, one speaks both truth and falsehood.
Thus words are touched by evil.

They meditated upon the Udgitha which functions through the eye, but the demons pierced it
through with evil. Therefore, one sees both what
is pleasing and what is ugly. Thus the eye is
touched by evil.

They meditated upon the Udgitha as hearing,
but the demons pierced it through with evil.
Therefore, one hears both good things and bad.
Thus the ear is touched by evil.

Then did they meditate upon the Udgitha as
the mind, but the demons pierced it through with
evil. Therefore, one thinks what is proper, true,
and good, and what is improper, false, and de-
praved. Thus the mind is touched by evil.

Chhandogya Upanishad (1, ii, 1–6)

HELLWELL lies at the top of the world and it leads
down to its roots.

It is probably as old as the world itself; and if it is
not, it should be, because it looks as if it were.

It begins with a doorway. There is a huge, burnished
metal door, erected by the First, that is heavy as sin,
three times the height of a man and half that distance
in width. It is a full cubit thick and bears a head-sized
ring of brass, a complicated pressure-plate lock and an
inscription that reads, roughly, "Go away. This is not a
place to be. If you do try to enter here, you will fail
and also be cursed. If somehow you succeed, then do
not complain that you entered unwarned, nor bother us
with your deathbed prayers." Signed, "The Gods."

It is set near the peak of a very high mountain
named Channa, in the midst of a region of very high
mountains called the Ratnagaris. In that place there is
always snow upon the ground, and rainbows ride like
fur on the backs of icicles, which sprout about the
frozen caps of cliffs. The air is sharp as a sword. The
sky is bright as the eye of a cat.

Very few feet have ever trod the trail that leads to
Hellwell. Of those who visited, most came only to look,
to see whether the great door really existed; and when
they returned home and told of having seen it, they
were generally mocked.

Telltale scratches about the lock plate testify that
some have actually sought entrance. Equipment sufficient to force the great door could not be transported or
properly positioned, however. The trail that leads to
Hellwell is less than ten inches in width for the final
three hundred feet of its ascent; and perhaps six men

could stand, with crowding, upon what remains of the
once wide ledge that faces that door.

It is told that Pannalal the Sage, having sharpened
his mind with meditation and divers asceticisms, had
divined the operation of the lock and entered Hellwell,
spending a day and a night beneath the mountain. He
was thereafter known as Pannalal the Mad.

The peak known as Channa, which holds the great
door, is removed by five days' journey from a small
village. This is within the far northern kingdom of
Malwa. This mountain village nearest to Channa has no
name itself, being filled with a fierce and independent
people who have no special desire that their town appear on the maps of the rajah's tax collectors. Of the
rajah, it is sufficient to tell that he is of middle height
and middle years, shrewd, slightly stout, neither pious
nor more than usually notorious and fabulously
wealthy. He is wealthy because he levies high taxes
upon his subjects. When his subjects begin to complain,
and murmurs of revolt run through the realm, he de-
clares war upon a neighboring kingdom and doubles
the taxes. If the war does not go well, he executes
several generals and has his Minister of Peace negotiate
a treaty. If, by some chance, it goes especially well, he
exacts tribute for whatever insult has caused the entire
affair. Usually, though, it ends in a truce, souring his
subjects on fighting and reconciling them to the high
tax rate. His name is Videgha and he has many children. He is fond of grak-birds, which can be taught to
sing bawdy songs, of snakes, to which he occasionally
feeds grak-birds who cannot carry a tune, and of gaming with dice. He does not especially like children.

Hellwell begins with the great doorway high in the
mountains at the northernmost corner of Videgha's
kingdom, beyond which there are no other kingdoms of
men. It begins there, and it corkscrews down through
the heart of the mountain Channa, breaking, like a
corkscrew, into vast cavernways uncharted by men,
extending far beneath the Ratnagari range, the deepest

passageways pushing down toward the roots of the world.

To this door came the traveler.

He was simply dressed, and he traveled alone, and he seemed to know exactly where he was going and what he was doing.

He climbed the trail up Channa, edging his way across its gaunt face.

It took him the better part of the morning to reach his destination, the door.

When he stood before it, he rested a moment, took a drink from his water bottle, wiped his mouth on the back of his hand, smiled.

Then he sat down with his back against the door and ate his lunch. When he had finished, he threw the leaf wrappings over the edge and watched them fall, drifting from side to side on the air currents, until they were out of sight. He lit his pipe then and smoked.

After he had rested, he stood and faced the door once again.

His hand fell upon the pressure plate, moved slowly through a series of gestures. There was a musical sound from within the door as his hand left the plate.

Then he seized upon the ring and drew back, his shoulder muscles straining. The door moved, slowly at first, then more rapidly. He stepped aside and it swung outward, passing beyond the ledge.

There was another ring, twin to the first, on the inner surface of the door. He caught at it as it passed him, dragging his heels to keep it from swinging so far as to place it beyond his reach.

A rush of warm air emerged from the opening at his back.

Drawing the door closed again behind him, he paused only to light one of the many torches he bore. Then he advanced along a corridor that widened as he moved ahead.

The floor slanted abruptly, and after a hundred paces the ceiling was so high as to be invisible.

After two hundred paces, he stood upon the lip of the well.

He was now in the midst of a vast blackness shot through with the flames of his torch. The walls had vanished, save for the one behind him and to the right. The floor ended a short distance before him.

Beyond that edge was what appeared to be a bottomless pit. He could not see across it, but he knew it to be roughly circular in shape; and he knew, too, that it widened in circumference as it descended.

He made his way down along the trail that wound about the well wall, and he could feel the rush of warm air rising from out of the depths. This trail was artificial. One could feel this, despite its steepness. It was precarious and it was narrow; it was cracked in many places, and in spots rubble had accumulated upon it. But its steady, winding slant bespoke the fact that there was purpose and pattern to its existence.

He moved along this trail, carefully. To his left was the wall. To his right there was nothing.

After what seemed an age and a half, he sighted a tiny flicker of light far below him, hanging in midair.

The curvature of the wall, however, gradually bent his way so that this light no longer hung in the distance, but lay below and slightly to his right.

Another twisting of the trail set it directly ahead of him.

When he passed the niche in the wall wherein the flame was cached, he heard a voice within his mind cry out:

"Free me, master, and I will lay the world at thy feet!"

But he hurried by, not even glancing at the almost-face within the opening.

Floating upon the ocean of black that lay beneath his feet, there were more lights now visible.

The well continued to widen. It was filled with brightening glimmers, like flame, but not flame; filled with shapes, faces, half-remembered images. From each there rose up a cry as he passed: "Free me! Free me!"

But he did not halt.

He came to the bottom of the well and moved across it, passing among broken stones and over fissures in the rocky floor. At last he reached the opposite wall, wherein a great orange fire danced.

It became cherry-red as he approached, and when he stood before it, it was the blue of a sapphire's heart.

It stood to twice his height, pulsing and twisting. From it, little flamelets licked out toward him, but they drew back as if they fell against an invisible barrier.

During his descent he had passed so many flames that he had lost count of their number. He knew, too, that more lay hidden within the caverns that open into the well bottom.

Each flame he had passed on the way down had addressed him, using its own species of communication, so that the words had sounded drumlike within his head: threatening words, and pleading, promising words. But no message came to him from this great blue blaze, larger than any of the others. No forms turned or twisted, tantalizing, within its bright heart. Flame it was, and flame it remained.

He kindled a fresh torch and wedged it beween two rocks.

"So, Hated One, you have returned!"

The words fell upon him like whiplashes. Steadying himself, he faced the blue flame then and replied:

"You are called Taraka?"

"He who bound me here should know what I am called," came the words. "Think not, oh Siddhartha, that because you wear a different body you go now unrecognized. I look upon the flows of energy which are your real being—not the flesh that masks them."

"I see," replied the other.

"Do you come to mock me in my prison?"

"Did I mock you in the days of the Binding?"

"No, you did not."

"I did that which had to be done, to preserve my own species. Men were weak and few in number. Your kind fell upon them and would have destroyed them."

"You stole our world, Siddhartha. You chained us here. What new indignity would you lay upon us?"

"Perhaps there is a way in which some reparation may be made."

"What is it that you want?"

"Allies."

"You want us to take your part in a struggle?"

"That is correct."

"And when it is over, you will seek to bind us again."

"Not if we can work out some sort of agreement beforehand."

"Speak to me your terms," said the flame.

"In the old days your people walked, visible and invisible, in the streets of the Celestial City."

"That is true."

"It is better fortified now."

"In what ways?"

"Vishnu the Preserver and Yama-Dharma, Lord of Death, have covered the whole of Heaven, rather than just the City—as it was in days of old—with what is said to be an impenetrable dome."

"There is no such thing as an impenetrable dome."

"I say only what I have heard."

"There are many ways into a city, Lord Siddhartha."

"You will find them all for me?"

"That is to be the price of my freedom?"

"Of your own freedom—yes."

"What of the others of my kind?"

"If they, too, are to be freed, you must all agree to help me lay siege to that City and take it."

"Free us, and Heaven shall fall!"

"You speak for the others?"

"I am Taraka. I speak for all."

"What assurance do you give, Taraka, that this bargain will be kept?"

"My word? I shall be happy to swear by anything you care to name—"

"A facility with oaths is not the most reassuring quality in a bargainer. And your strength is also your weakness in any bargaining at all. You are so strong as to be unable to grant to another the power to control you. You have no gods to swear by. The only thing you will honor is a gambling debt, and there are no grounds for gaming here."

"*You* possess the power to control us."

"Individually, perhaps. But not collectively."

"It *is* a difficult problem," said Taraka. "I should give anything I have to be free—but then, all that I have is power—pure power, in essence uncommittable. A greater force might subdue it, but that is not the answer. I do not really know how to give you satisfactory assurance that my promise will be kept. If I were you, *I* certainly would not trust me."

"It is something of a dilemma. So I will free you now—you alone—to visit the Pole and scout out the defenses of Heaven. In your absence, I will consider the problem further. Do you likewise, and perhaps upon your return an equitable arrangement can be made."

"Accepted! Release me from this doom!"

"Know then my power, Taraka," he said. "As I bind, so can I loose—thus!"

The flame boiled forward out of the wall.

It rolled into a ball of fire and spun about the well like a comet; it burned like a small sun, lighting up the darkness; it changed colors as it fled about, so that the rocks shone both ghastly and pleasing.

Then it hovered above the head of the one called Siddhartha, sending down its throbbing words upon him:

"You cannot know my pleasure to feel again my

strength set free. I've a mind to try your power once more."

The man beneath him shrugged.

The ball of flame coalesced. Shrinking, it grew brighter, and it slowly settled to the floor.

It lay there quivering, like a petal fallen from some titanic bloom; then it drifted slowly across the floor of Hellwell and re-entered the niche.

"Are you satisfied?" asked Siddhartha.

"Yes," came the reply, after a time. "Your power is undimmed, Binder. Free me once more."

"I grow tired of this sport, Taraka. Perhaps I'd best leave you as you are and seek assistance elsewhere."

"No! I gave you my promise! What more would you have?"

"I would have an absence of contention between us. Either you will serve me now in this matter, or you will not. That is all. Choose, and abide by your choice— and your word."

"Very well. Free me, and I will visit Heaven upon its mountain of ice, and report back to you of its weaknesses."

"Then go!"

This time, the flame emerged more slowly. It swayed before him, took on a roughly human outline.

"What is your power, Siddhartha? How do you do what you do?" it asked him.

"Call it electrodirection," said the other, "mind over energy. It is as good a term as any. But whatever you call it, do not seek to cross it again. I can kill you with it, though no weapon formed of matter may be laid upon you. Go now!"

Taraka vanished, like a firebrand plunged into a river, and Siddhartha stood among stones, his torch lighting the darkness about him.

He rested, and a babble of voices filled his mind— promising, tempting, pleading. Visions of wealth and of splendor flowed before his eyes. Wondrous harems were

paraded before him, and banquets were laid at his feet.
Essences of musk and champac, and the bluish haze of
burning incenses drifted, soothing his soul, about him.
He walked among flowers, followed by bright-eyed girls
who bore his wine cups, smiling; a silver voice sang to
him, and creatures not human danced upon the surface
of a nearby lake.

"Free us, free us," they chanted.

But he smiled and watched and did nothing.

Gradually, the prayers and the pleas and the promises turned to a chorus of curses and threats. Armored
skeletons advanced upon him, babies impaled upon
their blazing swords. There were pits all about him,
from which fires leapt up, smelling of brimstone. A
serpent dangled from a branch before his face, spitting
venom. A rain of spiders and toads descended upon
him.

"Free us—or infinite will be thy agony!" cried the
voices.

"If you persist," he stated, "Siddhartha shall grow
angry, and you will lose the one chance at freedom
which you really do possess."

Then all was still about him, and he emptied his
mind, drowsing.

He had two meals, there in the cavern, and then he
slept again.

Later, Taraka returned in the form of a great-taloned
bird and reported to him:

"Those of my kind may enter through the air vents,"
he said, "but men may not. There are also many eleva-
tor shafts within the mountain. Many men might ride
up the larger ones with ease. Of course, these are guarded. But if the guards were slain and the alarms discon-
nected, this thing might be accomplished. Also, there
are times when the dome itself is opened in various
places, to permit flying craft to enter and to depart."

"Very well," said Siddhartha. "I've a kingdom, some
weeks' journey hence, where I rule. A regent has been

seated in my place for many years, but if I return there I can raise me an army. A new religion moves now across the land. Men may now think less of the gods than once they did."

"You wish to sack Heaven?"

"Yes, I wish to lay open its treasures to the world."

"This is to my liking. It will not be easily won, but with an army of men and an army of my kind we should be able to do it. Let us free my people now, that we may begin."

"I believe I will simply have to trust you," said Siddhartha. "So yes, let us begin," and he moved across the floor of Hellwell toward the first deep tunnel heading downward.

That day he freed sixty-five of them, filling the caverns with their color and their movement and their light. The air sounded with mighty cries of joy and the noise of their passage as they swept about Hellwell, changing shape constantly and exulting in their freedom.

Without warning, then, one took upon itself the form of a flying serpent and swept down toward him, talons outstretched and slashing.

For a moment, his full attention lay upon it.

It uttered a brief, broken cry, and then it came apart, falling in a shower of blue-white sparks.

Then these faded, and it was utterly vanished.

There was silence in the caverns, and the lights pulsed and dipped about the walls.

Siddhartha directed his attention toward the largest point of light, Taraka.

"Did that one attack me in order to test my strength?" he inquired. "To see whether I can also kill, in the manner I told you I could?"

Taraka approached, hovered before him. "It was not by my bidding that he attacked," he stated. "I feel that he was half crazed from his confinement."

Siddhartha shrugged. "For a time now, disport yourselves as you would," he said. "I would have rest from this task," and he departed the smaller cavern.

He returned to the bottom of the well, where he lay down upon his blanket and dozed.

There came a dream.

He was running.

His shadow lay before him, and, as he ran upon it, it grew.

It grew until it was no longer his shadow but a grotesque outline.

Suddenly he knew that his shadow had been overrun by that of his pursuer: overrun, overwhelmed, submerged and surmounted.

Then he knew a moment of terrible panic, there upon the blind plain over which he fled.

He knew that it was now his own shadow.

The doom which had pursued him no longer lay at his back.

He knew that he was his own doom.

Knowing that he had finally caught up with himself, he laughed aloud, wanting really to scream.

When he awoke again, he was walking.

He was walking up the twisted wall-trail of Hellwell.

As he walked, he passed the imprisoned flames.

Again, each cried out to him as he went by:

"Free us, masters!"

And slowly, about the edges of the ice that was his mind, there was a thawing.

Masters.

Plural. Not singular.

Masters, they had said.

He knew then that he did not walk alone.

None of the dancing, flickering shapes moved through the darkness about him, below him.

The ones who had been imprisoned were still imprisoned. The ones he had freed were gone.

Now he climbed the high wall of Hellwell, no torch lighting his way. But still, he saw.

He saw every feature of the rocky trail, as though by moonlight.

He knew that his eyes were incapable of this feat.

And he had been addressed in the plural.

And his body was moving, but was not under the direction of his will.

He made an effort to halt, to stand still.

He continued to advance up the trail, and it was then that his lips moved, forming the words:

"You have awakened, I see. Good morning."

A question formed itself in his mind, to be answered immediately through his own mouth:

"Yes, and how does it feel to be bound yourself, Binder—in your own body?"

Siddhartha formed another thought:

"I did not think any of your kind capable of taking control of me against my will—even as I slept."

"To give you an honest answer," said the other, "neither did I. But then, I had at my disposal the combined powers of many of my kind. It seemed to be worth the attempt."

"And of the others? Where are they?"

"Gone. To wander the world until I summon them."

"And what of these others who remain bound? Had you waited, I would have freed them also."

"What care I of these others? I am free now, and in a body again! What else matters?"

"I take it, then, that your promised assistance means nothing?"

"Not so," replied the demon. "We shall return to this matter in, say, a lesser moon or so. The idea *does* appeal to me. I feel that a war with the gods would be a very excellent thing. But first I wish to enjoy the pleasures of the flesh for a time. Why should you begrudge me a little entertainment after the centuries of boredom and imprisonment you have wrought?"

"I must admit, however, that I do begrudge you this use of my person."

"Whatever the case, you must, for a time, put up with it. You, too, shall be in a position to enjoy what I enjoy, so why not make the best of it?"

"You state that you *do* intend to war against the gods?"

"Yes indeed. I wish I had thought of it myself in the old days. Perhaps, then, we should never have been bound. Perhaps there would no longer be men or gods upon this world. We were never much for concerted action, though. Independence of spirit naturally accompanies our independence of person. Each fought his own battles in the general conflict with mankind. I am a leader, true—by virtue of the fact that I am older and stronger and wiser than the others. They come to me for counsel, they serve me when I order them. But I have never ordered them all into battle. I shall, though, later. The novelty will do much to relieve the monotony."

"I suggest you do not wait, for there will be no 'later,' Taraka."

"Why not?"

"I came to Hellwell, the wrath of the gods swarming and buzzing at my back. Now sixty-six demons are loose in the world. Very soon, your presence will be felt. The gods will know who has done this thing, and they will take steps against us. The element of surprise will be lost."

"We fought the gods in the days of old . . ."

"And these are not the days of old, Taraka. The gods are stronger now, much stronger. Long have you been bound, and their might has grown over the ages. Even if you command the first army of Rakasha in history, and backing them in battle I raise me up a mighty army of men—even then, will the final result be a thing uncertain. To delay now is to throw everything away."

"I wish you would not speak to me like this, Siddhartha, for you trouble me."

"I mean to. For all your powers, if you meet the One in Red he will drink your life with his eyes. He will come here to the Ratnagaris, for he follows me. The freedom of demons is as a signpost, directing him hither. He may bring others with him. You may find them more than a match for all of you."

The demon did not reply. They reached the top of the well, and Taraka advanced the two hundred paces to the great door, which now stood open. He stepped out onto the ledge and looked downward.

"You doubt the power of the Rakasha, eh, Binder?" he asked. Then, "Behold!"

He stepped outward, over the edge.

They did not fall.

They drifted, like the leaves he had dropped—how long ago?

Downward.

They landed upon the trail halfway down the mountain called Channa.

"Not only do I contain your nervous system," said Taraka, "but I have permeated your entire body and wrapped it all about with the energies of my being. So send me your One in Red, who drinks life with his eyes. I should like to meet him."

"Though you can walk on air," said Siddhartha, "you speak rashly when you speak thus."

"The Prince Videgha holds his court not far from here, at Palamaidsu," said Taraka, "for I visited there on my return from Heaven. I understand he is fond of gaming. Therefore, thither fare we."

"And if the God of Death should come to join the game?"

"Let him!" cried the other. "You cease to amuse me, Binder. Good night. Go back to sleep!"

There was a small darkness and a great silence, growing and shrinking.

The days that followed were bright fragments.

There would come to him snatches of conversation or song, colorful vistas of galleries, chambers, gardens. And once he looked upon a dungeon where men were hung upon racks, and he heard himself laughing.

Between these fragments there came to him dreams and half dreams. They were lighted with fire, they ran with blood and tears. In a darkened, endless cathedral he rolled dice that were suns and planets. Meteors broke fire above his head, and comets inscribed blazing arcs upon a vault of black glass. There came to him a joy shot through with fear, and he knew it to be mainly that of another, but it was partly his, too. The fear— that was all his.

When Taraka drank too much wine, or lay panting on his wide, low couch in the harem, then was his grip loosened somewhat, upon the body that he had stolen. But Siddhartha was still weak with the mind-bruise, and his body was drunk or fatigued; and he knew that the time had not yet come to contest the mastery of the demon-lord.

There were times when he saw, not through the eyes of the body that had once been his, but saw as a demon saw, in all directions, and stripped flesh and bone from those among whom he passed, to behold the flames of their beings, colored with the hues and shades of their passions, flickering with avarice and lust and envy, darting with greed and hunger, smouldering with hate, waning with fear and pain. His hell was a many-colored place, somewhat mitigated only by the cold blue blaze of a scholar's intellect, the white light of a dying monk, the rose halo of a noble lady who fled his sight, and the dancing, simple colors of children at play.

He stalked the high halls and wide galleries of the royal palace at Palamaidsu, which were his winnings. The Prince Videgha lay in chains in his own dungeon. Throughout the kingdom, his subjects were not aware that a demon now sat upon the throne. Things seemed to be the same as they had always been. Siddhartha had

visions of riding through the streets of the town on the
back of an elephant. All the women of the town had
been ordered to stand before the doors of their dwell-
ings. Of these, he chose those who pleased him and
had them taken back to his harem. Siddhartha realized,
with a sudden shock, that he was assisting in the choosing, disputing with Taraka over the virtues of this or
that matron, maid or lady. He had been touched by the
lusts of the demon-lord, and they were becoming his
own. With this realization, he came into a greater wakefulness, and it was not always the hand of the demon
which raised the wine horn to his lips, or twitched the
whip in the dungeon. He came to be conscious for
greater periods of time, and with a certain horror he
knew that, within himself, as within every man, there
lies a demon capable of responding to his own kind.

Then, one day, he fought the power that ruled his
body and bent his mind. He had largely recovered, and
he coexisted with Taraka in all his doings, both as
silent watcher and active participant.

They stood on the balcony above the garden, looking
out across the day. Taraka had, with a single gesture,
turned all the flowers black. Lizardlike creatures had
come to dwell in the trees and the ponds, croaking and
flitting among the shadows. The incenses and perfumes
which filled the air were thick and cloying. Dark
smokes coiled like serpents along the ground.

There had been three attempts upon his life. The
captain of the palace guard had been the last to try.
But his blade had turned to a reptile in his hand and
struck at his face, taking out his eyes and filling his
veins with a venom that had caused him to darken and
swell, to die crying for a drink of water.

Siddhartha considered the ways of the demon, and in
that moment he struck.

His power had grown again, slowly, since that day in
Hellwell when last he had wielded it. Oddly independent of the brain of his body, as Yama had once told

him, the power turned like a slow pinwheel at the center of the space that was himself.

It spun again faster, and he hurled it against the force of the other.

A cry escaped Taraka, and a counterthrust of pure energy came back at Siddhartha like a spear.

Partly, he managed to deflect it, to absorb some of its force. Still, there was pain and turmoil within him as the brunt of the attack touched upon his being.

He did not pause to consider the pain, but struck again, as a spearman strikes into the darkened burrow of a fearsome beast.

Again, he heard his lips cry out.

Then the demon was building black walls against his power.

But one by one, these walls fell before his onslaught.

And as they fought, they spoke:

"Oh man of many bodies," said Taraka, "why do you begrudge me a few days within this one? It is not the body you were born into, and you, too, do but borrow it for a time. Why then, do you feel my touch to be a thing of defilement? One day you may wear another body, untouched by me. So why do you consider my presence a pollution, a disease? Is it because there is that within you which is like unto myself? Is it because you, too, know delight in the ways of the Rakasha, tasting the pain you cause like a pleasure, working your will as you choose upon whatsoever you choose? Is it because of this? Because you, too, know and desire these things, but also bear that human curse called guilt? If it is, I mock you in your weakness, Binder. And I shall prevail against you."

"It is because I am what I am, demon," said Siddhartha, hurling his energies back at him. "It is because I am a man who occasionally aspires to things beyond the belly and the phallus. I am not the saint the Buddhists think me to be, and I am not the hero out of legend. I am a man who knows much fear, and who occasionally feels guilt. Mainly, though, I am a man

who has set out to do a thing, and you are now block-
ing my way. Thus you inherit my curse—whether I win
or whether I lose now, Taraka, your destiny has already been altered. This is the curse of the Buddha—
you will never again be the same as once you were."

And all that day they stood upon the balcony, garments drenched with perspiration. Like a statue they
stood, until the sun had gone down out of the sky and
the golden trail divided the dark bowl of the night. A
moon leapt up above the garden wall. Later, another
joined it.

"What is the curse of the Buddha?" Taraka inquired,
over and over again. But Siddhartha did not reply.

He had beaten down the final wall, and they fenced
now with energies like flights of blazing arrows.

From a Temple in the distance there came the monot-
onous beating of a drum, and occasionally a garden
creature croaked, a bird cried out or a swarm of insects
settled upon them, fed, and swirled away.

Then, like a shower of stars, they came, riding upon
the night wind . . . the Freed of Hellwell, the other
demons who had been loosed upon the world.

They came in answer to Taraka's summons, adding
their powers to his own.

He became as a whirlwind, a tidal wave, a storm of
lightnings.

Siddhartha felt himself swept over by a titanic avalanche, crushed, smothered, buried.

The last thing he knew was the laughter within his
throat.

How long it was before he recovered, he did not
know. It was a slow thing this time, and it was in a
palace where demons walked as servants that he woke
up.

When the last anesthetic bonds of mental fatigue fell
away, there was strangeness about him.

The grotesque revelries continued. Parties were held
in the dungeons, where the demons would animate

corpses to pursue their victims and embrace them. Dark miracles were wrought, such as the grove of twisted trees which sprang from the marble flags of the throne room itself—a grove wherein men slept without awakening, crying out as old nightmares gave way to new. But a different strangeness had entered the palace.

Taraka was no longer pleased.

"What is the curse of the Buddha?" he inquired again, as he felt Siddhartha's presence pressing once more upon his own.

Siddhartha did not reply at once.

The other continued, "I feel that I will give you back your body one day soon. I grow tired of this sport, of this palace. I grow tired, and I think perhaps the day draws near when we should make war with Heaven. What say you to this, Binder? I told you I would keep my word."

Siddhartha did not answer him.

"My pleasures diminish by the day! Do you know why this is, Siddhartha? Can you tell me why strange feelings now come over me, dampening my strongest moments, weakening me and casting me down when I should be elated, when I should be filled with joy? Is *this* the curse of the Buddha?"

"Yes," said Siddhartha.

"Then lift your curse, Binder, and I will depart this very day. I will give you back this cloak of flesh. I long again for the cold, clean winds of the heights! Will you free me now?"

"It is too late, oh chief of the Rakasha. You have brought this thing upon yourself."

"What thing? How have you bound me this time?"

"Do you recall how, when we strove upon the balcony, you mocked me? You told me that I, too, took pleasure in the ways of the pain which you work. You were correct, for all men have within them both that which is dark and that which is light. A man is a thing of many divisions, not a pure, clear flame such as you once were. His intellect often wars with his emotions,

his will with his desires . . . his ideals are at odds with
his environment, and if he follows them, he knows
keenly the loss of that which was old—but if he does
not follow them, he feels the pain of having forsaken a
new and noble dream. Whatever he does represents
both a gain and a loss, an arrival and a departure.
Always he mourns that which is gone and fears some
part of that which is new. Reason opposes tradition.
Emotions oppose the restrictions his fellow men lay
upon him. Always, from the friction of these things,
there arises the thing you called the curse of man and
mocked—guilt!

"Know then, that as we existed together in the same
body and I partook of your ways, not always unwillingly, the road we followed was not one upon which all
the traffic moved in a single direction. As you twisted
my will to your workings, so was your will twisted, in
turn, by my revulsion at some of your deeds. You have
learned the thing called guilt, and it will ever fall as a
shadow across your meat and your drink. This is why
your pleasure has been broken. This is why you seek
now to flee. But it will do you no good. It will follow
you across the world. It will rise with you into the
realms of the cold, clean winds. It will pursue you
wherever you go. This is the curse of the Buddha."

Taraka covered his face with his hands.

"So this is what it is like to weep," he said, after a
time.

Siddhartha did not reply.

"Curse you, Siddhartha," he said. "You have bound
me again, to an even more terrible prison than Hellwell."

"You have bound yourself. It is you who broke our
pact. I kept it."

"Men suffer when they break pacts with demons,"
said Taraka, "but no Rakasha has ever suffered so
before."

Siddhartha did not reply.

On the following morning, as he sat to breakfast, there came a banging upon the door of his chambers.

"Who dares?" he cried out, and the door burst inward, its hinges tearing free of the wall, its bar snapping like a dry stick.

The head of a horned tiger upon the shoulders of an ape, great hooves for feet, talons for hands, the Rakasha fell forward into the room, smoke emerging from his mouth as he became transparent for a moment, returned to full visibility, faded once more, returned again. His talons were dripping something that was not blood and a wide burn lay across his chest. The air was filled with the odor of singed hair and charred flesh.

"Master!" it cried. "A stranger has come, asking audience of thee!"

"And you did not succeed in convincing him that I was not available?"

"Lord, a score of human guardsmen fell upon him, and he gestured. . . . He waved his hand at them, and there was a flash of light so bright that even the Rakasha might not look upon it. For an instant only it lasted—and they were all of them vanished, as if they had never existed. . . . There was also a large hole in the wall behind where they had stood. . . . There was no rubble. Only a smooth, clean hole."

"And then you fell upon him?"

"Many of the Rakasha sprang for him—but there is that about him which repels us. He gestured again and three of our own kind were gone, vanished in the light he hurls. . . . I did not take the full force of it, but was only grazed by his power. He sent me, therefore, to deliver his message. . . . I can no longer hold myself together—"

With that he vanished, and a globe of fire hung where the creature had lain. Now his words came into the mind, rather than being spoken across the air.

"He bids you come to him without delay. Else, he says he will destroy this palace."

"Did the three whom he burnt also take on again their own forms?"

"No," replied the Rakasha. "They are no more . . ."

"Describe this stranger!" ordered Siddhartha, forcing the words through his own lips.

"He stands very tall," said the demon, "and he wears black breeches and boots. Above the waist he has on him a strange garment. It is like a seamless white glove, upon his right hand only, which extends all the way up his arm and across his shoulders, wrapping his neck and rising tight and smooth about his entire head. Only the lower part of his face is visible, for he wears over his eyes large black lenses which extend half a span outward from his face. At his belt he wears a short sheath of the same white material as the garment—not containing a dagger, however, but a wand. Beneath the material of his garment, where it crosses his shoulders and comes up upon his neck, there is a hump, as if he wears there a small pack."

"Lord Agni!" said Siddhartha. "You have described the god of Fire!"

"Aye, this must be," said the Rakasha. "For as I looked beyond his flesh, to see the colors of his true being, I saw there a blaze like unto the heart of the sun. If there be a god of Fire, then this indeed is he."

"Now must we flee," said Siddhartha, "for there is about to be a great burning. We cannot fight with this one, so let us go quickly."

"I do not fear the gods," said Taraka, "and I should like to try the power of this one."

"You cannot prevail against the Lord of Flame," said Siddhartha. "His fire wand is invincible. It was given him by the deathgod."

"Then I shall wrest it from him and turn it against him."

"None may wield it without being blinded and losing a hand in the process! This is why he wears that strange garment. Let us waste no more time here!"

"I must see for myself," said Taraka. "I must."

"Do not let your new found guilt force you into flirting with self-destruction."

"Guilt?" said Taraka. "That puny, gnawing mind-rat of which you taught me? No, it is not guilt, Binder. It is that, where once I was supreme, save for yourself, new powers have arisen in the world. The gods were not this strong in the old days, and if they have indeed grown in power, then that power must be tested—by myself! It is of my nature, which is power, to fight every new power which arises, and to either triumph over it or be bound by it. I must test the strength of Lord Agni, to win over him."

"But we are two within this body!"

"That is true. . . . If this body be destroyed, then will I bear you away with me, I promise. Already have I strengthened your flames after the manner of my own kind. If this body dies, you will continue to live as a Rakasha. Our people once wore bodies, too, and I remember the art of strengthening the flames so that they may burn independent of the body. This has been done for you, so do not fear."

"Thanks a lot."

"Now let us confront the flame, and dampen it!"

They left the royal chambers and descended the stair. Far below, prisoner in his own dungeon, Prince Videgha whimpered in his sleep.

They emerged from the door that lay behind the hangings at the back of the throne. When they pushed aside these hangings, they saw that the great hall was empty, save for the sleepers within the dark grove and the one who stood in the middle of the floor, white arm folded over bare arm, a silver wand caught between the fingers of his gloved hand.

"See how he stands?" said Siddhartha. "He is confident of his power, and justly so. He is Agni of the Lokapalas. He can see to the farthest unobstructed horizon, as though it lies at his fingertips. And he can reach that far. He is said one night to have scored the moons themselves with that wand. If he but touch its base against a contact within his glove, the Universal Fire will leap forward with a blinding brilliance, obliterating matter and dispersing energies which lie in its path. It is still not too late to withdraw—"

"Agni!" he heard his mouth cry out. "You have requested audience with the one who rules here?"

The black lenses turned toward him. Agni's lips curled back to vanish into a smile which dissolved into words:

"I thought I'd find you here," he said, his voice nasal and penetrating. "All that holiness got to be too much and you had to cut loose, eh? Shall I call you Siddhartha, or Tathagatha, or Mahasamatman—or just plain Sam?"

"You fool," he replied. "The one who was known to you as the Binder of Demons—by all or any of those names—is bound now himself. You have the privilege of addressing Taraka of the Rakasha, Lord of Hellwell!"

There was a click, and the lenses became red.

"Yes, I perceive the truth of what you say," answered the other. "I look upon a case of demonic possession. Interesting. Doubtless cramped, also." He shrugged, and then added, "But I can destroy two as readily as one."

"Think you so?" inquired Taraka, raising both arms before him.

As he did, there was a rumbling and the black wood spread in an instant across the floor, engulfing the one who stood there, its dark branches writhing about him. The rumbling continued, and the floor moved several inches beneath their feet. From overhead, there came a creaking and the sound of snapping stone. Dust and gravel began to fall.

Then there was a blinding flash of light and the trees were gone, leaving short stumps and blackened smudges upon the floor.

With a groan and a mighty crash, the ceiling fell.

As they stepped back through the door that lay behind the throne, they saw the figure, which still stood in the center of the hall, raise his wand directly above his head and move it in a tiny circle.

A cone of brilliance shot upward, dissolving everything it touched. A smile still lay upon Agni's lips as the great stones rained down, none falling anywhere near him.

The rumbling continued, and the floor cracked and the walls began to sway.

They slammed the door and Sam felt a rushing giddiness as the window, which a moment before had lain at the far end of the corridor, flashed past him.

They coursed upward and outward through the heavens, and a tingling, bubbling feeling filled his body, as though he were a being of liquid through whom an electrical current was passing.

Looking back, with the sight of the demon who saw in all directions, he beheld Palamaidsu, already so distant that it could have been framed and hung upon the wall as a painting. On the high hill at the center of the town, the palace of Videgha was falling in upon itself, and great streaks of brilliance, like reversed lightning bolts, were leaping from the ruin into the heavens.

"That is your answer, Taraka," he said. "Shall we go back and try his power again?"

"I had to find out," said the demon.

"Now let me warn you further. I did not jest when I said that he can see to the farthest horizon. If he should free himself soon and turn his glance in this direction, he will detect us. I do not think you can move faster than light, so I suggest you fly lower and utilize the terrain for cover."

"I have rendered us invisible, Sam."

"The eyes of Agni can see deeper into the red and farther into the violet ranges than can those of a man."

They lost altitude then, rapidly. Before Palamaidsu, however, Sam saw that the only evidence which remained of the palace of Videgha was a cloud of dust upon a gray hillside.

Moving like a whirlwind, they sped far into the north, until at last the Ratnagaris lay beneath them. When they came to the mountain called Channa, they drifted down past its peak and came to a landing upon the ledge before the opened entrance to Hellwell.

They stepped within and closed the door.

"Pursuit will follow," said Sam, "and even Hellwell will not stand against it."

"How confident they are of their power," said Taraka, "to send only one!"

"Do you feel that confidence to be unwarranted?"

"No," said Taraka. "But what of the One in Red of whom you spoke, who drinks life with his eyes? Did you not think they would send Lord Yama, rather than Agni?"

"Yes," said Sam, as they moved back toward the well, "I was sure that he would follow, and I still feel that he will. When last I saw him, I caused him some distress. I feel he would hunt me anywhere. Who knows, he may even now be lying in ambush at the bottom of Hellwell itself."

They came to the lip of the well and entered upon the trail.

"He does not wait within," Taraka announced. "I would even now be contacted by those who wait, bound, if any but the Rakasha had passed this way."

"He will come," said Sam, "and when the Red One comes to Hellwell, he will not be stayed in his course."

"But many will try," said Taraka. "There is the first."

The first flame came into view, in its niche beside the trail.

As they passed by, Sam freed it, and it sprang into the air like a bright bird and spiraled down the well.

Step by step they descended, and from each niche

fire spilled forth and flowed outward. At Taraka's bidding, some rose and vanished over the edge of the well, departing through the mighty door which bore the words of the gods upon its outer face.

When they reached the bottom of the well, Taraka said, "Let us free those who lie locked in the caverns, also."

So they made their way through the passages and deep caverns, freeing the demons locked therein.

Then, after a time—how much time, he could never tell—they had all been freed.

The Rakasha assembled then about the cavern, standing in great phalanxes of flame, and their cries all came together into one steady, ringing note which rolled and rolled and beat within his head, until he realized, startled at the thought, that they were singing.

"Yes," said Taraka, "it is the first time in ages that they have done so."

Sam listened to the vibrations within his skull, catching something of the meaning behind the hiss and the blaze, the feelings that accompanied it falling into words and stresses that were more familiar to his own mind:

We are the legions of Hellwell, damned,
The banished ones of fallen flame.
We are the race undone by man.
So man we curse. Forget his name!

This world was ours before the gods,
In days before the race of men.
And when the men and gods have gone,
This world will then be ours again.

The mountains fall, the seas dry out,
The moons shall vanish from the sky.
The Bridge of Gold will one day fall,
And all that breathes must one day die.

But we of Hellwell shall prevail,

When fail the gods, when fail the men.
The legions of the damned die not.
We wait, we wait, to rise again!

Sam shuddered as they sang on and on, recounting
their vanished glories, confident of their ability to out-
last any circumstance, to meet any force with the cos-
mic judo of a push and a tug and a long wait, watching
anything of which they disapproved turn its strength
upon itself and pass. Almost, in that moment, he believed that what they sang was truth, and that one day
there would be none but the Rakasha, flitting above the
pocked landscape of a dead world.

Then he turned his mind to other matters and forced
the mood from him. But in the days that followed, and
even, on occasion, years afterward, it returned to plague
his efforts and mock his joys, to make him wonder,
know guilt, feel sadness and so be humbled.

After a time, one of the Rakasha who had left earlier
re-entered and descended the well. He hovered in the
air and reported what he had seen. As he spoke, his
fires flowed into the shape of a tau cross.

"This is the form of that chariot," he said, "which
blazed through the sky and then fell, coming to rest in
the valley beyond Southpeak."

"Binder, do you know this vessel?" asked Taraka.

"I have heard it described before," said Sam. "It is
the thunder chariot of Lord Shiva.

"Describe its occupant," he said to the demon.

"There were four, Lord."

"Four!"

"Yes. There is the one you have described as Agni,
Lord of the Fires. With him is one who wears the horns
of a bull set upon a burnished helm—his armor shows
like aged bronze, but it is not bronze; it is worked
about with the forms of many serpents, and it does not
seem to burden him as he moves. In his one hand he

holds a gleaming trident, and he bears no shield before his body."

"This one is Shiva," said Sam.

"And walking with these two there comes one all in red, whose gaze is dark. This one does not speak, but occasionally his glances fall upon the woman who walks by his side, to his left. She is fair of hair and complexion, and her armor matches his red. Her eyes are like the sea, and she smiles often with lips the color of the blood of men. About her throat she wears a necklace of skulls. She bears a bow, and upon her belt is a short sword. She holds in her hands a strange instrument, like a black scepter ending in a silver skull that is also a wheel."

"These two be Yama and Kali," said Sam. "Now hear me, Taraka, mightiest of the Rakasha, while I tell you what moves against us. The power of Agni you know full well, and of the One in Red have I already spoken. Now, she who walks at the left hand of Death bears also the gaze that drinks the life it beholds. Her scepter-wheel screams like the trumpets that signalize the ending of the Yuga, and all who come before its wailing are cast down and confused. She is as much to be feared as her Lord, who is ruthless and invincible. But the one with the trident is the Lord of Destruction himself. It is true that Yama is King of the Dead and Agni Lord of the Flames, but the power of Shiva is the power of chaos. His is the force which separates atom from atom, breaking down the forms of all things upon which he turns it. Against these four, the freed might of Hellwell itself cannot stand. Therefore, let us depart this place immediately, for they are most assuredly coming here."

"Did I not promise you, Binder," said Taraka, "that I would help you to fight the gods?"

"Yes, but that of which I spoke was to be a surprise attack. These have taken upon themselves their Aspects now, and have raised up their Attributes. Had they chosen, without even landing the thunder chariot,

Channa would no longer exist, but in the place of this mountain there would be a deep crater, here in the midst of the Ratnagaris. We must flee, to fight them another day."

"Do you remember the curse of the Buddha?" asked Taraka. "Do you remember how you taught me of guilt, Siddhartha? I remember, and I feel I owe you this victory. I owe you something for your pains, and I will give these gods into your hands in payment."

"No! If you would serve me at all, do it at another time than this! Serve me now by bearing me away from this place, far and fast!"

"Are you afraid of this encounter, Lord Siddhartha?"

"Yes, yes I am! For it is foolhardy! What of your song—'We wait, we wait, to rise again!'? Where is the patience of the Rakasha? You say you will wait for the seas to dry and the mountains to fall, for the moons to vanish from the sky—but you cannot wait for me to name the time and the battlefield! I know them far better than you, these gods, for once I was one of them. Do not do this rash thing now. If you would serve me, save me from this meeting!"

"Very well. I hear you, Siddhartha. Your words move me, Sam. But I would try their strength. So I shall send some of the Rakasha against them. But we shall journey far, you and I, far down to the roots of the world. There we will await the report of victory. If, somehow, the Rakasha should lose the encounter, then will I bear you far away from here and restore to you your body. I would wear it a few hours more, however, to savor your passions in this fighting."

Sam bowed his head.

"Amen," he said, and with a tingling, bubbling sensation, he felt himself lifted from the floor and borne along vast cavernways uncharted by men.

As they sped from chamber to vaulted chamber, down tunnels and chasms and wells, through labyrinths

and grottoes and corridors of stone, Sam set his mind
adrift, to move down the ways of memory and back.
He thought upon the days of his recent ministry, when
he had sought to graft the teachings of Gotama upon
the stock of the religion by which the world was ruled.
He thought upon the strange one, Sugata, whose hands
had held both death and benediction. Over the years,
their names would merge and their deeds would be
mingled. He had lived too long not to know how time
stirred the pots of legend. There had been a real Buddha, he knew that now. The teaching he had offered, no
matter how spuriously, had attracted this true believer,
this one who had somehow achieved enlightenment,
marked men's minds with his sainthood, and then gone
willingly into the hands of Death himself. Tathagatha
and Sugata would be part of a single legend, he knew,
and Tathagatha would shine in the light shed by his
disciple. Only the one Dhamma would survive. Then
his mind went back to the battle at the Hall of Karma,
and to the machinery still cached in a secret place. And
he thought then upon the countless transfers he had
undergone before that time, of the battles he had
fought, of the women he had loved across the ages; he
thought upon what a world could be and what this
world was, and why. Then he was taken again with his
rage against the gods. He thought upon the days when
a handful of them had fought the Rakasha and the
Nagas, the Gandharvas and the People-of-the-Sea, the
Kataputna demons and the Mothers of the Terrible
Glow, the Dakshinis and the Pretas, the Skandas and
the Pisakas, and had won, tearing a world loose from
chaos and building its first city of men. He had seen
that city pass through all the stages through which a
city can pass, until now it was inhabited by those who
could spin their minds for a moment and transform
themselves into gods, taking upon them an Aspect that
strengthened their bodies and intensified their wills and
extended the power of their desires into Attributes,
which fell with a force like magic upon those against

whom they turned them. He thought upon this city and these gods, and he knew of its beauty and its rightness, its ugliness and its wrongness. He thought of its splendor and its color, in contrast to that of the rest of the world, and he wept as he raged, for he knew that he could never feel either wholly right or wholly wrong in opposing it. This was why he had waited as long as he had, doing nothing. Now, whatever he did would result in both victory and defeat, a success and a failure; and whether the outcome of all his actions would be the passing or the continuance of the dream of the city, the burden of the guilt would be his.

They waited in darkness.

For a long, silent while they waited. Time passed like an old man climbing a hill.

They stood upon a ledge above a black pool, and waited.

"Should we not have heard by now?"

"Perhaps. Perhaps not."

"What shall we do?"

"What do you mean?"

"If they do not come at all. How long shall we wait here?"

"They will come, singing."

"I hope so."

But there came no singing, or movement. About them was the stillness of time that had no objects upon which to wear.

"How long have we waited?"

"I do not know. Long."

"I feel that all is not well."

"You may be right. Shall we rise a few levels and investigate, or shall I bear you to your freedom now?"

"Let us wait awhile longer."

"Very well."

Again, there was silence. They paced within it.

"What was that?"

"What?"

"A sound."

"I heard nothing and we are using the same ears."

"Not with the ears of the body—there it is again!"

"I heard nothing, Taraka."

"It continues. It is like a scream, but it does not end."

"Far?"

"Yes, quite distant. Listen my way."

"Yes! I believe it is the scepter of Kali. The battle, then, goes on."

"This long? Then the gods are stronger than I had supposed."

"No, the Rakasha are stronger than *I* had supposed."

"Whether we win or lose, Siddhartha, the gods are presently engaged. If we can get by them, their vessel may be unattended. Do you want it?"

"Steal the thunder chariot? That *is* a thought. . . . It is a mighty weapon, as well as transportation. What might our chances be?"

"I am certain the Rakasha can hold them for as long as is necessary—and it is a long climb up Hellwell. We need not use the trail ourself. I grow tired, but I can still bear us across the air."

"Let us rise a few levels and investigate."

They left their ledge by the black pool, and time beat again about them as they passed upward.

As they advanced, a globe of light moved to meet them. It settled upon the floor of the cavern and grew into a tree of green fire.

"How goes the battle?" asked Taraka.

"We hold them," it reported, "but we cannot close with them."

"Why not?"

"There is that about them which repels. I do not know how to call it, but we cannot draw too near."

"How then do you fight?"

"A steady storm of rocks rages about them. We hurl fire and water and great spinning winds, also."

"And how do they respond to this?"

"The trident of Shiva cuts a path through everything. But no matter how much he destroys, we raise up more against him. So he stands like a statue, uncreating storms we will not let end. Occasionally, he swerves to kill, while the Lord of Fires holds back the attack. The scepter of the goddess slows those who face upon it. Once slowed, they meet the trident or the hand or the eyes of Death."

"And you have not succeeded in harming them?"

"No."

"Where do they stand?"

"Part way down the well wall. They are still near to the top. They descend slowly."

"How many have we lost?"

"Eighteen."

"Then it was a mistake to end our waiting to begin this battle. The cost is too high and nothing is being gained. ... Sam, do you want to try for the chariot?"

"It is worth a risk. ... Yes, let us try."

"Go then," he instructed the Rakasha who branched and swayed before him. "Go, and we shall follow more slowly. We will rise along the side of the wall opposite them. When we begin the ascent, redouble your attack. Occupy them entirely until we have passed. Hold them then to give us time in which to steal their chariot from the valley. When this has been accomplished, I will return to you in my true form and we can put an end to the fighting."

"I obey," replied the other, and he fell upon the floor to become a green serpent of light, and slithered off ahead of them.

They rushed forward, running part of the way, to conserve the strength of the demon for the final necessary thrust against gravitation.

They had journeyed a great distance beneath the Ratnagaris, and the return trip seemed endless.

Finally, though, they came upon the floor of the well; and it was lighted sufficiently so that, even with the eyes of his body, Sam could see clearly about him. The noise was deafening. If he and Taraka had had to rely upon speech for communication, there would have been no communication.

Like some fantastic orchid upon an ebon bough, the fire bloomed upon the wall of the well. As Agni waved his wand, it changed its shape, writhing. In the air, like bright insects, danced the Rakasha. The rushing of winds was one loudness, and the rattling of many stones was another. Above it all was the ululating cry of the silver skull-wheel, which Kali waved like a fan before her face; and this was even more terrible when it rose beyond the range of hearing, but still screamed. Rocks split and melted and dissolved in midair, their white-hot fragments leaping like sparks from a forge, out and downward. They bounced and rolled, and glowed redly in the shadows of Hellwell. The surrounding walls of the well were pocked and gouged and scored in the places where the flame and the chaos had touched.

"Now," said Taraka, "we go!"

They rose into the air and moved up the side of the well. The power of the Rakasha's attack increased, to be answered with an intensified counterattack. Sam covered his ears with his hands, but it did no good against the burning needles behind his eyes, which stirred whenever the silver skull swept in his direction. A short distance to his left, a whole section of rock vanished abruptly.

"They have not detected us," said Taraka.

"Yet," answered Sam. "That accursed Fire god can look through a sea of ink to spot a shifting grain of sand. If he turns in this direction, I hope you can dodge his—"

"How was that?" asked Taraka, as they were suddenly forty feet higher and somewhat farther to the left.

They sped upward now, and a line of melting rock pursued them. Then this was interrupted as the demons set up a wailing and tore loose gigantic boulders, which they hurled upon the gods, with the accompaniment of hurricanes and sheets of fire.

They reached the lip of the well, passed above it and scurried back out of range.

"We must go all the way around now, to reach the corridor which leads to the door."

A Rakasha rose from out of the well and sped to their side.

"They retreat!" he cried. "The goddess has fallen. The One in Red supports her as they flee!"

"They do not retreat," said Taraka. "They move to cut us off. Block their way! Destroy the trail! Hurry!" -

The Rakasha dropped like a meteor back into the well.

"Binder, I grow tired. I do not know whether I can bear us from the ledge outside all the way to the ground below."

"Can you manage it part of the way?"

"Yes."

"That first three hundred feet or so where the trail is narrow?"

"I think so."

"Good!"

They ran.

As they fled along the rim of Hellwell, another Rakasha rose up and kept pace with them.

"I report!" he cried. "We have destroyed the trail twice. Each time, the Lord of Flames has burnt a new one!"

"Then naught more can be done! Stay with us now! We need your assistance in another matter."

It sped on ahead of them, a crimson wedge lighting their way.

They rounded the well and raced up the tunnel. When they reached its end, they hurled the door wide and stepped out onto the ledge. The Rakasha who had led the way slammed the door behind them, saying, "They pursue!"

Sam stepped over the ledge. As he fell, the door glowed for an instant, then melted above him.

With the help of the second Rakasha, they descended the entire distance to the base of Channa and moved up a trail and around a bend. The foot of a mountain now shielded them from the gods. But this rock was lashed with flame in an instant.

The second Rakasha shot high into the air, wheeled and vanished.

They ran along the trail, heading toward the valley that held the chariot. By the time they reached it, the Rakasha had returned.

"Kali and Yama and Agni descend," he stated. "Shiva stays behind, holding the corridor. Agni leads the pursuit. The One in Red helps the goddess, who is limping."

Before them, in the valley, lay the thunder chariot. Slim and unadorned, the color of bronze, though it was not bronze, it stood upon a wide, grassy plain. It looked like a fallen prayer tower or a giant's house key or some necessary part of a celestial instrument of music that had slipped free of a starry constellation and dropped to the ground. It seemed to be somehow incomplete, although the eye could not fault its lines. It held that special beauty that belongs to the highest orders of weapons, requiring function to make it complete.

Sam moved to its side, found the hatch, entered.

"You can operate this chariot, Binder?" asked Taraka. "Make it race through the heavens, spitting destruction across the land?"

"I'm sure Yama would keep the controls as simple as possible. He streamlines whenever he can. I've flown the jets of Heaven before, and I'm banking that this is of the same order."

He ducked into the cabin, settled into the control seat and stared at the panel before him.

"Damn!" he announced, his hand starting forward and twitching back.

The other Rakasha appeared suddenly, passing through the metal wall of the ship and hovering above the console.

"The gods move rapidly," he announced. "Particularly Agni."

Sam snapped a series of switches and pressed a button. Lights came on all over the instrument panel and a humming sound began within it.

"How far is he?" asked Taraka.

"Almost halfway down. He widened the trail with his flames. He runs upon it now, as if it were a roadway. He burns obstacles. He makes a clear path."

Sam drew back on a lever and adjusted a dial, reading the indicators before him. A shudder ran through the ship.

"Are you ready?" asked Taraka.

"I can't take off cold. It has to warm up. Also, this instrument board is trickier than I'd thought."

"We run a close race."

"Yes."

From the distance, there came the sounds of several explosions rising above the growing growl of the chariot. Sam pulled the lever forward another notch, readjusted the dial.

"I go to slow them," said the Rakasha, and vanished as he had come.

Sam drew the lever two notches farther, and somewhere something sputtered and died. The ship stood silent once more.

He pushed the lever back into its former position, spun the dial, pushed the button again.

And again a shudder ran through the chariot, and somewhere a purring began. Sam drew the lever one notch forward, adjusted the dial.

After a moment, he repeated it, and the purr became a soft growl.

"Gone," said Taraka. "Dead."

"Who? What?"

"The one who went to stop the Lord of Flames. He failed."

There were more explosions.

"Hellwell is being destroyed," said Taraka.

Perspiration upon his brow, Sam waited with his hand on the lever.

"He comes now—Agni!"

Sam looked through the long, slanted shield plate.

The Lord of Flames came into the valley.

"Good-bye, Siddhartha."

"Not yet," said Sam.

Agni looked at the chariot, raised his wand.

Nothing happened.

He stood, pointing the wand; and then he lowered it, shook it.

He raised it once more.

Again, no flame issued forth.

He reached behind his neck with his left hand, performed some adjustment upon his pack. As he did this, light streamed from the wand, burning a huge pit in the ground at his side.

He pointed the wand again.

Nothing.

Then he began running toward the ship.

"Electrodirection?" asked Taraka.

"Yes."

Sam drew back upon the lever, adjusted the dial farther. A huge roaring grew about him.

He pressed another button and there came a crackling sound from the rear of the vessel. He moved another dial as Agni reached the hatch.

There was a flash of flame and a metallic clanging.

He rose from his seat and moved out of the cabin and into the corridor.

Agni had entered, and he pointed the wand.

"Do not move—Sam! Demon!" he cried, above the roar of the engines; and as he spoke, his lenses clicked red and he smiled. "Demon," he stated. "Do not move, or you and your host will burn together!"

Sam sprang upon him.

Agni fell easily when he struck, for he had not believed that the other would reach him.

"Short circuit, eh?" said Sam, and hit him across the throat.

"Or sunspots?" and he struck him in the temple.

Agni fell to his side, and Sam hit him a final blow with the edge of his hand, just above the collarbone.

He kicked the wand the length of the corridor, and as he moved to close the hatch he knew that it was too late.

"Go now, Taraka," he said. "This is my fight from here on. You can do nothing more."

"I promised my assistance."

"You have none to give, now. Get out while still you can."

"If such is your will. But I have a final thing to say to you—"

"Save it! Next time I'm in the neighborhood—"

"Binder, it is this thing I learned of you—I am sorry. I—"

There was a terrible twisting, wrenching sensation within his body and mind, as the death-gaze of Yama fell upon him and struck deeper than his own being.

Kali, too, looked into his eyes; and as she did so, she raised her screaming scepter.

It was as the lifting of one shadow and the falling of another.

"Good-bye, Binder," came the words within his mind.

Then the skull began its screaming.

He felt himself falling.

There was a throbbing.

It was within his head. It was all about him.

He was awakened by throbbing, and he felt himself covered with aches, as with bandages.

There were chains upon his wrists and his ankles.

He was half seated on the floor of a small compartment. Beside the doorway sat the One in Red, smoking.

Yama nodded, said nothing.

"Why am I alive?" Sam asked him.

"You live for purposes of keeping an appointment made many years ago in Mahartha," said Yama. "Brahma is particularly anxious to see you once again."

"But I am not especially anxious to see Brahma."

"Over the years, that has become somewhat apparent."

"I see you got out of the mud all right."

The other smiled. "You are a nasty man," he said.

"I know. I practice."

"I gather your business deal fell through?"

"Unfortunately, yes."

"Perhaps you can try recouping your losses. We're halfway to Heaven."

"Think I'd have a chance?"

"You just might. Times change. Brahma could be a merciful god this week."

"My occupational therapist told me to specialize in lost causes."

Yama shrugged.

"What of the demon?" Sam asked. "The one who was with me?"

"I touched it," said Yama, "hard. I don't know whether I finished it or just drove it away. But you needn't worry about it again. I doused you with demon repellant. If the creature still lives, it will be a long time before it recovers from our contact. Maybe never. How did it happen in the first place? I thought you were the one man immune to demonic possession."

"So did I. What's demon repellant?"

"I found a chemical agent, harmless to us, which none of the energy beings can stand."

"Handy item. Could've used it in the days of the binding."

"Yes. We wore it into Hellwell."

"That was quite a battle, from what I saw of it."

"Yes," said Yama. "What is it like—demonic posses-

sion? What does it feel like to have another will over-
riding your own?"

"It is strange," said Sam, "and frightening, and
rather educating at the same time."

"In what ways?"

"It was their world first," said Sam. "We took it
away from them. Why shouldn't they be everything we
hate them for being? To them, we are the demons."

"But what does it feel like?"

"To have one's will overridden by that of another?
You should know."

Yama's smile vanished, then returned. "You would
like me to strike you, wouldn't you, Buddha? It would
make you feel superior. Unfortunately, I'm a sadist and
will not do it."

Sam laughed.

"Touché, Death," he said.

They sat in silence for a time.

"Can you spare me a cigarette?"

Yama passed him one, lit it.

"What's First Base like these days?"

"You'll hardly recognize the place," said Yama. "If
everyone in it were to die at this moment, it would still
be perfect ten thousand years from now. The flowers
would still bloom and the music would play and the
fountains would ripple the length of the spectrum.
Warm meals would still be laid within the garden pavilions. The City itself is immortal."

"A fitting abode, I suppose, for those who call themselves gods."

"Call themselves?" asked Yama. "You are wrong,
Sam. Godhood is more than a name. It is a condition of
being. One does not achieve it merely by being immortal, for even the lowliest laborer in the fields may
achieve continuity of existence. Is it then the condition-
ing of an Aspect? No. Any competent hypnotist can
play games with the self-image. Is it the raising up of
an Attribute? Of course not. I can design machines
more powerful and more accurate than any faculty a

man may cultivate. Being a god is the quality of being able to be yourself to such an extent that your passions correspond with the forces of the universe, so that those who look upon you know this without hearing your name spoken. Some ancient poet said that the world is full of echoes and correspondences. Another wrote a long poem of an inferno, wherein each man suffered a torture which coincided in nature with those forces which had ruled his life. Being a god is being able to recognize within one's self these things that are important, and then to strike the single note that brings them into alignment with everything else that exists. Then, beyond morals or logic or esthetics, one is wind or fire, the sea, the mountains, rain, the sun or the stars, the flight of an arrow, the end of a day, the clasp of love. One rules through one's ruling passions. Those who look upon gods then say, without even knowing their names, 'He is Fire. She is Dance. He is Destruction. She is Love.' So, to reply to your statement, they do not call themselves gods. Everyone else does, though, everyone who beholds them."

"So they play that on their fascist banjos, eh?"

"You choose the wrong adjective."

"You've already used up all the others."

"It appears that our minds will never meet on this subject."

"If someone asks you why you're oppressing a world and you reply with a lot of poetic crap, no. I guess there can't be a meeting of minds."

"Then let us choose another subject for conversation."

"I *do* look upon *you*, though, and say, 'He is Death.' "

Yama did not reply.

"Odd ruling passion. I've heard that you were old before you were young ..."

"You know that is true."

"You were a mechanical prodigy and a weapons master. You lost your boyhood in a burst of flame, and you became an old man that same day. Did death become your ruling passion in that moment? Or was it earlier? Or later?"

"It does not matter," said Yama.

"Do you serve the gods because you believe what you have said to me—or because you hate the larger portion of humanity?"

"I did not lie to you."

"Then Death is an idealist. Amusing."

"Not so."

"Or could it be, Lord Yama, that neither guess is correct? That your ruling passion—"

"You've mentioned her name before," said Yama, "in the same speech wherein you likened her to a disease. You were wrong then and you are still wrong. I do not care to hear that sermon over again, and since I am not at the moment sinking in quicksand, I will not."

"Peace," said Sam. "But tell me, do the ruling passions of the gods ever change?"

Yama smiled.

"The goddess of dance was once the god of war. So it would seem that anything can change."

"When I have died the real death," said Sam, "then will I be changed. But until that moment I will hate Heaven with every breath that I draw. If Brahma has me burnt, I will spit into the flames. If he has me strangled, I will attempt to bite the executioner's hand. If my throat is cut, may my blood rust the blade that does it. Is that a ruling passion?"

"You are good god material," said Yama.

"Good god!" said Sam.

"Before whatever may happen happens," said Yama, "I have been assured that you will be permitted to attend the wedding."

"Wedding? You and Kali? Soon?"

"At the full of the lesser moon," Yama replied. "So, whatever Brahma decides, at least I can buy you a drink before it occurs."

"For that I thank you, deathgod. But it has always been my understanding that weddings are not made in Heaven."

"That tradition is about to be broken," said Yama. "No tradition is sacred."

"Then good luck," said Sam.

Yama nodded, yawned, lit another cigarette.

"By the way," said Sam, "what is the latest vogue in celestial executions? I ask purely for informational purposes."

"Executions are not held in Heaven," said Yama, opening a cabinet and removing a chessboard.

$\mathcal{V}$

*From Hellwell to Heaven he went, there to commune
with the gods. The Celestial City holds many mysteries,
including some of the keys to his own past. Not all that
transpired during the time he dwelled there is known.
It is known, however, that he petitioned the gods on
behalf of the world, obtaining the sympathy of some,
the enmity of others. Had he chosen to betray humanity and accept the proffers of the gods, it is said by some
that he might have dwelled forever as a Lord of the
City and not have met his death beneath the claws of
the phantom cats of Kaniburrha. It is said by his
detractors, though, that he did accept these proffers, but
was later betrayed himself, so giving his sympathies
back to suffering mankind for the rest of his days,
which were few. . . .*

Girt about with lightnings, standard-bearer, armed
    with the sword, the wheel, the bow,
devourer, sustainer, Kali, night of destruction at
    Worldsend, who walketh the world by night,
protectress, deceiver, serene one, loved and lovely,
    Brahmani, Mother of the Vedas, dweller in
        the silent and most secret places,
well-omened, and gentle, all-knowing, swift as
    thought, wearer of skulls, possessed of
        power, the twilight, invincible leader,
        pitiful one,
opener of the way before those lost, granter of
    favors, teacher, valor in the form of woman,
chameleon-hearted, practitioner of austerities,
    magician, pariah, deathless and eternal. . . .
Āryatārābhattārikānāmāshtottarásatakastotra
(36–40)

THEN, as so often in the past, her snowy fur was sleeked by the wind.

She walked where the lemon-colored grasses stirred. She walked a winding track under dark trees and jungle flowers, crags of jasper rising to her right, veins of milk-white rock, shot through with orange streaks, open about her.

Then, as so often before, she moved on the great cushions of her feet, the wind sleeking her fur, white as marble, and the ten thousand fragrances of the jungle and the plain stirring about her; there, in the twilight of the place that only half existed.

Alone, she followed the ageless trail through the jungle that was part illusion. The white tiger is a solitary hunter. If others moved along a similar course, none cared for company.

Then, as so often before, she looked up at the smooth, gray shell of the sky and the stars that glistened there like shards of ice. Her crescent eyes widened, and she stopped and sat upon her haunches, staring upward.

What was it she was hunting?

A deep sound, like a chuckle ending in a cough, came from her throat. She sprang then suddenly to the top of a high rock, and sat there licking her shoulders. When a moon moved into view, she watched it. She seemed a figure molded of unmelting snow, topaz flames gleaming beneath her brows.

Then, as before, she wondered whether this was the true jungle of Kaniburrha in which she sat. She felt that she was still within the confines of the actual forest. But she could not really know.

What was it she was hunting?

Heaven exists upon a plateau that was once a range of mountains. These mountains were fused and smoothed to provide a level base. Topsoil was transported from the verdant south, to give it the growth that fleshed over this bony structure. Cupping the entire area is a transparent dome, protecting it against the polar cold and anything else unwanted within.

Heaven stands high and temperate and enjoys a long twilight and long, lazy days. Fresh airs, warmed as they are drawn within, circulate through the City and the forest. Within the dome itself, clouds can be generated. From within the clouds rains can be called forth, to fall upon almost any area. A snowfall could even be brought down in this manner, although this thing has never been done. It has always been summer in Heaven.

Within the summer of Heaven stands the Celestial City.

The Celestial City did not grow up as the cities of men grow up, about a port or near to good farmland, pasturage, hunting country, trade routes or a region rich in some natural resource that men desired and so settled beside. The Celestial City sprang from a conception in the minds of its first dwellers. Its growth was not slow and haphazard, a building added here, a thoroughfare rerouted there, one structure torn down to make way for another, and all parts coming together into an irregular and unseemly whole. No. Every demand of utility was considered and every inch of magnificence calculated by the first planners and the design-augmentation machines. These plans were coordinated and brought to fruition by an architectural artist without peer. Vishnu, the Preserver, held the entire Celestial City within his mind, until the day he circled Milehigh Spire on the back of the Garuda Bird, stared downward and the City was captured perfect in a drop of perspiration on his brow.

So Heaven sprang from the mind of a god, its conception stimulated by the desires of his fellows. It was laid by choice, rather than necessity, in a wilderness of ice and snow and rock, at the timeless Pole of the world, where only the mighty might make their home.

(What was it she was hunting?)

Beneath the dome of Heaven there stood, beside the

Celestial City, the great forest of Kaniburrha. Vishnu, in his wisdom, had seen that there must be a balance between the metropolis and the wilderness. While wilderness can exist independent of cities, that which dwells within a city requires more than the tamed plants of a pleasance. If the world were all city, he had reasoned, the dwellers within it would turn a portion of it into a wilderness, for there is that within them all which desires that somewhere there be an end to order and a beginning of chaos. So, within his mind there had grown up a forest, pumping forth streams and the smells of growth and decay, uttering the cries of the uncitied creatures who dwelled within its shadows, shrugging in the wind and glistening in the rain, falling down and growing up again.

The wilderness came to the edge of the City and stopped. It was forbidden to enter there, just as the City kept to its bounds.

But of the creatures who dwelled within the forest, some were predators; these knew no boundaries of limits, coming and going as they chose. Chief among these were the albino tigers. So it was written by the gods that the phantom cats might not look upon the Celestial City; and so it was laid upon their eyes, through the nervous systems that lay behind them, that there was no City. Within their white-cat brains, the world was only the forest of Kaniburrha. They walked the streets of Heaven, and it was a jungle trail they trod. If the gods stroked their fur as they passed them by, it was as the wind laying hands upon them. Should they climb a broad stairway, it was a rocky slope they mounted. The buildings were cliffs and the statues were trees; the passers-by were invisible.

Should one from the City enter the true forest, however, cat and god then dwelled upon the same plane of existence—the wilderness, the balancer.

She coughed again, as she had so often before, and her snowy fur was sleeked by the wind. She was a phantom cat, who for three days had stalked about the

wilderness of Kaniburrha, slaying and eating the raw
red flesh of her kill, crying out her great-throated cat-
challenge, licking her fur with her broad, pink tongue,
feeling the rain fall down upon her back, dripping from
off the high, hanging fronds, coming in torrents down
from the clouds, which coalesced, miraculously, in the
center of the sky; moving with fire in her loins, having
mated the night before with an avalanche of death-
colored fur, whose claws had raked her shoulders, the
smell of the blood driving them both into a great frenzy; purring, as the cool twilight came over her, bringing
with it the moons, like the changing crescents of her
eyes, golden and silver and dun. She sat upon the rock,
licking her paws and wondering what it was she had
hunted.

Lakshmi, in the Garden of the Lokapalas, lay with
Kubera, fourth keeper of the world, upon a scented
couch set beside the pool in which the Apsarases
played. The other three of the Lokapalas were absent
this evening. ... Giggling, the Apsarases splashed the
perfumed waters toward the couch. Lord Krishna the
Dark, however, chose that moment to blow upon his
pipes. The girls then turned away from Kubera the Fat
and Lakshmi the Lovely, to rest their elbows upon the
edges of the pool and stare at him, there beneath the
flowering tree where he lay sprawled amid wineskins
and the remains of several meals.

He ran up and down the scale and produced one
long wailing note and a series of goatlike bleats. Guari
the Fair, whom he had spent an hour undressing and
then had apparently forgotten, rose up from his side,
dove into the pool and vanished into one of the many
subaquaean caves. He hiccupped, began a tune,
stopped, began another.

"Is it true what they say about Kali?" asked
Lakshmi.

"What do they say?" grunted Kubera, reaching for a
bowl of soma.

She took the bowl from his hands, sipped at it, returned it to him. He quaffed it, and a servant refilled it as he placed it back upon the tray.

"That she wants a human sacrifice, to celebrate her wedding?"

"Probably," said Kubera. "Wouldn't put it past her. Bloodthirsty bitch, that one. Always transmigrating into some vicious animal for a holiday. Became a fire-hen once and clawed Sitala's face over something she'd said."

"When?"

"Oh, ten—eleven avatars back. Sitala wore a veil for a devilish long time, till her new body was ready."

"A strange pair," said Lakshmi into his ear, which she was biting. "Your friend Yama is probably the only one would live with her. Supposing she grew angry with a lover and cast her deadly look upon him? Who else could bear that gaze?"

"Jest not," said Kubera. "Thus did we lose Kartikeya, Lord of the Battles."

"Oh?"

"Aye. She's a strange one. Like Yama, yet not like him. He is deathgod, true. But his is the way of the quick, clean kill. Kali is rather like a cat."

"Does Yama ever speak of this fascination she holds for him?"

"Did you come here to gather gossip or to become some?"

"Both," she replied.

At that moment, Krishna took his Aspect upon him, raising up the Attribute of divine drunkenness. From his pipes there poured the bitter-dark sour-sweet melody contagious. The drunkenness within him expanded across the garden, in alternating waves of joy and sadness. He rose upon his lithe, dark legs and began to dance. His flat features were expressionless. His wet, dark hair lay in tight rings, like wire; even his beard was so curled. As he moved, the Apsarases came forth from the pool to follow him. His pipes wandered along the trails of the ancient melodies, growing more and more frenzied as he moved faster and faster, until finally he broke into the Rasa-lila, the Dance of Lust, and his retinue, hands on their hips, followed him with increasing speed through its gyrating movements.

Kubera's grip upon Lakshmi tightened.

"Now *there* is an Attribute," she said.

Rudra the Grim bent his bow and sent an arrow flying. The arrow sped on and on and finally came to rest in the center of a distant target.

At his side, Lord Murugan chuckled and lowered his bow.

"You win again," he said. "I can't beat that."

They unbraced their bows and moved toward the target after the arrows.

"Have you met him yet?" asked Murugan.

"I knew him a long time ago," said Rudra.

"Accelerationist?"

"He wasn't then. Wasn't much of anything, politically. He was one of the First, though, one of those who had looked upon Urath."

"Oh?"

"He distinguished himself in the wars against the People-of-the-Sea and against the Mothers of the Terrible Glow." Here, Rudra made a sign in the air. "Later," he continued, "this was remembered, and he was given charge of the northern marches in the wars against the demons. He was known as Kalkin in those days, and it was there that he came to be called Binder. He developed an Attribute which he could use against the demons. With it, he destroyed most of the Yakshas and bound the Rakasha. When Yama and Kali captured him at Hellwell in Malwa, he had already succeeded in freeing these latter. Thus, the Rakasha are again abroad in the world."

"Why did he do this thing?"

"Yama and Agni say that he had made a pact with their leader. They suspect he offered this one a lease on his body in return for the promise of demon troops to war against us."

"May we be attacked?"

"I doubt it. The demons are not stupid. If they could not defeat four of us in Hellwell, I doubt they would attack us all here in Heaven. And even now, Yama is in the Vasty Hall of Death designing special weapons."

"And where is his bride-to-be?"

"Who knows?" said Rudra. "And who cares?"

Murugan smiled.

"I once thought you more than passing fond of her yourself."

"Too cold, too mocking," said Rudra.

"She repulsed you?"

Rudra turned his dark face, which never smiled, upon the fair god of youth.

"You fertility deities are worse than Marxists," he said. "You think that's all that goes on between people. We were just friends for a time, but she is too hard on her friends and so loses them."

"She *did* repulse you?"

"I suppose so."

"And when she took Morgan, the poet of the plains, as her lover—he who one day incarnated as a jackbird and flew away—you then hunted jackbirds, until inside a month with your arrows you had slain near every one in Heaven."

"And I still hunt jackbirds."

"Why is that?"

"I do not care for their singing."

"She is too cold, too mocking," agreed Murugan.

"I do not like being mocked by *anyone*, youthgod. Could you outrun the arrows of Rudra?"

Murugan smiled again. "No," said he, "nor could my friends the Lokapalas—nor would they need to."

"When I assume my Aspect," said Rudra, "and take up my great bow, which was given me by Death himself, then can I send a heat-tracking arrow whistling

down the miles to pursue a moving target and strike it
like a thunderbolt, dead."

"Let us then talk of other matters," said Murugan,
suddenly interested in the target. "I gather that our
guest mocked Brahma some years ago in Mahartha and
did violence in holy places. I understand, though, that
he is the same one who founded the religion of peace
and enlightenment."

"The same."

"Interesting."

"An understatement."

"What will Brahma do."

Rudra shrugged. "Brahma only knows," he replied.

At the place called Worldsend, where there is nothing beyond the edge of Heaven but the distant flicker of
the dome and, far below, the blank ground, hidden
beneath a smoke-white mist, there stands the open-
sided Pavilion of Silence, upon whose round, gray roof
the rains never fall, and across whose balconies and
balustrades the fog boils in the morning and the winds
walk at twilight, and within whose airy chambers,
seated upon the stark, dark furniture, or pacing among
the gray columns, are sometimes to be found the gods
contemplative, the broken warriors or those injured in
love, who come to consider there all things hurtful or
futile, beneath a sky that is beyond the Bridge of the
Gods, in the midst of a place of stone where the colors
are few and the only sound is the wind—there, since
slightly after the days of the First, have sat the philoso-
pher and the sorceress, the sage and the magus, the
suicide, and the ascetic freed from the desire for rebirth
or renewal; there, in the center of renunciation and
abandonment, withdrawal and departure, are the five
rooms named Memory, Fear, Heartbreak, Dust and
Despair; and this place was built by Kubera the Fat,
who cared not a tittle for any of these sentiments, but
who, as a friend of Lord Kalkin, had done this con-
struction at the behest of Candi the Fierce, sometimes

known as Durga and as Kali, for he alone of all the gods possessed the Attribute of inanimate correspondence, whereby he could invest the works of his hands with feelings and passions to be experienced by those who dwelled among them.

They sat in the room called Heartbreak, and they drank of the soma but they were never drunken.

It was twilight all about the Pavilion of Silence, and the winds that circled through Heaven flowed past them.

They sat within black robes upon the dark seats, and his hand lay atop hers, there on the table that stood between them; and the horoscopes of all their days moved past them on the wall that separated Heaven from the heavens; and they were silent as they considered the pages of their centuries.

"Sam," she finally said, "were they not good?"

"Yes," he replied.

"And in those ancient days, before you left Heaven to dwell among men—did you love me then?"

"I do not really remember," he said. "It was so very long ago. We were both different people then—different minds, different bodies. Probably those two, whoever they were, loved one another. I cannot remember."

"But I recall the springtime of the world as though it were yesterday—those days when we rode together to battle, and those nights when we shook the stars loose from the fresh-painted skies! The world was so new and different then, with a menace lurking within every flower and a bomb behind every sunrise. Together we beat a world, you and I, for nothing really wanted us here and everything disputed our coming. We cut and burnt our way across the land and over the seas, and we fought under the seas and in the skies, until there was nothing left to oppose us. Then cities were built, and kingdoms, and we raised up those whom we chose to rule over them, until they ceased to amuse us and we cast them down again. What do the younger gods know of those days? How can they understand the power we knew, who were First?"

"They cannot," he replied.

"When we held court in our palace by the sea and I gave you many sons, and our fleets swept out to conquer the islands, were those days not fair and full of grace? And the nights things of fire and perfume and wine? . . . Did you not love me then?"

"I believe those two loved one another, yes."

"Those two? We are not that different. We are not that changed. Though ages slip away, there are some things within one's being which do not change, which do not alter, no matter how many bodies one puts upon oneself, no matter how many lovers one takes, no matter how many things of beauty and ugliness one looks upon or does, no matter how many thoughts one thinks or feelings one feels. One's self stands at the center of all this and watches."

"Open a fruit and there is a seed within it. Is that the center? Open the seed and there is nothing within it. Is that the center? We are two different persons from the master and the mistress of battles. It was good to have known those two, but that is all."

"Did you go to dwell outside of Heaven because you were tired of me?"

"I wanted a change of perspective."

"There have been long years over which I have hated you for departing. Then there have been times when I sat in the room called Despair, but was too much of a coward to walk beyond Worldsend. Then again, there have been times when I have forgiven you and invoked the seven Rishi to bring your image before me, so that I looked upon you as you went about your day, and it was almost as though we walked together once again. Other times I have desired your death, but you turned my executioner into a friend as you turn my wrath into forgiveness. Do you mean to say that you feel nothing for me?"

"I mean to say that I no longer love you. It would be

nice if there were some one thing constant and unchanging in the universe. If there is such a thing, then it is a thing which would have to be stronger than love, and it is a thing which I do not know."

"I have not changed, Sam."

"Think carefully, Lady, over all that you have said, over all that you have recalled for me this day. It is not really the man whom you have been remembering. It is the days of carnage through which the two of you rode together. The world is come into a tamer age now. You long for the fire and the steel of old. You think it is the man, but it is the destiny the two of you shared for a time, the destiny which is past, that stirs your mind, and you call it love."

"Whatever I call it, it has not changed! Its days are not past. It is a constant thing within the universe, and I call you to come share it with me once again!"

"What of Lord Yama?"

"What of him? You have dealt with those who would be numbered as his peers, did they still live."

"I take it, then, that it is his Aspect for which you care?"

She smiled, within the shadows and the wind.

"Of course."

"Lady, Lady, Lady, forget me! Go live with Yama and be his love. Our days are past, and I do not wish to recall them. They were good, but they are past. As there is a time for everything, there is a time also for the end of anything. This is an age for the consolidation of man's gains upon this world. This is a time for the sharing of knowledge, not the crossing of blades."

"Would you fight Heaven for this knowledge? Would you attempt to break the Celestial City, to open its vaults to the world?"

"You know that I would."

"Then we may yet have a common cause."

"No, Lady, do not deceive yourself. Your allegiance lies with Heaven, not with the world. You know that. If I won my freedom and you joined with me and we fought, perhaps you would be happy for a time. But win or lose, in the end I fear you would be unhappier than before."

"Hear me, soft-hearted saint of the purple grove. It is quite kind of you to anticipate my feelings, but Kali casts her allegiances where she will, owing nothing to anyone, but as she chooses. She is the mercenary goddess, remember that! Perhaps all that you have said is true, and she lies when she tells you she loves you still. Being ruthless and full of the battle lust, however, she follows the smell of blood. I feel that she may yet become an Accelerationist."

"Take care what you say, goddess. Who knows what may be listening?"

"None listens," said she, "for seldom are words spoken within this place."

"All the more reason for someone to be curious when they are."

She sat for a time in silence, then, "None listens," she said.

"Your powers have grown."

"Yes. What of yours?"

"About the same, I think."

"Then will you accept my sword, my wheel, my bow, in the name of Accelerationism?"

"No."

"Why not?"

"You give your promises too easily. You break them as readily as you make them, and because of this I can never trust you. If we fight and we win in the name of Accelerationism, it may also be the last great battle of this world. This is a thing you could not desire, nor permit to occur."

"You are a fool to speak of last great battles, Sam, for the last great battle is always the next one. Shall I come to you in a more comely shape to convince you that I speak the truth? Shall I embrace you in a body with the seal of virginity set upon it? Will this make you to trust my word?"

"Doubt, Lady, is the chastity of the mind, and I bear its seal upon my own."

"Then know that I did but bring you here to this place to torment you, and that you are correct—I spit upon your Accelerationism, and I have already numbered your days. I sought to give you false hopes, that you may be cast down from a greater height. It is only your stupidity and your weakness that have saved you from this."

"I am sorry, Kali—"

"I do not want your apology! I would have liked your love, though, so that I might have used it against you at the end of your days, to make them pass the harder. But, as you say, we have changed too much—and you are no longer worth the trouble. Do not think that I could *not* have made you love me again, either, with smiles and with caresses as of old. For I feel the heat within you, and it is an easy thing for me to fan it in a man. You are not worth a mighty death, however, falling from the heights of passion to the depths of despair. I do not have the time to give you more than my contempt."

The stars wheeled about them, frictionless and fiery, and her hand was gone from beneath his own, as she poured two more cups of soma to warm them against the night.

"Kali?"

"Yes?"

"If it will give you any satisfaction in the end, I still care for you. Either there is no such thing as love, or the word does not mean what I have thought it to mean on many different occasions. It is a feeling without a name, really—better to leave it at that. So take it and go away and have your fun with it. You know that we would both be at one another's throats again one day, as soon as we had run out of common enemies. We had many fine reconciliations, but were they ever worth the pain that preceded them? Know that you have won and that you are the goddess I worship—for are not worship and religious awe a combination of love and hate, desire and fear?"

They drank their soma in the room called Heartbreak, and the spell of Kubera lay about them.

Kali spoke:

"Shall I fall upon you and kiss you now, saying that I lied when I said I lied—so that you may laugh and say you lied, to achieve a final revenge? Go to, Lord Siddhartha! Better one of us died in Hellwell, for great is the pride of the First. We should not have come here—to this place."

"No."

"Shall we then depart?"

"No."

"In this, I agree. Let us sit here and worship one another for a time."

Her hand fell upon his own, caressed it. "Sam?"

"Yes?"

"Would you like to make love to me?"

"And so seal my doom? Of course."

"Then let us go into the room called Despair, where the winds stand stilled and where there is a couch . . ."

He followed her from Heartbreak to Despair, his pulse quickening in his throat, and when he had laid her bare on the couch and placed his hand upon the soft whiteness of her belly, he knew that Kubera was indeed the mightiest of the Lokapalas—for the feeling to which that room had been dedicated filled him, even as his desires mounted within him and he upon her— there came a loosening, a tightening, a sigh, and the ultimate tears burning to be shed.

"What is it you wish, Mistress Maya?"

"Tell me of Accelerationism, Tak of the Archives."

Tak stretched his great lean frame and his chair adjusted backward with a creak.

Behind him, the data banks were still, and certain rare records filled the long, high bookshelves with their colorful bindings and the air with their musty smells.

He handled the lady before him with his eyes, smiled and shook his head. She wore green, tightly, and an impatient look; her hair was an insolent red, and faint freckles flecked her nose and the hemispheres of her cheeks. Her hips and shoulders were wide, and her narrow waist tightly disciplined against this tendency.

"Why do you shake your head? Everyone comes to you for information."

"You are young, mistress. Three avatars, if I am not mistaken, lie behind you. At this point in your career, I am certain that you do not really wish to have your name placed upon the special list of those younger ones who seek this knowledge."

"List?"

"List."

"Why should there be a list of such inquirers?"

Tak shrugged. "Gods collect the strangest things, and certain among them save lists."

"I have always heard Accelerationism mentioned as a completely dead issue."

"So why this sudden interest in the dead?"

She laughed, and her green eyes bored into his gray ones.

The Archives exploded around him, and he stood in the ballroom halfway up Milehigh Spire. It was night, so late that it would soon be morning. A party had obviously been going on for a long while; but now the crowd in which he stood had come together in the corner of the room. They were leaning, and they were sitting and reclining, and all of them listening to the short, dark, husky man who stood beside the goddess Kali and talked. This was Great-Souled Sam the Buddha, who, with his warden, had just arrived. He was talking of Buddhism and Accelerationism, and of the days of the binding, and Hellwell, and the blasphemies of Lord Siddhartha in the city of Mahartha by the sea. He was talking, and his voice went on and on, hypnotic, and he radiated power and confidence and warmth, hypnotic, and his words went on and on and on, as the crowd slowly passed out and fell down around him. All of the women were quite ugly, except for Maya, who tittered then and clapped her hands, bringing back the Archives about them, and Tak again to his chair, his smile still upon his lips.

"So why this sudden interest in the dead?" he repeated.

"He is not dead, that one!"

"No?" said Tak. "He isn't? ... Mistress Maya, he was dead the moment he set foot within the Celestial City. Forget him. Forget his words. Let it be as if he never existed. Leave no trace of him within your mind. One day you will seek renewal—so know that the Masters of Karma will seek after this one within every mind that passes through their halls. The Buddha and his words are an abomination in the eyes of the gods."

"But why?"

"He is a bomb-throwing anarchist, a hairy-eyed revolutionary. He seeks to pull down Heaven itself. If you want more scientific information, I'll have to use the machines to retrieve the data. Would you care to sign an authorization for this?"

"No ..."

"Then put him out of your mind and lock the door."

"He is really that bad?"

"He's worse."

"Then why do you smile as you say these things?"

"Because I'm not a very serious person. Character has nothing to do with my message, however. So heed it."

"*You* seem to know all about it. Are archivists themselves immune to these lists?"

"Hardly. My name is first upon it. But this is not because I am an archivist. He is my father."

"That one? Your father?"

"Yes. You speak as one quite young, however. I doubt that he is even aware that he fathered me. What is paternity to the gods, who inhabit a succession of bodies, begetting scores of offspring by others who also change bodies four or five times a century? I am the son of a body he once inhabited, born of another who also passed through many, and I myself no longer live in the same body I was born into. The relationship, therefore, is quite intangible, and interesting primarily on levels of speculative metaphysics. What is the true father of a man? The circumstances which brought together the two bodies which begat him? Was it the fact that, for some reason, at one moment in time, these two pleased one another beyond any possible alternatives? If so, why? Was it the simple hunger of the flesh, or was it curiosity, or the will? Or was it something else? Pity? Loneliness? The desire to dominate? What feeling, or what thought was father to the body in which I first came into consciousness? I know that the man who inhabited that particular father-body at that particular instant of time is a complicated and powerful personality. Chromosomes mean nothing to us, not really. If we live, we do not carry these hallmarks down through the ages. We really inherit nothing at all, save for occasional endowments of property and cash. The bodies mean so little in the long run that it is far more interesting to speculate as to the mental processes which plucked us forth from chaos. I am pleased that it was he who called me to life, and I often conjecture as to the reasons. I see that your face is suddenly lacking in color, mistress. I did not mean to upset you with this talk, simply to satisfy your curiosity somewhat, and to lay upon your mind some of the thinking we old ones do upon these matters. One day you, too, will look upon it in this light, I am certain. But I am sorry to see you looking so distressed. Pray sit down. Forgive my prattle. You are the Mistress of Illusion. Are not the things of which I have spoken akin to the very stuff with which you work? I am certain that you can tell from the manner in which I speak why my name is first upon the list I mentioned. It is a case of hero worship, I suppose. My creator is quite distinguished. ... Now you are looking somewhat flushed. Would you care for

a cool drink? Wait here a moment. . . . There. Sip this.
Now then, about Accelerationism—it is a simple doctrine of sharing. It proposes that we of Heaven give
unto those who dwell below of our knowledge and
powers and substance. This act of charity would be
directed to the end of raising their condition of existence to a higher level, akin to that which we ourselves
occupy. Then every man would be as a god, you see.
The result of this, of course, would be that there would
no longer be any gods, only men. We would give them
knowledge of the sciences and the arts, which we possess, and in so doing we would destroy their simple
faith and remove all basis for their hoping that things
will be better—for the best way to destroy faith or hope
is to let it be realized. Why should we permit men to
suffer this burden of godhood collectively, as the Accelerationists wished, when we *do* grant it to them individually when they come to deserve it? In his sixtieth year
a man passes through the Halls of Karma. He is
judged, and if he has done well, observing the rules and
restrictions of his caste, paying the proper observances
to Heaven, advancing himself intellectually and morally, then this man will be incarnated into a higher caste,
eventually achieving godhood itself and coming to
dwell here in the City. Each man eventually receives
his just desserts—barring unfortunate accidents, of
course—and so each man, rather than society as a
sudden whole, may come into the divine inheritance
which the ambitious Accelerationists wished to scatter
wholesale before everyone, even those who were un-
ready. You can see that this attitude was dreadfully
unfair and proletarian-oriented. What they really
wanted to do was to lower the requirements for godhood. These requirements are necessarily strict. Would
you give the power of Shiva, of Yama, or of Agni into
the hands of an infant? Not unless you are a fool, you
wouldn't. Not unless you wished to wake up one morning and see that the world no longer existed. This is
what the Accelerationists would have wrought, though,

and this is why they were stopped. Now you know all about Accelerationism. . . . My, you look awfully warm. May I hang your garment while I get you another drink? . . . Very good. . . . Now, where were we, Maya? Oh yes—the beetles in the pudding. . . . Well, the Accelerationists claimed that everything I have just said would be true, excepting for the fact that the system is corrupt. They cast aspersions upon the probity of those who authorized incarnation. Some even dared claim that Heaven was comprised of an immortal aristocracy of wilful hedonists who played games with the world. Others dared to say that the best of men never achieve godhood, but meet ultimately with the real death or incarnation into a lower life form. Some others would even say that one such as yourself had been chosen for deification only because your original form and attitude struck the fancy of some lustful divinity, rather than for your other obvious virtues, my dear. . . . My, you're full of freckles, aren't you? . . . Yes, these are the things those thrice-damned Accelerationists preached. These are the things, the accusations, that the father of my spirit stands for, I am ashamed to say. What can one do with such a heritage but wonder at it? He rides a cycle of mighty days, and he represents the last great schism among the gods. Evil though he obviously is, he is a mighty figure, this father of my spirit, and I respect him as the sons of old did the fathers of their bodies. . . . Are you cold now? Here, let me. . . . There. . . . There. . . . There. . . . Come, now weave us an illusion, my lovely, where we walk in a world that is free of such foolishness. . . . This way now. Turn here. . . . Now let there be a new Eden within this bunker, my moist-lipped one of the green eyes. . . . What is that? . . . What is it that is paramount within me at this instant of time? . . . Truth, my love—and sincerity—and the desire to share . . ."

Ganesha the god-maker walked with Shiva in the forest of Kahiburrha.

"Lord of Destruction," he said, "I understand that you already seek reprisal against those here in the City who mark the words of Siddhartha with more than a smirk of dismissal."

"Of course," said Shiva.

"By so doing, you destroy his effectiveness."

" 'Effectiveness'? Explain what you mean."

"Kill me that green bird on yonder limb."

Shiva gestured with his trident and the bird fell.

"Now kill me its mate."

"I do not see her."

"Then kill me any other from among its flock."

"I see none."

"And now that it lies dead, you will not. So, if you wish, strike at the first who harken to the words of Siddhartha."

"I gather your meaning, Ganesha. He shall walk free, for a time. He shall."

Ganesha the god-maker regarded the jungle about him. Though he walked through the realm of the phantom cats, he feared no evil. For the Lord of Chaos walked by his side, and the Trident of Destruction comforted him.

Vishnu Vishnu Vishnu regarded regarded regarded Brahma Brahma Brahma . . .

They sat in the Hall of Mirrors.

Brahma held forth upon the Eightfold Path and the glory that is Nirvana.

After the space of three cigarettes, Vishnu cleared his throat.

"Yes, Lord?" asked Brahma.

"Why, may I inquire, this Buddhist tract?"

"Do you not find it fascinating?"

"Not particularly."

"That is indeed hypocritical of you."

"What do you mean?"

"A teacher should display at least a modicum of interest in his own lessons."

"Teacher? Lessons?"

"Of course, Tathagatha. Why else in recent years would the god Vishnu be moved to incarnate among men, other than to teach them the Way of Enlightenment?"

"I . . . ?"

"Hail, reformer, who has removed the fear of the real death from men's minds. Those who are not born again among men have now gone on to Nirvana."

Vishnu smiled. "Better to incorporate than struggle to extirpate?"

"Almost an epigram."

Brahma stood, considered the mirrors, considered Vishnu.

"So after we have disposed of Sam, you will have been the real Tathagatha."

"How shall we dispose of Sam?"

"I have not yet decided, but I am open to suggestions."

"Might I suggest that he be incarnated as a jackbird?"

"You might. But then, someone else might desire that the jackbird be reincarnated as a man. I feel that he is not without some supporters."

"Well, we do have time to consider the problem. There is no hurry now that he is in the custody of Heaven. I shall give you my thoughts on the matter as soon as I have some."

"That is sufficient, then, for now."

They they they walked walked walked from the from the Hall, then.

Vishnu passed from the Garden of Brahma's Joys; and as he departed, the Mistress of Death entered there. She addressed the eight-armed statue with the *veena* and it began to play upon it.

Hearing the music, Brahma approached.

"Kali! Lovely Lady . . ." he announced.

"Mighty is Brahma," she replied.

"Yes," Brahma agreed, "as mighty as might be desired. And it is so seldom that you visit here that I am mightily pleased. Come walk with me among the flowered paths and we shall talk. Your dress is lovely."

"Thank you."

They walked among the flowered paths. "How go the preparations for the wedding?"

"Well."

"Will you have honeymoon in Heaven?"

"We plan to take it far from here."

"Where, may I ask?"

"We have not yet agreed as to where."

"Time passes on the wings of the jackbird, my dear. If you wish, you and the Lord Yama may dwell in my Garden of Joys for a time."

"Thank you, Creator, but it is too splendid a place for the two destroyers to pass the time and feel at ease. We shall go forth, somewhere."

"As you wish." He shrugged. "What else lies upon your thinking?"

"What of the one called the Buddha?"

"Sam? Your old lover? What of him, indeed? What would you know concerning him?"

"How shall he be—dealt with?"

"I have not yet decided. Shiva has suggested we wait for a time before doing anything. Thus, we may assess his effect upon the community of Heaven. I have decided that Vishnu will have been the Buddha, for historical and theological purposes. As for Sam himself, I will give hearing to any reasonable suggestion."

"Did you not offer him godhood once?"

"Yes. He did not accept it, however."

"Supposing you did so again?"

"Why?"

"The present problem would not exist were he not a very talented individual. His talents would make him a worthy addition to the pantheon."

"This thought has occurred to me, also. Now, however, he would agree, whether he meant it or not. I am certain that he wishes to live."

"Yet, there are ways in which one can be sure in these matters."

"Such as?"

"Psych-probe."

"And if this shows a lack of commitment to Heaven—which it will . . . ?"

"Could not his mind itself be altered—by one such as Lord Mara?"

"I have never thought you guilty of sentiment, goddess. But it would seem you are most anxious for him to continue existing, in any form."

"Perhaps I am."

"You know that he might be—very changed. He will not be the same if this thing is done to him. His 'talent' may then be totally absent."

"In the course of ages all men change naturally—opinions, beliefs, convictions. Parts of the mind may sleep and other parts may awaken. Talent, I feel, is a difficult thing to destroy—as long as life itself remains. It is better to live than to die."

"I might be convinced of this, goddess—if you have the time, most lovely one."

"How much time?"

"Say, three days."

"Three days, then."

"Then let us adjourn to my Pavilion of Joys and discuss the matter fully."

"Very well."

"Where is Lord Yama now?"

"He labors in his workshop."

"A lengthy project, I trust."

"At least three days."

"Good. Yes, there may be some hope for Sam. It is against my better thinking, but then I *can* appreciate the notion. Yes, I can."

The eight-armed statue of the goddess who was blue played upon the *veena*, making music to fall about them as they walked in the garden, that summer.

Helba dwelled on the far side of Heaven, near to the wilderness' edge. So near to the forest, in fact, was the palace called Plunder that the animals stalked past the one transparent wall, brushing against it as they went. From the room called Rape, one could look out upon the shaded trails of the jungle.

It was within this room, its walls hung with the stolen treasures of lives past, that Helba entertained the one called Sam.

Helba was the god/goddess of thieves.

No one knew Helba's true sex, for Helba's was the habit of alternating gender with each incarnation.

Sam looked upon a lithe, dark-skinned woman who wore a yellow sari and yellow veil. Her sandals and nails were the color of cinnamon, and she wore a tiara that was golden upon her black hair.

"You have," said Helba, in a voice soft and purring, "my sympathy. It is only during those seasons of life when I incarnate as a man, Sam, that I wield my Attribute and engage in actual plunder."

"You must be able to take on your Aspect now."

"Of course."

"And raise up your Attribute?"

"Probably."

"But you will not?"

"Not while I wear the form of woman. As a man, I will undertake to steal anything from anywhere. . . . See there, upon the far wall, where some of my trophies are hung? The great blue-feather cloak belonged to Srit, Chief among the Kataputna demons. I stole it from out his cave as his hellhounds slept, drugged by myself. The shape-changing jewel I took from the very Dome of the Glow, climbing with suction discs upon my wrists and knees and toes, as the Mothers beneath me—"

"Enough!" said Sam. "I know all of these tales, Helba, for you tell them constantly. It has been so long since you have undertaken a daring theft, as of old, that I suppose these glories long past must be oft-repeated. Else, even the Elder Gods would forget what once you were. I can see that I have come to the wrong place, and I shall try elsewhere."

He stood, as to go.

"Wait," said Helba, stirring.

Sam paused. "Yes?"

"You could at least tell me of the theft you are contemplating. Perhaps I can offer advice—"

"What good would even your greatest advice be, Monarch of Thieves? I do not need words. I need actions."

"Perhaps, even . . . tell me!"

"All right," said Sam, "though I doubt you would be interested in a task this difficult—"

"You can skip over the child psychology and tell me what it is you want stolen."

"In the Museum of Heaven, which is a well-built and continuously guarded installation—"

"And one that is always open. Go on."

"In this building, within a computer-protected guard case—"

"These can be beaten, by one of sufficient skill."

"Within this case, upon a manikin, is hung a gray, scaled uniform. Many weapons lie about it."

"Whose?"

"This was the ancient habit of he who fought in the northern marches in the days of the wars against the demons."

"Was this not yourself?"

Sam tipped his smile forward and continued:

"Unknown to most, as a part of this display there is an item which was once known as the Talisman of the Binder. It may have lost all its virtue by now, but, on the other hand, it is possible that it has not. It served as a focus for the Binder's special Attribute, and he finds that he needs it once again."

"Which is the item you want stolen?"

"The great wide belt of shells which is clasped about the waist of the costume. It is pink and yellow in color.

It is also full of micro-miniature circuitry, which could probably not be duplicated today."

"That is not so great a theft. I just might consider it in this form—"

"I would need it in a hurry, or not at all."

"How soon?"

"Within six days, I fear."

"What would you be willing to pay me to deliver it into your hands?"

"I would be willing to pay you anything, if I had anything."

"Oh. You came to Heaven without a fortune?"

"Yes."

"Unfortunate."

"If I make good my escape, you can name your price."

"And if you do not, I receive nothing."

"It appears that way."

"Let me ponder. It may amuse me to do this thing and have you owe me the favor."

"Pray, do not ponder overlong."

"Come sit by me, Binder of Demons, and tell me of the days of your glory—when you, with the immortal goddess, rode abroad in the world, scattering chaos like seed."

"It was long ago," said Sam.

"Might those days come again if you win free?"

"They may."

"That is good to know. Yes ..."

"You will do this thing?"

"Hail, Siddhartha! Unbinder!"

"Hail?"

"And lightning and thunder. May they come again!"

"It is good."

"Now tell me of the days of your glory, and I will speak again of mine."

"Very well."

Dashing through the forest, clad in a leather belt,

Lord Krishna pursued the Lady Ratri, who had declined to couple with him after the rehearsal dinner. The day was clear and fragrant, but not half so fragrant as the midnight-blue sari he clutched in his left hand. She ran on ahead of him, beneath the trees; and he followed, losing sight of her for a moment as she turned up a side trail that led out into the open.

When he glimpsed her again, she stood upon a hillock, her bare arms upraised above her head, her fingertips touching. Her eyes were half closed, and her only garment, a long black veil, stirred about her white and gleaming form.

He realized then that she had taken on her Aspect, and might be about to wield an Attribute.

Panting, he raced up the hillside toward her; and she opened her eyes and smiled down upon him, lowering her arms.

As he reached for her, she swirled her veil in his face and he heard her laugh—somewhere within the immense night that covered him over.

It was black and starless and moonless, without a glint, shimmer, spark or glow from anywhere. It was a nighttime akin to blindness that had fallen upon him.

He snorted, and the sari was torn from his fingers. He halted, shaking, and he heard her laughter ringing about him.

"You have presumed too much, Lord Krishna," she told him, "and offended against the sanctity of Night. For this, I shall punish you by leaving this darkness upon Heaven for a time."

"I am not afraid of the dark, goddess," he replied, chuckling.

"Then your brains are indeed in your gonads, Lord, as hath often been said before—to stand lost and blinded in the midst of Kaniburrha, whose denizens need not to strike—and not to be afraid—I think this somewhat foolhardy. Good-bye, Dark One. Perhaps I'll see you at the wedding."

"Wait, lovely lady! Will you accept my apology?"

"Certainly, for I deserve it."

"Then lift this night you have laid upon this place."

"Another time, Krishna—when I am ready."

"But what shall I do until then?"

"It is said, sir, that by your piping you can charm the most fearsome of beasts. I suggest that if this be true you take up your pipes at this moment and begin your most soothing melody, until such a time as I see fit to let the light of day enter again into Heaven."

"Lady, you are cruel," said Krishna.

"Such is life, Lord of the Pipes," and she departed.

He began to play, thinking dark thoughts.

They came. Out of the sky, riding on the polar winds, across the seas and the land, over the burning snow, and under it and through it, they came. The shape-shifters drifted across the fields of white, and the sky-walkers fell down like leaves; trumpets sounded over the wastes, and the chariots of the snows thundered forward, light leaping like spears from their burnished sides; cloaks of fur afire, white plumes of massively breathed air trailing above and behind them, golden-gauntleted and sun-eyed, clanking and skidding, rushing and whirling, they came, in bright baldric, wer-mask, fire-scarf, devil-shoe, frost-greaves and power-helm, they came; and across the world that lay at their back, there was rejoicing in the Temples, with much singing and the making of offerings, and processions and prayers, sacrifices and dispensations, pageantry and color. For the much-feared goddess was to be wed with Death, and it was hoped that this would serve to soften both their dispositions. A festive spirit had also infected Heaven, and with the gathering of the gods and the demigods, the heroes and the nobles, the high priests and the favored rajahs and high-ranking Brahmins, this spirit obtained force and momentum and spun like an all-colored whirlwind, thundering in the heads of the First and latest alike.

So they came into the Celestial City, riding on the

backs of the cousins of the Garuda Bird, spinning down in sky gondolas, rising up through arteries of the mountains, blazing across the snow-soaked, ice-tracked wastes, to make Milehigh Spire to ring with their song, to laugh through a spell of brief and inexplicable darkness that descended and dispersed again, shortly; and in the days and nights of their coming, it was said by the poet Adasay that they resembled at least six different things (he was always lavish with his similes): a migration of birds, bright birds, across a waveless ocean of milk; a procession of musical notes through the mind of a slightly mad composer; a school of those deep-swimming fish whose bodies are whorls and runnels of light, circling about some phosphorescent plant within a cold and sea-deep pit; the Spiral Nebula, suddenly collapsing upon its center; a storm, each drop of which becomes a feather, songbird or jewel; and (and perhaps most cogent) a Temple full of terrible and highly decorated statues, suddenly animated and singing, suddenly rushing forth across the world, bright banners playing in the wind, shaking palaces and toppling towers, to meet at the center of everything, to kindle an enormous fire and dance about it, with the ever-present possibility of either the fire or the dance going completely out of control.

They came.

When the secret alarm rang in the Archives, Tak seized the Bright Spear from out its case on the wall. At various times during the day, the alarm would alert various sentinels. Having a premonition as to its cause, Tak was grateful that it did not ring at another hour. He elevated to the level of the City and made for the Museum on the hill.

It was already too late, though.

Open was the case and unconscious the attendant. The Museum was otherwise unoccupied, because of the activity in the City.

So near to the Archives was the building set, that

Tak caught the two on their way down the opposite side of the hill.

He waved the Bright Spear, afraid to use it. "Stop!" he cried.

They turned to him.

"You *did* trigger an alarm!" accused the other. He hurried to clasp the belt about his waist.

"Go on, get away!" he said. "I will deal with this one!"

"I could not have tripped an alarm!" cried his companion.

"Get out of here!"

He faced Tak, waiting. His companion continued to retreat down the hill. Tak saw that it was a woman.

"Take it back," said Tak, panting. "Whatever you have taken, take it back—and perhaps I can cover—"

"No," said Sam. "It is too late. I am the equal of anyone here now, and this is my only chance to depart. I know you, Tak of the Archives, and I do not wish to destroy you. Therefore, go—quickly!"

"Yama will be here in a moment! And—"

"I do not fear Yama. Attack me or leave me—now!"

"I cannot attack you."

"Then good-bye," and, so saying, Sam rose into the air like a balloon.

But as he drifted above the ground, the Lord Yama appeared upon the hillside with a weapon in his hands. It was a slender and gleaming tube that he held, with a small butt and a large trigger mechanism.

He raised it and pointed. "Your last chance!" he cried, but Sam continued to rise.

When he fired it, the dome was cracked, high overhead.

"He has taken on his Aspect and raised up an Attribute," said Tak. "He binds the energies of your weapon."

"Why did you not stop him?" asked Yama.

"I could not, Lord. I was taken by his Attribute."

"It does not matter," said Yama. "The third sentinel will overcome him."

Binding gravitation to his will, he rose.

As he fled, he grew conscious of a pursuing shadow.

Somewhere just at the periphery of his vision, it lurked. No matter how he turned his head it escaped his sight. But it was always there, and growing.

Ahead, there was a lock. A gate to the outside hovered above and ahead. The Talisman could unbind that lock, could warm him against the cold, could transport him anywhere in the world. . . .

There came a sound of wings, beating.

"Flee!" the voice thundered in his head. "Increase your speed, Binder! Flee faster! Flee faster!"

It was one of the strangest sensations he had ever experienced.

He felt himself moving forward, racing onward.

But nothing changed. The gate was no nearer. For all his sense of tremendous speed, he was not moving.

"Faster, Binder! Faster!" cried the wild, booming voice. "Seek to emulate the wind and the lightning in your going!"

He strove to halt the sense of motion that he felt.

Then the winds buffeted him, the mighty winds that circle through Heaven.

He fought them down, but the voice sounded right next to him now, though he saw nothing but shadow.

" 'The senses are horses and objects the roads they travel,' " said the voice. " 'If the intellect is related to a mind that is distracted, it loses then its discrimination,' " and Sam recognized the mighty words of the *Katha Upanishad* roaring at his back. " 'In this case,' " the voice went on, " 'the senses then become uncontrolled, like wild and vicious horses beneath the rein of a weak charioteer.' "

And the sky exploded with lightnings about him and the darkness wrapped him around.

He sought to bind the energies that assailed him, but found nothing with which to grapple.

"It is not real!" he cried out.

"What is real and what is not?" replied the voice. "Your horses escape you now."

There was a moment of terrible blackness, as if he moved through a vacuum of the senses. Then there was pain. Then nothing.

It is difficult to be the oldest youthgod in the business.

He entered the Hall of Karma, requested audience with a representative of the Wheel, was shown into the presence of the Lord, who had had to forego probing him two days before.

"Well?" he inquired.

"I am sorry for the delay, Lord Murugan. Our personnel had become involved in the wedding preparations."

"They are out reveling, when they should be preparing my new body?"

"You should not speak, Lord, as though it is truly *your* body. It is a body loaned you by the Great Wheel, in response to your present karmic needs—"

"And it is not ready because the staff is out reveling?"

"It is not ready because the Great Wheel turns in a manner—"

"I want it by tomorrow evening at the latest. If it is not ready, the Great Wheel may become as a juggernaut upon its ministers. Do you hear me and understand, Lord of Karma?"

"I hear you, but your speech is out of place in this—"

"Brahma recommended the transfer, and he would be pleased for me to appear at the wedding party at Milehigh Spire in my new form. Shall I inform him that the Great Wheel is unable to comply with his wishes because it turns exceeding slow?"

"No, Lord. It will be ready in time."

"Very good."

He turned and left.

The Lord of Karma made an ancient and mystical sign behind his back.

"Brahma."

"Yes, goddess?"

"Concerning my suggestion . . ."

"It shall be done as you requested, madam."

"I would have it otherwise."

"Otherwise?"

"Yea, Lord. I would have a human sacrifice."

"Not . . ."

"Yes."

"You are indeed even more sentimental than I had thought."

"Shall this thing be done, or shall it not?"

"To speak plainly—in the light of recent events, I should prefer it this way."

"Then it is resolved?"

"It shall be as you wish. There was more power present in that one than I had thought. If the Lord of Illusion had not been sentinel—well, I had not anticipated that one who had been so quiet for so long could also be as—*talented*, as you have put it."

"Will you give unto me the full disposition of this thing, Creator?"

"Gladly."

"And throw in the Monarch of Thieves, for dessert?"

"Yes. Let it be so."

"Thank you, mighty one."

"It is nothing."

"It will be. Good evening."

"Good evening."

It is said that on that day, that great day, the Lord Vayu stopped the winds of Heaven and a stillness came upon the Celestial City and the wood of Kaniburrha.

Citragupta, serving man to Lord Yama, built a mighty pyre at Worldsend, out of aromatic woods, gums, incenses, perfumes and costly cloths; and upon the pyre he laid the Talisman of the Binder and the great blue-feather cloak that had belonged to Srit, chief among the Kataputna demons; he also placed there the shape-changing jewel of the Mothers, from out the Dome of the Glow, and a robe of saffron from the purple grove of Alundil, which was said to have belonged to Ta-thagatha the Buddha. The silence of the morning after the night of the Festival of the First was complete. There was no movement to be seen in Heaven. It is said that demons flitted invisible through the upper air, but feared to draw near the gathering of power. It is said that there had been many signs and portents signi-fying the fall of the mighty. It was said, by the theolo-gians and holy historians, that the one called Sam had recanted his heresy and thrown himself upon the mercy of Trimurti. It is also said that the goddess Parvati, who had been either his wife, his mother, his sister, his daughter, or perhaps all of these, had fled Heaven, to dwell in mourning among the witches of the eastern continent, whom she counted as kin. With dawn, the great bird called Garuda, Mount of Vishnu, whose beak smashes chariots, had stirred for a moment into wakefulness and had uttered a single hoarse cry within his cage, a cry that rang through Heaven, stabbing glass into shards, echoing across the land, awakening the soundest sleeper. Within the still summer of Heaven, the day of Love and Death began.

The streets of Heaven were empty. The gods dwelled for a time indoors, waiting. All the portals of Heaven had been secured.

The thief and the one whose followers had called him Mahasamatman (thinking him a god) were re-leased. The air was of a sudden chill, with the laying of a weird.

High, high above the Celestial City, on a platform at the top of Milehigh Spire, stood the Lord of Illusion,

Mara the Dreamer. He had upon him his cloak of all colors. His arms were raised, and the powers of others among the gods flowed through him, adding to his own.

In his mind, a dream took shape. Then he cast his dream, as a high wave-front casts waters across a beach.

For all ages, since their fashioning by Lord Vishnu, the City and the wilderness had existed side by side, adjacent, yet not really touching, accessible, yet removed from one another by a great distance within the mind, rather than by a separation merely spatial in nature. Vishnu, being the Preserver, had done this for a reason. Now, he did not wholly approve of the lifting of his barrier, even in a temporary and limited way. He did not wish to see any of the wilderness enter into the City, which, in his mind, had grown into the perfect triumph of form over chaos.

Yet, by the power of the Dreamer was it given unto the phantom cats to look upon all of Heaven for a time.

They stirred, restlessly, upon the dark and ageless trails of the jungle that was part illusion. There, within the place that only half existed, a new seeing came into their eyes, and with it a restlessness and a summons to the hunt.

It was rumored among the seafaring folk, those worldwide gossips and carriers of tales, who seem to know all things, that some among the phantom cats who hunted on that day were not really cats at all. They say that it was told in the places of the world where the gods passed later, that some among the Celestial Party transmigrated on that day, taking upon themselves the bodies of white tigers out of Kaniburrha, to join in the hunt through the alleys of Heaven after the thief who had failed and the one who had been called Buddha.

It is said that, as he wandered the streets of the City, an ancient jackbird circled three times above him, then came to rest upon Sam's shoulder, saying:

"Are you not Maitreya, Lord of Light, for whom the world has waited, lo, these many years—he whose coming I prophesyed long ago in a poem?"

"No, my name is Sam," he replied, "and I am about to depart the world, not enter into it. Who are you?"

"I am a bird who was once a poet. All morning have I flown, since the yawp of Garuda opened the day. I was flying about the ways of Heaven looking for Lord Rudra, hoping to befoul him with my droppings, when I felt the power of a weird come over the land. I have flown far, and I have seen many things, Lord of Light."

"What things have you seen, bird who was a poet?"

"I have seen an unlit pyre set at the end of the world, with fogs stirring all about it. I have seen the gods who come late hurrying across the snows and rushing through the upper airs, circling outside the dome. I have seen the players upon the *ranga* and the *nepathya,* rehearsing the Masque of Blood, for the wedding of Death and Destruction. I have seen the Lord Vayu raise up his hand and stop the winds that circle through Heaven. I have seen all-colored Mara atop the spire of the highest tower, and I have felt the power of the weird he lays—for I have seen the phantom cats troubled within the wood, then hurrying in this direction. I have seen the tears of a man and of a woman. I have heard the laughter of a goddess. I have seen a bright spear uplifted against the morning, and I have heard an oath spoken. I have seen the Lord of Light at last, of whom I wrote, long ago:

> Always dying, never dead;
> Ever ending, never ended;
> Loathed in darkness,
> Clothed in light,
> He comes, to end a world,
> As morning ends the night.
> These lines were writ
> By Morgan, free,

Who shall, the day he dies,
See this prophecy."

The bird ruffled his feathers then and was still.

"I am pleased, bird, that you have had a chance to see many things," said Sam, "and that within the fiction of your metaphor you have achieved a certain satisfaction. Unfortunately, poetic truth differs considerably from that which surrounds most of the business of life."

"Hail, Lord of Light!" said the bird, and sprang into the air. As he rose, he was pierced through by an arrow shot from a nearby window by one who hated jackbirds.

Sam hurried on.

It is said that the phantom cat who had his life, and that of Helba a little later, was really a god or a goddess, which was quite possible.

It is said, also, that the phantom cat who killed them was not the first, or the second, to attempt this thing. Several tigers died beneath the Bright Spear, which passed into them, withdrew itself, vibrated clean of gore and returned then to the hand of its thrower. Tak of the Bright Spear fell himself, however, struck in the head by a chair thrown by Lord Ganesha, who had entered silently into the room at his back. It is said by some that the Bright Spear was later destroyed by Lord Agni, but others say that it was cast beyond Worldsend by the Lady Maya.

Vishnu was not pleased, later being quoted as having said that the City should not have been defiled with blood, and that wherever chaos finds egress, it will one day return. But he was laughed at by the younger of the gods, for he was accounted least among Trimurti, and his ideas were known to be somewhat dated, he being numbered among the First. For this reason, though, he disclaimed any part in the affair and retired into his tower for a time. Lord Varuna the Just turned away his face from the proceedings and visited the

Pavilion of Silence at Worldsend, where he sat for a spell in the room named Fear.

The Masque of Blood was quite lovely, having been written by the poet Adasay, who was noted for his elegant language, being of the anti-Morganic school. It was accompanied by powerful illusions cast by the Dreamer especially for the occasion. It is said that Sam, too, had walked in illusion on that day; and that, as a part of the weird, he had walked in partial darkness, amidst awful odors, through regions of wailing and shrieking, and that he had seen once again every terror he had known in his life conjured up before him, brilliant or swart, silent or trumpeting, fresh-torn from the fabric of his memory and dripping with the emotions of their birth into his life, before it was over.

What remained was taken in procession to the pyre at Worldsend, placed there upon it, burned amidst chanting. Lord Agni had raised his goggles, stared for a time, and then the flames had arisen. Lord Vayu had lifted up his hand and a wind had come to fan the fire. When it was finished, Lord Shiva had blasted the ashes beyond the world with a twist of his trident.

These things considered, it was thorough as well as impressive, the funeral.

Long unrehearsed in Heaven, the wedding came on with all the power of tradition. Milehigh Spire glistened, blindingly, like a stalagmite of ice. The weird had been withdrawn, and the phantom cats walked the streets of the City, blinded once more, their fur sleeked as if by the wind; and should they climb a broad stairway, it was a rocky slope they mounted; the buildings were cliffs and the statues were trees. The winds that circled through Heaven captured song and scattered it across the land. A sacred fire was kindled in the Square within the City's center Circle. Virgins, imported for the occasion, fed this fire with a clean, dry, aromatic wood, which crackled and burnt with very little smoke, save for occasional puffs of purest white. Surya, the sun, shone down with such brilliance that

the day fairly vibrated with clarity. The groom, attended by a great procession of friends and retainers decked
all in red, was escorted through the City to the Pavilion
of Kali, where all were taken within by her servants
and led into the great dining hall. There, Lord Kubera
served as host, seating the scarlet train, which was three
hundred in number, in chairs of black and chairs of
red, alternating, around the long black-wood tables,
which were inlaid with bone. There, in that hall, were
they all given to drink of *madhuparka,* which was of
honey and curds and psychedelic powders; and this
they drank in the company of the blue-garbed train of
the bride, which entered the hall bearing double cups.
The train of the bride numbered three hundred also;
and when all were seated and all had drunk of the
madhuparka, Kubera did then speak for a time, jesting
with them broadly and alternating his speech with
words of practical wisdom and occasional references to
the ancient scriptures. The legion of the groom then
departed to the pavilion in the Square, and that of the
bride advanced upon it from another direction. Yama
and Kali entered this pavilion separately and sat on
either side of a small curtain. There was much singing
of ancient songs and the curtain was removed by
Kubera, permitting the two to look upon one another
for the first time that day. Kubera did speak then,
giving Kali into the care of Yama in return for the
promises of goodness, wealth and pleasure to be given
unto her. Then Lord Yama clasped her hand and Kali
cast an offering of grain into the fire, about which
Yama led her, their garments having been knotted together by one of her retainers. After this, Kali trod
upon a millstone, and the two of them took seven steps
together, Kali treading upon a small pile of rice with
each step. Then was a light rain summoned down from
the sky for the space of several heartbeats, to sanctify
the occasion with the blessing of water. The retainers
and guests then combined into a single procession and
moved off through the town in the direction of the dark

pavilion of Yama, where great feasting and revelry was held, and where the Masque of Blood was presented.

As Sam had faced his final tiger, it had nodded its head slowly, knowing what it was hunting. There was no place for him to run, so he stood there, waiting. The cat took its time also. A horde of demons had tried to descend upon the City at that moment, but the power of the weird held them back. The goddess Ratri was seen to be weeping and her name was entered upon a list. Tak of the Archives was incarcerated for a time in the dungeons beneath Heaven. The Lord Yama was heard to say, "Life did not rise up," as though he had almost expected that it would.

All things considered, it was thorough as well as impressive, the death.

The wedding party lasted for seven days, and the Lord Mara spun dream after dream about the revelers. As if by a carpet of magic, he transported them through the lands of illusion, raising up palaces of colored smoke upon pillars of water and of fire, escalating the benches at which they sat down canyons of stardust, striving with coral and myrrh to bend their senses beyond themselves, bringing onto them all their Aspects, wherein he held them, rotating about the archetypes upon which they had based their powers, as Shiva danced in a graveyard the Dance of Destruction and the Dance of Time, celebrating the legend of his annihilation of the three flying cities of the Titans, and Krishna the Dark moved through the Wrestler's Dance in commemoration of his breaking of the black demon Bana, while Lakshmi danced the Dance of the Statue, and even Lord Vishnu was coerced into celebrating again the steps of the Dance of the Amphora, as Murugan, in his new body, laughed at the world clad in all her oceans, and did his dance of triumph upon those waters as upon a stage, the dance that he had danced after the slaying of Shura, who had taken refuge in the depths of the sea. When Mara gestured there was magic and color and music and wine. There was poetry and gaming. There was song and laughter. There was sport, in which mighty trials of strength and skill took place. In all, it required the stamina of a god to bear the entire seven days of pleasure.

These things considered, it was thorough as well as impressive, the wedding.

When it was over, the bride and the groom departed Heaven, to wander for a time about the world, to take in the pleasures of many places. They went, without servants or retainers, to wander free. They did not announce the order of their visitations, or the length of time they would spend—which was to be expected, their fellows being the celestial practical jokers that they were.

After their going, there was still some revelry. Lord Rudra, having consumed a magnificent quantity of soma, stood up upon a table and began to deliver a speech concerning the bride—a speech with which, had Yama been present, he would doubtless have taken issue. Such being the case, Lord Agni slapped Rudra across the mouth and was immediately challenged to a duel, in Aspect, across the length of Heaven.

Agni was flown to a mountaintop beyond Kaniburrha, and Lord Rudra took up a position near Worldsend. When the signal was given, Rudra sent a heat-tracking arrow whistling down the miles in the direction of his opponent. From fifteen miles away, however, Lord Agni spotted the arrow as it sped toward him and burnt it from out the air with a blast of the Universal Fire, which same power he then moved like a needle of light, to touch upon Rudra and burn him to ashes where he stood, also piercing through the dome at his back. Thus was the honor of the Lokapalas upheld, and a new Rudra was raised up from the ranks of the demigods to take the place of the old, who had fallen.

One rajah and two high priests died of poisoning, quite colorfully, and pyres were built to accommodate their bluish remains. Lord Krishna raised up his Aspect and played a music after which there is no music, and

Guari the Fair relented and came to him once more, her heart softened, after he had finished. Sarasvati in her glory did the Dance of Delight, and then Lord Mara re-created the flight of Helba and the Buddha through the City. This last dreaming troubled many, however, and more names were recorded at that time. A demon then dared enter into their midst, with the body of a youth and the head of a tiger, attacking Lord Agni with a terrible fury. He was repelled by the combined powers of Ratri and of Vishnu, but he succeeded in escaping into incorporeality before Agni could bring his wand to bear upon him.

In the days that followed, there were changes within Heaven.

Tak of the Archives and the Bright Spear was judged by the Lords of Karma and was transmigrated into the body of an ape; and there was a warning set within his mind that wherever he presented himself for renewal he was to be given again into the body of an ape, to wander the world in this form until such a time as Heaven saw fit to extend its mercy and lift this doom from him. He was then sent forth into the jungles of the south, and there released to work off his karmic burden.

Lord Varuna the Just gathered his servants about him and departed the Celestial City, to make his home elsewhere in the world. Some of his detractors likened his departure to that of Nirriti the Black, god of darkness and corruption, who had left Heaven filled with ill will and the miasma of many a dark curse. The detractors of Varuna were not so numerous, however, for it was common knowledge that he deserved the title Just, and his condemnation could easily be construed to reflect upon the worth of its speaker, so few spoke of him beyond the days immediately following his going.

Much later, others among the gods were exiled into the world, in the days of the Heavenly Purges. Their going, however, had its beginnings in these times, when Accelerationism entered again into Heaven.

Brahma, mightiest of the four orders of gods and the eighteen hosts of paradise, Creator of all, Lord of high Heaven and everything beneath it, from whose navel springs forth a lotus and whose hands churn the oceans —he, who in three strides encompasses all the worlds, the drum of whose glory strikes terror into the hearts of his enemies, upon whose right hand is the wheel of the law, who tethers catastrophes, using a snake for rope— Brahma was to feel more and more uncomfortable and distraught in the days that came to pass as a result of the promise rashly given to the Mistress of Death. But then, it is quite likely that he would have proceeded in the same manner without her persuasions. The major effect of her actions, then, was probably that it gave him, for a brief time, someone to blame his later troubles upon. He was also known as Brahma the Infallible.

The dome of Heaven was repaired in several places at the end of the time of the revels.

The Museum of Heaven was thereafter provided with an armed guard who remained upon the premises at all times.

Several demon-hunting parties were planned, but never got beyond the planning stage.

A new Archivist was appointed, one who had no knowledge whatsoever concerning his parentage.

The phantom cats of Kaniburrha were granted symbolic representation in Temples throughout the land.

On the last night of the revels, a lone god entered the Pavilion of Silence at Worldsend and dwelled for a long while in the room called Memory. Then he laughed long and returned to the Celestial City; and his laughter was a thing of youth and beauty and strength and purity, and the winds that circle through Heaven caught it up and bore it far across the land, where all who heard it marveled at the strange and vibrant note of triumph that it contained.

These things considered, it was thorough as well as impressive, the time of Love and Death, of Hate and Life, and of Folly.

vi

*During the time that followed the death of Brahma,
there came upon the Celestial City a period of turmoil.
Several among the gods were even expelled from Heav-
en. It was a time when just about everyone feared being
considered an Accelerationist; and, as fate would have
it, at some point or other during this period, just about
everyone was considered an Accelerationist. Though
Great-Souled Sam was dead, his spirit was said to live
on, mocking. Then, in the days of disaffection and
intrigue that led up to the Great Battle, it was rumored
that more than his spirit might have lived on. . . .*

> When the sun of suffering has set,
> there comes this peace,
> Lord of the quiet stars,
> this peace of creation,
> this place the mandala spins gray.
> The fool saith in his mind
> that his thoughts are only thoughts . . .
> *Saraha (98-99)*

IT WAS early morning. Near the pool of the purple lotus,
in the Garden of Joys, at the foot of the statue of the
blue goddess with the *veena,* Brahma was located.

The girl who found him first thought him to be
resting, for his eyes were still open. After a moment,
though, she realized that he was not breathing; and his
face, so contorted, underwent no changes of expression.

She trembled as she awaited the ending of the universe. God being dead, she understood that this normally followed. But after a time, she decided that the
internal cohesiveness of things might serve to hold the
universe together for another hour or so; and such

being the case, she thought it advisable to bring the matter of the imminent Yuga to the attention of someone better suited to cope with it.

She told Brahma's First Concubine, who went to see for herself, agreed that her Lord was indeed dead, addressed the statue of the blue goddess, who immediately began playing upon the *veena,* and then sent messages to Vishnu and Shiva to come at once to the Pavilion.

They did, bringing Lord Ganesha with them.

These viewed the remains, agreed as to their condition and confined both women to their quarters against execution.

Then they conferred.

"We need another creator in a hurry," said Vishnu. "The floor is open for nominations."

"I nominate Ganesha," said Shiva.

"I decline," said Ganesha.

"Why?"

"I do not like being on the scene. I would much rather remain off somewhere behind it."

"Then let us consider some alternative choices, quickly."

"Might it not be wise," asked Vishnu, "to ascertain the cause of this occurrence before proceeding?"

"No," said Ganesha. "The first order of business must be the selection of his successor. Even the postmortem must wait on that. Heaven must never be without a Brahma."

"What say you to one of the Lokapalas?"

"Perhaps."

"Yama?"

"No. He is too serious, too conscientious—a technician, not an administrator. Also, I think he's emotionally unstable."

"Kubera?"

"Too smart. I'm afraid of Kubera."

"Indra?"

"Too headstrong."

"Agni, then?"

"Maybe. Maybe not."

"Perhaps Krishna?"

"Too frivolous, never sober."

"Who would you suggest?"

"What is our greatest problem at the present time?"

"I do not feel that we have any great problems at the present time," said Vishnu.

"Then it might be wise to have one just about now," said Ganesha. "I feel that our greatest problem is Accelerationism. Sam came back, stirring, making clear waters muddy."

"Yes," said Shiva.

"Accelerationism? Why kick a dead dog?"

"Ah, but it is not dead. Not down among men. And it will also serve to direct attention away from the succession within Trimurti and regain at least surface solidarity here in the City. Unless, of course, you'd rather undertake a campaign against Nirriti and his zombies?"

"No thanks."

"Not now."

"Mmm . . . yes, then Accelerationism is our greatest problem at the present time."

"All right. Accelerationism is our greatest problem."

"Who hates it more than anyone else?"

"Yourself?"

"Nonsense. Except me."

"Tell us, Ganesha."

"Kali."

"I doubt this."

"I do not. The twin beasts, Buddhism and Accelerationism, draw a single chariot. The Buddha scorned her. She is a woman. She will carry on the campaign."

"It will mean renouncing her womanhood."

"Speak to me not of trifles."

"All right—Kali."

"But what of Yama?"

"What of him? Leave Yama to me."

"I'd rather."

"I also."

"Very well. Go you then forth across the world, within the thunder chariot and upon the back of the great bird Garuda. Find Yama and Kali. Return them to Heaven. I will wait upon your return and consider the matter of Brahma's passing."

"So be it."

"Agreed."

"Good morning."

"Good merchant Vama, wait! I would have words with thee."

"Yea, Kabada. What wouldst thou?"

"It is difficult to find the words I would have with thee. But they do concern a certain state of affairs which hath aroused considerable sentiment on the parts of thy various adjacent neighbors."

"Oh? Speak on then."

"Concerning the atmosphere . . ."

"The atmosphere?"

"The winds and breezes, perhaps . . ."

"Winds? Breezes?"

"And the things they bear."

"Things? Such as . . . ?"

"Odors, good Vama."

"Odors? What odors?"

"Odors of—well, odors of—of fecal matter."

"Of . . . ? Oh! Yes. True. True enough. There may be a few such. I had forgotten, having grown used to them."

"Might I inquire as to their cause?"

"They are caused by the product of defecation, Kabada."

"Of this I am aware. I meant to make inquiry as to *why* they are present, rather than their source and nature."

"They are present because of the buckets in my back room, which are filled with such—items."

"Oh?"

"Yes. I have been saving the products of my family in this manner. I have been doing this for the past eight days."

"Against what use, worthy Vama?"

"Hast thou not heard of a thing, a wondrous thing, a thing into which these items are discharged—into water—and then a lever pulled, and then, with a mighty rushing sound, these things are borne away, far beneath the ground?"

"I have heard some talk of such . . ."

"Oh, 'tis true, 'tis true. There *is* such a thing. It has but recently been invented by one whom I should not name, and it involves great pipes and a seat without a bottom, or a top, really. It is the most wonderful discovery of the age—and I will have me one within a matter of moons!"

"Thou? Such a thing?"

"Yea. It shall be installed in the small room I have built onto the back of my home. I may even give a dinner that night and permit all my neighbors to take use of it."

"This is indeed wondrous—and thou generous."

"I feel so."

"But—of the—smells . . . ?"

"They are caused by the buckets of items, which I am preserving against the installation of this thing."

"Why?"

"I should rather have it on my karmic record that this thing was used for these items beginning with eight days ago, rather than several moons from now. It will show my rapid advancement in life."

"Ah! I see now the wisdom of thy ways, Vama. I did not wish it to appear that we stood in the way of any man who seeks to better himself. Forgive me if I gave this impression."

"Thou art forgiven."

"Thy neighbors do love thee, smells and all. When

thou art advanced to a higher state, please remember this."

"Of course."

"Such progress must be expensive."

"Quite."

"Worthy Vama, we shall take delight in the atmosphere, with all its pungent portents."

"This is only my second lifetime, good Kabada, but already I feel that destiny touches upon me."

"And I, also. The winds of Time do shift, and they bear to mankind many wondrous things. The gods keep thee."

"Thou also. But forget not the blessing of the Enlightened One, whom my second cousin Vasu sheltered in his purple grove."

"How could I? Mahasamatman was a god also. Some say Vishnu."

"They lie. He was the Buddha."

"Add then his blessings."

"Very good. Good day, Kabada."

"Good day, worthy one."

Yama and Kali entered into Heaven. They descended upon the Celestial City on the back of the bird called Garuda. In the company of Vishnu, they entered into the City. They did not pause for any purpose, but went directly to the Pavilion of Brahma. In the Garden of Joys they met with Shiva and with Ganesha.

"Hear me, Death and Destruction," said Ganesha, "Brahma is dead and only we five now know of it."

"How did this thing come to pass?" asked Yama.

"It appears that he was poisoned."

"Has there been an autopsy?"

"No."

"Then I shall perform one."

"Good. But now there is another matter, of even graver consideration."

"Name it."

"His successor."

"Yes. Heaven cannot be without a Brahma."

"Exactly. . . . Kali, tell me, would you consider being Brahma, of the golden saddle and silver spurs?"

"I don't know . . ."

"Then begin thinking about it, and quickly. You are considered the best choice."

"What of Lord Agni?"

"Not so high on the list. It does not appear he is so anti-Accelerationist as Madam Kali."

"I see."

"And I."

"Therefore, he is a good god, but not a great one."

"Yes. Who might have killed Brahma?"

"I have no idea. Have you?"

"Not yet."

"But you will find him, Lord Yama?"

"Aye, with my Aspect upon me."

"You two may wish to confer."

"We do."

"Then will we leave you now. An hour hence we shall dine together in the Pavilion."

"Yes."

"Yes."

"Till then . . ."

"Till then."

"Till then."

"Lady?"

"Yes?"

"With a changing of bodies one is automatically divorced, unless a continuation contract be signed."

"Yes."

"Brahma must needs be a man."

"Yes."

"Refuse it."

"My Lord . . ."

"You hesitate?"

"It is all so sudden, Yama . . ."

"You pause even to consider it?"

"I must."

"Kali, you distress me."

"Such was not my intention."

"And I bid you refuse the offer."

"I am a goddess in my own right, as well as your wife, Lord Yama."

"What does that mean?"

"I make my own decisions."

"If you accept, Kali, then all things are come to an end between us."

"That is apparent."

"What, in the names of the Rishis, is Accelerationism but a storm over an ant hill? Why are they suddenly so against it?"

"It must be that they feel a need to be against something."

"Why choose you to head it?"

"I do not know."

"Unless there is some special reason for you to be anti-Accelerationist, my dear?"

"I do not know."

"I am but young, as gods go, but I have heard it said that in the early days of the world the hero with whom you rode—Kalkin—was the same as the one called Sam. If you had reason to hate your ancient Lord, and Sam was truly he, then could I see their enlisting you against this thing he had started. Might this be true?"

"It might."

"Then if you love me—and you are truly my lady—then let another be Brahma."

"Yama . . ."

"They will want a decision within the hour."

"And I will have one for them."

"What will it be?"

"I am sorry, Yama . . ."

Yama departed the Garden of Joys before dinner-time. Though it seemed an unhealthy breach of etiquette, Yama, among all the gods, was deemed hardest to discipline and was aware of this fact, as well as the reasons that lay behind it. So he left the Garden of Joys and journeyed to the place where Heaven stops.

He dwelled that day and that night at Worldsend, nor was he disturbed by any callers. He spent time in each of the five rooms in the Pavilion of Silence. His thoughts being his own, you leave them alone, too. In the morning, he returned to the Celestial City.

There, he learned of the death of Shiva.

His trident had burnt another hole in the dome, but his head had been smashed in by means of a blunt instrument, as yet unlocated.

Yama went to his friend Kubera.

"Ganesha, Vishnu and the new Brahma have already approached Agni, to fill the place of the Destroyer," said Kubera. "I believe he will accept."

"Excellent, for Agni," said Yama. "Who killed God?"

"I have thought much upon it," said Kubera, "and I believe that in the case of Brahma it must have been someone with whom he was sufficiently familiar to have taken refreshment, and in the case of Shiva, someone well enough known to have surprised him. More than this deponent knoweth not."

"The same person?"

"I'd bet money."

"Could it be part of an Accelerationist plot?"

"I find this difficult to believe. Those who are sympathetic to Accelerationism have no real organization. Accelerationism is returned too recently to Heaven for it to amount to more than that. A cabal, perhaps. Most likely a single individual did it, independent of backers."

"What other reasons might be present?"

"A vendetta. Or some minor deity out to become a major one. Why does anybody kill anybody?"

"Can you think of anyone in particular?"

"The biggest problem, Yama, will be eliminating suspects, not finding them. Has the investigation been given into your hands?"

"I am no longer certain. I think so. But I will find who did it, whatever his station, and kill him."

"Why?"

"I have need of something to do, someone to . . ."

"Kill?"

"Yes."

"I am sorry, my friend."

"I, also. It is my privilege and my intention, however."

"I wish you had not spoken with me at all, concerning this matter. It is obviously quite confidential."

"I won't tell anyone if you won't."

"I assure you I shan't."

"And you know I'll take care of the karmic trackings, against the psych-probe."

"That is why I mentioned it, and spoke of Shiva also. Let it be so."

"Good day, my friend."

"Good day, Yama."

Yama departed the Pavilion of the Lokapalas. After a time, the goddess Ratri entered there.

"Hail, Kubera."

"Hail, Ratri."

"Why sit you there alone?"

"Because I have none to make me unalone. Why come you here—alone?"

"Because I had none to talk with, till now."

"Seek you counsel, or conversation?"

"Both."

"Sit down."

"Thank you. I am afraid."

"Are you hungry, too?"

"No."

"Have a piece of fruit and a cup of soma."

"All right."

"What is it that you fear, and how may I help you?"

"I saw Lord Yama leaving here . . ."

"Yes."

"I realized when I looked upon his face that there *is*

a god of Death, and that there is a power which even gods might fear . . ."

"Yama is strong, and he is my friend. Death is mighty, and is no one's friend. The two exist together though, and it is strange. Agni is strong also, and is Fire. *He* is my friend. Krishna could be strong if he wished. But he never wishes so. He wears out bodies at a fantastic rate. He drinks soma and makes music and women. He hates the past and the future. He is my friend. I am least among the Lokapalas, and I am not strong. Whatever body I wear goes quickly to fat. I am more father than brother to my three friends. Of them, I can appreciate the drunkenness and the music and the loving and the fire, for these are things of life, and so can I love my friends as men or as gods. But the other Yama makes me to be afraid, also, Ratri. For when he takes upon him his Aspect he is a vacuum, which sets this poor fat a-tremble. Then he is no one's friend. So do not feel awkward if you fear my friend. You know that when a god is troubled, then his Aspect rushes to comfort him, oh goddess of the Night, as even now if becomes twilight within this bower, though the day is far from ended. Know that you passed a troubled Yama."

"He returned fairly suddenly."

"Yes."

"May I ask why?"

"I am afraid the matter is confidential."

"Does it concern Brahma?"

"Why do you ask?"

"I believe Brahma is dead. I fear that Yama was summoned to find his slayer. I fear he will find me, though I call down a century of night upon Heaven. He will find me, and I cannot face the vacuum."

"What do you know regarding this alleged slaying?"

"I believe I was either the last to see Brahma alive or the first to see him dead, depending upon what his twitching signified."

"What were the circumstances?"

"I had gone to his Pavilion early yesterday morning, to intercede with him that he might lift his wrath and permit the return of Lady Parvati. I was told to seek him in the Garden of His Joys, and I walked there—"

"Told? Who told you?"

"One of his women. I don't know her name."

"Go ahead. What happened then?"

"I found him at the foot of the blue statue which plays upon the *veena*. He was twitching. There was no breathing. Then he stopped twitching even and was still. There was no heartbeat and no pulse that I could feel. So I called back a portion of the night to cloak me in shadows and departed the Garden."

"Why did you not summon assistance? It still might not have been too late."

"Because I wanted him to die, of course. I hated him for what he did to Sam, and for the driving away of Parvati and Varuna, and for what he did to the Archivist, Tak, and for—"

"Enough. One could go on all day thus. Did you depart directly from the Garden, or did you stop back at the Pavilion?"

"I passed the Pavilion and saw the same girl. I made myself visible to her and told her that I could not locate Brahma and would return later. . . . He *is* dead, isn't he? What shall I do now?"

"Have another piece of fruit and some more soma. Yes, he's dead."

"Will Yama come after me?"

"Of course. He will go after everyone who was seen anywhere near there. It was doubtless a reasonably quick-acting poison, and you were there right near the time of death. So naturally he will go after you—and he will have you psych-probed, along with all the others. This will reveal that you did not do it. So I suggest you simply await being called into custody. Do not tell anyone else this story."

"What shall I tell Yama?"

"If he reaches you before I reach him, tell him

everything, including the fact that you have spoken with me. This is because I am not even supposed to know that this thing has occurred. The passing of one among Trimurti is always kept secret for as long as possible, even at the expense of lives."

"But the Lords of Karma would read it from your memory when you stood to a judgment."

"Just so they do not read it from your memory today. The knowledge of Brahma's passing will be kept to as small a group as possible. Since Yama may be conducting the official investigation and is also the designer of the psych-probe, I don't think any yellow wheel people will be dragged in to run the machines. Still, I must confirm this fact with Yama—or suggest it to him—immediately."

"Before you go . . ."

"Yes?"

"You said that only a few may know of this thing, even if lives must be spent. Does this mean that I . . . ?"

"No. You will live, because I will protect you."

"Why will you?"

"Because you are my friend."

Yama operated the machine that probes the mind. He probed thirty-seven subjects, all of whom could have had access to Brahma in his Garden during the entire day prior to the deicide. Of these, eleven were gods or goddesses, including Ratri, Sarasvati, Vayu, Mara, Lakshmi, Murugan, Agni and Krishna.

Of these thirty-seven, gods and men, none was found to be guilty.

Kubera the artificer stood at Yama's side, and he regarded the psych-tapes.

"What now, Yama?"

"I do not know."

"Mayhap the killer was invisible."

"Perhaps."

"But you think not?"

"I think not."

"Supposing everybody in the City were made to stand the probe?"

"There are many arrivals and departures every day, via many entrances and exits."

"Have you given thought to the possibility of its having been one of the Rakasha? They are again abroad in the world, as well you know—and they hate us."

"The Rakasha do not poison their victims. Also, I do not believe one could enter the Garden, because of the demon-repelling incense."

"What now?"

"I shall return to my laboratory, and think."

"May I accompany you to the Vasty Hall of Death?"

"If you wish."

Kubera returned with Yama; and while Yama thought, Kubera perused his master-tapes index, which he had set up when experimenting with the first probe-machines. They were discarded, they were incomplete, of course; only the Lords of Karma kept up to date life-record tapes on everyone in the Celestial City. Kubera knew this, of course.

The printing press was rediscovered in a place called Keenset, by the river Vedra. Experiments with sophisticated plumbing were also going on in this place. Two very fine Temple artists also appeared on the scene, and an old glasscutter made a pair of bifocals and began grinding out more. Therefore, indications were that one of the city-states was undergoing a renaissance.

Brahma decided it was time to move against Accelerationism.

A war party was raised in Heaven, and the Temples of cities adjacent to Keenset sent out the call to the faithful to be ready for a holy war.

Shiva the Destroyer bore only a token trident, for his real faith lay with the wand of fire that he wore at his side.

Brahma, of the golden saddle and silver spurs, bore a sword, a wheel and a bow.

The new Rudra bore the bow and quiver of the old.

Lord Mara wore a shimmering cloak, which changed colors constantly, and none could tell what manner of weapons he bore or what sort of chariot he mounted. For to stare upon him overlong was to feel one's head swim, and things changed their shapes about him, save for his horses, whose mouths constantly dripped blood, which smoked where it fell.

Then, from among the demigods were fifty chosen, still struggling to discipline erratic Attributes, eager to strengthen Aspect and gain merit through battle.

Krishna declined battle and went off to play his pipes in Kaniburrha.

He found him lying upon a grassy hillside beyond the City, staring up into the star-filled sky.

"Good evening."

He turned his head and nodded.

"How goes it with you, good Kubera?"

"Well enough, Lord Kalkin. And yourself?"

"Quite well. Have you a cigarette upon your most impressive person?"

"I am never far from them."

"Thank you."

"Light?"

"Yes."

"Was that a jackbird that circled the Buddha before Madam Kali tore his guts out?"

"Let us speak of pleasanter matters."

"You killed a weak Brahma and a mighty one has replaced him."

"Oh?"

"You killed a strong Shiva, but an equal strength replaces his."

"Life is full of changes."

"What did you hope to gain? Revenge?"

"Revenge is part of the illusion of self. How can a

man kill that which neither lives nor dies truly, but which exists only as a reflection of the Absolute?"

"You did a pretty good job of it, though, even if, as you say, it was only a rearrangement."

"Thank you."

"But why did you do it? . . . And I'd prefer an answer to a tract."

"I intended to wipe out the entire hierarchy of Heaven. It would seem now, though, that this must go the way of all good intentions."

"Tell me why you did it."

"If you'll tell me how you found me out . . ."

"Fair enough. Tell me, why?"

"I decided that mankind could live better without gods. If I disposed of them all, people could start having can openers and cans to open again, and things like that, without fearing the wrath of Heaven. We've stepped on these poor fools enough. I wanted to give them a chance to be free, to build what they wanted."

"But they live, and they live and they live."

"Sometimes, and sometimes not. So do the gods."

"You were about the last Accelerationist left in the world, Sam. No one would have thought you were also the deadliest."

"How did you find me out?"

"It occurred to me that Sam would be the number one suspect, except for the fact that he was dead."

"I had assumed that to be sufficient defense against detection."

"So I asked myself if there was any means by which Sam could have escaped death. I could think of none, other than a change of bodies. Who, I then asked myself, took upon him a new body the day Sam died? There was only Lord Murugan. This did not seem logical, however, because he did it *after* Sam's death, not before it. I dismissed that part for a moment. You—Murugan—having been among the thirty-seven suspects, were probed and passed upon as innocent by Lord Yama. It seemed I had surely taken to a false trail then—until I thought of a very simple way to test the notion. Yama can beat the psych-probe himself, so why could not someone else be able to do it? I recalled at this point that Kalkin's Attribute *had* involved the control of lightnings and electromagnetic phenomena. He could have sabotaged the machine with his mind so that it saw there no evil. The way of testing it, therefore, was not to consider what the machine had read, but rather *how* it had read it. Like the prints of the palms and the fingers of the hands, no two minds register the same patterns. But from body to body one does retain a similar mind-matrix, despite the fact that a different brain's involved. Regardless of the thoughts passing through the mind, the thought patterns record themselves unique to the person. I compared yours with a record of Murugan's which I found in Yama's laboratory. They were not the same. I do not know how you accomplished the body-change, but I knew you for what you were."

"Very clever, Kubera. Who else is familiar with this strange reasoning?"

"No one, yet. Yama, soon though, I fear. He always solves problems."

"Why do you place your life in jeopardy by seeking me thus?"

"One does not generally achieve your age, my age, without being somewhat reasonable. I knew you would at least listen to me before striking. I know, too, that since what I have to say is good no harm will come to me."

"What do you propose?"

"I am sufficiently sympathetic with what you have done to assist you in escaping from Heaven."

"Thank you, no."

"You would like to win this contest, would you not?"

"Yes, and I'll do it in my own way."

"How?"

"I will return to the City now and destroy as many

of them as I can before they stop me. If enough of the great ones fall, the others will not be able to hold this place together."

"And if you fall? What then of the world, and of the cause you have championed? Will you be able to rise again to defend it?"

"I do not know."

"How *did* you manage the comeback?"

"One time was I possessed of a demon. He rather took a liking to me, and he told me at a time when we were in peril that he had 'strengthened my flames,' so that I could exist independent of my body. I had forgotten this until I saw my mangled corpse lying beneath me upon the streets of Heaven. I knew of only one place where I might get me another body, that being the Pavilion of the Gods of Karma. Murugan was there demanding service. As you say, my power is electrodirection. I learned there that it works without a brain to back it, as the circuits were momentarily interrupted and I went into Murugan's new body and Murugan went to hell."

"The fact that you tell me all of this seems to indicate that you intend to send me after him."

"I am sorry, good Kubera, for I like you. If you will give me your word that you will forget what you have learned and that you will wait for some other to discover it, then I will permit you to live and depart."

"Risky."

"I know that you have never given your word and broken it, though you are as old as the hills of Heaven."

"Who is the first god you would slay?"

"Lord Yama, of course, for he must be closest upon my heels."

"Then must you kill me, Sam, for he is a brother Lokapala and my friend."

"I am sure we will both regret it if I have to kill you."

"Then has your acquaintanceship with the Rakasha

perhaps given you some of their taste for a wager?"

"Of what sort?"

"You win, and you have my word not to speak of this. I win, and you flee with me upon the back of Garuda."

"And of the contest?"

"Irish stand-down."

"With you, fat Kubera? And me in my magnificent new body?"

"Yes."

"Then you may strike first."

On a dark hill on the far side of Heaven, Sam and Kubera stood facing one another.

Kubera drew back his right fist and sent it forward against Sam's jaw.

Sam fell, lay still for a moment, rose slowly to his feet.

Rubbing his jaw, he returned to the spot where he had stood.

"You are stronger than you seem, Kubera," he said, and struck forward.

Kubera lay upon the ground, sucking in air.

He tried to rise, thought better of it, moaned once, then struggled back to his feet.

"I didn't think you'd get up," said Sam.

Kubera moved to face him, a dark, moist line descending his chin.

As he took his ground, Sam flinched.

Kubera waited, still breathing deeply.

Run down the gray night wall. Flee! Beneath a rock. Hide! The fury turns thy bowels to water. The friction of this crossing grates upon thy spine. . . .

"Strike!" said Sam, and Kubera smiled and hit him.

He lay there quivering, and the voices of the night, compounded of insect sounds and the wind and the sighing of grasses came to him.

Tremble, like the last loosening leaf of the year. There is a lump of ice in thy chest. There are no words within thy brain, only the colors of panic move there. . . .

Sam shook his head and rose to his knees.

Fall again, curl thyself into a ball and weep. For this is how man began, and this is how he ends. The universe is a black ball, rolling. It crusheth what it toucheth. It rolls to thee. Flee! Thou might a moment gain, an hour perhaps, before it comes upon thee. . . .

He raised his hands to his face, lowered them, glared up at Kubera, stood.

"You built the room called Fear," he said, "at the Pavilion of Silence. I remember now your power, old god. It is not sufficient."

An invisible horse races through pastures of thy mind. Thou knowest him by his hoof marks, each of which is a wound. . . .

Sam took his position, clenched his fist.

The sky creaks above thee. The ground may open beneath thy feet. And what is that tall, shadowlike thing that comes to stand at thy back?

Sam's fist shook, but he drove it forward.

Kubera rocked back upon his heels and his head snapped to the side, but he did not lose his footing.

Sam stood there trembling as Kubera drew back his right arm for the final blow.

"Old god, you cheat," he said.

Kubera smiled through his blood, and his fist came forward like a black ball.

Yama was talking to Ratri when the cry of awakened Garuda broke the night.

"This thing has never happened before," he said.

Slowly, the heavens began to open.

"Perhaps Lord Vishnu goes forth . . ."

"He has never done so at night. And when I spoke with him a short time ago he said nothing of this."

"Then some other god would dare his mount."

"No! To the pens, Lady! Quickly! I may have need of thy powers."

He dragged her forward with him, toward the steel aerie of the Bird.

Garuda was awake and untethered, but the hood was still upon him.

Kubera, who had carried Sam to the pens, strapped him into the saddle seat, still unconscious.

He climbed down to the floor and activated a final control. The top of the cage rolled away. Then he took up the long metal pinion hook and moved back to the rope ladder. The bird smell was overpowering. Garuda shifted restlessly and ruffled feathers twice the size of a man.

Slowly, he climbed.

As he was strapping himself into place, Yama and Ratri approached the cage.

"Kubera! What madness is this?" cried Yama. "You have never been fond of the heights!"

"Urgent business, Yama," he replied, "and it would take a day to finish servicing the thunder chariot."

"What business, Kubera? And why not take a gondola?"

"Garuda's faster. I'll tell you about it on my return."

"Perhaps I can be of help."

"No. Thank you."

"But Lord Murugan can?"

"In this case, yes."

"You two were never on the best of terms."

"Nor are we now. But I have need of his services."

"Hail, Murugan! . . . Why does he not reply?"

"He sleeps, Yama."

"There is blood upon your face, brother."

"I had a small accident earlier."

"And Murugan appears somewhat mishandled also."

"It was the same accident."

"Something is amiss here, Kubera. Wait, I'm coming into the cage."

"Stay out, Yama!"

"The Lokapalas do not order one another about. We are equals."

"Stay out, Yama! I'm raising Garuda's hood!"

"Don't do it!"

Yama's eyes suddenly flashed and he stood taller within his red.

Kubera leaned forward with the hook and raised the hood from the Bird's high head. Garuda threw his head back and cried once more.

"Ratri," said Yama, "lay shadows upon Garuda's eyes, that he may not see."

Yama moved toward the entrance of the cage. Darkness, like a thundercloud, hid the head of the Bird.

"Ratri!" said Kubera. "Lift this darkness and lay it upon Yama, or all is lost!"

Ratri hesitated only a moment, and this was done.

"Come to me quickly!" he cried. "Come mount Garuda and ride with us! We need you, badly!"

She entered the cage and was lost to sight, as the darkness kept spreading and spreading, like a pool of ink, Yama groping his way through it.

The ladder jerked and swayed, and Ratri mounted Garuda.

Garuda screamed then and leapt into the air, for Yama had moved forward, blade in hand, and had cut at the first thing he had felt.

The night rushed about them and Heaven lay far below.

When they reached a mighty height, the dome began to close.

Garuda sped toward the gate, screaming again.

They were through it before it closed, and Kubera prodded the Bird.

"Where are we going?" asked Ratri.

"To Keenset, by the river Vedra," he answered. "And this is Sam. He is still alive."

"What has happened?"

"He is the one Yama seeks."

"Will he seek him in Keenset?"

"Doubtless, lady. Doubtless. But ere he finds him, we may be better prepared."

In the days that preceded the Great Battle, the defenders came to Keenset. Kubera and Sam and Ratri brought the warning. Keenset was already aware of the raising of its neighbors, but not of the heavenly avengers who were to come.

Sam drilled the troops who would fight against gods, and Kubera drilled those who would fight against men.

Black armor was forged for the goddess of Night, of whom it has been said, "Guard us from the she-wolf and the wolf, and guard us from the thief, of Night."

And on the third day there was a tower of fire before Sam's tent on the plane outside the city.

"It is the Lord of Hellwell come to keep his promise, oh Siddhartha!" said the voice that rang within his head.

"Taraka! How did you find me—recognize me?"

"I look upon the flames, which are your true being, not the flesh which masks them. You know that."

"I thought you dead."

"I nearly was. Those two *do* drink life with their eyes! Even the life of one such as I."

"I told you that. Do you bring your legions with you?"

"Yes, I bring my legions."

"It is good. The gods will move against this place soon."

"I know. Many times have I visited Heaven atop its mountain of ice, and my spies remain there yet. So I know that they make ready to come to this place. They also invite humans to share in the battle. Though they do not feel they need the assistance of men, they think it good that they join in the destruction of the city Keenset."

"Yes, that is understandable," said Sam, studying the

great vortex of yellow flame. "What other news have you?"

"The One in Red comes."

"I expected him."

"To his death. I must defeat him."

"He will have demon-repellant upon him."

"Then I will find a way to remove it, or kill him from a distance. He will be here by nightfall."

"How does he come?"

"In a flying machine—not so large as the chariot of thunder we tried to steal—but very fast. I could not attack it in flight."

"Comes he alone?"

"Yes—save for machines."

"Machines?"

"Many machines. His flying machine is filled with strange equipment."

"This may bode ill."

The tower spun orange.

"But others come also."

"You just said he comes alone."

"This is true."

"Then riddle me your true meaning."

"The others do not come from Heaven."

"Where, then?"

"I have traveled much since your departure for Heaven, going up and down in the world and seeking allies among those who also hate the Gods of the City. By the way, in your last incarnation I *did* try to save you from the cats out of Kaniburrha."

"I know."

"The gods *are* strong—stronger than they have ever been before."

"But tell me who is coming to aid us."

"Lord Nirriti the Black, who hates all things, hates the Gods of the City most of all. So he is sending a thousand unliving ones to fight on the plains beside the Vedra. He said that, after the battle, we of the Rakasha may take our choice from the bodies which yet remain among the mindless ones he has grown."

"I do not relish aid from the Black One, but I am in no position to discriminate. How soon will these arrive?"

"Tonight. But Dalissa will be here sooner. Even now, I feel her approaching."

"Dalissa? Who . . . ?"

"The last of the Mothers of the Terrible Glow. She alone escaped into the depths when Durga and Lord Kalkin rode to the dome by the sea. All her eggs were smashed and she can lay no more, but she bears within her body the burning power of the sea-glow."

"And you think she would aid *me?*"

"She would aid no other. She is the last of her kind. She will only assist a peer."

"Then know that the one who was known as Durga now wears the body of Brahma, chief among our enemies."

"Yes, which makes both of you men. She might have taken the other side, had Kali remained a woman. But she has committed herself now. You were her choice."

"That helps to even things a bit."

"The Rakasha herd elephants and slizzards and great cats at this time, to drive against our enemies."

"Good."

"And they summon fire elementals."

"Very good."

"Dalissa is near here now. She will wait at the bottom of the river, to rise up when she is needed."

"Say hello to her for me," said Sam, turning to re-enter his tent.

"I will."

He dropped the flap behind him.

When the God of Death came down out of the sky onto the plains beside the Vedra, Taraka of the Rakasha set upon him in the form of a great cat out of Kaniburrha.

But immediately he fell back. The demon repellant lay upon Yama, and Taraka could not close with him because of it.

The Rakasha swirled away, dropping the cat form he had assumed, to become a whirlwind of silver motes.

"Deathgod!" the word exploded in Yama's head. "Remember Hellwell?"

Immediately, rocks and stones and sandy soil were sucked up into the vortex and hurled across the air toward Yama, who swirled his cloak and muffled his eyes with its hem, but did not otherwise stir.

After a time, the fury died.

Yama had not moved. The ground about him was strewn with debris, but none lay near him.

Yama lowered his cloak and glared into the whirlwind.

"What sorcery is this?" came the words. "How is it you manage to stand?"

Yama continued to stare at Taraka. "How is it you manage to swirl?" he asked.

"I am greatest among the Rakasha. I bore your death-gaze before."

"And I am greatest among the gods. I stood against your entire legion at Hellwell."

"You are a lackey to Trimurti."

"You are wrong. I have come here to fight against Heaven, in this place, in the name of Accelerationism. Great is my hatred, and I have brought weapons to be used against Trimurti."

"Then I suppose I must forego the pleasure of continuing our combat at this time . . ."

"I should deem it advisable."

"And you doubtless wish to be taken to our leader?"

"I can find my own way."

"Then, until we meet again, Lord Yama . . ."

"Good-bye, Rakasha."

Taraka shot like a burning arrow into the heavens and was gone from sight.

Some say that Yama had solved his case as he stood there in the great birdcage, amidst the darkness and the droppings. Others say that he duplicated Kubera's reasoning a short while later, using the tapes in the Vasty Hall of Death. Whichever it was, when he entered the tent on the plains by the Vedra he greeted the man inside with the name Sam. This man laid his hand upon his blade and faced him.

"Death, you precede the battle," he said.

"There has been a change," Yama replied.

"What sort of change?"

"Position. I have come here to oppose the will of Heaven."

"In what way?"

"Steel. Fire. Blood."

"Why this change?"

"Divorces are made in Heaven. And betrayals. And shamings. The lady has gone too far, and I know now the reason, Lord Kalkin. I neither embrace your Accelerationism nor do I reject it. Its only mattering to me is that it represents the one force in the world to oppose Heaven. I will join you, with this understanding, if you will accept my blade."

"I accept your blade, Lord Yama."

"And I will raise it against any of the heavenly horde—saving only Brahma himself, whom I will not face."

"Agreed."

"Then permit me to serve as your charioteer."

"I would, only I have no chariot of battle."

"I brought one, a very special one. For a long time have I labored upon it, and it is not yet complete. But it will suffice. I must assemble it this night, however, for the battle will commence tomorrow at dawn."

"I have felt that it might. The Rakasha have warned me as to the movement of troops near here."

"Yes, I saw them as I passed overhead. The main attack should come from the northeast, across the plains. The gods will join in later. But there will doubtless be parties coming from all directions, including up the river."

"We control the river. Dalissa of the Glow waits at its bottom. When the time comes, she can raise up mighty waves, making it to boil and overflow its banks."

"I had thought the Glow extinguished!"

"Save for her, it is. She is the last."

"I take it the Rakasha will be fighting with us?"

"Yes, and others . . ."

"What others?"

"I have accepted assistance—bodies without minds—a war party of such—from Lord Nirriti."

Yama's eyes narrowed and his nostrils flared.

"This is not good, Siddhartha. Sooner or later, he will have to be destroyed, and it is not good to be in the debt of such a one."

"I know that, Yama, but I am desperate. They arrive tonight . . ."

"If we win, Siddhartha, toppling the Celestial City, breaking the old religion, freeing man for industrial progress, still will there be opposition. Nirriti, who has waited all these centuries for the passing of the gods, will then have to be fought and beaten himself. It will either be this or the same thing all over again—and at least the Gods of the City have some measure of grace in their unfair doings."

"I think he would have come to our assistance whether invited or not."

"Yes, but by inviting him, or accepting his offer, you owe him this thing."

"Then I will have to deal with that situation when it arises."

"That's politics, I guess. But I like it not."

Sam poured them of the sweet dark wine of Keenset. "I think Kubera would like to see you later," he said, offering a goblet.

"What is he doing?" asked Yama, accepting it and draining it off in a single swallow.

"Drilling troops and giving classes on the internal combustion engine to all the local savants," said Sam. "Even if we lose, some may live and go elsewhere."

"If it is to be put to any use, they will need to know more than engine design . . ."

"He's been talking himself hoarse for days, and the scribes are taking it all down—geology, mining, metallurgy, petroleum chemistry . . ."

"Had we more time, I would give my assistance. As it is, if ten per cent is retained it may be sufficient. Not tomorrow, or even the next day, but . . ."

Sam finished his wine, refilled the goblets. "To the morrow, charioteer!"

"To the blood, Binder, to the blood and the killing!"

"Some of the blood may be our own, deathgod. But so long as we take sufficient of the enemy with us . . ."

"I cannot die, Siddhartha, save by my own choosing."

"How can that be, Lord Yama?"

"Let Death keep his own small secrets, Binder. For I may choose not to exercise my option in this battle."

"As you would, Lord."

"To your health and long life!"

"To yours."

The day of the battle dawned pink as the fresh-bitten thigh of a maiden.

A small mist drifted in from the river. The Bridge of the Gods glistened all of gold in the east, reached back, darkening, into retreating night, divided the heavens like a burning equator.

The warriors of Keenset waited outside the city, upon the plain by the Vedra. Five thousand men, with blades and bows, pikes and slings, waited for the battle. A thousand zombies stood in the front ranks, led by the living sergeants of the Black One, who guided all their movements by the drum, scarves of black silk curling in the breeze like snakes of smoke upon their helms.

Five hundred lancers were held to the rear. The

silver cyclones that were the Rakasha hung in the middle air. Across the half-lit world the occasional growl of a jungle beast could be heard. Fire elementals glowed upon tree limb, lance and pennon pole.

There were no clouds in the heavens. The grasses of the plain were still moist and sparkling. The air was cool, the ground still soft enough to gather footprints readily. Gray and green and yellow were the colors that smote the eye beneath the heavens; and the Vedra swirled within its banks, gathering leaves from its escort of trees. It is said that each day recapitulates the history of the world, coming up out of darkness and cold into confused light and beginning warmth, consciousness blinking its eyes somewhere in midmorning, awakening thoughts a jumble of illogic and unattached emotion, and all speeding together toward the order of noontide, the slow, poignant decline of dusk, the mystical vision of twilight, the end of entropy that is night once more.

The day began.

A dark line was visible at the far end of the field. A trumpet note cut the air and that line advanced.

Sam stood in his battle chariot at the head of the formation, wearing burnished armor and holding a long, gray lance of death. He heard the words of Death, who wore red and was his charioteer:

"Their first wave is of slizzard cavalry."

Sam squinted at the distant line.

"It is," said his charioteer.

"Very well."

He gestured with his lance, and the Rakasha moved forward like a tidal wave of white light. The zombies began their advance.

When the white wave and the dark line came together there was a confusion of voices, hisses and the rattle of arms.

The dark line halted, great gouts of dust fuming above it.

Then came the sounds of the aroused jungle as the

gathered beasts of prey were driven upon the flank of the enemy.

The zombies marched to a slow, steady drumbeat, and the fire elementals flowed on before them and the grasses withered where they passed.

Sam nodded to Death, and his chariot moved slowly forward, riding upon its cushion of air. At his back, the army of Keenset stirred. Lord Kubera slept, drugged to the sleep that is like unto death, in a hidden vault beneath the city. The Lady Ratri mounted a black mare at the rear of the lancers' formation.

"Their charge has been broken," said Death.

"Yes."

"All their cavalry was cast down and the beasts still rage among them. They have not yet reformed their ranks. The Rakasha hurl avalanches like rain from the heavens down upon their heads. Now there comes the flow of fire."

"Yes."

"We will destroy them. Even now they see the mindless minions of Nirriti coming upon them as a single man, all in step and without fear, their drums keeping time, perfect and agonizing, and nothing behind their eyes, nothing at all. Looking above their heads then, they see us here as within a thundercloud, and they see that Death drives your chariot. Within their hearts there comes a quickening and there is a coldness upon their biceps and their thighs. See how the beasts pass among them?"

"Yes."

"Let there be no bugles within our ranks, Siddhartha. For this is not battle, but slaughter."

"Yes."

The zombies slew everything they passed, and when they fell they went down without a word, for it was all the same with them, and words mean nothing to the unliving.

They swept the field, and fresh waves of warriors came at them. But the cavalry had been broken. The foot soldiers could not stand before the lancers and the Rakasha, the zombies and the infantry of Keenset.

The razor-edged battle chariot driven by Death cut through the enemy like a flame through a field. Missiles and hurled spears turned in mid-flight to speed off at right angles before they could touch upon the chariot or its occupants. Dark fires danced within the eyes of Death as he gripped the twin rings with which he directed the course of the vehicle. Again and again, he drove down without mercy upon the enemy, and Sam's lance darted like the tongue of a serpent as they passed through the ranks.

From somewhere, the notes of a retreat were sounded. But there were very few who answered the call.

"Wipe your eyes, Siddhartha," said Death, "and call a new formation. The time has come to press the attack. Manjusri of the Sword must order a charge."

"Yes, Death, I know."

"We hold the field, but not the day. The gods are watching, judging our strength."

Sam raised his lance in signal and there was fresh movement among the troops. Then a new stillness hung about them. Suddenly, there was no wind, no sound. The sky was blue. The ground was a gray-green trampled thing. Dust, like a specter hedge, hovered in the distance.

Sam surveyed the ranks, moved his lance forward.

At that moment, there came a clap of thunder.

"The gods will enter the field," said Death, looking upward.

The thunder chariot passed overhead. No rain of destruction descended, however.

"Why are we still alive?" asked Sam.

"I believe they would rather our defeat be more ignominious. Also, they may be afraid to attempt to use the thunder chariot against its creator—justly afraid."

"In that case . . ." said Sam, and he gave the signal for the troops to charge.

The chariot bore him forward.

At his back, the forces of Keenset followed.

They cut down the stragglers. They smashed through the guard that attempted to delay them. In the midst of a storm of arrows, they broke the archers. Then they faced the body of the holy crusaders who had sworn to level the city of Keenset.

Then there came the notes of Heaven upon a trumpet.

The opposing lines of human warriors parted.

The fifty demigods rode forth.

Sam raised his lance.

"Siddhartha," said Death, "Lord Kalkin was never beaten in battle."

"I know."

"I have with me the Talisman of the Binder. That which was destroyed upon the pyre at Worldsend was a counterfeit. I retained the original to study it. I never had the chance. Hold but a moment and I will brace it about you."

Sam raised his arms and Death clasped the belt of shells around his waist.

He gave sign then to the forces of Keenset to halt.

Death drove him forward, alone, to face the half-gods.

About the heads of some there played the nimbus of early Aspect. Others bore strange weapons to focus their strange Attributes. Fires came down and licked about the chariot. Winds lashed at it. Great smashing noises fell upon it. Sam gestured with his lance and the first three of his opponents reeled and fell from the backs of their slizzards.

Then Death drove his chariot among them.

Its edges are razors and its speed three times that of a horse and twice that of a slizzard.

A mist sprang up about him as he rode, a mist tinged with blood. Heavy missiles sped toward him and vanished to one side or the other. Ultrasonic screams assailed his ears, but somehow were partly deadened.

His face expressionless, Sam raised his lance high above his head.

A look of sudden fury crossed over his face, and the lightnings leapt from its tip.

Slizzards and riders baked and crisped.

The smell of charred flesh came to his nostrils.

He laughed, and Death wheeled the chariot for another pass.

"Are you watching me?" Sam screamed at the heavens. "Watch on, then! And watch out! You just made a mistake!"

"Don't!" said Death. "It is too soon! Never mock a god until he is passed!"

And the chariot swept through the ranks of the demigods once again, and none could touch upon it.

Trumpet notes filled the air, and the holy army rushed to succor its champions.

The warriors of Keenset moved forward to engage them.

Sam stood in the chariot and the missiles fell heavy about it, always missing. Death drove him through the ranks of the enemy, now like a wedge, now like a rapier. He sang as he moved, and his lance was the tongue of a serpent, sometimes crackling as it fell with bright flashes. The Talisman glowed with a pale fire about his waist.

"We'll take them!" he said.

"There are only demigods and men upon the field," said Death. "They are still testing our strength. There are very few who remember the full power of Kalkin."

"The *full* power of Kalkin?" asked Sam. "That has never been released, oh Death. Not in all the ages of the world. Let them come against me now and the heavens will weep upon their bodies and the Vedra run the color of blood! ... Do you hear me? Do you hear me, gods? Come against me! I challenge you, here upon this field! Meet me with your strength, in this place!"

"No!" said Death. "Not yet!"

Overhead, the thunder chariot passed once again.

Sam raised his lance and pyrotechnic hell broke loose about the passing vessel.

"You should not have let them know you could do that! Not yet!"

The voice of Taraka came to him then, across the din of the battle and the song within his brain.

"They come up the river now, oh Binder! And another party assails the gates of the city!"

"Call then upon Dalissa to rise up and make the Vedra to boil with the power of the Glow! Take you of the Rakasha to the gates of Keenset and destroy the invader!"

"I hear, Binder!" and Taraka was gone.

A beam of blinding light fell from the thunder chariot and cut through the ranks of the defenders.

"The time has come," said Death, and he waved his cloak in gesture.

In the rearmost rank, the Lady Ratri stood up in the stirrups of her mount, the black mare. She raised the black veil that she wore over her armor.

There were screams from both sides as the sun covered its face and darkness descended upon the field. The stalk of light vanished from beneath the thunder chariot and the burning ceased.

Only a faint phosphorescence, with no apparent source, occurred about them. This happened as the Lord Mara swept onto the field in his cloudy chariot of colors, drawn by the horses who vomited rivers of smoking blood.

Sam headed toward him, but a great body of warriors interposed themselves; and before they won through, Mara had driven across the field, slaying everyone in his path.

Sam raise his lance and scowled, but his target blurred and shifted; and the lightnings always fell behind or to the side.

Then, in the distance, within the river, a soft light began. It pulsed warmly, and something like a tentacle seemed to wave for a moment above the surface of the waters.

Sounds of fighting came from the city. The air was full of demons. The ground seemed to move beneath the feet of the armies.

Sam raised his lance and a jagged line of light ran up into the heavens, provoking a dozen more to descend upon the field.

More beasts growled, coughed and wailed, racing through both ranks, killing as they passed those of both sides.

The zombies continued to slay, beneath the prodding of the dark sergeants, to the steady beating of the drums; and fire elementals clung to the breasts of the corpses, as though feeding.

"We have broken the demigods," said Sam. "Let us try Lord Mara next."

They sought him across the field, amidst screams and wails, crossing over those who were soon to become corpses and those who already were.

When they saw the colors of his chariot, they gave chase.

He turned and faced them finally, in a corridor of darkness, the sounds of the battle dim and distant. Death drew rein also, and they stared across the night into each other's glowing eyes.

"Will you stand to battle, Mara?" cried Sam. "Or must we run you down like a dog?"

"Speak not to me of your kin, the hound and the bitch, oh Binder!" he answered. "It *is* you, isn't it, Kalkin? That's your belt. This is your sort of war. Those were your lightnings striking friend and foe alike. You *did* live, somehow, eh?"

"It is I," said Sam, leveling his lance.

"And the carrion god to drive your wagon!"

Death raised his left hand, palm forward.

"I promise you death, Mara," he said. "If not by the hand of Kalkin, then by my own. If not today, then another day. But it is between us also, now."

To the left, the pulsing in the river became more and more frequent.

Death leaned forward and the chariot sped toward Mara.

The horses of the Dreamer reared and blew fire from their nostrils. They leapt ahead.

The arrows of Rudra sought them in the dark, but these were also turned aside as they blazed toward Death and his chariot. They exploded upon either side, adding for a moment to the faint illumination.

In the distance, elephants lumbered, raced and squealed, pursued by the Rakasha across the plains.

There came a mighty roaring sound.

Mara grew into a giant, and his chariot was a mountain. His horses spanned eternities as they galloped forward. Lightning leapt from Sam's lance, like spray from a fountain. A blizzard suddenly swirled about him, and the cold of interstellar space itself entered into his bones.

At the last possible instant, Mara swerved his chariot and leapt down from it.

They struck it broadside and there came a grinding sound from beneath them as they settled slowly to the ground.

By then the roaring was deafening and the pulses of light from the river had grown into a steady glow. A wave of steaming water swept across the field as the Vedra overflowed its banks.

There were more screams, and the clash of arms continued. Faintly, the drums of Nirriti still beat within the darkness, and there came a strange sound from overhead as the thunder chariot sped toward the ground.

"Where'd he go?" cried Sam.

"To hide," said Death. "But he cannot hide forever."

"Damn it! Are we winning or losing?"

"That's a good question. I don't know the answer, though."

The waters foamed about the grounded chariot.

"Can you get us moving again?"

"Not in this darkness, with the water all around us."

"Then what do we do now?"

"Cultivate patience and smoke cigarettes." He leaned back and struck a light.

After a time, one of the Rakasha came and hovered in the air above them.

"Binder!" reported the demon. "The new attackers of the city wear upon them that-which-repels!"

Sam raised his lance and a line of lightning fled from its point.

For one photoflash of an instant, the field was illuminated.

The dead lay everywhere. Small groups of men huddled together. Some lay twisting in combat upon the ground. The bodies of animals were strewn among them. A few large cats still wandered, feeding. The fire elementals had fled from the water, which had coated the fallen with mud and soaked those who still could stand. Broken chariots and dead slizzards and horses made mounds upon the field. Across the scene, empty-eyed and continuing to follow orders, the zombies wandered, slaying anything living that moved before them. In the distance, one drum still beat, with an occasional falter. From the city there came the sounds of continued battle.

"Find the lady in black," said Sam to the Rakasha, "and tell her to break the darkness."

"Yes," said the demon, and fled back toward the city.

The sun shone again and Sam shielded his eyes against it.

The carnage was even worse under the blue sky and the golden bridge.

Across the field, the thunder chariot rested upon high ground.

The zombies slew the last of the men in sight. Then, as they turned to seek more life, the drumming ceased and they fell to the ground themselves.

Sam stood with Death within the chariot. They looked about them for signs of life.

"Nothing moves," said Sam. "Where are the gods?"

"Perhaps in the thunder chariot."

The Rakasha came to them once more.

"The defenders cannot hold the city," he reported.

"Have the gods joined in that assault?"

"Rudra is there, and his arrows work much havoc."

"The Lord Mara. Brahma, too, I think—and there are many others. There is much confusion. I hurried."

"Where is the Lady Ratri?"

"She entered into Keenset and abides there in her Temple."

"Where are the rest of the gods?"

"I do not know."

"I will go on to the city," said Sam, "and aid in its defense."

"And I to the thunder chariot," said Death, "to take it and use it against the enemy—if it can still be used. If not, there is still Garuda."

"Yes," said Sam, and levitated.

Death sprang down from the chariot. "Fare thee well."

"Thou also."

They crossed the place of carnage, each in his own fashion.

He climbed the small rise, his red leather boots soundless on the turf.

He swept his scarlet cloak back over his right shoulder and surveyed the thunder chariot.

"It was damaged by the lightnings."

"Yes," he agreed.

He looked back toward the tail assembly, at the one who had spoken.

His armor shone like bronze, but it was not bronze.

It was worked about with the forms of many serpents.

He wore the horns of a bull upon his burnished helm, and in his left hand he held a gleaming trident.

"Brother Agni, you have come up in the world."

"I am no longer Agni, but Shiva, Lord of Destruction."

"You wear his armor upon a new body and you carry his trident. But none could master the trident of Shiva so quickly. This is why you wear the white gauntlet on your right hand, and the goggles upon your brow."

Shiva reached up and lowered the goggles over his eyes.

"It is true, I know. Throw away your trident, Agni. Give me your glove and your wand, your belt and your goggles."

He shook his head.

"I respect your power, deathgod, your speed and your strength, your skill. But you stand too far away for any of these to aid you now. You cannot come at me but I will burn you before you reach me here. Death, you shall die."

He reached for the wand at his belt.

"You seek to turn the gift of Death against its giver?" The blood-red scimitar came into his hand as he spoke.

"Good-bye, Dharma. Your days are come to an end."

He drew the wand.

"In the name of a friendship which once existed," said the one in red, "I will give you your life if you surrender to me."

The wand wavered.

"You killed Rudra to defend the name of my wife."

"It was to preserve the honor of the Lokapalas that I did it. Now I am God of Destruction, and one with Trimurti!"

He pointed the fire wand, and Death swirled his scarlet cloak before him.

There came a flash of light so blinding that two miles

away upon the walls of Keenset the defenders saw it and wondered.

The invaders had entered Keenset. There were fires now, screams, and the blows of metal upon wood, metal upon metal.

The Rakasha pushed down buildings upon the invaders with whom they could not close. The invaders as well as the defenders were few in number. The main bodies of both forces had perished upon the plains.

Sam stood atop the highest tower of the Temple and stared down into the falling city.

"I could not save you, Keenset," he stated. "I tried, but was not sufficient."

Far below, in the street, Rudra strung his bow.

Seeing him, Sam raised his lance.

The lightnings fell upon Rudra and the arrow exploded in their midst.

When the air cleared, where Rudra had been standing there was now a small crater in the center of a space of charred ground.

Lord Vayu appeared upon a distant rooftop and called forth the winds to fan the flames. Sam raised his lance once more, but then a dozen Vayus stood upon a dozen rooftops.

"Mara!" said Sam. "Show yourself, Dreamer! If you dare!"

There was laughter all around him.

"When I am ready, Kalkin," came the voice, out of the smoky air, "I *will* dare. The choice, though, is mine to make. . . . Are you not dizzy? What would happen if you were to cast yourself down toward the ground? Would the Rakasha come to bear you up? Would your demons save you?"

Lightnings fell upon all the buildings near the Temple then, but above the noise came the laughter of Mara. It faded away into the distance as fresh fires crackled.

Sam seated himself and watched the city burn. The

sounds of fighting died down and ceased. There was only flame.

A sharp pain came and went in his head. Then it came and would not go. Then it racked his entire body, and he cried out.

Brahma, Vayu, Mara and four demigods stood below in the street.

He tried to raise his lance, but his hand shook so that it fell from his grasp, rattled on brick, was gone.

The scepter that is a skull and a wheel was pointed in his direction.

"Come down, Sam!" said Brahma, moving it slightly so that the pains shifted and burned. "You and Ratri are the only ones left alive! You are the last! Surrender!"

He struggled to his feet and clasped his hands upon his glowing belt.

He swayed and said the words through clenched teeth:

"Very well! I shall come down, as a bomb into your midst!"

But then the sky was darkened, lightened, darkened.

A mighty cry rose above the sound of the flames.

"It is Garuda!" said Mara.

"Why should Vishnu come—now?"

"Garuda was stolen! Do you forget?"

The great Bird dived upon the burning city, like a titan phoenix toward its flaming nest.

Sam twisted his head upward and saw the hood suddenly fall over Garuda's eyes. The Bird fluttered his wings, then plummeted toward the gods, where they stood before the Temple.

"Red!" cried Mara. "The rider! He wears red!"

Brahma spun and turned the screaming scepter, holding it with both hands toward the head of the diving Bird.

Mara gestured, and Garuda's wings seemed to take fire.

Vayu raised both arms, and a wind like a hurricane

hammered the mount of Vishnu, whose beak smashes chariots.

He cried once more, opening his wings, slowing his descent. The Rakasha then rushed about his head, urging him downward with buffets and stings.

He slowed, slowed, but could not stop.

The gods scattered.

Garuda struck the ground and the ground shuddered.

From among the feathers of his back, Yama came forth, blade in hand, took three steps, and fell to the ground. Mara emerged from a ruin and struck him across the back of his neck, twice, with the edge of his hand.

Sam sprang before the second blow descended, but he did not reach the ground in time. The scepter screamed once more and everything spun about him. He fought to break his fall. He slowed.

The ground was forty feet below him—thirty—twenty . . .

The ground was clouded by a blood-dimmed haze, then black.

"Lord Kalkin has finally been beaten in battle," someone said softly.

Brahma, Mara, and two demigods named Bora and Tikan were the only ones who remained to bear Sam and Yama from the dying city of Keenset by the river Vedra. The Lady Ratri walked before them, a cord looped about her neck.

They took Sam and Yama to the thunder chariot, which was even more damaged than it had been when they left it, having a great gaping hole in its right side and part of its tail assembly missing. They secured their prisoners in chains, removing the Talisman of the Binder and the crimson cloak of Death. They sent a message then to Heaven, and after a time sky gondolas came to return them to the Celestial City.

"We have won," said Brahma. "Keenset is no more."

"A costly victory, I think," said Mara.

"But we have won!"

"And the Black One stirs again."

"He sought but to test our strength."

"And what must he think of it? We lost an entire army? And even gods have died this day."

"We fought with Death, the Rakasha, Kalkin, Night and the Mother of the Glow. Nirriti will not lift up his hand against us again, not after a winning such as this."

"Mighty is Brahma," said Mara, and turned away.

The Lords of Karma were called to stand in judgment of the captives.

The Lady Ratri was banished from the City and sentenced to walk the world as a mortal, always to be incarnated into middle-aged bodies of more than usually plain appearance, bodies that could not bear the full power of her Aspect or Attributes. She was shown this mercy because she was judged an incidental accomplice only, one misled by Kubera, whom she had trusted.

When they sent after Lord Yama, to bring him to judgment, he was found to be dead in his cell. Within his turban, there had been a small metal box. This box had exploded.

The Lords of Karma performed an autopsy and conferred.

"Why did he not take poison if he wished to die?" Brahma had asked. "It would be easier to conceal a pill than that box."

"It is barely possible," said one of the Lords of Karma, "that somewhere in the world he had another body, and that he sought to transmigrate by means of a broadcast unit, which was set to destroy itself after use."

"Could this thing be done?"

"No, of course not. Transfer equipment is bulky and complicated. But Yama boasted he could do anything. He once tried to convince me that such a device could be built. But the contact between the two bodies must be direct and by means of many leads and cables. And no unit that tiny could have generated sufficient power."

"Who built you the psych-probe?" asked Brahma.

"Lord Yama."

"And Shiva, the thunder chariot? And Agni, the fire wand? Rudra, his terrible bow? The Trident? The Bright Spear?"

"Yama."

"I should like to advise you then, that at approximately the same time as that tiny box must have been operating, a great generator, as of its own accord, turned itself on within the Vasty Hall of Death. It functioned for less than five minutes, and then turned itself off again."

"Broadcast power?"

Brahma shrugged.

"It is time to sentence Sam."

This was done. And since he had died once before, without much effect, it was decided that a sentence of death was not in order.

Accordingly, he was transmigrated. Not into another body.

A radio tower was erected, Sam was placed under sedation, transfer leads were attached in the proper manner, but there was no other body. They were attached to the tower's converter.

His *atman* was projected upward through the opened dome, into the great magnetic cloud that circled the entire planet and was called the Bridge of the Gods.

Then he was given the unique distinction of receiving a second funeral in Heaven. Lord Yama received his first; and Brahma, watching the smoke arise from the pyres, wondered where he really was.

"The Buddha has gone to nirvana," said Brahma. "Preach it in the Temples! Sing it in the streets! Glorious was his passing! He has reformed the old religion, and we are better now than ever before! Let all who would think otherwise remember Keenset!"

This thing was done also.

But they never found Lord Kubera.

The demons were free.

Nirriti was strong.

And elsewhere in the world there were those who remembered bifocal glasses and toilets that flushed, petroleum chemistry and internal combustion engines, and the day the sun had hidden its face from the justice of Heaven.

Vishnu was heard to say that the wilderness had come into the City at last.

vii

Another name by which he is sometimes called is Maitreya, meaning Lord of Light. After his return from the Golden Cloud, he journeyed to the Palace of Kama at Khaipur, where he planned and built his strength against the Day of the Yuga. A sage once said that one never sees the Day of the Yuga, but only knows it when it is past. For it dawns like any other day and passes in the same wise, recapitulating the history of the world.

He is sometimes called Maitreya, meaning Lord of Light . . .

The world is a fire of sacrifice, the sun its fuel, sunbeams its smoke, the day its flames, the points of the compass its cinders and sparks. In this fire the gods offer faith as libation. Out of this offering King Moon is born.

Rain, oh Gautama, is the fire, the year its fuel, the clouds its smoke, the lightning its flame, cinders, sparks. In this fire the gods offer King Moon as libation. Out of this offering the rain is born.

The world, oh Gautama, is the fire, the earth its fuel, fire its smoke, the night its flame, the moon its cinders, the stars its sparks. In this fire the gods offer rain as libation. Out of this offering food is produced.

Man, oh Gautama, is the fire, his open mouth its fuel, his breath its smoke, his speech its flame, his eye its cinders, his ear its sparks. In this fire the gods offer food as libation. Out of this offering the power of generation is born.

Woman, oh Gautama, is the fire, her form its fuel, her hair its smoke, her organs its flame, her pleasures its cinders and its sparks. In this flame the gods offer the power of generation as libation. Out of this offering a man is born. He lives for so long as he is to live.

When a man dies, he is carried to be offered in the fire. The fire becomes his fire, the fuel his fuel, the smoke his smoke, the flame his flame, the cinders his cinders, the sparks his sparks. In this fire the gods offer the man as libation. Out of this offering the man emerges in radiant splendor.

Brihadaranyaka Upanishad (VI, ii, 9-14)

IN A high, blue palace of slender spires and filigreed gates, where the tang of salt sea spray and the crying of sea-wights came across the bright air to season the senses with life and delight, Lord Nirriti the Black spoke with the man who had been brought to him.

"Sea captain, what is your name?" he asked.

"Olvagga, Lord," answered the captain. "Why did you kill my crew and let me live?"

"Because I would question *you,* Captain Olvagga."

"Regarding what?"

"Many things. Things such as an old sea captain might know, through his travels. How stands my control of the southern sea lanes?"

"Stronger than I thought, or you'd not have me here."

"Many others are afraid to venture out, are they not?"

"Yes."

Nirriti moved to a window overlooking the sea. He turned his back upon his captive. After a time, he spoke again:

"I hear there has been much scientific progress in the north since, oh, the battle of Keenset."

"I, too, have heard this. Also, I know it to be true. I have seen a steam engine. The printing press is now a part of life. Dead slizzard legs are made to jump with galvanic currents. A better grade of steel is now being forged. The microscope and the telescope have been rediscovered."

Nirriti turned back to him, and they studied one another.

Nirriti was a small man, with a twinkling eye, a facile smile, dark hair, restrained by a silver band, an upturned nose and eyes the color of his palace. He wore black and lacked a suntan.

"Why do the Gods of the City fail to stop this thing?"

"I feel it is because they are weakened, if that is what you want to hear, Lord. Since the disaster by the Vedra they have been somewhat afraid to squelch the progress of mechanism with violence. It has also been said that there is internal strife in the City, between the demigods and what remains of their elders. Then there is the matter of the new religion. Men no longer fear Heaven so much as they used to. They are more willing to defend themselves; and now that they are better equipped, the gods are less willing to face them."

"Then Sam *is* winning. Across the years, he is beating them."

"Yes, Renfrew. I feel this to be true."

Nirriti glanced at the two guards who flanked Olvagga.

"Leave," he ordered. Then, when they had gone, "You know me?"

"Yes, chaplin. For I am Jan Olvegg, captain of the *Star of India.*"

"Olvegg. That seems moderately impossible."

"True, nevertheless. I received this now ancient body the day Sam broke the Lords of Karma at Mahartha. I was there."

"One of the First, and—yes!—a Christian!"

"Occasionally, when I run out of Hindi swear words."

Nirriti placed a hand on his shoulder. "Then your very being must ache at this blasphemy they have wrought!"

"I'm none too fond of them—nor they of me."

"I daresay. But of Sam—he did the same thing—compounding this plurality of heresies—burying the true Word even deeper . . ."

"A weapon, Renfrew," said Olvegg. "Nothing more. I'm sure he didn't want to be a god any more than you or I."

"Perhaps. But I wish he had chosen a different weapon. If he wins their souls are still lost."

Olvegg shrugged. "I'm no theologian, such as yourself . . ."

"But will you help me? Over the ages I have built up a mighty force. I have men and I have machines. You say our enemies are weakened. My soulless ones—born not of man or woman—they are without fear. I have sky gondolas—many. I can reach their City at the Pole. I can destroy their Temples here in the world. I think the time is at hand to cleanse the world of this abomination. The true faith must come again! Soon! It *must* be soon . . ."

"As I said, I'm no theologian. But I, too, would see the City fall," said Olvegg. "I will help you, in any way I can."

"Then we will take a few of their cities and defile their Temples, to see what action this provokes."

Olvegg nodded.

"You will advise me. You will provide moral support," said Nirriti, and bowed his head.

"Join me in prayer," he ordered.

The old man stood for a long while outside the Palace of Kama in Khaipur, staring at its marble pillars. Finally, a girl took pity on him and brought him bread and milk. He ate the bread.

"Drink the milk, too, grandfather. It is nourishing and will help sustain thy flesh."

"Damn!" said the old man. "Damn milk! And damn my flesh! My spirit, also, for that matter!"

The girl drew back. "That is hardly the proper reply upon the receipt of charity."

"It is not your charity to which I object, wench. It is your taste in beverages. Could you not spare me a draught of the foulest wine from the kitchen? ... That which the guests have disdained to order and the cook will not even slop over the cheapest pieces of meat? I crave the squeezings of grapes, not cows."

"Perhaps I could bring you a menu? Depart! Before I summon a servant!"

He stared into her eyes. "Take not offense, lady, I pray. Begging comes hard to me."

She looked into his pitch-dark eyes in the midst of a ruin of wrinkles and tan. His beard was streaked with black. The tiniest smile played about the corners of his lips.

"Well ... follow me around to the side. I'll take you into the kitchen and see what can be found. I don't really know why I should, though."

His fingers twitched as she turned, and his smile widened as he followed, watching her walk.

"Because I want you to," he said.

Taraka of the Rakasha was uneasy. Flitting above the clouds that moved through the middle of the day, he thought upon the ways of power. He had once been mightiest. In the days before the binding there had been none who could stand against him. Then Siddhartha the Binder had come. He had known of him earlier, known of him as Kalkin and had known him to be strong. Sooner or later, he had realized, they would have to meet, that he might test the power of that Attribute which Kalkin was said to have raised up. When they had come together, on that mighty, gone day when the mountaintops had flared with their fury, on that day the Binder had won. And in their second encounter, ages afterward, he had somehow beaten him even more fully. But he had been the only one, and now he was gone from out the world. Of all creatures, only the Binder had bested the Lord of Hellwell. Then the gods had come to challenge his power. They had been puny in the early days, struggling to discipline their mutant powers with drugs, hypnosis, meditation, neuro-surgery—forging them into Attributes—and across the ages, those powers had grown. Four of them had entered Hellwell, only four, and his legions had not been able to repel them. The one called Shiva was strong, but the Binder had later slain him. This was as it should be, for Taraka recognized the Binder as a peer. The woman he dismissed. She was only a woman, and she had required assistance from Yama. But Lord Agni, whose soul had been one bright, blinding flame—*this* one he had almost feared. He recalled the day Agni had walked into the palace at Palamaidsu, alone, and had challenged him. He could not stop that one, though he had tried, and he had seen the palace itself destroyed by the power of his fires. And nothing in Hellwell could stop him either. He had made a promise then to himself that he must test this power, as he had that of Siddhartha, to defeat it or be bound by it. But he never did. The Lord of Fires had fallen himself, before the One in Red—who had been the fourth in Hellwell—who had somehow turned his fires back upon him, that day beside the Vedra in the battle for Keenset. This meant that *he* was the greatest. For had not even the Binder warned him of Yama-Dharma, god of Death? Yes, the one whose eyes drink life was the mightiest yet remaining in the world. He had almost fallen to his strength within the thunder chariot. He had tested this strength once, briefly, but had relented be-cause they were allies in that fight. It was told that Yama had died afterward, in the City. Later, it was told that he still walked the world. As Lord of the Dead it was said that he could not die himself, save by his own choosing. Taraka accepted this as a fact, know-ing what this acceptance meant. It meant that he, Taraka, would return to the south, to the island of the blue palace, where the Lord of Evil, Nirriti the Black, awaited his answer. He would give his assent. Starting at Mahartha and working northward from the sea, the

Rakasha would add their power to his dark own, destroying the Temples of the six largest cities of the southwest, one after another, filling the streets of those cities with the blood of their citizens and the flameless legions of the Black One—until the gods came to their defense, and so met their doom. If the gods failed to come, then their true weakness would be known. The Rakasha would then storm Heaven, and Nirriti would level the Celestial City; Milehigh Spire would fall, the dome would be shattered, the great white cats of Kaniburrha would look upon ruins, and the pavilions of the gods and the demigods would be covered with the snows of the Pole. And all of this for one reason, really—aside from relieving the boredom, aside from hastening the final days of gods and of men in the world of the Rakasha. Whenever there is great fighting and the doing of mighty deeds and bloody deeds and flaming deeds—he comes, Taraka knew—the One in Red comes from somewhere, always, for his Aspect draws him to the realm that is his. Taraka knew he would search, wait, do anything, for however long it took, until that day he stared into the black fires that burn behind the eyes of Death. . . .

Brahma stared at the map, then looked back to the screen of crystal, about which a bronze Naga twisted, tail in teeth.

"Burning, oh priest?"

"Burning, Brahma . . . the whole warehouse district!"

"Order the people to quench the fires."

"They are already doing so, Mighty One."

"Then why trouble me with the matter?"

"There is fear, Great One."

"Fear? Fear of what?"

"The Black One, whose name I may not speak in your presence, whose strength has grown steadily in the south, he who controls the sea lanes, cutting off trade."

"Why should you be afraid to speak the name of

Nirriti before me? I know of the Black One. Do you feel he started the fires?"

"Yes, Great One—or rather some accursed one in his pay did it. There is much talk that he seeks to cut us off from the rest of the world, to drain our wealth, destroy our stores and weaken our spirits, because he plans—"

"To invade you, of course."

"You have said it, Potent One."

"It may be true, my priest. So tell me, do you feel your gods will not stand by you if the Lord of Evil attacks?"

"There has never been any doubt, Most Puissant One. We simply wanted to remind you of the possibility and renew our perpetual supplication for mercy and divine protection."

"You have made your point, priest. Fear not."

Brahma ended the transmission. "He will attack."

"Of course."

"And how strong is he, I wonder? No one really knows how strong he is, Ganesha. Do they?"

"You ask me, my Lord? Your humble policy adviser?"

"I do not see anyone else present, humble godmaker. Do you know of anyone who might have information?"

"No, Lord. I do not. Everyone avoids the foul one as though he were the real death. Generally, he is. As you are aware, the three demigods I sent south did not return."

"They were strong, too, whatever their names, weren't they? How long ago was that?"

"The last was a year ago, when we sent the new Agni."

"Yes, he wasn't very good, though—still used incendiary grenades . . . but strong."

"Morally, perhaps. When there are fewer gods one must settle for demigods."

"In the old days, I would have taken the thunder chariot—"

"In the old days there was no thunder chariot. Lord Yama—"

"Silence! We have a thunder chariot now. I think the tall man of smoke who wears a wide hat shall bend above Nirriti's palace."

"Brahma, I think Nirriti can stop the thunder chariot."

"Why so?"

"From some firsthand reports I've heard, I believe that he has used guided missiles against warships sent after his brigands."

"Why did you not tell me of this sooner?"

"They are very recent reports. This is the first chance I have had to broach the subject."

"Then you do not feel we should attack?"

"No. Wait. Let *him* move first, that we may judge his strength."

"This would involve sacrificing Mahartha, would it not?"

"So? Have you never seen a city fall? ... How will Mahartha benefit him, by itself, and for a time? If we cannot reclaim it, *then* let the man of smoke nod his wide white hat—over Mahartha."

"You are right. It will be worth it, to assess his power properly and to drain a portion of it away. In the meantime, we must prepare."

"Yes. What will your order be?"

"Alert all the powers in the City. Recall Lord Indra from the eastern continent, at once!"

"Thy will be done."

"And alert the other five cities of the river—Lananda, Khaipur, Kilbar—"

"Immediately."

"Go then!"

"I am already gone."

Time like an ocean, space like its water, Sam in the middle, standing, decided.

"God of Death," he called out, "enumerate our strengths."

Yama stretched and yawned, then rose from the scarlet couch upon which he had been dozing, almost invisible. He crossed the room, stared into Sam's eyes.

"Without raising Aspect, here is my Attribute."

Sam met his gaze, held it. "This is in answer to my question?"

"Partly," replied Yama, "but mainly it was to test your own power. It appears to be returning. You bore my death-gaze longer than any mortal could."

"I know my power is returning. I can feel it. Many things are returning now. During the weeks we have dwelled here in Ratri's palace I have meditated upon my past lives. They were not all failures, deathgod. I have decided this today. Though Heaven has beaten me at every turn, each victory has cost them much."

"Yes, it would seem you are rather a man of destiny. They are actually weaker now than they were the day you challenged their power at Mahartha. They are also relatively weaker. This is because men are stronger. The gods broke Keenset, but they did not break Acceleration. Then they tried to bury Buddhism within their own teachings, but they could not. I cannot really say whether your religion helped with the plot of this tale you are writing, by encouraging Acceleration in any way whatsoever, but then none of the gods could say either. It served as a good fog, though—it diverted their attention from mischief they might have been doing, and since it did happen to 'take' as a teaching, their efforts against it served to arouse some anti-Deicrat sentiment. You would seem inspired if you didn't seem shrewd."

"Thank you. Do you want my blessing?"

"No, do you want mine?"

"Perhaps, Death, later. But you did not answer my question. Please tell me what strengths lie with us."

"Very well. Lord Kubera will arrive shortly . . ."

"Kubera? Where is he?"

"He has dwelled in hiding over the years, leaking scientific knowledge into the world."

"Over so *many* years? His body must be ancient! How could he have managed?"

"Do you forget Narada?"

"My old physician from Kapil?"

"The same. When you dispersed your lancers after your battle in Mahartha, he retreated into the back-lands with a service of retainers. He packed with him all the equipment you had taken from the Hall of Karma. I located him many years ago. Subsequent to Keenset, after my escape from Heaven by the Way of the Black Wheel, I brought Kubera out from his vault beneath that fallen city. He later allied himself with Narada, who now runs a bootleg body shop in the hills. They work together. We have set up several others in various places, also."

"And Kubera comes? Good!"

"And Siddhartha is still Prince of Kapil. A call for troops from that principality would still be heard. We have sounded them out."

"A handful, probably. But still good to know—yes."

"And Lord Krishna."

"Krishna? What is he doing on our side? Where is he?"

"He was here. I found him the day we arrived. He had just moved in with one of the girls. Quite pathetic."

"How so?"

"Old. Pitifully old and weak, but still a drunken lecher. His Aspect served him still, however, periodically summoning up some of his ancient charisma and a fraction of his colossal vitality. He had been expelled from Heaven after Keenset, but because he would not fight against Kubera and myself, as did Agni. He has wandered the world for over half a century, drinking and loving and playing his pipes and growing older. Kubera and I have tried several times to locate him, but he did considerable traveling. This is generally a requirement for renegade fertility deities."

"What good will he be to us?"

"I sent him to Narada for a new body on the day I found him. He will be riding in with Kubera. His powers always take to the transfer quickly, too."

"But what *good* will he be to us?"

"Do not forget that it was he who broke the black demon Bana, whom even Indra feared to face. When he is sober, he is one of the deadliest fighting men alive. Yama, Kubera, Krishna, and if you're willing—Kalkin! We will be the new Lokapalas, and we will stand together."

"I am willing."

"So be it, then. Let them send a company of their trainee gods against us! I've been designing new weapons. It is a shame that there must be so many separate and exotic ones. It is quite a drain on my genius to make each a work of art, rather than to mass-produce a particular species of offense. But the plurality of the paranormal dictates it. Someone always has an Attribute to stand against any one weapon. Let them face, though, the Gehenna Gun and be fibrillated apart, or cross blades with the Electrosword, or stand before the Fountain Shield, with its spray of cyanide and dimethyl sulfoxide, and they will know that it is the Lokapalas they face!"

"I see now, Death, why it is that any god—even Brahma—may pass and be succeeded by another—save for yourself."

"Thank you. Have you a plan of any sort?"

"Not yet. I will need more information as to the strength within the City. Has Heaven demonstrated its power in recent years?"

"No."

"If there were some way of testing them without showing our hand. . . . Perhaps the Rakasha . . ."

"No, Sam. I do not trust them."

"Nor I. But they can sometimes be dealt with."

"As you dealt with them in Hellwell and Pala-maidsu?"

"Well answered. Maybe you are right. I will give it more thought. I wonder about Nirriti, though. How go things with the Black One?"

"In recent years, he has come to dominate the seas. Rumor has it that his legions grow, and that he builds machines of war. I once told you, though, of my fears in this matter. Let us stay as far away from Nirriti as possible. He has but one thing in common with us—the desire to topple Heaven. Neither Accelerationist nor Deicrat, should he succeed he would set up a Dark Age worse than the one we're beginning to come out of. Perhaps our best course of action would bē to provoke a battle between Nirriti and the Gods of the City, lie low and then shoot at the winners."

"You may be right, Yama. But how to do this?"

"We may not have to. It may happen of its own accord—soon. Mahartha crouches, cowering back from the sea it faces. You are the strategist, Sam. I'm only a tactician. We brought you back to tell us what to do. Pray think about it carefully, now that you are yourself once more."

"You are always stressing those last words."

"Yea, preacher. For you have not been battle-tested since your return from bliss. . . . Tell me, can you make the Buddhists fight?"

"Probably, but I might have to assume an identity I now find distasteful."

"Well . . . perhaps not. Keep it in mind, in case we're hard put. To be safe, though, practice every night in front of a mirror with that esthetics lecture you gave back at Ratri's monastery."

"I'd rather not."

"I know, but do it anyway."

"Better I should practice with a blade. Fetch me one and I'll give you a lesson."

"Ho! Fair enough! Make it a good lesson and you've got yourself a convert."

"Then let us adjourn to the courtyard, where I will proceed to enlighten you."

As, within the blue palace, Nirriti raised his arms, the rockets screamed skyward from the decks of his launch ships to arc above the city of Mahartha.

As his black breastplate was buckled into place, the rockets came down upon that city and the fires began.

As he donned his boots, his fleet entered into the harbor.

As his black cloak was clasped about his throat and his black steel helm placed upon his head, his sergeants began a soft drumbeat beneath the decks of his ships.

As his sword belt was hung about his waist, the soulless ones stirred within the holds of the vessels.

As he put on his gauntlets of leather and steel, his fleet, driven by winds fanned by the Rakasha, approached the port.

As he motioned to his young steward, Olvagga, to follow him into the courtyard, the warriors who never spoke mounted the decks of the ships and faced the burning harbor.

As the engines within the dark sky gondola rumbled and the door was opened before them, the first of his ships dropped anchor.

As they entered the gondola, the first of his troops entered Mahartha.

When they reached Mahartha, the city had fallen.

Birds sang in the high, green places of the garden. Fish, like old coins, lay at the bottom of the blue pool. The flowers in bloom were mainly red and big-petaled; but there were also occasional yellow wunlips about her jade bench. There was a white, wrought-iron back to it, upon which she rested her left hand while she regarded the flagstones across which his boots scuffed as he moved in her direction.

"Sir, this is a private garden," she stated.

He stopped before the bench and looked down at

her. He was beefy, tanned, dark of eye and beard, expressionless until he smiled. He wore blue and leather.

"Guests do not come here," she added, "but do use the gardens in the other wing of the building. Go through yon archway—"

"You were always welcome in *my* garden, Ratri," he said.

"Your . . . ?"

"Kubera."

"Lord Kubera! You are not—"

"Fat. I know. New body, and it's been working hard. Building Yama's weapons, transporting them . . ."

"When did you arrive?"

"This minute. I brought Krishna back, along with a load of firepacks, grenades and antipersonnel mines . . ."

"Gods! It's been so long . . ."

"Yes. Very. But an apology is still due you, so I have come to give it. It has bothered me these many years. I am sorry, Ratri, about that night, long ago, when I dragged you into this thing. I needed your Attribute, so I drafted you. I do not like to use people so."

"I would have left the City soon, at any rate, Kubera. So do not feel overly guilty. I should prefer a more comely form, though, than this which I now wear. This is not essential, however."

"I'll get you another body, lady."

"Another day, Kubera. Pray sit down. Here. Are you hungry? Are you thirsty?"

"Yes, and yes."

"Here is fruit, and soma. Or would you prefer tea?"

"Soma, thank you."

"Yama says Sam is recovered from his sainthood."

"Good, the need for him is growing. Has he made any plans yet—for us to act upon?"

"Yama has not told me. But perhaps Sam has not told Yama."

The branches shook violently in a nearby tree and Tak dropped to the ground, landing upon all fours. He crossed the flagstones and stood beside the bench.

"All this talk has awakened me," he growled. "Who is this fellow, Ratri?"

"Lord Kubera, Tak."

"If thou beest he—then oh, how changed!" said Tak.

"And the same might be said of yourself, Tak of the Archives. Why are you still an ape? Yama could transmigrate you."

"I am more useful as an ape," said Tak. "I am an excellent spy—far better than a dog. I am stronger than a man. And who can tell one ape from another? I will remain in this form until there is no longer any need for my special services."

"Commendable. Has there been further news of Nirriti's movements?"

"His vessels move nearer the large ports than was their wont in the past," said Tak. "There appear to be more of them, also. Beyond this, nothing. It would seem the gods fear him, for they do not destroy him."

"Yes," said Kubera, "for now he is an unknown. I'm inclined to think of him as Ganesha's mistake. It was he who permitted him to leave Heaven unmolested, and to take what equipment he did with him. I think Ganesha wanted someone available as an enemy of Heaven, should the need for one ever arise in a hurry. He must never have dreamed a nontechnical could have put the equipment to the uses he did, and build up the forces he now commands."

"There is logic in what you say," said Ratri. "Even I have heard that Ganesha often moves in such a manner. What will he do now?"

"Give Nirriti the first city he attacks, to observe his means of offense and assess his strength—if he can persuade Brahma to hold back. *Then* strike at Nirriti. Mahartha must fall, and *we* must stand near. It would be interesting even to watch."

"But you feel we will do more than watch?" asked Tak.

"Indeed. Sam knows we must be on hand to make more pieces of the pieces, and then to pick some up. We will have to move as soon as someone else does, Tak, which may be soon."

"At last," said Tak. "I have always wanted to go to battle at the side of the Binder."

"In the weeks to come, I am certain that almost as many wishes will be granted as broken."

"More soma? More fruit?"

"Thank you, Ratri."

"And you, Tak?"

"A banana, perhaps."

Within the shadow of the forest, at the peak of a high hill, Brahma sat, like a statue of a god mounted upon a gargoyle, staring downward into Mahartha.

"They defile the Temple."

"Yes," answered Ganesha. "The Black One's feelings have not changed over the years."

"In a way, it is a pity. In another way, it is frightening. His troops had rifles and sidearms."

"Yes. They are very strong. Let us return to the gondola."

"In a moment."

"I fear, Lord ... they may be too strong—at this point."

"What do you suggest?"

"They cannot sail up the river. If they would attack Lananda they must go overland."

"True. Unless he has sufficient sky vessels."

"And if they would attack Khaipur they must go even farther."

"Aye! And if they would attack Kilbar they must go farther yet! Get to your point! What are you trying to say?"

"The farther they go, the greater their logistic problems, the more vulnerable they become to guerrilla tactics along the way—"

"Are you proposing I do nothing but harass them? That I let them march across the land, taking city after city? They will dig in until reinforcements come to hold what they have gained, *then* they will move on. Only a fool would do otherwise. If we wait—"

"Look down below!"

"What? What is it?"

"They are preparing to move out."

"Impossible!"

"Brahma, you forget that Nirriti is a fanatic, a madman. He doesn't want Mahartha, or Lananda or Khaipur either. He wants to destroy our Temples and ourselves. The only other things he cares about in those cities are souls, not bodies. He will move across the land destroying every symbol of our religion that he comes upon, until we choose to carry the fight to him. If we do nothing, he will probably then send in missionaries."

"Well, we must do something!"

"Then weaken him as he moves. When he is weak enough, strike! Give him Lananda. Khaipur, too, if necessary. Even Kilbar and Hamsa. When he is weak enough, smash him. We can spare the cities. How many have we destroyed ourselves? You cannot even remember!"

"Thirty-six," said Brahma. "Let us return to Heaven while I consider this thing. If I follow your advice and he withdraws before he becomes too weakened, then we have lost much."

"I'm willing to gamble that he won't."

"The dice are not yours to cast, Ganesha, but mine. And see, he has those cursed Rakasha with him! Let us depart quickly, before they detect us."

"Yes, quickly!"

They turned their slizzards back toward the forest.

Krishna put aside his pipes when the messenger was brought to him.

"Yes?" he asked.

"Mahartha has fallen . . ."

Krishna stood.

"And Nirriti prepares to march upon Lananda."

"What have the gods done in defense?"

"Nothing. Nothing at all."

"Come with me. The Lokapalas are about to confer."

Krishna left his pipes upon the table.

That night, Sam stood upon the highest balcony of Ratri's palace. The rains fell about him, coming like cold nails through the wind. Upon his left hand, an iron ring glowed with an emerald radiance.

The lightning fell and fell and fell, and remained.

He raised his hand and the thunders roared and roared, like the death cries of all the dragons who might ever have lived, sometime, somewhere. . . .

The night fell back as the fire elementals stood before the Palace of Kama.

Sam raised both hands together, and they climbed into the air as one and hovered high in the night.

He gestured and they moved above Khaipur, passing from one end of the city to the other.

Then they circled.

Then they split apart and danced within the storm.

He lowered his hands.

They returned and stood once more before him.

He did not move. He waited.

After a hundred heartbeats, it came and spoke to him out of the night:

"Who are you, to command the slaves of the Rakasha?"

"Bring me Taraka," said Sam.

"I take orders from no mortal."

"Then look upon the flames of my true being, ere I

bind you to yon metal flagpole for so long as it shall stand."

"Binder! You live!"

"Bring me Taraka," he repeated.

"Yes, Siddhartha. Thy will be done."

Sam clapped his hands and the elementals leapt skyward and the night was dark about him once more.

The Lord of Hellwell took upon him a manlike form and entered the room where Sam sat alone.

"The last ever I saw of you was upon the day of the Great Battle," he stated. "Later, I heard that they had found a way of destroying you."

"As you can see, they did not."

"How came you into the world again?"

"Lord Yama fetched me back—the One in Red."

"His power is indeed great."

"It proved sufficient. How go things with the Rakasha these days?"

"Well. We continue your fight."

"Really? In what ways?"

"We aid your old ally—the Black One, Lord Nirriti—in his campaign against the gods."

"I suspected this. It is the reason I have contacted you."

"You wish to ride with him?"

"I have thought it over carefully, and despite my comrades' objections I *do* wish to ride with him—provided he will make an agreement with us. I want you to carry my message to him."

"What is the message, Siddhartha?"

"The message is that the Lokapalas—these being Yama, Krishna, Kubera and myself—will ride to battle with him against the gods, bringing all our supporters, powers, and machineries to bear upon them, if he will agree not to war against the followers of either Buddhism or Hinduism as they exist in the world, for purposes of converting them to his persuasion—and further, that he will not seek to suppress Accelerationism, as the gods have done, should we prove victorious. Look upon his flames as he speaks his answer, and tell me whether he speaks it true."

"Do you think he will agree to this, Sam?"

"I do. He knows that, if the gods were no longer present to enforce Hinduism as they do, then he would gain converts. He can see this from what I managed to do with Buddhism, despite their opposition. He feels that his way is the only right way and that it is destined to prevail in the face of competition. I think he would agree to *fair* competition for this reason. Take him this message and bring me his answer. All right?"

Taraka wavered. His face and left arm became smoke.

"Sam . . ."

"What?"

"Which one *is* the right way?"

"Huh? You're asking me *that?* How should I know?"

"Mortals call you Buddha."

"That is only because they are afflicted with language and ignorance."

"No. I have looked upon your flames and name you Lord of Light. You bind them as you bound us, you loose them as you loosed us. Yours was the power to lay a belief upon them. You are what you claimed to be."

"I lied. I never believed in it myself, and I still don't. I could just as easily have chosen another way—say, Nirriti's religion—only crucifixion hurts. I might have chosen one called Islam, only I know too well how it mixes with Hinduism. My choice was based upon calculation, not inspiration, and I am nothing."

"You are the Lord of Light."

"Go deliver my message now. We can discuss religion another day."

"The Lokapalas, you say, are Yama, Krishna, Kubera and yourself?"

"Yes."

"Then he *does* live. Tell me, Sam, before I go ... could you defeat Lord Yama in battle?"

"I do not know. I don't think so, though. I don't think anybody could."

"But could he defeat you?"

"Probably, in a fair fight. Whenever we met as enemies in the past, I was sometimes lucky and sometimes I managed to trick him. I've fenced with him recently and he is without peer. He is too versatile in the ways of destruction."

"I see," said Taraka, his right arm and half his chest drifting away. "Then good night upon you, Siddhartha. I take your message with me."

"Thank you, and good night upon yourself."

Taraka became all smoke and fled forth into the storm.

High above the world, spinning: Taraka.

The storm raged about him, but he took scant notice of its fury.

The thunders fell and the rain came down and the Bridge of the Gods was invisible.

But none of these things bothered him.

For he was Taraka of the Rakasha, Lord of Hellwell . . .

And he had been the mightiest creature in the world, save for the Binder.

Now the Binder had told him that there was One Greater . . . and they were to fight together, as before.

How insolently he had stood in his Red and his Power! That day. Over half a century ago. By the Vedra.

To destroy Yama-Dharma, to defeat Death, would prove Taraka supreme. . . .

To prove Taraka supreme was more important than defeating the gods, who must one day pass, anyhow, for they were not of the Rakasha.

Therefore, the Binder's message to Nirriti—to which he had said Nirriti would agree—would be spoken only

to the storm, and Taraka would look upon its flames
and know that it spoke true.

For the storm never lies . . . and it always says *No!*

The dark sergeant brought him into camp. He had
been resplendent in his armor, with its bright trappings,
and he had not been captured; he had walked up to
him and stated that he had a message for Nirriti. For
this reason, the sergeant decided against slaying him
immediately. He took his weapons, conducted him into
the camp—there in the wood near Lananda—and left
him under guard while he consulted his leader.

Nirriti and Olvegg sat within a black tent. A map of
Lananda was spread before them.

When they permitted him to bring the prisoner into
the tent, Nirriti regarded him and dismissed the sergeant.

"Who are you?" he asked.

"Ganesha of the City. The same who aided you in
your flight from Heaven."

Nirriti appeared to consider this.

"Well do I remember my one friend from the old
days," he said. "Why have you come to me?"

"Because the time is propitious to do so. You have
finally undertaken the great crusade."

"Yes."

"I would hold privy counsel with you concerning it."

"Speak then."

"What of this fellow?"

"To speak before Jan Olvegg is to speak before me.
Say what is on your mind."

"Olvegg?"

"Yes."

"Just so. I have come to tell you that the Gods of the
City are weak. Too weak, I feel, to defeat you."

"I had felt this to be true."

"But they are not so weak as to be unable to hurt
you immensely when they do move. Things might hang

in the balance if they muster all their forces at the proper moment."

"I came to battle with this in mind, also."

"Better your victory be less costly. You know I am a Christian sympathizer."

"What is it you have in mind?"

"I volunteered to lead some guerrilla fighting solely to tell you that Lananda is yours. They will not defend it. If you continue to move as you have—not consolidating your gains—and you move upon Khaipur, Brahma will not defend it either. But when you come to Kilbar, your forces weakened from the battles for the first three cities and from these, our raids along the way, then will Brahma strike with the full might of Heaven, that you may go down to defeat before the walls of Kilbar. All the powers of the Celestial City have been readied. They wait for you to dare the gates of the fourth city of the river."

"I see. That is good to know. Then they do fear that which I bear."

"Of course. Will you bear it as far as Kilbar?"

"Yes. And I will win in Kilbar, also. I shall send for my mightiest weapons before we attack that city. The powers which I have held back to use upon the Celestial City itself will be unleashed upon my enemies when they come to the defense of doomed Kilbar."

"They, too, will bring mighty weapons."

"Then, when we meet, the outcome will lie neither in their hands nor in my hands, really."

"There is a way to tip the balance even further, Renfrew."

"Oh? What else have you in mind?"

"Many of the demigods are dissatisfied with the situation in the City. They had wanted a prolonged campaign against Accelerationism and against the followers of Tathagatha. They were disappointed when this did not follow Keenset. Also, Lord Indra has been recalled from the eastern continent, where he was carrying the war against the witches. Indra could be made to appre-

ciate the sentiments of the demigods—and his followers
will come hot from another battlefield."

Ganesha adjusted his cloak.

"Speak on," said Nirriti.

"When they come to Kilbar," said Ganesha, "it may
be that they will not fight in its defense."

"I see. What will you gain from all this, Ganesha?"

"Satisfaction."

"Nothing more?"

"I would that you recall one day that I made this
visit."

"So be it. I shall not forget, and you shall have
reward of me afterward. . . . Guard!"

The tent flap was opened, and the one who had
brought Ganesha re-entered the tent.

"Escort this man wherever he wants to be taken, and
release him unharmed," Nirriti ordered.

"You would trust this one?" asked Olvegg, after he
had gone.

"Yes," said Nirriti, "but I would give him his silver
afterward."

The Lokapalas sat to counsel within Sam's chamber
at the Palace of Kama in Khaipur. Also present were
Tak and Ratri.

"Taraka tells me that Nirriti will not have us on our
terms," said Sam.

"Good," said Yama. "I half feared he would agree."

"And in the morning they attack Lananda. Taraka
feels they will take the city. It will be a little more
difficult than Mahartha was, but he is certain they will
win. I am too."

"And I."

"And I."

"Then he will move on to this city, Khaipur. Then
Kilbar, then Hamsa, then Gayatri. Somewhere along
this route, he knows the gods will move against him."

"Of course."

"So we are in the middle and we have several choices

before us. We could not make a deal with Nirriti. Do you think we could make one with Heaven?"

"No!" said Yama, slamming his fist upon the table. "Which side are you on, Sam?"

"Acceleration," he replied. "If it can be procured through negotiation, rather than unnecessary bloodshed, so much the better."

"I'd rather deal with Nirriti than Heaven!"

"So let us vote upon it as we did upon making the contact with Nirriti."

"And you require only one assent to win."

"Those were my terms upon entering the Lokapalas. You asked me to lead you, so I require the power to break a tie. Let me explain my reasoning, though, before we talk of a vote."

"Very well—talk!"

"Heaven has, in recent years, developed a more liberal attitude toward Acceleration, as I understand it. There has been no official change of position, but no steps have been taken against Acceleration either— presumably because of the beating they took at Keenset. Am I not correct?"

"Essentially," said Kubera.

"It seems that they have decided such actions would be too costly every time Science rears its ugly head. There were people, humans, fighting against them in that battle. Against Heaven. And people, unlike ourselves, have families, have ties which weaken them— and they are bound to keep a clean karmic record if they desire rebirth. Still, they fought. Accordingly, Heaven has been moved to greater lenience in recent years. Since this is the situation as it actually exists, they have nothing to lose by acknowledging it. In fact, they could make it show to their favor, as a benign gesture of divine graciousness. I think that they would be willing to make the concessions Nirriti would not—"

"I want to see Heaven fall," said Yama.

"Of course. So do I. But think carefully. Just with what you've given to humans over the past half century—can Heaven hold this world in fief much longer? Heaven fell that day at Keenset. Another generation, perhaps two, and its power over mortals will have passed. In this battle with Nirriti they will be hurt further, even in victory. Give them a few more years of decadent glory. They become more and more impotent with every season. They have reached their peak. Their decline has set in."

Yama lit a cigarette.

"Is it that you want someone to kill Brahma for you?" asked Sam.

Yama sat silently, drew upon the cigarette, exhaled. Then, "Perhaps," he said. "Perhaps that is it. I do not know. I don't like to think about it. It is probably true, though."

"Would you like my guarantee that Brahma will die?"

"No! If you try it, I'll kill you!"

"You feel that you do not really know whether you want Brahma dead or alive. Perhaps it is that you love and hate simultaneously. You were old before you were young, Yama, and she was the only thing you ever cared for. Am I right?"

"Yes."

"Then I have no answer for you, for your own troubles, but you must separate yourself this much from the problem at hand."

"All right, Siddhartha. I vote to stop Nirriti here at Khaipur, if Heaven will back us."

"Does anybody have any objections to this?"

There was silence.

"Then let us journey to the Temple and commandeer its communications unit."

Yama put out his cigarette.

"But I will not speak with Brahma," he said.

"I'll do the talking," said Sam.

Ili, the fifth note of the harp, buzzed within the Garden of the Purple Lotus.

When Brahma activated the screen within his Pavilion, he saw a man who wore the blue-green turban of Urath.

"Where is the priest?" asked Brahma.

"Tied up outside. I can have him dragged in, if you'd like to hear a prayer or two . . ."

"Who are you that wears the turban of the First and goes armed in the Temple?"

"I have a strange feeling of having been through all this once before," said the man.

"Answer my questions!"

"Do you want Nirriti stopped, Lady? Or do you want to give him all these cities along the river?"

"You try the patience of Heaven, mortal? You shall not leave the Temple alive."

"Your threats of death mean nothing to the chief of the Lokapalas, Kali."

"The Lokapalas are no more, and they had no chief."

"You look upon him, Durga."

"*Yama?* Is that you?"

"No, but he is here with me—as are Krishna, and Kubera."

"Agni is dead. Every new Agni has died since . . ."

"Keenset. I know, Candi. I was not a member of the original team. Rild didn't kill me. The phantom cat who shall remain nameless did a good job, but it wasn't good enough. And now I've crossed back over the Bridge of the Gods. The Lokapalas have chosen me as their leader. We will defend Khaipur and break Nirriti, if Heaven will help us."

"Sam . . . it couldn't be you!"

"Then call me Kalkin, or Siddhartha, or Tathagatha, or Mahasamatman, or Binder, or Buddha, or Maitreya. It's Sam, though. I have come to worship thee and make a bargain."

"Name it."

"Men have been able to live with Heaven, but Nirriti is another matter. Yama and Kubera have brought weapons into the city. We can fortify it and whip up a good defense. If Heaven will add its power to our own, Nirriti will meet his downfall at Khaipur. We will do this, if Heaven will sanction Acceleration and religious freedom, and end the reign of the Lords of Karma."

"That's quite a bit, Sam . . ."

"The first two merely amount to agreeing that something does exist and has a right to go on. The third will come to pass whether you like it or not, so I'm giving you a chance to be graceful about it."

"I'll have to think . . ."

"Take a minute. I'll wait. If the answer is no, though, we'll pull out and let Renfrew have this city, defile this Temple. After he's taken a few more, you'll have to meet him. We won't be around then, though. We'll wait till it's all over. If you're still in business then, you won't be in any position to decide about those terms I just gave you. If you're not, I think we'll be able to take the Black One on and best him and what will be left of his zombies. Either way, we get what we want. This way is easier on you, though."

"All right! I'll muster the forces immediately. We will ride together in this last battle, Kalkin. Nirriti dies at Khaipur! Keep someone there in the comm-room, so we can stay in contact."

"I'll make this my headquarters."

"Now untie the priest and bring him here. He is about to receive some divine orders, and, shortly, a divine visitation."

"Yes, Brahma."

"Sam, wait! After the battle, should we live, I would talk with you—concerning mutual worship."

"You wish to become a Buddhist?"

"No, a woman again . . ."

"There is a place and a moment for all things, and this is neither."

"When the time and the moment occur, I will be there."

"I'll get you your priest now. Hold the line."

Now after the fall of Lananda, Nirriti held a service amid the ruins of that city, praying for victory over the other cities. His dark sergeants beat the drums slowly and the zombies fell to their knees. Nirriti prayed until the perspiration covered his face like a mask of glass and light, and it ran down inside his prosthetic armor, which gave him the strength of many. Then he lifted up his face to the heavens, looked upon the Bridge of the Gods and said, "Amen."

Then he turned and headed toward Khaipur, his army rising at his back.

When Nirriti came to Khaipur, the gods were waiting.

The troops from Kilbar were waiting, as well as those of Khaipur.

And the demigods and the heroes and the nobles were waiting.

And the high-ranking Brahmins and many of the followers of Mahasamatman were waiting. These latter having come in the name of the Divine Esthetic.

Nirriti looked across the mined field that led to the walls of the city, and he saw the four horsemen who were the Lokapalas waiting by the gate, the banners of Heaven flaring beside them in the wind.

He lowered his visor and turned to Olvegg.

"You were right. I wonder if Ganesha waits within?"

"We will know soon enough."

Nirriti continued his advance.

This was the day when the Lord of Light held the field. The minions of Nirriti never entered Khaipur. Ganesha fell beneath the blade of Olvegg, as he was attempting to backstab Brahma, who had closed with Nirriti upon a hillock. Olvegg then fell, clutching his stomach, and began crawling toward a rock.

Brahma and the Black One then faced one another on foot and Ganesha's head rolled into a gully.

"That one told me Kilbar," said Nirriti.

"That one wanted Kilbar," said Brahma, "and tried to make it Kilbar. Now I know why."

They sprang together and Nirriti's armor fought for him with the strength of many.

Yama spurred his horse toward the rise and was enveloped in a swirling of dust and sand. He raised his cloak to his eyes and laughter rang about him.

"Where is your death-gaze now, Yama-Dharma?"

"Rakasha!" he snarled.

"Yes. It is I, Taraka!"

And Yama was suddenly drenched with gallons of water; and his horse reared, falling over backward.

He was upon his feet with his blade in his hand, when the flaming whirlwind coalesced into a manlike form.

"I've washed you clean of that-which-repels, deathgod. Now you shall go down to destruction at my hand!"

Yama lunged forward with his blade.

He cut through his gray opponent from shoulder to thigh, but no blood came and there was no sign of the passage of his blade.

"You cannot cut me down as you would a man, oh Death! But see what I can do to you!"

Taraka leapt upon him, pinning his arms to his sides and bearing him to the ground. A fountain of sparks arose.

In the distance, Brahma had his knee upon Nirriti's spine and was bending his head backward, against the power of the black armor. This was when Lord Indra leapt down from the back of his slizzard and raised his sword Thunderbolt against Brahma. He heard Nirriti's neck break.

"It is your cloak that protects you!" Taraka cried out, from where he wrestled on the ground; and then he looked into the eyes of Death. . . .

Yama felt Taraka weaken sufficiently to push him away.

He sprang to his feet and raced toward Brahma

without stopping to pick up his blade. There on the
hill, Brahma parried Thunderbolt again and again,
blood spurting from the stump of his severed left arm
and streaming from wounds of the head and chest.
Nirriti held his ankle in a grip of steel.

Yama cried out as he charged, drawing his dagger.

Indra drew back, out of range of Brahma's blade,
and turned to face him.

"A dagger against Thunderbolt, Red One?" he asked.

"Aye," said Yama, striking with his right hand and
dropping the blade into his left for the true strike.

The point entered Indra's forearm.

Indra dropped Thunderbolt and struck Yama in the
jaw. Yama fell, but he swept Indra's legs out from
under him, carrying him to the ground.

His Aspect possessed him completely then, and as he
glared Indra seemed to wither beneath his gaze. Taraka
leapt upon his back just as Indra died. Yama tried to
free himself, but it felt as if a mountain lay across his
shoulders.

Brahma, who lay beside Nirriti, tore off his harness,
which had been soaked with demon repellant. With his
right hand he cast it across the space that separated
them, so that it fell beside Yama.

Taraka withdrew, and Yama turned and gazed upon
him. Thunderbolt then leapt up from where it had
fallen upon the ground and sped toward Yama's breast.

Yama seized the blade with both hands, its point
inches away from his heart. It began to move forward
and the blood dripped from the palms of his hands and
fell upon the ground.

Brahma turned a death-gaze upon the Lord of Hellwell, a gaze that drew now upon the force of life itself
within him.

The point touched Yama.

Yama threw himself to the side, turning, and it
gouged him from breastbone to shoulder as it passed.

Then his eyes were two spears, and the Rakasha lost

his manlike form and became smoke. Brahma's head
fell upon his breast.

Taraka screamed as Siddhartha rode toward him
upon a white horse, the air crackling and smelling of
ozone:

"No, Binder! Hold your power! My death belongs to
Yama . . ."

"Oh foolish demon!" said Sam. "It need not have
been . . ."

But Taraka was no more.

Yama fell to his knees beside Brahma and tied a
tourniquet about what remained of his left arm.

"Kali!" he said. "Don't die! Talk to me, Kali!"

Brahma gasped and his eyes flickered open, but
closed again.

"Too late," mumbled Nirriti. He turned his head and
looked at Yama. "Or rather, just in time. You're Azra-
el, aren't you? The Angel of Death . . ."

Yama slapped him, and the blood upon his hand was
smeared across Nirriti's face.

" 'Blessed are the poor in spirit, for theirs is the
kingdom of heaven,' " said Nirriti. " 'Blessed are they
that mourn, for they shall be comforted. Blessed are the
meek, for they shall inherit the earth.' "

Yama slapped him again.

" 'Blessed are they which do hunger and thirst after
righteousness, for they shall be filled. Blessed are the
merciful, for they shall obtain mercy. Blessed are the
pure in heart, for they shall see God. . . .' "

" 'And blessed are the peacemakers,' " said Yama,
" 'for they shall be called the children of God.' How do
you fit into the picture, Black One? Whose child are
you, to have wrought as you have done?"

Nirriti smiled and said, " 'Blessed are they who are
persecuted for righteousness' sake, for theirs is the kingdom of heaven.' "

"You are mad," said Yama, "and I will not take
your life for that reason. Give it away yourself, when
you are ready, which should be soon."

He lifted Brahma then in his arms and began walking back toward the city.

" 'Blessed are ye, when men shall revile you,' " said Nirriti, " 'and persecute you, and say all manner of evil things against you falsely, for my sake. . . .' "

"Water?" asked Sam, unstoppering his canteen and raising Nirriti's head.

Nirriti looked at him, licked his lips, nodded slightly. He trickled the water into his mouth.

"Who are you?" he asked.

"Sam."

"You? *You* rose again?"

"It doesn't count," said Sam. "I didn't do it the hard way."

Tears filled the Black One's eyes. "It means you'll win, though," he gasped. "I can't understand why He permitted it . . ."

"This is only one world, Renfrew. Who knows what goes on elsewhere? And that isn't really the fight I wanted to win, anyhow. You know that. I'm sorry for you, and I'm sorry about the whole thing. I agree with everything you said to Yama, and so do the followers of the one they called the Buddha. I don't recall any longer whether I was really that one, or whether it was another. But I am gone away from that one now. I shall return to being a man, and I shall let the people keep the Buddha who is in their hearts. Whatever the source, the message was pure, believe me. That is the only reason it took root and grew."

Renfrew swallowed another drink.

" 'Even so every good tree bringeth forth good fruit,' " he said. "It was a will greater than mine that determined I die in the arms of the Buddha, that decided upon this Way for this world. . . . Give me your blessing, oh Gautama. I die now . . ."

Sam bowed his head.

" 'The wind goeth toward the south, and turneth about unto the north. It whirleth about continually, and the wind returneth again according to his circuits. All the rivers run into the sea, yet the sea is not full. Unto the place from whence the rivers come, thither they return again. The thing that hath been, it is that which shall be, and that which is done is that which shall be done. There is no remembrance of former things, neither shall there be any remembrance of things that are to come with those that shall come after. . . ."

Then he covered the Black One with his cloak of white, for he had died.

Jan Olvegg was borne in a litter into the town. Sam sent for Kubera and for Narada to meet him at the Hall of Karma, for it was apparent Olvegg would not be long alive in his present body.

When they entered the Hall, Kubera stumbled over the dead man who lay within the archway.

"Who . . . ?" he asked.

"A Master."

Three more wearers of the yellow wheel lay within the corridor that led to their transfer rooms. All of them bore arms.

They found another near the machinery. The thrust of a blade had caught him precisely in the center of his yellow circle, and he looked like a well-used target. His mouth was still opened for the scream he'd never screamed.

"Could the townsmen have done this?" asked Narada. "The Masters have grown more unpopular in recent years. Perhap they took advantage of the battle frenzy . . ."

"No," said Kubera, as he raised the stained sheet that covered the body upon the operating table, looked beneath it, lowered it. "No, it wasn't the townsmen."

"Who, then?"

He glanced back at the table.

"That's Brahma," he said.

"Oh."

"Someone must have told Yama he couldn't use the machinery to try a transfer."

"Then where's Yama?"

"I have no idea. But we'd better work fast if we're going to manage Olvegg."

"Yes. Move!"

The tall youth strode into the Palace of Kama and asked after Lord Kubera. He bore a long, gleaming spear across his shoulder, and he paced without pause as he waited.

Kubera entered the chamber, glanced at the spear, at the youth, said one word.

"Yes, it is Tak," replied the spearman. "New spear, new Tak. No need to remain an ape any longer, so I didn't. The time of departure is near, so I came to say good-bye—to you and to Ratri . . ."

"Where will you go, Tak?"

"I'd like to see the rest of the world, Kubera, before you manage to mechanize all the magic out of it."

"That day is nowhere near at hand, Tak. Let me persuade you to stay a while longer . . ."

"No, Kubera. Thank you, but Captain Olvegg is anxious to get along. He and I are moving out together."

"Where will you be going?"

"East, west . . . who knows? Whatever quarter beckons. . . . Tell me, Kubera, who owns the thunder chariot now?"

"It belonged to Shiva originally, of course. But there no longer is a Shiva. Brahma used it for a long while . . ."

"But there no longer is a Brahma. Heaven is without one for the first time—as Vishnu rules, preserving. So . . ."

"Yama built it. If it belongs to anyone, it belongs to him . . ."

"And he has no use for it," finished Tak. "So I think Olvegg and I will borrow it for our journeying."

"What mean you he has no use for it? No one has seen him these three days since the battle—"

"Hello, Ratri," said Tak, and the goddess of Night

entered the room. "'Guard us from the she-wolf and the wolf, and guard us from the thief, oh Night, and so be good for us to pass.'"

He bowed and she touched his head.

Then he looked up into her face, and for one splendid moment the goddess filled wide space, to its depths and its heights. Her radiance drove out the dark. . . .

"I must go now," he said. "Thank you, thank you—for your blessing."

He turned quickly and started from the chamber.

"Wait!" said Kubera. "You spoke of Yama. Where is he?"

"Seek him at the Inn of the Three-Headed Fire-Hen," Tak said, over his shoulder, "if you must seek him, that is. Perhaps 'twere better you wait till he seeks you, though."

Then Tak was gone.

As Sam approached the Palace of Kama, he saw Tak hurrying down the stair.

"Tak, a good morning to you!" he called, but Tak did not answer until he was almost upon him. Then he halted abruptly and shielded his eyes, as against the sun.

"Sir! Good morning."

"Where hurry you, Tak? Fresh from trying out your new body and off to lunch?"

Tak chuckled. "Aye, Lord Siddhartha. I've an appointment with adventure."

"So I've heard. I spoke with Olvegg last night. . . . Fare thee well upon thy journeying."

"I wanted to tell you," said Tak, "that I knew you'd win. I knew you'd find the answer."

"It wasn't *the* answer, but it was an answer, and it wasn't much, Tak. It was just a small battle. They could have done as well without me."

"I mean," said Tak, "everything. You figured in everything that led up to it. You had to be there."

"I suppose I did ... yes, I do suppose I did. ... Something always manages to draw me near the tree that lightning is about to fall upon."

"Destiny, sir."

"Rather an accidental social conscience and some right mistake-making, I fear."

"What will you do now, Lord?"

"I don't know, Tak. I haven't decided yet."

"Come with Olvegg and me? Ride with us about the world? Adventure with us?"

"Thank you, no. I'm tired. Maybe I'll ask for your old job and become Sam of the Archives."

Tak chuckled once more.

"I doubt it. I'll see you again, Lord. Good-bye now."

"Good-bye. ... There is something ..."

"What?"

"Nothing. For a moment, something you did reminded me of someone I once knew. It was nothing. Good luck!"

He clasped him on the shoulder and walked by.

Tak hurried on.

The innkeeper told Kubera that they did have a guest who fit that description, second floor, rear room, but that perhaps he should not be disturbed.

Kubera climbed to the second floor.

No one answered his knocking, so he tried the door.

It was bolted within, so he pounded upon it.

Finally, he heard Yama's voice:

"Who is it?"

"Kubera."

"Go away, Kubera."

"No. Open up, or I'll wait here till you do."

"Bide a moment, then."

After a time, he heard a bar lifted and the door swung several inches inward.

"No liquor on your breath, so I'd say it's a wench," he stated.

"No," said Yama, looking out at him. "What do you want?"

"To find out what's wrong. To help you, if I can."

"You can't, Kubera."

"How do you know? I, too, am an artificer—of a different sort, of course."

Yama appeared to consider this, then he opened the door and stepped aside. "Come in," he said.

The girl sat on the floor, a heap of various objects before her. She was scarcely more than a child, and she hugged a brown and white puppy and looked at Kubera with wide, frightened eyes, until he gestured and she smiled.

"Kubera," said Yama.

"Koo-bra," said the girl.

"She is my daughter," said Yama. "Her name is Murga."

"I never knew you had a daughter."

"She is retarded. She suffered some brain damage . . ."

"Congenital, or transfer effect?" asked Kubera.

"Transfer effect."

"I see."

"She is my daughter," repeated Yama, "Murga."

"Yes," said Kubera.

Yama dropped to his knees at her side and picked up a block.

"Block," he said.

"Block," said the girl.

He held up a spoon. "Spoon," he said.

"Spoon," said the girl.

He picked up a ball and held it before her. "Ball," he said.

"Ball," said the girl.

He picked up the block and held it before her again.

"Ball," she repeated.

Yama dropped it.

"Help me, Kubera," he said.

"I will, Yama. If there is a way, we will find it."

He sat down beside him and raised his hands.

The spoon came alive with spoon-ness and the ball with ball-ness and the block with block-ness, and the girl laughed. Even the puppy seemed to study the objects.

"The Lokapalas are never defeated," said Kubera, and the girl picked up the block and stared at it for a long time before she named it.

Now it is known that Lord Varuna returned to the Celestial City after Khaipur. The promotion system within the ranks of Heaven began to break down at about this same time. The Lords of Karma were replaced by the Wardens of Transfer, and their function was divorced from the Temples. The bicycle was rediscovered. Seven Buddhist shrines were erected. Nirriti's Palace was made into an art gallery and Kama Pavilion. The Festival of Alundil continued to be held every year, and its dancers were without equal. The purple grove still stands, tended by the faithful.

Kubera remained with Ratri in Khaipur. Tak departed with Olvegg in the thunder chariot, for an unknown destination. Vishnu ruled in Heaven.

Those who prayed to the seven Rishi thanked them for the bicycle and for the timely avatar of the Buddha, whom they named Maitreya, meaning Lord of Light, either because he could wield lightnings or because he refrained from doing so. Others continued to call him Mahasamatman and said he was a god. He still preferred to drop the Maha- and the -atman, however, and continued to call himself Sam. He never claimed to be a god. But then, of course, he never claimed not to be a god. Circumstances being what they were, neither admission could be of any benefit. Also, he did not remain with his people for a sufficient period of time to warrant much theological by-play. Several conflicting stories are told concerning the days of his passing.

The one thing that is common to all the legends is that a large red bird with a tail thrice the length of its body came to him one day at dusk as he rode upon his horse beside the river.

He departed Khaipur before sunrise the following day and was not seen again.

Now some say the occurrence of the bird was coincidental with his departure, but in no way connected with it. He departed to seek anonymous peace of a saffron robe because he had finished the task for which he had returned, they say, and he was already tired of the noise and fame of his victory. Perhaps the bird reminded him how quickly such brightness passes. Or perhaps it did not, if he had already made up his mind.

Others say that he did not take up the robe again, but that the bird was a messenger of the Powers Beyond Life, summoning him back again to the peace of Nirvana, to know forever the Great Rest, the perpetual bliss, and to hear the songs the stars sing upon the shores of the great sea. They say he has crossed beyond the Bridge of the Gods. They say he will not return.

Others say that he took upon him a new identity, and that he walks among mankind still, to guard and guide in the days of strife, to prevent the exploitation of the lower classes by those who come into power.

Still others say that the bird was a messenger, not of the next world, but of this one, and that the message it bore was not meant for him, but for the wielder of Thunderbolt, Lord Indra, who had looked into the eyes of Death. Such a bird as the red one had never been seen before, though their kind is now known to exist upon the eastern continent, where Indra had held battle against the witches. If the bird bore something like intelligence within its flaming head, it might have carried the message of some need in that far-off land. It must be remembered that the Lady Parvati, who had been either his wife, his mother, his sister, his daughter, or perhaps all of these to Sam, had fled to that place at the time the phantom cats looked upon Heaven, to dwell there with the witches, whom she counted as kin. If the bird bore such a message, the tellers of this tale do not doubt but that he departed immediately for the eastern continent, to effect her delivery from whatever peril was present.

These are the four versions of Sam and the Red Bird Which Signalled His Departure, as told variously by the moralists, the mystics, the social reformers, and the romantics. One may, I daresay, select whichever version suits his fancy. He should, however, remember that such birds definitely are not found upon the western continent, but seem to be quite prolific in the east.

Approximately a half year later, Yama-Dharma departed Khaipur. Nothing specific is known of the days of the deathgod's going, which most people consider ample information. He left his daughter Murga in the care of Ratri and Kubera and she grew into a strikingly beautiful woman. He may have ridden into the east, possibly even crossing over the sea. For there is a legend in another place of how One in Red went up against the power of the Seven Lords of Komlat in the land of the witches. Of this, we cannot be certain, any more than we can know the real end of the Lord of Light.

But look around you ...

Death and Light are everywhere, always, and they begin, end, strive, attend, into and upon the Dream of the Nameless that is the world, burning words within Samsara, perhaps to create a thing of beauty.

As the wearers of the saffron robe still meditate upon the Way of Light, and the girl who is named Murga visits the Temple daily, to place before her dark one in his shrine the only devotion he receives, of flowers.